Night Art School
Cooper Union

W9-AEK-341

THE LIFE & OPINIONS

OF

TRISTRAM SHANDY
Gentleman

THE
LIFE & OPINIONS
OF
TRISTRAM SHANDY
Gentleman

Ταράσσει τοὺς Ἀνθρώπους οὐ τὰ Πράγματα,
Ἀλλά τὰ περὶ τῶν Πραγμάτων Δόγματα.

BY
LAURENCE STERNE

.

Volume I

With an Introduction by Christopher Morley

and Illustrations by
T. M. CLELAND

new york
THE LIMITED EDITIONS CLUB
1935

MELZ Colker
PR
3714
.T7
1935
V. 1

WITHDRAWN FROM
COOPER UNION LIBRARY

A
094/35
8 839 T
v. 1

94856

THE SPECIAL CONTENTS OF THIS EDITION ARE
COPYRIGHT, 1935, BY THE LIMITED EDITIONS CLUB, INC.

INTRODUCTION

NOTHING NEW is likely to be said at this date in a note on *Tristram Shandy*. I always like to think of the astonished mirth of its very earliest readers. Zounds! they must have said to themselves. It did not concern them (nor does it us) that much of manner and matter was lifted from Rabelais and Burton. As Professor Saintsbury said in his essay on Sterne (which I wish might be reprinted in every edition; so manly, temperate and wise): "Where he is best he does not steal at all, and that is the only point of real importance."

Reading *Tristram Shandy* for the first time is one of those initiations that should not be deferred too late. I suppose it most often happens in college. I've never forgotten the bewildered excitement of my volatile classmate Mifflin McGill (at Haverford) when, during our sophomore year, he went about for months on end bursting into sudden cackles, repeating passages that had seized his fancy, and still scarcely believing it possible that so much of human absurdity had really been put into print. I suppose that same discovery is made perennially by several hundred or several thousand young readers. There is too much snigger in Sterne's laughter, sometimes; but those who would read the book only for love of smut are always defeated by its difficulty.

Much of the wealth of Sterne's wisdom (and lubricity) will escape the 'prentice reader. Lorry was a mature man (aged 45) when he began to write *Tristram*, and some of his japing (and tenderness) requires a fairly long perspective of grievance and folly. But, when the reader is fit, he will probably agree that the random, idiotic and grotesquely physical paradoxes of carnal clay have nowhere else been so brilliantly suggested. One of Sterne's subtle remarks is that

"Attitudes are nothing, madam—'tis the transition from one attitude to another—like the preparation and resolution of the discord into harmony—which is all in all."

As an axiom of literary virtuosity, this shrewd saying is exquisitely illustrated in Sterne's writing. He modulates from one key to another with superb address. And perhaps no writer has ever lingered with more tender and malicious effect upon the momentary postures which betray our human oddity. It is a profound instinct, for the highest art of fiction is to seem to make life stand still, unconscious of itself, long enough to be looked at. Consider (as he bids us) the occasion of Corporal Trim dropping his hat, to illustrate the finality of death. Consider My Father pausing on the stairs; My Mother listening at the door (the door with the imperfect hinge).

There are plenty more instances, and more mischievous ones, that show Sterne's cunning at setting the scene. The famous episodes of Trim's knee, or the "concupiscible" widow in the sentry-box, are familiar enough. The Fly, the Oath, have become stock examples in every textbook. But we prefer sometimes to look for marks of genius in less intentional show passages. So don't miss that scene in the kitchen, and the "fat foolish scullion".

    *   *   *   *

Perhaps *Tristram Shandy* should be read first at not over 20 years, and again at not less than 40. After that, or even between those ages, you may use your judgment. Few, except the proofreader and Professor Saintsbury and Governor Cross, read every word. I would not for anything be the proofreader, as *Tristram* contradicts every rule on which the printer forms his rigid cosmos. Every detail of punctuation and typography is absolutely Sterne's own, studied to convey the effect he had in mind. The biographers sometimes comment on the fact that Sterne always went up to London to be on hand for the publication of successive batches of volumes. Surely it was to have a last precautionary look at those difficult proofs. The stereotyped reader, unaccustomed to tricks, is often taken aback by these typographical freaks. Many booksellers have had the experience of copies returned by innocent customers, complaining that the book is defective because some pages are blank, or blacked out, or some chapters transposed. That is not really a very subtle form of mirth, though it always seems so to the green reader. Sterne's finest touches are less obvious.

It is said that *Tristram* was begun in the hope of recouping Sterne's losses in farming. If so, no agricultural depression was ever better justified. Great books make great demands on their readers. In essence you can regard it as a soliloquy of some 200,000 words (only a guess, I haven't counted them) for the purpose of introducing one very gross episode. The final remark of Tristram's guileless mother—"L—d! said my mother, what is all this story about?"—might well have been made the motto of the whole work. Or you can think of it as a treatise on midwifery, on education, on "the construction and come-at-ability of that animal called Woman", or on the endearing simplicity of two delightful old men. Myself, I sometimes grow weary of Sterne's more deliberate bids for laughter: the asterisks and aposiopeses, the typographic vaudeville, the ancient after-dinner-speaker's device of insisting that the bawdy thought he has suggested isn't at all what he meant. Our parson does all these better than anyone else; but there's a whoreson lot of it. To me the greatest thing in the book is its echo of a vanished soldiery. Sterne was an army child and his earliest memories were of Marlborough's veterans. Like Shakespeare before him, and Kipling after, he saw that certain unique qualities and savors of English character came to their highest pitch, both comic and pathetic, in the art of war. They went to war in kindness, in a very special mood of simplicity and rude mirth. The moving absurdity and seriousness of Uncle Toby and Corporal Trim are what, above all, list this book among the superior few. It is all very well for Sterne to tell us that *Tristram* was written "against the spleen"—viz. to cause laughter. Yes, much of it was, but it had also larger intentions. Great captain of innuendo and the double entendre, he also knew how to achieve his purpose by saying nothing. You might meditate on the genius with which My Mother is conveyed to us, though she is almost always offstage (abed, usually). How well we know her! "She never asked the meaning of what she didn't understand."

*   *   *   *

It's very human that poor Lorry, who seems to have made rather an unhappy mess of his own marriage, should set out to compose so confident an essay on conjugal dynamics. More than once it almost seems as though he had said the last word on the topic—but that will never be said. The joint and diverse ejaculation of Uncle Toby and My Father—

God bless ⎱ 'em all—said my uncle Toby and
Deuce take ⎰ my father, each to himself—

comes as near it as we are likely to get on the masculine side. But how about the distaff? Do women read *Tristram?* I doubt it. I wish some intrepid scholiast would compile me a list of the great books of the world which are, by the peculiar astringence of their humor, less likely to appeal to ladies. That is a roundabout way of saying, more bluntly, the books Women Don't Care For. The only purpose of so silly a list would be to set them on to reading them.

As to the much palavered theme of Sterne's lewdness, let's at least be frank. You will find none of his lubricities, no not one, which most of us have not grinned at (however ruefully or secretly) in our own thought. He plunged home to perennial springs of shameful human glee. Condemn him, we condemn ourselves. It's a pity, we have already admitted, that there's too much snigger in his woodpile. He goes far beyond good taste. But laughter often does. It is godlike, knowing not good nor evil.

*   *   *   *

We say to ourselves, let's not be too solemn about the masterpieces of comedy. The grisly legend of poor Yorick is that his corpse was taken by bodysnatchers and dissected by the anatomists at Cambridge. That legend has been enacted more than once in too pick-thank comment on his book. But great things, however light their tone, compel us to take them respectfully. Digressions are the sunshine of reading, Sterne says somewhere. This book, which is all digression, is also all sunshine. It is impossible to imagine that any writer ever had more fun than our deplorable vicar dipping his wicked quill. He had that singularly rich fun that can only be had by one writing for highly intelligent readers.

And if you suppose that the much advertised "stream of consciousness" method is anything new, where will you find it more accurately employed than in *Tristram Shandy?* When the very newest shock-merchant is too wildly acclaimed for qualities supposed unprecedented, I am sometimes tempted to whistle *Lillabullero*—and pace a few toises with Uncle Toby. As I write this note I see a new novel reviewed thus: "defies classification . . . a cock-eyed book; mad, repellent, weird and perverse, provocative, sometimes brilliant, many times beautiful, always exciting." If *Tristram Shandy* were published to-day for the first time, I wonder what adjectives we would have left for it?

CHRISTOPHER MORLEY

CONTENTS

To the Right Honourable

Mr. PITT

SIR,

NEVER poor Wight of a Dedicator had less hopes from his Dedication, than I have from this of mine; for it is written in a bye corner of the kingdom, and in a retired thatched house, where I live in a constant endeavour to fence against the infirmities of ill health, and other evils of life, by mirth; being firmly persuaded that every time a man smiles,——but much more so, when he laughs, it adds something to this Fragment of Life.

I humbly beg, Sir, that you will honour this book, by taking it——(not under your Protection,——it must protect itself, but)——into the country with you; where, if I am ever told, it has made you smile; or can conceive it has beguiled you of one moment's pain——I shall think myself as happy as a minister of state;——perhaps much happier than any one (one only excepted) that I have read or heard of.

I am, great sir,

(and what is more to your Honour)

I am, good sir,

Your Well-wisher, and

most humble Fellow-subject,

THE AUTHOR.

THE

LIFE

AND

OPINIONS

OF

TRISTRAM SHANDY
Gentleman

BOOK I

Chapter I

I wish either my father or my mother, or indeed both of them, as they were in duty both equally bound to it, had minded what they were about when they begot me; had they duly considered how much depended upon what they were then doing;—that not only the production of a rational Being was concerned in it, but that possibly the happy formation and temperature of his body, perhaps his genius and the very cast of his mind; —and, for aught they knew to the contrary, even the fortunes of his whole house might take their turn from the humours and dispositions which were then upper-most;——Had they duly weighed and considered all this, and proceeded accordingly,——I am verily persuaded I should have made a quite different figure in the world, from that in which the reader is likely to see me.—Believe me, good folks, this is not so inconsiderable a thing as many of you may think it;—you have all, I dare say, heard of the animal spirits, as how they are transfused from father to son etc. etc.—and a great deal to that purpose:—Well, you may take my word, that nine parts in ten of a man's sense or his nonsense, his successes and miscarriages in this world depend upon their motions and activity, and the different tracts and trains you put them into, so that when they are once set a-going, whether right or wrong, 'tis not a halfpenny matter,—away they go cluttering like hey-go mad; and by tread-ing the same steps over and over again, they presently make a road of it, as plain and as smooth as a garden-walk, which, when they are once used to, the Devil him-self sometimes shall not be able to drive them off it.

"Pray, my Dear," quoth my mother, "have you not forgot to wind up the clock?"———"Good G—!" cried my father, making an exclamation, but taking care to moderate his voice at the same time,——"Did ever woman, since the creation of the world, interrupt a man with such a silly question?" Pray, what was your father saying?——Nothing.

Chapter II

———THEN, positively, there is nothing in the question
that I can see, either good or bad.———Then, let
me tell you, Sir, it was a very unseasonable question at
least,—because it scattered and dispersed the animal
spirits, whose business it was to have escorted and gone
hand in hand with the HOMUNCULUS, and conducted
him safe to the place destined for his reception.

The Homunculus, Sir, in however low and ludicrous
a light he may appear, in this age of levity, to the eye of
folly or prejudice;—to the eye of reason in scientific re-
search, he stands confessed—a Being guarded and cir-
cumscribed with rights.———The minutest philosophers,
who, by the bye, have the most enlarged understandings,
(their souls being inversely as their enquiries) shew us
incontestably, that the Homunculus is created by the
same hand,—engendered in the same course of nature,
—endowed with the same locomotive powers and faculties with us:—That he consists as we do, of skin, hair,
fat, flesh, veins, arteries, ligaments, nerves, cartilages,
bones, marrow, brains, glands, genitals, humours, and
articulations;—is a Being of as much activity,—and, in
all senses of the word, as much and as truly our fellow-
creature as my Lord Chancellor of England.—He may
be benefited,—he may be injured,—he may obtain re-
dress;—in a word, he has all the claims and rights of
humanity, which Tully, Puffendorf, or the best ethic
writers allow to arise out of that state and relation.

Now, dear Sir, what if any accident had befallen him

in his way alone!—or that, through terror of it, natural to
so young a traveller, my little Gentleman had got to his
journey's end miserably spent;—his muscular strength
and virility worn down to a thread;—his own animal
spirits ruffled beyond description,—and that in this sad
disordered state of nerves, he had lain down a prey to
sudden starts, or a series of melancholy dreams and
fancies, for nine long, long months together.—I tremble
to think what a foundation had been laid for a thousand
weaknesses both of body and mind, which no skill of the
physician or the philosopher could ever afterwards have
set thoroughly to rights.

CHAPTER III

To my uncle Mr. Toby Shandy do I stand indebted
for the preceding anecdote, to whom my father, who
was an excellent natural philosopher, and much given to
close reasoning upon the smallest matters, had oft, and
heavily complained of the injury; but once more particularly, as my uncle Toby well remembered, upon his observing a most unaccountable obliquity, (as he called it)
in my manner of setting up my top, and justifying the
principles upon which I had done it,—the old gentleman
shook his head, and in a tone more expressive by half of
sorrow than reproach,—he said his heart all along foreboded, and he saw it verified in this, and from a thousand other observations he had made upon me, That I
should neither think nor act like any other man's child:
—"But alas!" continued he, shaking his head a second

time, and wiping away a tear which was trickling down his cheeks, "My Tristram's misfortunes began nine months before ever he came into the world."

—My mother, who was sitting by, looked up,—but she knew no more than her backside what my father meant,—but my uncle, Mr. Toby Shandy, who had been often informed of the affair,—understood him very well.

Chapter IV

I know there are readers in the world, as well as many other good people in it, who are no readers at all,— who find themselves ill at ease, unless they are let into the whole secret from first to last, of everything which concerns you.

It is in pure compliance with this humour of theirs, and from a backwardness in my nature to disappoint any one soul living, that I have been so very particular already. As my life and opinions are likely to make some noise in the world, and, if I conjecture right, will take in all ranks, professions, and denominations of men whatever,—be no less read than the *Pilgrim's Progress* itself —and in the end, prove the very thing which Montaigne dreaded his Essays should turn out, that is, a book for a parlour-window;—I find it necessary to consult every one a little in his turn; and therefore must beg pardon for going on a little further in the same way: For which cause, right glad I am, that I have begun the history of myself in the way I have done; and that I am able to go on, tracing every thing in it, as Horace says, *ab Ovo*.

Horace, I know does not recommend this fashion altogether: But that gentleman is speaking only of an epic poem or a tragedy;—(I forget which,)—besides, if it was not so, I should beg Mr. Horace's pardon;—for in writing what I have set about, I shall confine myself neither to his rules, nor to any man's rules that ever lived.

To such, however, as do not choose to go so far back into these things, I can give no better advice, than that they skip over the remaining part of this chapter; for I declare before-hand, 'tis wrote only for the curious and inquisitive.

BOOK I

————————Shut the door————————

I was begot in the night, betwixt the first Sunday and
the first Monday in the month of March, in the year of
our Lord one thousand seven hundred and eighteen. I
am positive I was,—But how I came to be so very particular in my account of a thing which happened before
I was born, is owing to another small anecdote known
only in our own family, but now made public for the
better clearing up this point.

My father, you must know, who was originally a
Turkey merchant, but had left off business for some
years, in order to retire to, and die upon, his paternal
estate in the county of ————, was, I believe, one of the
most regular men in everything he did, whether 'twas
matter of business, or matter of amusement, that ever
lived. As a small specimen of this extreme exactness of
his, to which he was in truth a slave,—he had made it a

CHAP. IV

rule for many years of his life,—on the first Sunday-night of every month throughout the whole year,—as certain as ever the Sunday-night came,——to wind up a large house-clock, which we had standing on the back-stairs head, with his own hands:—And being somewhere between fifty and sixty years of age at the time I have been speaking of,—he had likewise gradually brought some other little family concernments to the same period, in order, as he would often say to my uncle Toby, to get them all out of the way at one time, and be no more plagued and pestered with them the rest of the month.

It was attended with but one misfortune, which, in a great measure, fell upon myself, and the effects of which I fear I shall carry with me to my grave; namely, that from an unhappy association of ideas, which have no connection in nature, it so fell out at length, that my poor mother could never hear the said clock wound up, —but the thoughts of some other things unavoidably popped into her head—and *vice versa:*——Which strange combination of ideas, the sagacious Locke, who certainly understood the nature of these things better than most men, affirms to have produced more wry actions than all other sources of prejudice whatsoever.

But this by the bye.

Now it appears by a memorandum in my father's pocket-book, which now lies upon the table, "That on Lady-day, which was on the 25th of the same month in which I date my geniture,—my father set out upon his journey to London, with my eldest brother Bobby, to fix him at Westminster school"; and, as it appears from the same authority, "That he did not get down to his wife and family till the second week in May following," —it brings the thing almost to a certainty. However, what follows in the beginning of the next chapter, puts it beyond all possibility of doubt.

——But pray, Sir, What was your father doing all December,—January, and February?——Why, Madam, —he was all that time afflicted with a Sciatica.

Chapter V

O N the fifth day of November, 1718, which to the era fixed on, was as near nine calendar months as any husband could in reason have expected,—was I Tristram Shandy, Gentleman, brought forth into this scurvy and disastrous world of ours.——I wish I had been born in the Moon, or in any of the planets, (except Jupiter or Saturn, because I never could bear cold weather) for it could not well have fared worse with me in any of them (though I will not answer for Venus) than it has in this vile, dirty planet of ours,—which, o' my conscience, with reverence be it spoken, I take to be made up of the shreds and clippings of the rest;——not but the planet is well enough, provided a man could be born in it to a great title or to a great estate; or could any how contrive to be called up to public charges, and employments of dignity or power;——but that is not my case;——and therefore every man will speak of the fair as his own market has gone in it;——for which cause I affirm it over again to be one of the vilest worlds that ever was made;—for I can truly say, that from the first hour I drew my breath in it, to this, that I can now scarce draw it at all, for an asthma I got in skating against the wind in Flanders;— I have been the continual sport of what the world calls Fortune; and though I will not wrong her by saying, She has ever made me feel the weight of any great or signal evil;——yet with all the good temper in the world, I affirm it of her, that in every stage of my life, and at every turn and corner where she could get fairly at me, the ungracious duchess has pelted me with a set of as pitiful misadventures and cross accidents as ever small Hero sustained.

Chapter VI

In the beginning of the last chapter, I informed you exactly when I was born; but I did not inform you how. No, that particular was reserved entirely for a chapter by itself;—besides, Sir, as you and I are in a manner perfect strangers to each other, it would not have been proper to have let you into too many circumstances relating to myself all at once.—You must have a little patience. I have undertaken, you see, to write not only my life, but my opinions also; hoping and expecting that your knowledge of my character, and of what kind of a mortal I am, by the one, would give you a better relish for the other: As you proceed farther with me, the slight acquaintance, which is now beginning betwixt us, will grow into familiarity; and that, unless one of us is in fault, will terminate in friendship.—*O diem praeclarum!* —then nothing which has touched me will be thought trifling in its nature, or tedious in its telling. Therefore, my dear friend and companion, if you should think me somewhat sparing of my narrative on my first setting out—bear with me,—and let me go on, and tell my story my own way:—Or, if I should seem now and then to trifle upon the road,—or should sometimes put on a fool's cap with a bell to it, for a moment or two as we pass along,—don't fly off,—but rather courteously give me credit for a little more wisdom than appears upon my outside;—and as we jog on, either laugh with me, or at me, or in short do any thing,—only keep your temper.

CHAPTER VII

In the same village where my father and my mother dwelt, dwelt also a thin, upright, motherly, notable, good old body of a midwife, who with the help of a little plain good sense, and some years' full employment in her business, in which she had all along trusted little to her own efforts, and a great deal to those of dame Nature,— had acquired, in her way, no small degree of reputation in the world:——by which word *world*, need I in this place inform your worship, that I would be understood to mean no more of it, than a small circle described upon the circle of the great world, of four English miles diameter, or thereabouts, of which the cottage where the good old woman lived, is supposed to be the centre?—She had been left, it seems, a widow in great distress, with three or four small children, in her forty-seventh year; and as she was at that time a person of decent carriage,—grave deportment,—a woman moreover of few words, and withal an object of compassion, whose distress, and silence under it, called out the louder for a friendly lift: the wife of the parson of the parish was touched with pity; and having often lamented an inconvenience, to which her husband's flock had for many years been exposed, inasmuch as there was no such thing as a midwife, of any kind or degree, to be got at, let the case have been never so urgent, within less than six or seven long miles riding; which said seven long miles in dark nights and dismal roads, the country thereabouts being nothing but a deep clay, was almost equal to fourteen; and that in effect was sometimes next to having no midwife at all; it came into her head, that it would be doing as seasonable a kindness to the whole parish, as to the poor creature herself, to get her a little instructed in some of the plain principles of the business, in order to set her up in it. As no woman thereabouts was better qualified to execute the plan she had formed than herself, the gentlewoman very charitably undertook it; and having great influence over the female part of the parish, she found no difficulty in effecting it to the utmost of her wishes. In truth, the parson joined his interest with his wife's in the whole affair; and in order to do things as they should be, and give the poor soul as good a title by law to practice, as his wife had given by institution,—he cheerfully paid the fees for the ordinary's licence himself, amounting in the whole, to the sum of eighteen shillings and fourpence; so that betwixt them both, the good woman was fully invested in the real and corporal possession of her office, together with all its rights, members, and appurtenances whatsoever.

These last words, you must know, were not according to the old form in which such licences, faculties, and powers usually ran, which in like cases had heretofore been granted to the sisterhood. But it was according to a neat Formula of Didius his own devising, who having a particular turn for taking to pieces, and new framing over again, all kinds of instruments in that way, not only hit upon this dainty amendment, but coaxed many of the old licensed matrons in the neighbourhood, to open their faculties afresh, in order to have this wham-wham of his inserted.

I own I never could envy Didius in these kinds of fancies of his:—But every man to his own taste.—Did not Dr. Kunastrokius, that great man, at his leisure hours, take the greatest delight imaginable in combing of asses' tails, and plucking the dead hairs out with his teeth, though he had tweezers always in his pocket? Nay, if you come to that, Sir, have not the wisest of men in all ages, not excepting Solomon himself,—have they not had their Hobby-Horses;—their running horses,—their coins and their cockle-shells, their drums and their trumpets, their fiddles, their pallets,—their maggots and their butterflies?—and so long as a man rides his Hobby-Horse peaceably and quietly along the King's highway, and neither compels you or me to get up behind him,— pray, Sir, what have either you or I to do with it?

CHAP. VII

CHAPTER VIII

—*De gustibus non est disputandum;*—that is, there is
no disputing against Hobby-Horses; and for my
part, I seldom do; nor could I with any sort of grace, had
I been an enemy to them at the bottom; for happening,
at certain intervals and changes of the moon, to be both
fiddler and painter, according as the fly stings:—Be it
known to you, that I keep a couple of pads myself, upon
which, in their turns, (nor do I care who knows it) I frequently ride out and take the air;—though sometimes, to
my shame be it spoken, I take somewhat longer journeys
than what a wise man would think altogether right.—
But the truth is,—I am not a wise man;—and besides am a
mortal of so little consequence in the world, it is not much
matter what I do: so I seldom fret or fume at all about
it: Nor does it much disturb my rest, when I see such
great Lords and tall Personages as hereafter follow;—
such, for instance, as my Lord A, B, C, D, E, F, G, H, I,
K, L, M, N, O, P, Q, and so on, all of a row, mounted
upon their several horses, some with large stirrups, getting on in a more grave and sober pace;——others on
the contrary, tucked up to their very chins, with whips
across their mouths, scouring and scampering it away
like so many little party-coloured devils astride a mort-
gage,—and as if some of them were resolved to break
their necks.——So much the better—say I to myself;—
for in case the worst should happen, the world will make
a shift to do excellently well without them: and for the
rest,——why——God speed them——e'en let them ride

on without opposition from me; for were their lordships unhorsed this very night—'tis ten to one but that many of them would be worse mounted by one half before to-morrow morning.

Not one of these instances therefore can be said to break in upon my rest.——But there is an instance, which I own puts me off my guard, and that is, when I see one born for great actions, and what is still more for his honour, whose nature ever inclines him to good ones; —when I behold such a one, my Lord, like yourself, whose principles and conduct are as generous and noble as his blood, and whom, for that reason, a corrupt world cannot spare one moment;—when I see such a one, my Lord, mounted, though it is but for a minute beyond the time which my love to my country has prescribed to him, and my zeal for his glory wishes,—then, my Lord, I cease to be a philosopher, and in the first transport of an honest impatience, I wish the Hobby-Horse, with all his fraternity, at the Devil.

"My Lord,

"I maintain this to be a dedication, notwithstanding its singularity in the three great essentials of matter, form, and place: I beg, therefore, you will accept it as such, and that you will permit me to lay it, with the most respectful humility, at your Lordship's feet,—when you are upon them,—which you can be when you please;

CHAP. VIII

—and that is, my Lord, whenever there is occasion for it, and I will add, to the best purposes too. I have the honour to be,

"*My Lord,*
Your Lordship's most obedient,
and most devoted,
and most humble servant,

TRISTRAM SHANDY."

CHAPTER IX

I SOLEMNLY declare to all mankind, that the above dedication was made for no one Prince, Prelate, Pope, or Potentate,—Duke, Marquis, Earl, Viscount, or Baron, of this, or any other Realm in Christendom;——nor has it yet been hawked about, or offered publicly or privately, directly or indirectly, to any one person or personage, great or small; but is honestly a true Virgin-Dedication untried on, upon any soul living.

I labour this point so particularly, merely to remove any offence or objection which might arise against it from the manner in which I propose to make the most of it;—which is the putting it up fairly to public sale; which I now do.

——Every author has a way of his own in bringing his points to bear;—for my own part, as I hate chaffering and higgling for a few guineas in a dark entry;—I resolved within myself, from the very beginning, to deal

squarely and openly with your Great Folks in this affair,
and try whether I should not come off the better by it.

If therefore there is any one Duke, Marquis, Earl,
Viscount, or Baron, in these his Majesty's dominions,
who stands in need of a tight, genteel dedication, and
whom the above will suit (for by the bye, unless it suits
in some degree I will not part with it)——it is much at
his service for fifty guineas;——which I am positive is
twenty guineas less than it ought to be afforded for, by
any man of genius.

My Lord, if you examine it over again, it is far from
being a gross piece of daubing, as some dedications are.
The design, your Lordship sees, is good,—the colouring
transparent,—the drawing not amiss;—or to speak more
like a man of science,—and measure my piece in the
painter's scale, divided into 20,—I believe, my Lord, the
outlines will turn out as 12,—the composition as 9,—
the colouring as 6,—the expression 13 and a half,—and
the design,—if I may be allowed, my Lord, to understand my own design, and supposing absolute perfection
in designing, to be as 20,—I think it cannot well fall
short of 19. Besides all this,—there is keeping in it, and
the dark strokes in the Hobby-Horse, (which is a second-
ary figure, and a kind of back-ground to the whole) give
great force to the principal lights in your own figure, and
make it come off wonderfully;——and besides, there is
an air of originality in the *tout ensemble*.

Be pleased, my good Lord, to order the sum to be
paid into the hands of Mr. Dodsley, for the benefit of
the author, and in the next edition care shall be taken

CHAP. IX

that this chapter be expunged, and your Lordship's titles, distinctions, arms, and good actions, be placed at the front of the preceding chapter: All which, from the words, *De gustibus non est disputandum*, and whatever else in this book relates to Hobby-Horses, but no more, shall stand dedicated to your Lordship.—The rest I dedicate to the Moon, who, by the bye, of all the Patrons or Matrons I can think of, has most power to set my book agoing, and make the world run mad after it.

    Bright Goddess,
If thou art not too busy with Candid and Miss Cunegund's affairs,—take Tristram Shandy's under thy protection also.

Chapter X

WHATEVER degree of small merit the act of benignity in favour of the midwife might justly claim, or in whom that claim truly rested,—at first sight seems not very material to this history;——certain however it was, that the gentlewoman, the parson's wife, did run away at that time with the whole of it: And yet, for my life, I cannot help thinking but that the parson himself, though he had not the good fortune to hit upon the design first, —yet, as he heartily concurred in it the moment it was laid before him, and as heartily parted with his money to carry it into execution, had a claim to some share of it,—if not to a full half of whatever honour was due to it.

The world at that time was pleased to determine the matter otherwise.

Lay down the book, and I will allow you half a day to give a probable guess at the grounds of this procedure.

Be it known then, that, for about five years before the date of the midwife's licence, of which you have had so circumstantial an account,—the parson we have to do with had made himself a country-talk by a breach of all decorum, which he had committed against himself, his station, and his office;—and that was in never appearing better, or otherwise mounted, than upon a lean, sorry, jack-ass of a horse, value about one pound fifteen shillings; who, to shorten all description of him, was full brother to Rosinante, as far as similitude congenial could make him; for he answered his description to a hair-breadth in every thing,—except that I do not remember 'tis any where said, that Rosinante was broken-winded; and that, moreover, Rosinante, as is the happiness of most Spanish horses, fat or lean,—was undoubtedly a horse at all points.

I know very well that the Hero's horse was a horse of chaste deportment, which may have given grounds for the contrary opinion; But it is as certain at the same time, that Rosinante's continency (as may be demonstrated from the adventure of the Yanguesian carriers) proceeded from no bodily defect or cause whatsoever, but from the temperance and orderly current of his blood.—And let me tell you, Madam, there is a great deal of very good chastity in the world, in behalf of which you could not say more for your life.

Let that be as it may, as my purpose is to do exact justice to every creature brought upon the stage of this

CHAP. X

dramatic work,—I could not stifle this distinction in favour of Don Quixote's horse;—in all other points, the parson's horse, I say, was just such another,—for he was as lean, and as lank, and as sorry a jade, as Humility herself could have bestrided.

In the estimation of here and there a man of weak judgment, it was greatly in the parson's power to have helped the figure of this horse of his,—for he was master of a very handsome demi-peaked saddle, quilted on the seat with green plush, garnished with a double row of silver-headed studs, and a noble pair of shining brass stirrups, with a housing altogether suitable, of grey superfine cloth, with an edging of black lace, terminating in a deep, black, silk fringe, *poudré d'or,*—all which he had purchased in the pride and prime of his life, together with a grand embossed bridle, ornamented at all points as it should be.——But not caring to banter his beast, he had hung all these up behind his study door:—and, in lieu of them, had seriously befitted him with just such a bridle and such a saddle, as the figure and value of such a steed might well and truly deserve.

In the several sallies about his parish, and in the neighbouring visits to the gentry who lived around him, —you will easily comprehend, that the parson, so appointed, would both hear and see enough to keep his philosophy from rusting. To speak the truth, he never could enter a village, but he caught the attention of both old and young.——Labour stood still as he passed—the bucket hung suspended in the middle of the well,—the spinning-wheel forgot its round,——even chuck-farthing and shuffle-cap themselves stood gaping till he had got out of sight; and as his movement was not of the quickest, he had generally time enough upon his hands to make his observations,—to hear the groans of the serious,—and the laughter of the light-hearted;—all which he bore with excellent tranquillity.—His character was, —he loved a jest in his heart—and as he saw himself in the true point of ridicule, he would say he could not be angry with others for seeing him in a light, in which he so strongly saw himself: So that to his friends, who knew his foible was not the love of money, and who therefore made the less scruple in bantering the extravagance of his humour,—instead of giving the true cause,—he chose rather to join in the laugh against himself; and as he never carried one single ounce of flesh upon his own bones, being altogether as spare a figure as his beast,—

CHAP. X

he would sometimes insist upon it, that the horse was as good as the rider deserved;—that they were, centaur-like,—both of a piece. At other times, and in other moods, when his spirits were above the temptation of false wit,—he would say, he found himself going off fast in a consumption; and, with great gravity, would pretend, he could not bear the sight of a fat horse, without a dejection of heart, and a sensible alteration in his pulse; and that he had made choice of the lean one he rode upon, not only to keep himself in countenance, but in spirits.

At different times he would give fifty humorous and apposite reasons for riding a meek-spirited jade of a broken-winded horse, preferably to one of mettle;—for on such a one he could sit mechanically, and meditate as delightfully *de vanitate mundi et fugâ saeculi,* as with the advantage of a death's-head before him;—that, in all other exercitations, he could spend his time, as he rode slowly along,—to as much account as in his study; that he could draw up an argument in his sermon,—or a hole in his breeches, as steadily on the one as in the other;—that brisk trotting and slow argumentation, like wit and judgment, were two incompatible movements.—But that upon his steed—he could unite and reconcile every thing, —he could compose his sermon,—he could compose his cough,——and, in case nature gave a call that way, he could likewise compose himself to sleep.—In short, the parson upon such encounters would assign any cause but the true cause,—and he withheld the true one, only out of a nicety of temper, because he thought it did honour to him.

But the truth of the story was as follows: In the first years of this gentleman's life, and about the time when the superb saddle and bridle were purchased by him, it had been his manner, or vanity, or call it what you will, —to run into the opposite extreme.—In the language of the county where he dwelt, he was said to have loved a good horse, and generally had one of the best in the whole parish standing in his stable always ready for saddling; and as the nearest midwife, as I told you, did not live nearer to the village than seven miles, and in a vile country,—it so fell out that the poor gentleman was scarce a whole week together without some piteous application for his beast; and as he was not an unkind-hearted man, and every case was more pressing and more distressful than the last,—as much as he loved his beast, he had never a heart to refuse him; the upshot of which was generally this, that his horse was either clapped, or spavined, or greazed;—or he was twitter-boned, or broken-winded, or something, in short, or other had befallen him, which would let him carry no flesh;—so that he had every nine or ten months a bad horse to get rid of,—and a good horse to purchase in his stead.

What the loss in such a balance might amount to, *communibus annis*, I would leave to a special jury of sufferers in the same traffic, to determine;—but let it be what it would, the honest gentleman bore it for many years without a murmur, till at length, by repeated ill accidents of the kind, he found it necessary to take the thing under consideration; and upon weighing the whole,

CHAP. X

and summing it up in his mind, he found it not only dis-
proportioned to his other expenses, but withal so heavy
an article in itself, as to disable him from any other act
of generosity in his parish: Besides this, he considered
that with half the sum thus galloped away, he could do
ten times as much good;—and what still weighed more
with him than all other considerations put together, was
this, that it confined all his charity into one particular
channel, and where, as he fancied, it was the least wanted,
namely to the child-bearing and child-getting part of his
parish; reserving nothing for the impotent,—nothing for
the aged,—nothing for the many comfortless scenes he
was hourly called forth to visit, where poverty, and sick-
ness, and affliction dwelt together.

For these reasons he resolved to discontinue the expense; and there appeared but two possible ways to
extricate him clearly out of it;—and these were, either
to make it an irrevocable law never more to lend his
steed upon any application whatever,—or else be content to ride the last poor devil, such as they had made
him, with all his aches and infirmities, to the very end of
the chapter.

As he dreaded his own constancy in the first—he
very cheerfully betook himself to the second; and though
he could very well have explained it, as I said, to his
honour,—yet, for that very reason, he had a spirit above
it; choosing rather to bear the contempt of his enemies,
and the laughter of his friends, than undergo the pain of
telling a story, which might seem a panegyric upon himself.

I have the highest idea of the spiritual and refined sentiments of this reverend gentleman, from this single stroke in his character, which I think comes up to any of the honest refinements of the peerless knight of La Mancha, whom, by the bye, with all his follies, I love more, and would actually have gone farther to have paid a visit to, than the greatest hero of antiquity.

But this is not the moral of my story: The thing I had in view was to shew the temper of the world in the whole of this affair.—For you must know, that so long as this explanation would have done the parson credit, the devil a soul could find it out,—I suppose his enemies would not, and that his friends could not.——But no sooner did he bestir himself in behalf of the midwife, and pay the expenses of the ordinary's licence to set her up, —but the whole secret came out; every horse he had lost, and two horses more than ever he had lost, with all the circumstances of their destruction, were known and distinctly remembered.—The story ran like wild-fire— "The parson had a returning fit of pride which had just seized him; and he was going to be well mounted once again in his life; and if it was so, 'twas plain as the sun at noon-day, he would pocket the expense of the licence, ten times told, the very first year:—So that every body was left to judge what were his views in this act of charity."

What were his views in this, and in every other action of his life,—or rather what were the opinions which floated in the brains of other people concerning it, was a thought which too much floated in his own, and too often

CHAP. X

broke in upon his rest, when he should have been sound asleep.

About ten years ago this gentleman had the good fortune to be made entirely easy upon that score,—it being just so long since he left his parish,—and the whole world at the same time behind him,—and stands accountable to a Judge of whom he will have no cause to complain.

But there is a fatality attends the actions of some men: Order them as they will, they pass thro' a certain medium, which so twists and refracts them from their true directions——that, with all the titles to praise which a rectitude of heart can give, the doers of them are nevertheless forced to live and die without it.

Of the truth of which, this gentleman was a painful example.——But to know by what means this came to pass,—and to make that knowledge of use to you, I insist upon it that you read the two following chapters, which contain such a sketch of his life and conversation, as will carry its moral along with it.—When this is done, if nothing stops us in our way, we will go on with the midwife.

CHAPTER XI

YORICK was this parson's name, and, what is very remarkable in it, (as appears from a most ancient account of the family, wrote upon strong vellum, and now in perfect preservation) it had been exactly so spelt for near,——I was within an ace of saying nine hundred years;——but I would not shake my credit in telling an improbable truth, however indisputable in itself;—and therefore I shall content myself with only saying—It had been exactly so spelt, without the least variation or transposition of a single letter, for I do not know how long; which is more than I would venture to say of one half of the best surnames in the kingdom; which, in a course of years, have generally undergone as many chops and changes as their owners.—Has this been owing to the pride, or to the shame of the respective proprietors? —In honest truth, I think sometimes to the one, and sometimes to the other, just as the temptation has wrought. But a villainous affair it is, and will one day so blend and confound us altogether, that no one shall be able to stand up and swear, "That his own great grandfather was the man who did either this or that."

This evil had been sufficiently fenced against by the prudent care of the Yorick's family, and their religious preservation of these records I quote, which do farther inform us, That the family was originally of Danish extraction, and had been transplanted into England as early as in the reign of Horwendillus, king of Denmark, in whose court, it seems, an ancestor of this Mr. Yorick's, and from whom he was lineally descended, held a considerable post to the day of his death. Of what nature this considerable post was, this record saith not;—It only adds, That, for near two centuries, it had been totally abolished, as altogether unnecessary, not only in that court, but in every other court of the Christian world.

It has often come into my head, that this post could be no other than that of the king's chief Jester;—and

CHAP. XI

that Hamlet's Yorick, in our Shakespeare, many of whose plays, you know, are founded upon authenticated facts, was certainly the very man.

I have not the time to look into Saxo-Grammaticus's Danish history to know the certainty of this;—but if you have leisure, and can easily get at the book, you may do it full as well yourself.

I had just time, in my travels through Denmark with Mr. Noddy's eldest son, whom, in the year 1741, I accompanied as governor, riding along with him at a prodigious rate thro' most parts of Europe, and of which original journey performed by us two, a most delectable narrative will be given in the progress of this work; I had just time, I say, and that was all, to prove the truth of an observation made by a long sojourner in that country;——namely, "That nature was neither very lavish, nor was she very stingy in her gifts of genius and capacity to its inhabitants;—but, like a discreet parent, was moderately kind to them all; observing such an equal tenor in the distribution of her favours, as to bring them, in those points, pretty near to a level with each other; so that you will meet with few instances in that kingdom of refined parts; but a great deal of good plain household understanding amongst all ranks of people, of which every body has a share"; which is, I think, very right.

With us, you see, the case is quite different:—we are all ups and downs in this matter;—you are a great genius; or 'tis fifty to one, Sir, you are a great dunce and a blockhead;—not that there is a total want of intermediate steps,—no,—we are not so irregular as that comes to;—

but the two extremes are more common, and in a greater degree in this unsettled island, where nature, in her gifts and dispositions of this kind, is most whimsical and capricious; fortune herself not being more so in the bequest of her goods and chattels than she.

This is all that ever staggered my faith in regard to Yorick's extraction, who, by what I can remember of him, and by all the accounts I could ever get of him, seemed not to have had one single drop of Danish blood in his whole crasis; in nine hundred years, it might possibly have all run out:——I will not philosophize one moment with you about it; for happen how it would, the fact was this:—That instead of that cold phlegm and exact regularity of sense and humours, you would have looked for, in one so extracted;—he was, on the contrary, as mercurial and sublimated a composition,—as heteroclite a creature in all his declensions;—with as much life and whim, and *gaité de cœur* about him, as the kindliest climate could have engendered and put together. With all this sail, poor Yorick carried not one ounce of ballast; he was utterly unpractised in the world: and, at the age of twenty-six, knew just about as well how to steer his course in it, as a romping, unsuspicious girl of thirteen: So that upon his first setting out, the brisk gale of his spirits, as you will imagine, ran him foul ten times in a day of somebody's tackling; and as the grave and more slow-paced were oftenest in his way,—— you may likewise imagine, 'twas with such he had generally the ill luck to get the most entangled. For aught I know there might be some mixture of unlucky wit at the

CHAP. XI

bottom of such Fracas:——For, to speak the truth, Yorick had an invincible dislike and opposition in his nature to gravity;—not to gravity as such;—for where gravity was wanted, he would be the most grave or serious of mortal men for days and weeks together;—but he was an enemy to the affectation of it, and declared open war against it, only as it appeared a cloak for ignorance, or for folly: and then, whenever it fell in his way, however sheltered and protected, he seldom gave it much quarter.

Sometimes, in his wild way of talking, he would say, that Gravity was an errant scoundrel, and he would add, —of the most dangerous kind too,—because a sly one; and that he verily believed, more honest, well-meaning people were bubbled out of their goods and money by it in one twelve-month, than by pocket-picking and shop-lifting in seven. In the naked temper which a merry heart discovered, he would say there was no danger,— but to itself:—whereas the very essence of gravity was design, and consequently deceit;—'twas a taught trick to gain credit of the world for more sense and knowledge than a man was worth; and that, with all its pretensions, —it was no better, but often worse, than what a French wit had long ago defined it,—viz. "A mysterious carriage of the body to cover the defects of the mind";—which definition of gravity, Yorick, with great imprudence, would say, deserved to be wrote in letters of gold.

But, in plain truth, he was a man unhackneyed and unpractised in the world, and was altogether as indiscreet and foolish on every other subject of discourse where policy is wont to impress restraint. Yorick had no impression but one, and that was what arose from the nature of the deed spoken of; which impression he would usually translate into plain English without any periphrasis;—and too oft without much distinction of either person, time, or place;—so that when mention was made of a pitiful or an ungenerous proceeding——he never gave himself a moment's time to reflect who was the hero of the piece,——what his station,——or how far he had power to hurt him hereafter;——but if it was a dirty action,—without more ado,—The man was a dirty fellow,—and so on.—And as his comments had usually the ill fate to be terminated either in a *bon mot*, or to be enlivened throughout with some drollery or humour of expression, it gave wings to Yorick's indiscretion. In a word, tho' he never sought, yet, at the same time, as he seldom shunned occasions of saying what came uppermost, and without much ceremony:——he had but too many temptations in life, of scattering his wit and his humour,—his gibes and his jests about him.——They were not lost for want of gathering.

What were the consequences, and what was Yorick's catastrophe thereupon, you will read in the next chapter.

CHAP. XI

Chapter XII

THE Mortgager and Mortgagee differ the one from the other, not more in length of purse, than the Jester and Jestée do, in that of memory. But in this the comparison between them runs, as the scholiasts call it, upon all-four; which, by the bye, is upon one or two legs more than some of the best of Homer's can pretend to;—namely, That the one raises a sum, and the other a laugh at your expense, and thinks no more about it. Interest, however, still runs on in both cases;—the periodical or accidental payments of it, just serving to keep the memory of the affair alive; till, at length, in some evil hour,—pop comes the creditor upon each, and by demanding principal upon the spot, together with full interest to the very day, makes them both feel the full extent of their obligations.

As the reader (for I hate your *ifs*) has a thorough knowledge of human nature, I need not say more to satisfy him, that my Hero could not go on at this rate without some slight experience of these incidental mementos. To speak the truth, he had wantonly involved himself in a multitude of small book-debts of this stamp, which, notwithstanding Eugenius's frequent advice, he too much disregarded; thinking, that as not one of them was contracted thro' any malignancy;—but, on the contrary, from an honesty of mind, and a mere jocundity of humour, they would all of them be crossed out in course.

Eugenius would never admit this; and would often tell him, that one day or other he would certainly be

reckoned with; and he would often add, in an accent of
sorrowful apprehension,—to the uttermost mite. To
which Yorick, with his usual carelessness of heart, would
as often answer with a pshaw!—and if the subject was
started in the fields,—with a hop, skip, and a jump at
the end of it; but if close pent up in the social chimney-
corner, where the culprit was barricadoed in, with a
table and a couple of arm-chairs, and could not so readily
fly off in a tangent,—Eugenius would then go on with
his lecture upon discretion in words to this purpose,
though somewhat better put together.

Trust me, dear Yorick, this unwary pleasantry of
thine will sooner or later bring thee into scrapes and difficulties, which no after-wit can extricate thee out of.
——In these sallies, too oft, I see, it happens, that a
person laughed at, considers himself in the light of a person injured, with all the rights of such a situation belonging to him; and when thou viewest him in that light too,
and reckons up his friends, his family, his kindred and
allies,——and musters up with them the many recruits
which will list under him from a sense of common danger;
——'tis no extravagant arithmetic to say, that for every
ten jokes,—thou hast got an hundred enemies; and till
thou hast gone on, and raised a swarm of wasps about
thine ears, and art half stung to death by them, thou
wilt never be convinced it is so.

I cannot suspect it in the man whom I esteem, that
there is the least spur from spleen or malevolence of intent in these sallies——I believe and know them to be
truly honest and sportive:—But consider, my dear lad,

CHAP. XII

that fools cannot distinguish this,—and that knaves will not: and thou knowest not what it is, either to provoke the one, or to make merry with the other:——whenever they associate for mutual defence, depend upon it, they will carry on the war in such a manner against thee, my dear friend, as to make thee heartily sick of it, and of thy life too.

Revenge from some baneful corner shall level a tale of dishonour at thee, which no innocence of heart or integrity of conduct shall set right.——The fortunes of thy house shall totter,—thy character, which led the way to them, shall bleed on every side of it,—thy faith questioned,—thy works belied,—thy wit forgotten,—thy learning trampled on. To wind up the last scene of thy tragedy, Cruelty and Cowardice, twin ruffians, hired and set on by Malice in the dark, shall strike together at all thy infirmities and mistakes:——The best of us, my dear lad, lie open there,——and trust me,——trust me, Yorick, when to gratify a private appetite, it is once resolved upon, that an innocent and an helpless creature shall be sacrificed, 'tis an easy matter to pick up sticks enough from any thicket where it has strayed, to make a fire to offer it up with.

Yorick scarce ever heard this sad vaticination of his destiny read over to him, but with a tear stealing from his eye, and a promissory look attending it, that he was resolved, for the time to come, to ride his tit with more sobriety.—But, alas, too late!—a grand confederacy, with ***** and ***** at the head of it, was formed before the first prediction of it.—The whole plan of the attack,

just as Eugenius had foreboded, was put in execution all
at once,—with so little mercy on the side of the allies,—
and so little suspicion in Yorick, of what was carrying on
against him,—that when he thought, good easy man!
full surely preferment was o' ripening,—they had smote
his root, and then he fell, as many a worthy man had
fallen before him.

Yorick, however, fought it out with all imaginable
gallantry for some time; till, overpowered by numbers,
and worn out at length by the calamities of the war,—
but more so, by the ungenerous manner in which it was
carried on,—he threw down the sword; and though he
kept up his spirits in appearance to the last, he died,
nevertheless, as was generally thought, quite broken-
hearted.

What inclined Eugenius to the same opinion was as
follows:

A few hours before Yorick breathed his last, Eugenius
stept in with an intent to take his last sight and last farewell of him. Upon his drawing Yorick's curtain, and ask-
ing how he felt himself, Yorick looking up in his face
took hold of his hand,—and after thanking him for the
many tokens of his friendship to him, for which, he said,
if it was their fate to meet hereafter,—he would thank
him again and again,—he told him, he was within a few
hours of giving his enemies the slip for ever.—I hope not,
answered Eugenius, with tears trickling down his cheeks,
and with the tenderest tone that ever man spoke.—I
hope not, Yorick, said he.——Yorick replied, with a look
up, and a gentle squeeze of Eugenius's hand, and that

CHAP. XII

was all,—but it cut Eugenius to his heart.—Come,—
come, Yorick, quoth Eugenius, wiping his eyes, and
summoning up the man within him,—my dear lad, be
comforted,—let not all thy spirits and fortitude forsake
thee at this crisis when thou most wants them;—who
knows what resources are in store, and what the power
of God may yet do for thee?——Yorick laid his hand
upon his heart, and gently shook his head;—For my

BOOK I

part, continued Eugenius, crying bitterly as he uttered the words,—I declare I know not, Yorick, how to part with thee, and would gladly flatter my hopes, added Eugenius, cheering up his voice, that there is still enough left of thee to make a bishop, and that I may live to see it.——I beseech thee, Eugenius, quoth Yorick, taking off his night-cap as well as he could with his left hand,—his right being still grasped close in that of Eugenius, ——I beseech thee to take a view of my head.—I see nothing that ails it, replied Eugenius. Then, alas! my friend, said Yorick, let me tell you, that 'tis so bruised and mis-shapened with the blows which ***** and *****, and some others have so unhandsomely given me in the dark, that I might say with Sancho Pança, that should I recover, and "Mitres thereupon be suffered to rain down from heaven as thick as hail, not one of them would fit it."——Yorick's last breath was hanging upon his trembling lips ready to depart as he uttered this:—yet still it was uttered with something of a Cervantick tone;—and as he spoke it, Eugenius could perceive a stream of lambent fire lighted up for a moment in his eyes;—faint picture of those flashes of his spirit, which (as Shakespeare said of his ancestor) were wont to set the table in a roar!

Eugenius was convinced from this, that the heart of his friend was broke: he squeezed his hand,——and then walked softly out of the room, weeping as he walked. Yorick followed Eugenius with his eyes to the door,—he then closed them,—and never opened them more.

He lies buried in the corner of his church-yard, in the parish of ——, under a plain marble slab, which his friend Eugenius, by leave of his executors, laid upon his grave, with no more than these three words of inscription, serving both for his epitaph and elegy,

> Alas, poor YORICK!

Ten times a day has Yorick's ghost the consolation to hear his monumental inscription read over with such a variety of plaintive tones, as denote a general pity and esteem for him;——a foot-way crossing the church-yard close by the side of his grave,—not a passenger goes by without stopping to cast a look upon it,—and sighing as he walks on,

Alas, poor YORICK!

CHAP. XII

CHAPTER XIII

I T is so long since the reader of this rhapsodical work has been parted from the midwife, that it is high time to mention her again to him, merely to put him in mind that there is such a body still in the world, and whom, upon the best judgment I can form upon my own plan at present,—I am going to introduce to him for good and all: But as fresh matter may be started, and much unexpected business fall out betwixt the reader and myself, which may require immediate dispatch;——'twas right to take care that the poor woman should not be lost in the meantime;—because when she is wanted we can no way do without her.

I think I told you that this good woman was a person of no small note and consequence throughout our whole village and township;—that her fame had spread itself to the very out-edge and circumference of that circle of importance, of which kind every soul living, whether he has a shirt to his back or no,——has one surrounding him;—which said circle, by the way, whenever 'tis said that such a one is of great weight and importance in the world,——I desire may be enlarged or contracted in your worship's fancy, in a compound ratio of the station, profession, knowledge, abilities, height and depth (measuring both ways) of the personage brought before you.

In the present case, if I remember, I fixed it about four or five miles, which not only comprehended the whole parish, but extended itself to two or three of the adjacent hamlets in the skirts of the next parish; which made a considerable thing of it. I must add, That she was, moreover, very well looked on at one large grange-house, and some other odd houses and farms within two or three miles, as I said, from the smoke of her own chimney:——But I must here, once for all, inform you, that all this will be more exactly delineated and explained in a map, now in the hands of the engraver, which with many other pieces and developements of this work, will be added to the end of the twentieth volume,—not to swell the work,—I detest the thought of such a thing;—but by way of commentary, scholium, illustration, and key to such passages, incidents, or innuendos as shall be thought to be either of private interpretation, or of dark or doubtful meaning, after my life and my opinions shall have been read over (now don't forget the meaning of the word) by all the world;—which, betwixt you and me, and in spite of all the gentlemen-reviewers in Great Britain, and of all that their worships shall undertake to write or say to the contrary,—I am determined shall be the case.—I need not tell your worship, that all this is spoke in confidence.

Chapter XIV

Upon looking into my mother's marriage-settlement, in order to satisfy myself and reader in a point necessary to be cleared up, before we could proceed any farther in this history;—I had the good fortune to pop upon the very thing I wanted before I had read a day and a half straight forwards,—it might have taken me up a month;

—which shews plainly that when a man sits down to write a history,—tho' it be but the history of Jack Hickathrift or Tom Thumb, he knows no more than his heels what lets and confounded hindrances he is to meet with in his way,—or what a dance he may be led, by one excursion or another, before all is over. Could a historiographer drive on his history, as a muleteer drives on his mule,—straight forward;——for instance, from Rome all the way to Loretto, without ever once turning his head aside either to the right hand or to the left,——he might venture to foretell you to an hour when he should get to his journey's end:——but the thing is, morally speaking, impossible: For, if he is a man of the least spirit he will have fifty deviations from a straight line to make with this or that party as he goes along, which he can no ways avoid. He will have views and prospects to himself perpetually soliciting his eye, which he can no more help standing still to look at than he can fly; he will moreover have various

    Accounts to reconcile:
    Anecdotes to pick up:
    Inscriptions to make out:
    Stories to weave in:
    Traditions to sift:
    Personages to call upon:
    Panegyrics to paste up at this door;
    Pasquinades at that:——All which both the man and his mule are quite exempt from. To sum up all; there are archives at every stage to be looked into, and rolls, records, documents, and endless genealogies, which justice

ever and anon calls him back to stay the reading of:—In short, there is no end of it;—for my own part, I declare I have been at it these six weeks, making all the speed I possibly could,—and am not yet born:—I have just been able, and that's all, to tell you *when* it happened, but not *how;*—so that you see the thing is yet far from being accomplished.

These unforeseen stoppages, which I own I had no conception of when I first set out;—but which, I am convinced now, will rather increase than diminish as I advance,—have struck out a hint which I am resolved to follow;—and that is,—not to be in a hurry; but to go on leisurely, writing and publishing two volumes of my life every year;—which, if I am suffered to go on quietly, and can make a tolerable bargain with my bookseller, I shall continue to do as long as I live.

Chapter XV

THE article in my mother's marriage-settlement, which I told the reader I was at the pains to search for, and which, now that I have found it, I think proper to lay before him,—is so much more fully expressed in the deed itself, than ever I can pretend to do it, that it would be barbarity to take it out of the lawyer's hand:—It is as follows.

"𝕬nd this 𝕴ndenture further witnesseth, That the said Walter Shandy, merchant, in consideration of the said intended marriage to be had, and, by God's blessing, to be well and truly solemnized and consummated be-

tween the said Walter Shandy and Elizabeth Mollineux
aforesaid, and divers other good and valuable causes and
considerations him thereunto specially moving,—doth
grant, covenant, condescend, consent, conclude, bargain,
and fully agree to and with John Dixon, and James
Turner, Esqrs., the above-named Trustees, &c. &c.—
to wit,—That in case it should hereafter so fall out, chance,
happen, or otherwise come to pass,—That the said
Walter Shandy, merchant, shall have left off business
before the time or times, that the said Elizabeth Mollineux shall, according to the course of nature or otherwise, have left off bearing and bringing forth children;—
and that, in consequence of the said Walter Shandy having so left off business, he shall in despite, and against
the free-will, consent, and good-liking of the said Elizabeth Mollineux,—make a departure from the city of
London, in order to retire to, and dwell upon, his estate
at Shandy Hall, in the county of ——, or at any other
country-seat, castle, hall, mansion-house, messuage or
grange-house, now purchased, or hereafter to be purchased, or upon any part or parcel thereof:—That then,
and as often as the said Elizabeth Mollineux shall happen
to be enceint with child or children severally and law-
fully begot, or to be begotten, upon the body of the said
Elizabeth Mollineux, during her said coverture,—he the
said Walter Shandy shall, at his own proper cost and
charges, and out of his own proper monies, upon good
and reasonable notice, which is hereby agreed to be within
six weeks of her the said Elizabeth Mollineux's full reckoning, or time of supposed and computed delivery,—pay,

or cause to be paid, the sum of one hundred and twenty pounds of good and lawful money, to John Dixon, and James Turner, Esqrs. or assigns,—upon TRUST and confidence, and for and unto the use and uses, intent, end, and purpose following:—𝕿𝖍𝖆𝖙 𝖎𝖘 𝖙𝖔 𝖘𝖆𝖞,—That the said sum of one hundred and twenty pounds shall be paid into the hands of the said Elizabeth Mollineux, or to be otherwise applied by them the said Trustees, for the well and truly hiring of one coach, with able and sufficient horses, to carry and convey the body of the said Elizabeth Mollineux, and the child or children which she shall be then and there enceint and pregnant with,—unto the city of London; and for the further paying and defraying of all other incidental costs, charges, and expenses whatsoever,—in and about, and for, and relating to, her said intended delivery and lying-in, in the said city or suburbs thereof. And that the said Elizabeth Mollineux shall and may, from time to time, and at all such time and times as are here covenanted and agreed upon,—peaceably and quietly hire the said coach and horses, and have free ingress, egress, and regress throughout her journey, in and from the said coach, according to the tenor, true intent, and meaning of these presents, without any let, suit, trouble, disturbance, molestation, discharge, hindrance, forfeiture, eviction, vexation, interruption, or incumbrance whatsoever.—And that it shall moreover be lawful to and for the said Elizabeth Mollineux, from time to time, and as oft or often as she shall well and truly be advanced in her said pregnancy, to the time heretofore stipulated and agreed upon,—to live and re-

CHAP. XV

side in such place or places, and in such family or families, and with such relations, friends, and other persons within the said city of London, as she at her own will and pleasure, notwithstanding her present coverture, and as if she was a *femme sole* and unmarried,—shall think fit.—And this Indenture further witnesseth, That for the more effectually carrying of the said covenant into execution, the said Walter Shandy, merchant, doth hereby grant, bargain, sell, release, and confirm unto the said John Dixon, and James Turner, Esqrs. their heirs, executors, and assigns, in their actual possession now being, by virtue of an indenture of bargain and sale for a year to them the said John Dixon, and James Turner, Esqrs. by him the said Walter Shandy, merchant, thereof made; which said bargain and sale for a year, bears date the day next before the date of these presents, and by force and virtue of the statute for transferring of uses into possession,—All that the manor and lordship of Shandy, in the county of ——, with all the rights, members, and appurtenances thereof; and all and every the messuages, houses, buildings, barns, stables, orchards, gardens, backsides, tofts, crofts, garths, cottages, lands, meadows, feedings, pastures, marshes, commons, woods, underwoods, drains, fisheries, waters, and water-courses;—together with all rents, reversions, services, annuities, fee-farms, knights' fees, views of frankpledge, escheats, reliefs, mines, quarries, goods and chattels of felons and fugitives, felons of themselves, and put in exigent, deodands, free warrens, and all other royalties and seigniories, rights and jurisdictions, privileges and hereditaments whatsoever.——*And also* the advowson, donation, presentation, and free disposition of the rectory or parsonage of Shandy aforesaid, and all and every the tenths, tithes, glebe-lands."——In three words,——"My mother was to lay in, (if she chose it) in London."

But in order to put a stop to the practice of any unfair play on the part of my mother, which a marriage-article of this nature too manifestly opened a door to, and which indeed had never been thought of at all, but for my uncle Toby Shandy;—a clause was added in security of my father, which was this:—"That in case my mother hereafter should, at any time, put my father to the trouble and expense of a London journey, upon false cries and tokens;——that for every such instance, she should forfeit all the right and title which the covenant gave her to the next turn;——but to no more,—and so on, *toties quoties*, in as effectual a manner, as if such a covenant betwixt them had not been made."—This, by the way, was no more than what was reasonable;—and yet, as reasonable as it was, I have ever thought it hard that the whole weight of the article should have fallen entirely, as it did, upon myself.

But I was begot and born to misfortunes:—for my poor mother, whether it was wind or water—or a compound of both,—or neither;—or whether it was simply the mere swell of imagination and fancy in her;—or how far a strong wish and desire to have it so, might mislead her judgment:—in short, whether she was deceived or deceiving in this matter, it no way becomes me to decide. The fact was this, That in the latter end of September

CHAP. XV

1717, which was the year before I was born, my mother having carried my father up to town much against the grain,—he peremptorily insisted upon the clause;—so that I was doomed, by marriage-articles, to have my nose squeezed as flat to my face, as if the destinies had actually spun me without one.

How this event came about,—and what a train of vexatious disappointments, in one stage or other of my life, have pursued me from the mere loss, or rather compression, of this one single member,—shall be laid before the reader all in due time.

CHAPTER XVI

MY father, as any body may naturally imagine, came down with my mother into the country, in but a pettish kind of a humour. The first twenty or five-and-twenty miles he did nothing in the world but fret and teaze himself, and indeed my mother too, about the cursed expense, which he said might every shilling of it have been saved;—then what vexed him more than every thing else was, the provoking time of the year,—which, as I told you, was towards the end of September, when his wall-fruit and green gages especially, in which he was very curious, were just ready for pulling:——"Had he been whistled up to London, upon a Tom Fool's errand, in any other month of the whole year, he should not have said three words about it."

For the next two whole stages, no subject would go down, but the heavy blow he had sustained from the loss

of a son, whom it seems he had fully reckoned upon in
his mind, and registered down in his pocket-book, as a
second staff for his old age, in case Bobby should fail
him. The disappointment of this, he said, was ten times
more to a wise man, than all the money which the journey, etc., had cost him, put together,—rot the hundred
and twenty pounds,——he did not mind it a rush.

From Stilton, all the way to Grantham, nothing in
the whole affair provoked him so much as the condolences
of his friends, and the foolish figure they should both
make at church, the first Sunday;——of which, in the
satirical vehemence of his wit, now sharpened a little by
vexation, he would give so many humorous and provoking descriptions,—and place his rib and self in so many

CHAP. XVI

tormenting lights and attitudes in the face of the whole congregation;—that my mother declared, these two stages were so truly tragi-comical, that she did nothing but laugh and cry in a breath, from one end to the other of them all the way.

From Grantham, till they had crossed the Trent, my father was out of all kind of patience at the vile trick and imposition which he fancied my mother had put upon him in this affair—"Certainly," he would say to himself, over and over again, "the woman could not be deceived herself——if she could,——what weakness!"—tormenting word!—which led his imagination a thorny dance, and before all was over, played the deuce and all with him;—for sure as ever the word weakness was uttered, and struck full upon his brain—so sure it set him upon running divisions upon how many kinds of weaknesses there were;—that there was such a thing as weakness of the body,—as well as weakness of the mind,—and then he would do nothing but syllogize within himself for a stage or two together, How far the cause of all these vexations might, or might not, have arisen out of himself.

In short, he had so many little subjects of disquietude springing out of this one affair, all fretting successively in his mind as they rose up in it, that my mother, whatever was her journey up, had but an uneasy journey of it down.—In a word, as she complained to my uncle Toby, he would have tired out the patience of any flesh alive.

Chapter XVII

Though my father travelled homewards, as I told you, in none of the best of moods,—pshawing and pishing all the way down,—yet he had the complaisance to keep the worst part of the story still to himself;—which was the resolution he had taken of doing himself the justice, which my uncle Toby's clause in the marriage-settlement empowered him; nor was it till the very night in which I was begot, which was thirteen months after, that she had the least intimation of his design: when my father, happening, as you remember, to be a little chagrined and out of temper,—took occasion as they lay chatting gravely in bed afterwards, talking over what was to come,——to let her know that she must accommodate herself as well as she could to the bargain made between them in their marriage-deeds; which was to lie-in of her next child in the country, to balance the last year's journey.

My father was a gentleman of many virtues,—but he had a strong spice of that in his temper, which might, or might not, add to the number.—'Tis known by the name of perseverance in a good cause,—and of obstinacy in a bad one: Of this my mother had so much knowledge, that she knew 'twas to no purpose to make any remonstrance,—so she e'en resolved to sit down quietly, and make the most of it.

Chapter XVIII

As the point was that night agreed, or rather determined, that my mother should lie-in of me in the country, she took her measures accordingly; for which purpose, when she was three days, or thereabouts, gone with child, she began to cast her eyes upon the midwife, whom you have so often heard me mention; and before the week was well got round, as the famous Dr. Manningham was not to be had, she had to come to a final determination in her mind,—notwithstanding there was a scientific operator within so near a call as eight miles of us, and who, moreover, had expressly wrote a five shillings book upon the subject of midwifery, in which he had exposed, not only the blunders of the sisterhood itself,—but had likewise super-added many curious improvements for the quicker extraction of the foetus in cross births, and some other cases of danger, which belay us in getting into the world; notwithstanding all this, my mother, I say, was absolutely determined to trust her life, and mine with it, into no soul's hand but this old woman's only.—Now this I like;—when we cannot get at the very thing we wish—never to take up with the next best in degree to it:—no; that's pitiful beyond description;—it is no more than a week from this very day, in which I am now writing this book for the edification of the world;—which is March 9, 1759,——that my dear, dear Jenny, observing I looked a little grave, as she stood cheapening a silk of five-and-twenty shillings a yard,—told the mercer, she was sorry she had given him so much trouble;—and immediately went and bought herself a yard-wide stuff of ten-pence a yard.—'Tis the duplication of one and the same greatness of soul; only what lessened the honour of it, somewhat, in my mother's case, was that she could not heroine it into so violent and hazardous an extreme, as one in her situation might have wished, because the old midwife had really some little claim to be depended upon,—as much, at least, as success could give her; having, in the course of her practice of near twenty years in the parish, brought every mother's son of them into the world without any one slip or accident which could fairly be laid to her account.

These facts, tho' they had their weight, yet did not altogether satisfy some few scruples and uneasiness which hung upon my father's spirits in relation to this choice. —To say nothing of the natural workings of humanity and justice—or of the yearnings of parental and connubial love, all which prompted him to leave as little to hazard as possible in a case of this kind;—he felt himself concerned in a particular manner, that all should go right in the present case;—from the accumulated sorrow he lay open to, should any evil betide his wife and child in lying-in at Shandy Hall.—He knew the world judged by events, and would add to his afflictions in such a misfortune, by loading him with the whole blame of it.—— "Alas o' day;—had Mrs. Shandy, poor gentlewoman! had but her wish in going up to town just to lie-in and come down again;—which, they say, she begged and prayed for upon her bare knees,—and which, in my opinion, considering the fortune which Mr. Shandy got

CHAP. XVIII

with her,—was no such mighty matter to have complied with, the lady and her babe might both of 'em have been alive at this hour."

This exclamation, my father knew, was unanswerable;—and yet, it was not merely to shelter himself,—nor was it altogether for the care of his offspring and wife that he seemed so extremely anxious about this point;—my father had extensive views of things,——and stood moreover, as he thought, deeply concerned in it for the public good, from the dread he entertained of the bad uses an ill-fated instance might be put to.

He was very sensible that all political writers upon the subject had unanimously agreed and lamented, from the beginning of Queen Elizabeth's reign down to his own time, that the current of men and money towards the metropolis, upon one frivolous errand or another,—set in so strong,—as to become dangerous to our civil rights,—though, by the bye,—a current was not the image he took most delight in,—a distemper was here his favourite metaphor, and he would run it down into a perfect allegory, by maintaining it was identically the same in the body national as in the body natural, where the blood and spirits were driven up into the head faster than they could find their ways down;——a stoppage of circulation must ensue, which was death in both cases.

There was little danger, he would say, of losing our liberties by French politics or French invasions;—nor was he so much in pain of a consumption from the mass of corrupted matter and ulcerated humours in our constitution, which he hoped was not so bad as it was imagined;—but he verily feared, that in some violent push, we should go off, all at once, in a state-apoplexy;—and then he would say, "The Lord have mercy upon us all."

My father was never able to give the history of this distemper,—without the remedy along with it.

"Was I an absolute prince," he would say, pulling up his breeches with both his hands, as he rose from his arm-chair, "I would appoint able judges, at every avenue of my metropolis, who should take cognizance of every fool's business who came there;—and if, upon a fair and candid hearing, it appeared not of weight sufficient to leave his own home, and come up, bag and baggage, with his wife and children, farmer's sons, etc. etc., at his back-side, they should be all sent back, from constable to constable, like vagrants as they were, to the place of their legal settlements. By this means I shall take care, that my metropolis tottered not thro' its own weight;—that the head be no longer too big for the body;—that the extremes, now wasted and pinned in, be restored to their due share of nourishment, and regain with it their natural strength and beauty:—I would effectually provide, That the meadows and corn-fields of my dominions, should laugh and sing;—that good cheer and hospitality flourish once more;—and that such weight and influence be put thereby into the hands of the Squirality of my kingdom, as should counterpoise what I perceive my Nobility are now taking from them.

"Why are there so few palaces and gentlemen's seats," he would ask, with some emotion, as he walked across the room, "throughout so many delicious provinces in

CHAP. XVIII

France? Whence is it that the few remaining Chateaus amongst them are so dismantled,—so unfurnished, and in so ruinous and desolate a condition?——Because, Sir," (he would say) "in that kingdom no man has any country-interest to support;—the little interest of any kind which any man has anywhere in it, is concentrated in the court, and the looks of the Grand Monarch: by the sunshine of whose countenance, or the clouds which pass across it, every French man lives or dies."

Another political reason which prompted my father so strongly to guard against the least evil accident in my mother's lying-in in the country,——was, That any such instance would infallibly throw a balance of power, too great already, into the weaker vessels of the gentry, in his own, or higher stations;——which, with the many other usurped rights which that part of the constitution was hourly establishing,—would, in the end, prove fatal to the monarchical system of domestic government established in the first creation of things by God.

In this point he was entirely of Sir Robert Filmer's opinion, That the plans and institutions of the greatest monarchies in the eastern parts of the world, were, originally, all stolen from that admirable pattern and prototype of this household and paternal power;—which, for a century, he said, and more, had gradually been degenerating away into a mixed government;——the form of which, however desirable in great combinations of the species,——was very troublesome in small ones,—and seldom produced any thing, that he saw, but sorrow and confusion.

For all these reasons, private and public, put together, —my father was for having the man-midwife by all means,—my mother by no means. My father begged and intreated, she would for once recede from her prerogative in this matter, and suffer him to choose for her; —my mother, on the contrary, insisted upon her privilege in this matter, to choose for herself,—and have no mortal's help but the old woman's.—What could my father do? He was almost at his wits' end;——talked it over with her in all moods;—placed his arguments in all lights;—argued the matter with her like a christian,— like a heathen,—like a husband,—like a father,—like a patriot,—like a man:—My mother answered every thing only like a woman; which was a little hard upon her;— for as she could not assume and fight it out behind such a variety of characters,—'twas no fair match:—'twas seven to one.—What could my mother do?——She had the advantage (otherwise she had been certainly overpowered) of a small reinforcement of chagrin personal at the bottom, which bore her up, and enabled her to dispute the affair with my father with so equal an advantage,——that both sides sung *Te Deum*. In a word, my mother was to have the old woman,—and the operator was to have licence to drink a bottle of wine with my father and my uncle Toby Shandy in the back parlour, —for which he was to be paid five guineas.

I must beg leave, before I finish this chapter, to enter a caveat in the breast of my fair reader;—and it is this, ——Not to take it absolutely for granted, from an unguarded word or two which I have dropped in it,——

CHAP. XVIII

"That I am a married man."—I own, the tender appellation of my dear, dear Jenny,—with some other strokes of conjugal knowledge, interspersed here and there, might, naturally enough, have misled the most candid judge in the world into such a determination against me.—All I plead for, in this case, Madam, is strict justice, and that you do so much of it, to me as well as to yourself,—as not to prejudge, or receive such an impression of me, till you have better evidence than, I am positive, at present can be produced against me.—Not that I can be so vain or unreasonable, Madam, as to desire you should therefore think, that my dear, dear Jenny is my kept mistress; —no,—that would be flattering my character in the other extreme, and giving it an air of freedom, which, perhaps, it has no kind of right to. All I contend for, is the utter impossibility, for some volumes, that you, or the most penetrating spirit upon earth, should know how this matter really stands.—It is not impossible, but that my dear, dear Jenny! tender as the appellation is, may be my child.——Consider,—I was born in the year eighteen.—Nor is there anything unnatural or extravagant in the supposition, that my dear Jenny may be my friend. —Friend!—My friend.—Surely, Madam, a friendship between the two sexes may subsist, and be supported without——Fy! Mr. Shandy:——Without any thing, Madam, but that tender and delicious sentiment, which ever mixes in friendship, where there is a difference of sex. Let me intreat you to study the pure and sentimental parts of the best French Romances;—it will really, Madam, astonish you to see with what a variety of

chaste expressions this delicious sentiment, which I have
the honour to speak of, is dressed out.

Chapter XIX

I WOULD sooner undertake to explain the hardest problem in geometry, than pretend to account for it, that
a gentleman of my father's great good sense,——knowing, as the reader must have observed him, and curious
too in philosophy,—wise also in political reasoning,—and
in polemical (as he will find) no way ignorant,—could be
capable of entertaining a notion in his head, so out of the
common track,—that I fear the reader, when I come to
mention it to him, if he is the least of a choleric temper,
will immediately throw the book by; if mercurial, he will
laugh most heartily at it;—and if he is of a grave and
saturnine cast, he will, at first sight, absolutely condemn
as fanciful and extravagant; and that was in respect to
the choice and imposition of christian names, on which
he thought a great deal more depended than what super-
ficial minds were capable of conceiving.

His opinion, in this matter, was, That there was a
strange kind of magic bias, which good or bad names, as
he called them, irresistibly impressed upon our characters
and conduct.

The hero of Cervantes argued not the point with more
seriousness,——nor had he more faith,——or more to
say on the powers of necromancy in dishonouring his
deeds,—or on Dulcinea's name, in shedding lustre upon
them, than my father had on those of Trismegistus or

Archimedes, on the one hand—or of Nyky and Simkin
on the other. How many Caesars and Pompeys, he would
say, by mere inspiration of the names, have been rendered worthy of them? And how many, he would add, are
there, who might have done exceeding well in the world,
had not their characters and spirits been totally depressed and Nicodemused into nothing?

I see plainly, Sir, by your looks, (or as the case happened) my father would say—that you do not heartily
subscribe to this opinion of mine,—which, to those, he
would add, who have not carefully sifted it to the bottom,
—I own has an air more of fancy than of solid reasoning
in it;——and yet, my dear Sir, if I may presume to know
your character, I am morally assured, I should hazard
little in stating a case to you,—not as a party in the dispute,—but as a judge, and trusting my appeal upon it to
your own good sense and candid disquisition in this
matter;—you are a person free from any narrow prejudices of education as most men;—and, if I may presume
to penetrate farther into you,—of a liberality of genius
above bearing down an opinion, merely because it wants
friends. Your son,—your dear son,—from whose sweet
and open temper you have so much to expect.—Your
Billy, Sir!—would you, for the world, have called him
Judas?—Would you, my dear Sir, he would say, laying
his hand upon your breast, with the genteelest address,
—and in that soft and irresistible piano of voice, which
the nature of the *argumentum ad hominem* absolutely requires,—Would you, Sir, if a Jew of a godfather had proposed the name for your child, and offered you his purse

along with it, would you have consented to such a dese-
cration of him?——O my God! he would say, looking up,
if I know your temper right, Sir—you are incapable of it;
——you would have trampled upon the offer; you would
have thrown the temptation at the tempter's head with
abhorrence.

Your greatness of mind in this action, which I admire,
with that generous contempt of money, which you shew
me in the whole transaction, is really noble;—and what
renders it more so, is the principle of it;—the workings of
a parent's love upon the truth and conviction of this
very hypothesis, namely, That was your son called Judas,
—the sordid and treacherous idea, so inseparable from
the name, would have accompanied him through life like
his shadow, and, in the end, made a miser and a rascal of
him, in spite, Sir, of your example.

I never knew a man able to answer this argument.
——But, indeed, to speak of my father as he was;—he
was certainly irresistible; both in his orations and dis-
putations;—he was born an orator;—Θεοδίδακτος.—Per-
suasion hung upon his lips, and the elements of Logic
and Rhetoric were so blended up in him,—and, withal,
he had so shrewd a guess at the weaknesses and passions
of his respondent,——that Nature might have stood up
and said,—"This man is eloquent."—In short, whether
he was on the weak or the strong side of the question,
'twas hazardous in either case to attack him.—And yet,
'tis strange he had never read Cicero, nor Quintilian
de Oratore, nor Isocrates, nor Aristotle, nor Longinus
amongst the ancients;—nor Vossius, nor Scioppius, nor

CHAP. XIX

Ramus, nor Farnaby amongst the moderns;—and what
is more astonishing, he had never in his whole life the
least light or spark of subtlety struck into his mind, by
one single lecture upon Crackenthorp or Burgersdicius,
or any Dutch logician or commentator;—he knew not so
much as in what the difference of an argument *ad igno-
rantiam* and an argument *ad hominem* consisted; so that
I well remember, when he went up along with me to enter
my name at Jesus College in ****,—it was a matter of
just wonder with my worthy tutor, and two or three
fellows of that learned society,—that a man who knew
not so much as the names of his tools, should be able to
work after that fashion with them.

To work with them in the best manner he could, was
what my father was, however, perpetually forced upon;
—for he had a thousand little sceptical notions of the
comic kind to defend—most of which notions, I verily
believe, at first entered upon the footing of mere whims,
and of a *vive la Bagatelle;* and as such he would make
merry with them for half an hour or so, and having
sharpened his wit upon them, dismiss them till another
day.

I mention this, not only as matter of hypothesis or
conjecture upon the progress and establishment of my
father's many odd opinions,—but as a warning to the
learned reader against the indiscreet reception of such
guests, who, after a free and undisturbed entrance, for
some years, into our brains,—at length claim a kind of
settlement there,——working sometimes like yeast;—
but more generally after the manner of the gentle passion,

beginning in jest,—but ending in downright earnest.

Whether this was the case of the singularity of my father's notions—or that his judgment, at length, became the dupe of his wit;—or how far, in many of his notions, he might, though odd, be absolutely right;—— the reader, as he comes at them, shall decide. All that I maintain here, is, that in this one, of the influence of christian names, however it gained footing, he was serious;—he was all uniformity;—he was systematical, and, like all systematic reasoners, he would move both heaven and earth, and twist and torture every thing in nature, to support his hypothesis. In a word, I repeat it over again;—he was serious; and, in consequence of it, he would lose all kind of patience whenever he saw people, especially of condition, who should have known better, ——as careless and as indifferent about the name they imposed upon their child,—or more so, than in the choice of Ponto or Cupid for their puppy-dog.

This, he would say, looked ill;—and had, moreover, this particular aggravation in it, viz., That when once a vile name was wrongfully or injudiciously given, 'twas not like the case of a man's character, which, when wronged, might hereafter be cleared;——and, possibly, some time or other, if not in the man's life, at least after his death,—be, somehow or other, set to rights with the world: But the injury of this, he would say, could never be undone;—nay, he doubted even whether an act of parliament could reach it:——He knew as well as you, that the legislature assumed a power over surnames;— but for very strong reasons, which he could give, it had

CHAP. XIX

never yet adventured, he would say, to go a step farther.

It was observable, that tho' my father, in consequence of this opinion, had, as I have told you, the strongest likings and dislikings towards certain names;—that there were still numbers of names which hung so equally in the balance before him, that they were absolutely indifferent to him. Jack, Dick, and Tom were of this class: These my father called neutral names;—affirming of them, without a satire, That there had been as many knaves and fools, at least, as wise and good men, since the world began, who had indifferently borne them;—so that, like equal forces acting against each other in contrary directions, he thought they mutually destroyed each other's effects; for which reason, he would often declare, He would not give a cherry-stone to choose amongst them. Bob, which was my brother's name, was another of these neutral kinds of christian names, which operated very little either way; and as my father happened to be at Epsom, when it was given him,—he would ofttimes thank Heaven it was no worse. Andrew was something like a negative quantity in Algebra with him;—'twas worse, he said, than nothing.—William stood pretty high:—Numps again was low with him:—and Nick, he said, was the Devil.

But, of all the names in the universe, he had the most unconquerable aversion for Tristram;—he had the lowest and most contemptible opinion of it of any thing in the world,—thinking it could possibly produce nothing in *rerum naturâ*, but what was extremely mean and pitiful: So that in the midst of a dispute on the subject, in which, by the bye, he was frequently involved,—he would sometimes break off in a sudden and spirited Epiphonema, or rather Erotesis, raised a third, and sometimes a full fifth above the key of the discourse,—and demand it categorically of his antagonist, Whether he would take upon him to say, he had ever remembered,—whether he had ever read,—or even whether he had ever heard tell of a man, called Tristram, performing any thing great or worth recording?—No,—he would say,—Tristram!—The thing is impossible.

What could be wanting in my father but to have wrote a book to publish this notion of his to the world? Little boots it to the subtle speculatist to stand single in his opinions,—unless he gives them proper vent:—It was the identical thing which my father did:—for in the year sixteen, which was two years before I was born, he was at the pains of writing an express Dissertation simply upon the word Tristram,—shewing the world, with great candour and modesty, the grounds of his great abhorrence to the name.

When this story is compared with the title-page,—Will not the gentle reader pity my father from his soul? —to see an orderly and well-disposed gentleman, who tho' singular,—yet inoffensive in his notions,—so played upon in them by cross purposes;——to look down upon the stage, and see him baffled and overthrown in all his little systems and wishes; to behold a train of events perpetually falling out against him, and in so critical and cruel a way, as if they had purposedly been planned and pointed against him, merely to insult his speculations.

CHAP. XIX

——In a word, to behold such a one, in his old age, ill-fitted for troubles, ten times in a day suffering sorrow;—ten times in a day calling the child of his prayers Tristram!—Melancholy dissyllable of sound! which, to his ears, was unison to Nincompoop, and every name vituperative under heaven.——By his ashes! I swear it,—if ever malignant spirit took pleasure, or busied itself in traversing the purposes of mortal man,—it must have been here;—and if it was not necessary I should be born before I was christened, I would this moment give the reader an account of it.

Chapter XX

—How could you, Madam, be so inattentive in reading the last chapter? I told you in it, That my mother was not a Papist.——Papist! You told me no such thing, Sir.—Madam, I beg leave to repeat it over again, that I told you as plain, at least, as words, by direct inference, could tell you such a thing.—Then, Sir, I must have missed a page.—No, Madam,—you have not missed a word.——Then I was asleep, Sir.—My pride, Madam, cannot allow you that refuge.——Then, I declare, I know nothing at all about the matter.—That, Madam, is the very fault I lay to your charge; and as a punishment for it, I do insist upon it, that you immediately turn back, that is, as soon as you get to the next full stop, and read the whole chapter over again. I have imposed this penance upon the lady, neither out of wantonness nor cruelty; but from the best of motives; and therefore

shall make her no apology for it when she returns back:
—'Tis to rebuke a vicious taste, which has crept into
thousands besides herself,—of reading straight forwards,
more in quest of the adventures, than of the deep erudition and knowledge which a book of this cast, if read
over as it should be, would infallibly impart with them
——The mind should be accustomed to make wise reflections, and draw curious conclusions as it goes along;
the habitude of which made Pliny the younger affirm,
"That he never read a book so bad, but he drew some
profit from it." The stories of Greece and Rome, run
over without this turn and application,—do less service,
I affirm it, than the history of Parismus and Parismenus,
or of the Seven Champions of England, read with it.

——But here comes my fair lady. Have you read
over again the chapter, Madam, as I desired you?—You
have: And did you not observe the passage, upon the
second reading, which admits the inference?——Not a
word like it! Then, Madam, be pleased to ponder well
the last line but one of the chapter, where I take upon
me to say, "It was necessary I should be born before I
was christened." Had my mother, Madam, been a Papist,
that consequence did not follow.

It is a terrible misfortune for this same book of mine,
but more so to the Republic of letters;—so that my own
is quite swallowed up in the consideration of it,—that
this self-same vile pruriency for fresh adventures in all
things, has got so strongly into our habit and humour,—
and so wholly intent are we upon satisfying the impatience of our concupiscence that way,—that nothing but

CHAP. XX

the gross and more carnal parts of a composition will go
down:—The subtle hints and sly communications of
science fly off, like spirits upwards,——the heavy moral
escapes downwards; and both the one and the other are
as much lost to the world, as if they were still left in the
bottom of the ink-horn.

I wish the male-reader has not passed by many a one,
as quaint and curious as this one, in which the female-
reader has been detected. I wish it may have its effects;
—and that all good people, both male and female, from
her example, may be taught to think as well as read.[1]

Mémoire présenté à Messieurs les Docteurs de Sorbonne[2]

Un Chirurgien Accoucheur représente à Messieurs les
Docteurs de Sorbonne, qu'il y a des cas, quoique très
rares, où une mere ne sçauroit accoucher, & même où

[1] The Romish Rituals direct the baptizing of the child, in cases of danger,
before it is born;—but upon this proviso, That some part or other of the
child's body be seen by the baptizer:——But the Doctors of the Sorbonne, by
a deliberation held amongst them, April 10, 1733,—have enlarged the powers
of the midwives, by determining, That though no part of the child's body
should appear,——that baptism shall, nevertheless, be administered to it by
injection,—*par le moyen d'une petite canulle,*—Anglicè *a squirt.*——'Tis very
strange that St. Thomas Aquinas, who had so good a mechanical head, both
for tying and untying the knots of school-divinity,—should, after so much
pains bestowed upon this,—give up the point at last, as a second *La chose
impossible,*—"Infantes in maternis uteris existentes (quoth St. Thomas!)
baptizari possunt *nullo modo.*"—O Thomas! Thomas!

If the reader has the curiosity to see the question upon baptism by injection, as presented to the Doctors of the Sorbonne, with their consultation
thereupon, it is as follows.

[2] Vide Deventer, Paris edit., 4to, 1734, p. 366.

l'enfant est tellement renfermé dans le sein da sa mère, qu'il ne fait parôitre aucune partie de son corps, ce qui seroit un cas, suivant les Rituels, de lui conférer, du moins sous condition, le baptême. Le Chirurgien, qui consulte, prétend, par le moyen d'une petite canulle, de pouvoir baptiser immediatement l'enfant, sans faire aucun tort à la mère.——Il demand si ce moyen, qu'il vient de proposer, est permis & légitimé, & s'il peut s'en servir dans les cas qu'il vient d'exposer.

Réponse

Le Conseil estime, que la question proposée souffre de grandes difficultés. Les Théologiens posent d'un côté pour principe, que le baptême, qui est une naissance spirituelle, suppose une première naissance; il faut être né dans le monde, pour renaître en Jésus-Christ, comme ils l'enseignent. S. Thomas, 3 part. quaest. 88, artic. 11, suit cette doctrine comme une vérité constante; l'on ne peut, dit ce S. Docteur, baptiser les enfans qui sont renfermés dans le sein de leurs mères, & S. Thomas est fondé sur ce, que les enfans ne sont point nés, & ne peuvent être comptés parmi les autres hommes; d'où il conclud, qu'ils ne peuvent être l'objet d'une action extérieure, pourre çevoir par leur ministère, les sacremens nécessaires au salut: *Pueri in maternis uteris existentes nondum prodierunt in lucem ut cum aliis hominibus vitam ducant; unde non possunt subjici actioni humanae, ut per eorum ministerium sacramenta recipiant ad salutem.* Les rituels ordonnent dans la pratique ce que les théologiens ont établi sur les mêmes matières, & ils deffendent tous

CHAP. XX

d'une manière uniforme, de baptiser les enfans qui sont
renfermés dans le sein de leurs mères, s'ils ne font
paroître quelque partie de leurs corps. Le concours des
théologiens, & des rituels, qui sont les règles des diocèses,
paroît former une autorité qui termine la question présente; cependant le conseil de conscience considérant d'un
côté, que le raisonnement des théologiens est uniquement
fondé sur une raison de convenance, & que la deffense
des rituels suppose que l'on ne peut baptiser immédiate-
ment les enfans ainsi renfermés dans le sein de leurs
mères, ce qui est contre la supposition présente; & d'un
autre côté, considérant que les mêmes théologiens enseignent, que l'on peut risquer les sacremens que Jésus-
Christ a établis comme des moyens faciles, mais nécessaires pour sanctifier les hommes; & d'ailleurs estimant,
que les enfans renfermés dans le sein de leurs mères,
pourroient être capables de salut, parcequ'ils sont capables de damnation;—pour ces considérations, & en
egard à l'exposé, suivant lequel on assure avoir trouvé
un moyen certain de baptiser ces enfans ainsi renfermés,
sans faire aucun tort à la mère, le Conseil estime que l'on
pourroit se servir du moyen proposé, dans la confiance
qu'il a, que Dieu n'a point laissé ces sortes d'enfans sans
aucuns secours, & supposant, comme il est exposé, que le
moyen dont il s'agit est propre à leur procurer le baptême; cependant comme il s'agiroit, en autorisant la
pratique proposée, de changer une règle universellement
établie, le Conseil croît que celui qui consulte doit s'addresser à son évêque, & à qui il appartient de juger de
l'utilité, & du danger du moyen proposé, & comme, sous

le bon plaisir de l'évêque, le Conseil estime qu'il faudroit recourir au Pape, qui a le droit d'expliquer les règles de l'église, & d'y déroger dans le cas, où la loi ne sçauroit obliger, quelque sage & quelque utile que paroisse la manière de baptiser dont il s'agit, le Conseil ne pourroit l'approuver sans le concours de ces deux autorités. On conseile au moins à celui qui consulte, de s'addresser à son évêque, & de lui faire part de la présente décision, afin que, si le prélat entre dans les raisons sur lesquelles les docteurs soussignés s'appuyent, il puisse être autorisé dans le cas de nécessité, ou il risqueroit trop d'attendre que la permission fût demandée & accordée d'employer le moyen qu'il propose si avantageux au salut de l'enfant. Au reste, le Conseil, en estimant que l'on pourroit s'en servir, croît cependant, que si les enfans dont il s'agit, venoient au monde, contre l'espérance de ceux qui se seroient servis du même moyen, il seroit nécessaire de les baptiser sous condition; & en cela le Conseil se conforme à tous les rituels, qui en autorisant le baptême d'un enfant qui fait paroître quelque partie de son corps, enjoignent néantmoins, & ordonnent de le baptiser sous condition, s'il vient heureusement au monde.

Déliberé en Sorbonne, le 10 Avril, 1733.

A. Le Moyne.
L. De Romigny.
De Marcilly.

Mr. Tristram Shandy's compliments to Messrs. Le Moyne, De Romigny, and De Marcilly; hopes they all rested well the night after so tiresome a consultation.—

CHAP. XX

He begs to know, whether after the ceremony of marriage, and before that of consummation, the baptizing all the Homunculi at once, slapdash, by injection, would not be a shorter and safer cut still; on condition, as above, That if the Homunculi do well, and come safe into the world after this, that each and every of them shall be baptized again (*sous condition*)——And provided, in the second place, That the thing can be done, which Mr. Shandy apprehends it may, *par le moyen d'une petite canulle*, and *sans faire aucun tort au père*.

CHAPTER XXI

——I wonder what's all that noise, and running backwards and forwards for, above stairs, quoth my father, addressing himself, after an hour and a half's silence, to my uncle Toby,——who, you must know, was sitting on the opposite side of the fire, smoking his social pipe all the time, in mute contemplation of a new pair of black plush breeches which he had got on:—What can they be doing, brother?—quoth my father,—we can scarce hear ourselves talk.

I think, replied my uncle Toby, taking his pipe from his mouth, and striking the head of it two or three times upon the nail of his left thumb, as he began his sentence,——I think, says he:——But to enter rightly into my uncle Toby's sentiments upon this matter, you must be made to enter first a little into his character, the outlines of which I shall just give you, and then the dialogue between him and my father will go on as well again.

Pray what was that man's name,—for I write in such a hurry, I have no time to recollect or look for it,—who first made the observation, "That there was great inconsistency in our air and climate"? Whoever he was, 'twas a just and good observation in him.—But the corollary drawn from it, namely, "That it is this which has furnished us with such a variety of odd and whimsical characters";—that was not his;—it was found out by another man, at least a century and a half after him: Then again,—that this copious storehouse of original materials, is the true and natural cause that our Comedies are so much better than those of France, or any others that either have, or can be wrote upon the Continent:——that discovery was not fully made till about the middle of King William's reign,—when the great Dryden, in writing one of his long prefaces, (if I mistake

CHAP. XXI

not) most fortunately hit upon it. Indeed toward the latter end of Queen Anne, the great Addison began to patronize the notion, and more fully explained it to the world in one or two of his *Spectators;*—but the discovery was not his.—Then, fourthly and lastly, that this strange irregularity in our climate, producing so strange an irregularity in our characters,——doth thereby, in some sort, make us amends, by giving us somewhat to make us merry with when the weather will not suffer us to go out of doors,—that observation is my own;—and was struck out by me this very rainy day, March 26, 1759, and betwixt the hours of nine and ten in the morning.

Thus—thus, my fellow-labourers and associates in this great harvest of our learning, now ripening before our eyes; thus it is, by slow steps of casual increase, that our knowledge physical, metaphysical, physiological, polemical, nautical, mathematical, enigmatical, technical, biographical, romantical, chemical, and obstetrical, with fifty other branches of it, (most of 'em ending as these do, in *ical*) have for these two centuries and more, gradually been creeping upwards towards that ᾿ακμή of their perfections, from which, if we may form a conjecture from the advances of these last seven years, we cannot possibly be far off.

When that happens, it is to be hoped, it will put an end to all kind of writings whatsoever;—the want of all kind of writing will put an end to all kind of reading;—and that in time, As war begets poverty; poverty peace,——must, in course, put an end to all kind of knowledge,

—and then——we shall have all to begin over again; or, in other words, be exactly where we started.

——Happy! thrice happy times! I only wish that the era of my begetting, as well as the mode and manner of it, had been a little altered,—or that it could have been put off, with any convenience to my father or mother, for some twenty or five-and-twenty years longer, when a man in the literary world might have stood some chance.—

But I forget my uncle Toby, whom all this while we have left knocking the ashes out of his tobacco-pipe.

His humour was of that particular species, which does honour to our atmosphere; and I should have made no scruple of ranking him amongst one of the first-rate productions of it, had not there appeared too many strong lines in it of a family-likeness, which shewed that he derived the singularity of his temper more from blood, than either wind or water, or any modifications or combinations of them whatever: And I have, therefore, oft-times wondered, that my father, tho' I believe he had his reasons for it, upon his observing some tokens of eccentricity, in my course, when I was a boy,—should never once endeavour to account for them in this way: for all the Shandy Family were of an original character throughout:——I mean the males,—the females had no character at all,—except, indeed, my great aunt Dinah, who, about sixty years ago, was married and got with child by the coachman, for which my father, according to his hypothesis of christian names, would often say, She might thank her godfathers and godmothers.

CHAP. XXI

It will seem very strange,—and I would as soon think of dropping a riddle in the reader's way, which is not my interest to do, as set him upon guessing how it could come to pass, that an event of this kind, so many years after it had happened, should be reserved for the interruption of the peace and unity, which otherwise so cordially subsisted, between my father and my uncle Toby. One would have thought, that the whole force of the misfortune should have spent and wasted itself in the family at first,—as is generally the case.—But nothing ever wrought with our family after the ordinary way. Possibly at the very time this happened, it might have something else to afflict it; and as afflictions are sent down for our good, and that as this had never done the Shandy Family any good at all, it might lie waiting till apt times and circumstances should give it an opportunity to discharge its office.——Observe, I determine nothing upon this.——My way is ever to point out to the curious, different tracts of investigation, to come at the first springs of the events I tell;—not with a pedantic Fescue,—or in the decisive manner of Tacitus, who outwits himself and his reader;—but with the officious humility of a heart devoted to the assistance merely of the inquisitive;—to them I write,——and by them I shall be read,——if any such reading as this could be supposed to hold out so long,—to the very end of the world.

Why this cause of sorrow, therefore, was thus reserved for my father and uncle, is undetermined by me. But how and in what direction it exerted itself so as to become the cause of dissatisfaction between them, after it began to operate, is what I am able to explain with great exactness, and is as follows:

My uncle Toby Shandy, Madam, was a gentleman, who, with the virtues which usually constitute the character of a man of honour and rectitude,—possessed one in a very eminent degree, which is seldom or never put into the catalogue; and that was a most extreme and unparalleled modesty of nature;—though I correct the word nature, for this reason, that I may not prejudge a point which must shortly come to a hearing, and that is, Whether this modesty of his was natural or acquired.— Whichever way my uncle Toby came by it, 'twas nevertheless modesty in the truest sense of it; and that is, Madam, not in regard to words, for he was so unhappy as to have very little choice in them—but to things;— and this kind of modesty so possessed him, and it arose to such a height in him, as almost to equal, if such a thing could be, even the modesty of a woman: That female nicety, Madam, and inward cleanliness of mind and fancy, in your sex, which makes you so much the awe of ours.

You will imagine, Madam, that my uncle Toby had contracted all this from this very source;—that he had spent a great part of his time in converse with your sex; and that from a thorough knowledge of you, and the force of imitation which such fair examples render irresistible, he had acquired this amiable turn of mind.

I wish I could say so,—for unless it was with his sister-in-law, my father's wife and my mother—my uncle Toby scarce exchanged three words with the sex in as many

CHAP. XXI

years;——no, he got it, Madam, by a blow.——A blow!
—Yes, Madam, it was owing to a blow from a stone,
broke off by a ball from the parapet of a horn-work at
the siege of Namur, which struck full upon my uncle
Toby's groin.—Which way could that affect it? The
story of that, Madam, is long and interesting;—but it
would be running my history all upon heaps to give it
you here.——'Tis for an episode hereafter; and every
circumstance relating to it, in its proper place, shall be
faithfully laid before you:—'Till then, it is not in my
power to give farther light into this matter, or say more
than what I have said already,——That my uncle Toby
was a gentleman of unparalleled modesty, which happening to be somewhat subtilized and rarefied by the
constant heat of a little family pride,—they both so
wrought together within him, that he could never bear
to hear the affair of my aunt Dinah touched upon, but
with the greatest emotion.—The least hint of it was
enough to make the blood fly into his face;—but when
my father enlarged upon the story in mixed companies,
which the illustration of his hypothesis frequently obliged
him to do,—the unfortunate blight of one of the fairest
branches of the family would set my uncle Toby's honour
and modesty o'bleeding; and he would often take my
father aside, in the greatest concern imaginable, to expostulate and tell him, he would give him any thing in
the world, only to let the story rest.

My father, I believe, had the truest love and tenderness for my uncle Toby, that ever one brother bore
towards another, and would have done anything in

nature, which one brother in reason could have desired of another, to have made my uncle Toby's heart easy in this, or any other point. But this lay out of his power.

——My father, as I told you, was a philosopher in grain, — speculative, — systematical; — and my aunt Dinah's affair was a matter of as much consequence to him, as the retrogradation of the planets to Copernicus: —The backslidings of Venus in her orbit fortified the Copernican system, called so after his name; and the backslidings of my aunt Dinah in her orbit, did the same service in establishing my father's system, which, I trust, will for ever hereafter be called the Shandean System, after his.

In any other family dishonour, my father, I believe, had as nice a sense of shame as any man whatever;—and neither he, nor, I dare say, Copernicus, would have divulged the affair in either case, or have taken the least notice of it to the world, but for the obligations they owed, as they thought, to truth.—*Amicus Plato*, my father would say, construing the words to my uncle Toby, as he went along, *Amicus Plato*; that is, Dinah was my aunt;—*sed magis amica veritas*—but Truth is my sister.

This contrariety of humours betwixt my father and my uncle, was the source of many a fraternal squabble. The one could not bear to hear the tale of family disgrace recorded,—and the other would scarce ever let a day pass to an end without some hint at it.

For God's sake, my uncle Toby would cry,—and for my sake, and for all our sakes, my dear brother Shandy, —do let this story of our aunt's and her ashes sleep in

CHAP. XXI

peace;——how can you,——how can you have so little
feeling and compassion for the character of our family?
——What is the character of a family to an hypothesis?
my father would reply.——Nay, if you come to that—
what is the life of a family?——The life of a family!—
my uncle Toby would say, throwing himself back in his
arm chair, and lifting up his hands, his eyes, and one leg.
——Yes, the life,—my father would say, maintaining
his point. How many thousands of 'em are there every
year that come cast away, (in all civilized countries at
least)—and considered as nothing but common air, in
competition of an hypothesis. In my plain sense of things,
my uncle Toby would answer,—every such instance is
downright Murder, let who will commit it.—There lies
your mistake, my father would reply;——for, *in Foro
Scientiae* there is no such thing as Murder,—'tis only
Death, brother.

My uncle Toby would never offer to answer this by
any other kind of argument, than that of whistling half
a dozen bars of *Lillabullero*.——You must know it was
the usual channel thro' which his passions got vent, when
any thing shocked or surprised him:——but especially
when any thing, which he deemed very absurd, was
offered.

As not one of our logical writers, nor any of the com-
mentators upon them, that I remember, have thought
proper to give a name to this particular species of argument,—I here take the liberty to do it myself, for two
reasons. First, That, in order to prevent all confusion in
disputes, it may stand as much distinguished for ever,

from every other species of argument——as the *Argumentum ad Verecundiam, ex Absurdo, ex Fortiori*, or any other argument whatsoever:——And, secondly, That it may be said by my children's children, when my head is laid to rest,—that their learned grandfather's head had been busied to as much purpose once, as other people's; —That he had invented a name,—and generously thrown it into the Treasury of the *Ars Logica*, for one of the most unanswerable arguments in the whole science. And, if the end of disputation is more to silence than convince, —they may add, if they please, to one of the best arguments too.

I do therefore, by these presents, strictly order and command, That it be known and distinguished by the name and title of the *Argumentum Fistulatorium*, and no other;—and that it rank hereafter with the *Argumentum Baculinum* and the *Argumentum ad Crumenam*, and for ever hereafter be treated of in the same chapter.

As for the *Argumentum Tripodium*, which is never used but by the woman against the man;—and the *Argumentum ad Rem*, which, contrarywise, is made use of by the man only against the woman;—As these two are enough in conscience for one lecture;——and, moreover, as the one is the best answer to the other,—let them likewise be kept apart, and be treated of in a place by themselves.

CHAP. XXI

Chapter XXII

THE learned Bishop Hall, I mean the famous Dr. Joseph Hall, who was Bishop of Exeter in King James the First's reign, tells us in one of his *Decads*, at the end of his divine art of meditation, imprinted at London, in the year 1610, by John Beal, dwelling in Aldersgate-street, "That it is an abominable thing for a man to commend himself";——and I really think it is so.

And yet, on the other hand, when a thing is executed in a masterly kind of a fashion, which thing is not likely to be found out;—I think it is full as abominable, that a man should lose the honour of it, and go out of the world with the conceit of it rotting in his head.

This is precisely my situation.

For in this long digression which I was accidentally led into, as in all my digressions (one only excepted) there is a master-stroke of digressive skill, the merit of which has all along, I fear, been overlooked by my reader, —not for want of penetration in him,—but because 'tis an excellence seldom looked for, or expected indeed, in a digression;—and it is this: That tho' my digressions are all fair, as you observe,—and that I fly off from what I am about, as far, and as often too, as any writer in Great Britain; yet I constantly take care to order affairs so that my main business does not stand still in my absence.

I was just going, for example, to have given you the great outlines of my uncle Toby's most whimsical character;—when my aunt Dinah and the coachman came across us, and led us a vagary some millions of miles into

the very heart of the planetary system: Notwithstanding all this, you perceive that the drawing of my uncle
Toby's character went on gently all the time;—not the
great contours of it,—that was impossible,—but some
familiar strokes and faint designations of it, were here
and there touched on, as we went along, so that you are
much better acquainted with my uncle Toby now than
you was before.

By this contrivance the machinery of my work is of a
species by itself; two contrary motions are introduced
into it, and reconciled, which were thought to be at vari-
ance with each other. In a word, my work is digressive,
and it is progressive too,—and at the same time.

This, Sir, is a very different story from that of the
earth's moving round her axis, in her diurnal rotation,
with her progress in her elliptic orbit which brings about
the year, and constitutes that variety and vicissitude
of seasons we enjoy;—though I own it suggested the
thought,—as I believe the greatest of our boasted improvements and discoveries have come from such trifling
hints.

Digressions, incontestably, are the sunshine;——they
are the life, the soul of reading!—take them out of this
book, for instance,—you might as well take the book
along with them;—one cold eternal winter would reign
in every page of it; restore them to the writer;—he steps
forth like a bridegroom,—bids All-hail; brings in variety,
and forbids the appetite to fail.

All the dexterity is in the good cookery and management of them, so as to be not only for the advantage

CHAP. XXII

of the reader, but also of the author, whose distress, in this matter, is truly pitiable: For, if he begins a digression,—from that moment, I observe, his whole work stands stock still;—and if he goes on with his main work, —then there is an end of his digression.

——This is vile work.—For which reason, from the beginning of this, you see, I have constructed the main work and the adventitious parts of it with such intersections, and have so complicated and involved the digressive and progressive movements, one wheel within another, that the whole machine, in general, has been kept a-going;—and, what's more, it shall be kept a-going these forty years, if it pleases the fountain of health to bless me so long with life and good spirits.

Chapter XXIII

I HAVE a strong propensity in me to begin this chapter very nonsensically, and I will not baulk my fancy.— Accordingly I set off thus:

If the fixture of Momus's glass in the human breast, according to the proposed emendation of that arch-critic, had taken place,——first, This foolish consequence would certainly have followed,—That the very wisest and very gravest of us all, in one coin or other, must have paid window-money every day of our lives.

And, secondly, That had the said glass been there set up, nothing more would have been wanting, in order to have taken a man's character, but to have taken a chair and gone softly, as you would to a dioptrical bee-hive, and looked in,—viewed the soul stark naked;—observed all her motions,—her machinations;—traced all her maggots from their first engendering to their crawling forth;—watched her loose in her frisks, her gambols, her capricios; and after some notice of her more solemn deportment, consequent upon such frisks, etc.,——then taken your pen and ink and set down nothing but what you had seen, and could have sworn to:—But this is an advantage not to be had by the biographer in this planet; —in the planet Mercury (belike) it may be so, if not better still for him;——for there the intense heat of the country, which is proved by computators, from its vicinity to the sun, to be more than equal to that of red-hot iron,—must, I think, long ago have vitrified the bodies of the inhabitants, (as the efficient cause) to suit them for the climate (which is the final cause;) so that betwixt them both, all the tenements of their souls, from top to bottom, may be nothing else, for aught the soundest philosophy can shew to the contrary, but one fine transparent body of clear glass (bating the umbilical knot)— so that, till the inhabitants grow old and tolerably wrinkled, whereby the rays of light, in passing through them, become so monstrously refracted,——or return reflected from their surfaces in such transverse lines to the eye, that a man cannot be seen through;—his soul might as well, unless for mere ceremony, or the trifling advantage which the umbilical point gave her,—might, upon all other accounts, I say, as well play the fool out o' doors as in her own house.

But this, as I said above, is not the case of the inhab-

CHAP. XXIII

itants of this earth;—our minds shine not through the body, but are wrapt up here in a dark covering of un-crystallized flesh and blood; so that, if we would come to the specific characters of them, we must go some other way to work.

Many, in good truth, are the ways, which human wit has been forced to take, to do this thing with exactness.

Some, for instance, draw all their characters with wind-instruments.—Virgil takes notice of that way in the affair of Dido and Aeneas;—but it is as fallacious as the breath of fame;—and, moreover, bespeaks a narrow genius. I am not ignorant that the Italians pretend to a mathematical exactness in their designations of one par-ticular sort of character among them, from the *forte* or *piano* of a certain wind-instrument they use,—which they say is infallible.—I dare not mention the name of the instrument in this place;—'tis sufficient we have it amongst us,—but never think of making a drawing by it;—this is enigmatical, and intended to be so, at least *ad populum*:—And therefore, I beg, Madam, when you come here, that you read on as fast as you can, and never stop to make any inquiry about it.

There are others again, who will draw a man's char-acter from no other helps in the world, but merely from his evacuations;—but this often gives a very incorrect outline,—unless, indeed, you take a sketch of his reple-tions too; and by correcting one drawing from the other, compound one good figure out of them both.

I should have no objection to this method, but that I think it must smell too strong of the lamp—and be ren-

dered still more operose, by forcing you to have an eye
to the rest of his Non-naturals.——Why the most natural
actions of a man's life should be called his Non-naturals,
—is another question.

There are others, fourthly, who disdain every one of
these expedients;—not from any fertility of their own,
but from the various ways of doing it, which they have
borrowed from the honourable devices which the Penta-
graphic Brethren[1] of the brush have shewn in taking
copies.—These, you must know, are your great historians.

One of these you will see drawing a full-length character against the light;—that's illiberal,—dishonest,—
and hard upon the character of the man who sits.

Others, to mend the matter, will make a drawing of
you in the Camera;—that is most unfair of all,—because,
there you are sure to be represented in some of your
most ridiculous attitudes.

To avoid all and every one of these errors in giving
you my uncle Toby's character, I am determined to draw
it by no mechanical help whatever;——nor shall my
pencil be guided by any one wind-instrument which ever
was blown upon, either on this, or on the other side of
the Alps;—nor will I consider either his repletions or his
discharges,—or touch upon his Non-naturals;—but, in a
word, I will draw my uncle Toby's character from his
Hobby-Horse.

---

[1] Pentagraph, an instrument to copy prints and pictures mechanically,
and in any proportion.

CHAP. XXIII

Chapter XXIV

I f I was not morally sure that the reader must be out of all patience for my uncle Toby's character,——I would here previously have convinced him that there is no instrument so fit to draw such a thing with, as that which I have pitched upon.

A man and his Hobby-Horse, tho' I cannot say that they act and re-act exactly after the same manner in which the soul and body do upon each other: Yet doubtless there is a communication between them of some kind; and my opinion rather is, that there is something in it more of the manner of electrified bodies,—and that, by means of the heated parts of the rider, which come immediately into contact with the back of the Hobby-Horse,—by long journeys and much friction, it so happens, that the body of the rider is at length filled as full of Hobby-Horsical matter as it can hold;——so that if you are able to give but a clear description of the nature of the one, you may form a pretty exact notion of the genius and character of the other.

Now the Hobby-Horse which my uncle Toby always rode upon, was in my opinion an Hobby-Horse well worth giving a description of, if it was only upon the score of his great singularity;—for you might have travelled from York to Dover,—from Dover to Penzance in Cornwall, and from Penzance to York back again, and not have seen such another upon the road; or if you had seen such a one, whatever haste you had been in, you must infallibly have stopped to have taken a view of him. Indeed, the gait and figure of him was so strange, and so utterly unlike was he, from his head to his tail, to any one of the whole species, that it was now and then made a matter of dispute,——whether he was really a Hobby-Horse or no: but as the Philosopher would use no other argument to the Sceptic, who disputed with him against the reality of motion, save that of rising up upon his legs, and walking across the room;—so would my uncle Toby use no other argument to prove his Hobby-Horse was a Hobby-Horse indeed, but by getting upon his back and riding him about;—leaving the world, after that, to determine the point as it thought fit.

In good truth, my uncle Toby mounted him with so much pleasure, and he carried my uncle Toby so well, ——that he troubled his head very little with what the world either said or thought about it.

It is now high time, however, that I give you a description of him:—But to go on regularly, I only beg you will give me leave to acquaint you first, how my uncle Toby came by him.

Chapter XXV

THE wound in my uncle Toby's groin, which he received at the siege of Namur, rendering him unfit for the service, it was thought expedient he should return to England, in order, if possible, to be set to rights.

He was four years totally confined,—part of it to his bed, and all of it to his room: and in the course of his cure, which was all that time in hand, suffered unspeakable miseries,—owing to a succession of exfoliations from the *os pubis*, and the outward edge of that part of the *coxendix* called the *os illium*,——both which bones were dismally crushed, as much by the irregularity of the stone, which I told you was broke off the parapet,—as by its size,—(tho' it was pretty large) which inclined the surgeon all along to think, that the great injury which it had done my uncle Toby's groin, was more owing to the gravity of the stone itself, than to the projectile force of it,—which he would often tell him was a great happiness.

My father at that time was just beginning business in London, and had taken a house;—and as the truest friendship and cordiality subsisted between the two brothers,—and that my father thought my uncle Toby could no where be so well nursed and taken care of as in his own house,——he assigned him the very best apartment in it.—And what was a much more sincere mark of his affection still, he would never suffer a friend or an acquaintance to step into the house on any occasion, but he would take him by the hand, and lead him upstairs to see his brother Toby, and chat an hour by his bedside.

The history of a soldier's wound beguiles the pain of it;—my uncle's visitors at least thought so, and in their daily calls upon him, from the courtesy arising out of that belief, they would frequently turn the discourse to that subject,—and from that subject the discourse would generally roll on to the siege itself.

These conversations were infinitely kind; and my uncle Toby received great relief from them, and would have received much more, but that they brought him into some unforeseen perplexities, which, for three months together, retarded his cure greatly; and if he had not hit upon an expedient to extricate himself out of them, I verily believe they would have laid him in his grave.

What these perplexities of my uncle Toby were,— 'tis impossible for you to guess;—If you could,—I should blush; not as a relation,—not as a man,—nor even as a woman,—but I should blush as an author; inasmuch as I set no small store by myself upon this very account, that my reader has never yet been able to guess at any thing. And in this, Sir, I am of so nice and singular a humour, that if I thought you was able to form the least judgment or probable conjecture to yourself, of what was to come in the next page,—I would tear it out of my book.

CHAP. XXV

BOOK II

Chapter I

I HAVE begun a new book, on purpose that I might have room enough to explain the nature of the perplexities in which my uncle Toby was involved, from the many discourses and interrogations about the siege of Namur, where he received his wound.

I must remind the reader, in case he has read the history of King William's wars,—but if he has not,—I then inform him, that one of the most memorable attacks in that siege, was that which was made by the English and Dutch upon the point of the advanced counterscarp, between the gate of St. Nicolas, which inclosed the great sluice or water-stop, where the English were terribly exposed to the shot of the counter-guard and demi-bastion of St. Roch: The issue of which hot dispute, in three words, was this; That the Dutch lodged themselves upon

the counter-guard,—and that the English made themselves masters of the covered-way before St. Nicolas-gate,
notwithstanding the gallantry of the French officers,
who exposed themselves upon the glacis sword in hand.

As this was the principal attack of which my uncle
Toby was an eye witness at Namur,——the army of the
besiegers being cut off, by the confluence of the Maes
and Sambre, from seeing much of each other's operations,——my uncle Toby was generally more eloquent
and particular in his account of it; and the many perplexities he was in, arose out of the almost insurmountable difficulties he found in telling his story intelligibly,
and giving such clear ideas of the differences and distinctions between the scarp and counterscarp,—the glacis
and covered-way,—the half-moon and ravelin,—as to
make his company fully comprehend where and what he
was about.

Writers themselves are too apt to confound these
terms; so that you will the less wonder, if in his endeavours to explain them, and in opposition to many miscon-
ceptions, that my uncle Toby did oft-times puzzle his
visitors, and sometimes himself too.

To speak the truth, unless the company my father
led up stairs were tolerably clear-headed, or my uncle
Toby was in one of his explanatory moods, 'twas a difficult thing, do what he could, to keep the discourse free
from obscurity.

What rendered the account of this affair the more
intricate to my uncle Toby, was this,—that in the attack
of the counterscarp, before the gate of St. Nicolas, ex-

tending itself from the bank of the Maes, quite up to the great water-stop,—the ground was cut and cross cut with such a multitude of dykes, drains, rivulets, and sluices, on all sides,—and he would get so sadly bewildered, and set fast amongst them, that frequently he could neither get backwards or forwards to save his life; and was oft-times obliged to give up the attack upon that very account only.

These perplexing rebuffs gave my uncle Toby Shandy more perturbations than you would imagine: and as my father's kindness to him was continually dragging up fresh friends and fresh enquirers,——he had but a very uneasy task of it.

No doubt my uncle Toby had great command of himself,—and could guard appearances, I believe, as well as most men;—yet any one may imagine, that when he could not retreat out of the ravelin without getting into the half-moon, or get out of the covered-way without falling down the counterscarp, nor cross the dyke without danger of slipping into the ditch, but that he must have fretted and fumed inwardly:—He did so;—and the little and hourly vexations, which may seem trifling and of no account to the man who has not read Hippocrates, yet, whoever has read Hippocrates, or Dr. James Mackenzie, and has considered well the effects which the passions and affections of the mind have upon the digestion—(Why not of a wound as well as of a dinner?)—may easily conceive what sharp paroxysms and exacerbations of his wound my uncle Toby must have undergone upon that score only.

CHAP. I

—My uncle Toby could not philosophize upon it;—
'twas enough he felt it was so,—and having sustained
the pain and sorrows of it for three months together, he
was resolved some way or other to extricate himself.

He was one morning lying upon his back in his bed,
the anguish and nature of the wound upon his groin
suffering him to lie in no other position, when a thought
came into his head, that if he could purchase such a
thing, and have it pasted down upon a board, as a large
map of the fortification of the town and citadel of Namur,
with its environs, it might be a means of giving him ease.
—I take notice of his desire to have the environs along
with the town and citadel, for this reason,—because my
uncle Toby's wound was got in one of the traverses,
about thirty toises from the returning angle of the trench,
opposite to the salient angle of the demi-bastion of St.
Roch:——so that he was pretty confident he could stick
a pin upon the identical spot of ground where he was
standing on when the stone struck him.

All this succeeded to his wishes, and not only freed
him from a world of sad explanations, but, in the end, it
proved the happy means, as you will read, of procuring
my uncle Toby his Hobby-Horse.

CHAPTER II

THERE is nothing so foolish, when you are at the expense of making an entertainment of this kind, as to
order things so badly, as to let your critics and gentry of
refined taste run it down: Nor is there any thing so likely

to make them do it, as that of leaving them out of the party, or, what is full as offensive, of bestowing your attention upon the rest of your guests in so particular a way, as if there was no such thing as a critic (by occupation) at table.

——I guard against both; for, in the first place, I have left half a dozen places purposely open for them;—and in the next place, I pay them all court.—Gentlemen, I kiss your hands, I protest no company could give me half the pleasure,—by my soul I am glad to see you——I beg only you will make no strangers of yourselves, but sit down without any ceremony, and fall on heartily.

I said I had left six places, and I was upon the point of carrying my complaisance so far, as to have left a seventh open for them,—and in this very spot I stand on; but being told by a Critic, (tho' not by occupation, —but by nature) that I had acquitted myself well enough, I shall fill it up directly, hoping, in the mean time, that I shall be able to make a great deal of more room next year.

——How, in the name of wonder! could your uncle Toby, who, it seems was a military man, and whom you have represented as no fool,——be at the same time such a confused, pudding-headed, muddle-headed fellow, as —Go look.

So, Sir Critic, I could have replied; but I scorn it.— 'Tis language unurbane,—and only befitting the man who cannot give clear and satisfactory accounts of things, or dive deep enough into the first causes of human ignorance and confusion. It is moreover the reply valiant—

CHAP. II

and therefore I reject it: for tho' it might have suited my
uncle Toby's character as a soldier excellently well,—
and had he not accustomed himself, in such attacks, to
whistle the *Lillabullero*, as he wanted no courage, 'tis the
very answer he would have given; yet it would by no
means have done for me. You see as plain as can be, that
I write as a man of erudition; that even my similes, my
allusions, my illustrations, my metaphors, are erudite,—
and that I must sustain my character properly, and contrast it properly too,—else what would become of me?
Why, Sir, I should be undone:—at this very moment
that I am going here to fill up one place against a critic,
—I should have made an opening for a couple.

——Therefore I answer thus:

Pray, Sir, in all the reading which you have ever read,
did you ever read such a book as Locke's Essay upon the
Human Understanding?——Don't answer me rashly—
because many, I know, quote the book, who have not
read it—and many have read it who understand it not:
—If either of these is your case, as I write to instruct, I
will tell you in three words what the book is.—It is a
history.—A history! of who? what? where? when? Don't
hurry yourself——It is a history-book, Sir, (which may
possibly recommend it to the world) of what passes in a
man's own mind; and if you will say so much of the
book, and no more, believe me, you will cut no contemptible figure in a metaphysic circle.

But this by the way.

Now if you will venture to go along with me, and
look down into the bottom of this matter, it will be

found that the cause of obscurity and confusion, in the mind of a man, is threefold.

Dull organs, dear Sir, in the first place. Secondly, slight and transient impressions made by the objects, when the said organs are not dull. And thirdly, a memory like unto a sieve, not able to retain what it has received. —Call down Dolly your chamber-maid, and I will give you my cap and bell along with it, if I make not this matter so plain that Dolly herself should understand it as well as Malebranch.——When Dolly has indited her epistle to Robin, and has thrust her arm into the bottom of her pocket hanging by her right side;—take that opportunity to recollect that the organs and faculties of perception can, by nothing in this world be so aptly typified and explained as by that one thing which Dolly's hand is in search of.—Your organs are not so dull that I should inform you—'tis an inch, Sir, of red seal-wax.

When this is melted and dropped upon the letter, if Dolly fumbles too long for her thimble, till the wax is over hardened, it will not receive the mark of her thimble from the usual impulse which was wont to imprint it. Very well. If Dolly's wax, for want of better, is bees-wax, or of a temper too soft—tho' it may receive,—it will not hold the impression, how hard soever Dolly thrusts against it; and last of all, supposing the wax good, and eke the thimble, but applied thereto in care-less haste, as her Mistress rings the bell;——in any one of these three cases the print left by the thimble will be as unlike the prototype as a brass-jack.

CHAP. II

Now you must understand that not one of these was the true cause of the confusion in my uncle Toby's discourse; and it is for that very reason I enlarge upon them so long, after the manner of great physiologists—to shew the world, what it did *not* arise from.

What it did arise from, I have hinted above, and a fertile source of obscurity it is,—and ever will be,—and that is the unsteady uses of words, which have perplexed the clearest and most exalted understandings.

It is ten to one (at Arthur's) whether you have ever read the literary histories of past ages;—if you have, what terrible battles, 'yclept logomachies, have they occasioned and perpetuated with so much gall and ink-shed, —that a good-natured man cannot read the accounts of them without tears in his eyes.

Gentle critic! when thou hast weighed all this, and considered within thyself how much of thy own knowledge, discourse, and conversation has been pestered and disordered, at one time or other, by this, and this only: —What a pudder and racket in Councils about οὐσία and ὑπόστασις; and in the Schools of the learned about power and about spirit;—about essences, and about quintessences;——about substances and about space. ——What confusion in greater Theatres from words of little meaning, and as indeterminate a sense! when thou considerest this, thou wilt not wonder at my uncle Toby's perplexities,—thou wilt drop a tear of pity upon his scarp and his counterscarp;—his glacis and his covered way;—his ravelin and his half-moon: 'Twas not by ideas,—by Heaven; his life was put in jeopardy by words.

BOOK II

CHAPTER III

WHEN my uncle Toby got his map of Namur to his mind, he began immediately to apply himself, and with the utmost diligence, to the study of it; for nothing being of more importance to him than his recovery, and his recovery depending, as you have read, upon the passions and affections of his mind, it behoved him to take the nicest care to make himself so far master of his subject, as to be able to talk upon it without emotion.

In a fortnight's close and painful application, which, by the bye, did my uncle Toby's wound, upon his groin, no good,—he was enabled, by the help of some marginal documents at the feet of the elephant, together with

Gobesius's military architecture and pyroballogy, translated from the Flemish, to form his discourse with passable perspicuity; and before he was two full months
gone,—he was right eloquent upon it, and could make
not only the attack of the advanced counterscarp with
great order;——but having, by that time, gone much
deeper into the art, than what his first motive made
necessary, my uncle Toby was able to cross the Maes
and Sambre; make diversions as far as Vauban's line,
the abbey of Salsines, etc., and give his visitors as distinct a history of each of their attacks, as of that of the
gate of St. Nicolas, where he had the honour to receive
his wound.

But desire of knowledge, like the thirst of riches, increases ever with the acquisition of it. The more my
uncle Toby pored over his map, the more he took a liking
to it!—by the same process and electrical assimilation,
as I told you, through which I ween the souls of connoisseurs themselves, by long friction and incumbition,
have the happiness, at length, to get all be-virtued—bepictured,—be-butterflied, and be-fiddled.

The more my uncle Toby drank of this sweet fountain of science, the greater was the heat and impatience
of his thirst, so that before the first year of his confinement had well gone round, there was scarce a fortified
town in Italy or Flanders, of which, by one means or
other, he had not procured a plan, reading over as he got
them, and carefully collating therewith the histories of
their sieges, their demolitions, their improvements, and
new works, all which he would read with that intense

application and delight, that he would forget himself, his wound, his confinement, his dinner.

In the second year my uncle Toby purchased Ramelli and Cataneo, translated from the Italian;—likewise Stevinus, Moralis, the Chevalier de Ville, Lorini, Cochorn, Sheeter, the Count de Pagan, the Marshal Vauban, Mons. Blondel, with almost as many more books of military architecture, as Don Quixote was found to have of chivalry, when the curate and barber invaded his library.

Towards the beginning of the third year, which was in August, ninety-nine, my uncle Toby found it necessary to understand a little of projectiles:—and having judged it best to draw his knowledge from the fountain-head, he began with N. Tartaglia, who it seems was the first man who detected the imposition of a cannon-ball's doing all that mischief under the notion of a right line— This N. Tartaglia proved to my uncle Toby to be an impossible thing.

——Endless is the search of Truth.

No sooner was my uncle Toby satisfied which road the cannon-ball did not go, but he was insensibly led on, and resolved in his mind to enquire and find out which road the ball did go: For which purpose he was obliged to set off afresh with old Maltus, and studied him devoutly.—He proceeded next to Galileo and Torricellius, wherein, by certain Geometrical rules, infallibly laid down, he found the precise part to be a Parabola—or else an Hyperbola,—and that the parameter, or *latus rectum*, of the conic section of the said path, was to the quantity and amplitude in a direct ratio, as the whole line to the sine of double the angle of incidence, formed by the breech upon an horizontal plane;—and that the semi-parameter,——stop! my dear uncle Toby——stop! —go not one foot farther into this thorny and bewildered track,—intricate are the steps! intricate are the mazes of this labyrinth! intricate are the troubles which the pursuit of this bewitching phantom Knowledge will bring upon thee.—O my uncle;—fly—fly, fly from it as from a serpent.—Is it fit—good-natured man! thou should'st sit up, with the wound upon thy groin, whole nights baking thy blood with hectic watchings?—Alas! 'twill exasperate thy symptoms,—check thy perspirations— evaporate thy spirits—waste thy animal strength,—dry up thy radical moisture, bring thee into a costive habit of body,—impair thy health,—and hasten all the infirmities of thy old age.—O my uncle! my uncle Toby.

Chapter IV

I WOULD not give a groat for that man's knowledge in pen-craft, who does not understand this,—That the best plain narrative in the world, tacked very close to the last spirited apostrophe to my uncle Toby—would have felt both cold and vapid upon the reader's palate;—therefore I forthwith put an end to the chapter, though I was in the middle of my story.

——Writers of my stamp have one principle in common with painters. Where an exact copying makes our pictures less striking, we choose the less evil; deeming it even more pardonable to trespass against truth, than beauty. This is to be understood *cum grano salis;* but be it as it will,—as the parallel is made more for the sake of letting the apostrophe cool, than any thing else,—'tis not very material whether upon any other score the reader approves of it or not.

In the latter end of the third year, my uncle Toby perceiving that the parameter and the semi-parameter of the conic section angered his wound, he left off the study of projectiles in a kind of a huff, and betook himself to the practical part of fortification only; the pleasure of which, like a spring held back, returned upon him with redoubled force.

It was in this year that my uncle began to break in upon the daily regularity of a clean shirt,——to dismiss his barber unshaven,——and to allow his surgeon scarce time sufficient to dress his wound, concerning himself so little about it, as not to ask him once in seven times dressing, how it went on: when, lo!—all of a sudden, for the change was quick as lightning, he began to sigh heavily for his recovery,——complained to my father, grew impatient with the surgeon:——and one morning, as he heard his foot coming up stairs, he shut up his books, and thrust aside his instruments, in order to expostulate with him upon the protraction of the cure, which, he told him, might surely have been accomplished at least by that time:—He dwelt long upon the miseries he had undergone, and the sorrows of his four years' melancholy imprisonment;——adding, that had it not

CHAP. IV

been for the kind looks and fraternal cheerings of the best of brothers,—he had long since sunk under his misfortunes.——My father was by: My uncle Toby's eloquence brought tears into his eyes;——'twas unexpected:——My uncle Toby, by nature was not eloquent;—it had the greater effect:——The surgeon was confounded;——not that there wanted grounds for such, or greater marks of impatience,—but 'twas unexpected too; in the four years he had attended him, he had never seen any thing like it in my uncle Toby's carriage; he had never once dropped one fretful or discontented word;——he had been all patience,—all submission.

—We lose the right of complaining sometimes by forbearing it;—but we often treble the force:—The surgeon was astonished; but much more so, when he heard my uncle Toby go on, and peremptorily insist upon his healing up the wound directly,—or sending for Monsieur Ronjat, the king's serjeant-surgeon, to do it for him.

The desire of life and health is implanted in man's nature;——the love of liberty and enlargement is a sister-passion to it: These my uncle Toby had in common with his species;——and either of them had been sufficient to account for his earnest desire to get well and out of doors;——but I have told you before, that nothing wrought with our family after the common way;—— and from the time and manner in which this eager desire shewed itself in the present case, the penetrating reader will suspect there was some other cause or crotchet for it in my uncle Toby's head:——There was so, and 'tis the subject of the next chapter to set forth what that cause

and crotchet was. I own, when that's done, 'twill be time
to return back to the parlour fire-side, where we left my
uncle Toby in the middle of his sentence.

CHAPTER V

WHEN a man gives himself up to the government of
a ruling passion,—or, in other words, when his
Hobby-Horse grows headstrong,—farewell cool reason
and fair discretion!

My uncle Toby's wound was near well, and as soon
as the surgeon recovered his surprise, and could get leave
to say as much——he told him, 'twas just beginning to
incarnate; and that if no fresh exfoliation happened,
which there was no sign of,—it would be dried up in five
or six weeks. The sound of as many Olympiads, twelve
hours before, would have conveyed an idea of shorter
duration to my uncle Toby's mind.—The succession of
his ideas was now rapid,—he broiled with impatience to
put his design in execution;——and so, without consult-
ing farther with any soul living,—which, by the bye, I
think is right, when you are predetermined to take no one
soul's advice,——he privately ordered Trim, his man, to
pack up a bundle of lint and dressings, and hire a chariot-
and-four to be at the door exactly by twelve o'clock that
day, when he knew my father would be upon 'Change.
——So leaving a bank-note upon the table for the surgeon's care of him, and a letter of tender thanks for his
brother's—he packed up his maps, his books of fortification, his instruments, etc., and by the help of a crutch on

one side, and Trim on the other,——my uncle Toby embarked for Shandy Hall.

The reason, or rather the rise of this sudden demi-
gration was as follows:

The table in my uncle Toby's room, and at which,
the night before this change happened, he was sitting
with his maps, etc., about him—being somewhat of the
smallest, for that infinity of great and small instruments
of knowledge which usually lay crowded upon it—he
had the accident, in reaching over for his tobacco-box, to
throw down his compasses, and in stooping to take the
compasses up, with his sleeve he threw down his case of
instruments and snuffers;—and as the dice took a run
against him, in his endeavouring to catch the snuffers in
falling——he thrust Monsieur Blondel off the table, and
Count de Pagan o' top of him.

'Twas to no purpose for a man, lame as my uncle
Toby was, to think of redressing these evils by himself,
—he rung his bell for his man Trim;——Trim, quoth my
uncle Toby, prithee see what confusion I have here been
making—I must have some better contrivance, Trim,
——Can'st not thou take my rule, and measure the
length and breadth of this table, and then go and bespeak me one as big again?——Yes, an' please your
Honour, replied Trim, making a bow; but I hope your
Honour will be soon well enough to get down to your
country-seat, where,—as your Honour takes so much
pleasure in fortification, we could manage this matter to
a T.

I must here inform you, that this servant of my

uncle Toby's, who went by the name of Trim, had been
a corporal in my uncle's own company,—his real name
was James Butler,—but having got the nick-name of
Trim in the regiment, my uncle Toby, unless when he
happened to be very angry with him, would never call
him by any other name.

CHAP. V

The poor fellow had been disabled for the service, by a wound on his left knee by a musket-bullet, at the battle of Landen, which was two years before the affair of Namur;—and as the fellow was well-beloved in the regiment, and a handy fellow into the bargain, my uncle Toby took him for his servant; and of an excellent use was he, attending my uncle Toby in the camp and in his quarters as a valet, groom, barber, cook, sempster, and nurse; and indeed, from first to last, waited upon him and served him with great fidelity and affection.

My uncle Toby loved the man in return, and what attached him more to him still, was the similitude of their knowledge.——For Corporal Trim, (for so, for the future, I shall call him) by four years' occasional attention to his Master's discourse upon fortified towns, and the advantage of prying and peeping continually into his Master's plans, etc., exclusive and besides what he gained Hobby-Horsically, as a body-servant, *Non Hobby Horsical per se*;——had become no mean proficient in the science; and was thought, by the cook and chamber-maid, to know as much of the nature of strong-holds as my uncle Toby himself.

I have but one more stroke to give to finish Corporal Trim's character,——and it is the only dark line in it.—The fellow loved to advise,—or rather to hear himself talk; his carriage, however, was so perfectly respectful, 'twas easy to keep him silent when you had him so; but set his tongue a-going,—you had no hold of him—he was voluble—the eternal interlardings of "your Honour," with the respectfulness of Corporal Trim's manner, interceding so strong in behalf of his elocution, that though you might have been incommoded,——you could not well be angry. My uncle Toby was seldom either the one or the other with him—or, at least, this fault, in Trim, broke no squares with them. My uncle Toby, as I said, loved the man;——and besides, as he ever looked upon a faithful servant,—but as an humble friend,—he could not bear to stop his mouth.——Such was Corporal Trim.

If I durst presume, continued Trim, to give your Honour my advice, and speak my opinion in this matter. —Thou art welcome, Trim, quoth my uncle Toby— speak,——speak what thou thinkest upon the subject, man, without fear. Why then, replied Trim, (not hanging his ears and scratching his head like a country-lout, but) stroking his hair back from his forehead, and standing erect as before his division,—I think, quoth Trim, advancing his left, which was his lame leg, a little forwards,—and pointing with his right hand open towards a map of Dunkirk, which was pinned against the hangings,——I think, quoth Corporal Trim, with humble submission to your Honour's better judgment,——that these ravelins, bastions, curtins, and hornworks, make but a poor, contemptible, fiddle-faddle piece of work of it here upon paper, compared to what your Honour and I could make of it were we in the country by ourselves, and had but a rood, or a rood and a half of ground to do what we pleased with: As summer is coming on, continued Trim, your Honour might sit out of doors, and give me the nography—(Call it ichnography, quoth my

CHAP. V

uncle),——of the town or citadel, your Honour was pleased to sit down before,—and I will be shot by your Honour upon the glacis of it, if I did not fortify it to your Honour's mind——I dare say thou would'st, Trim, quoth my uncle.—For if your Honour, continued the Corporal, could but mark me the polygon, with its exact lines and angles—That I could do very well, quoth my uncle.—I would begin with the fossé, and if your Honour could tell me the proper depth and breadth—I can to a hair's breadth, Trim, replied my uncle.—I would throw out the earth upon this hand towards the town for the scarp,—and on that hand towards the campaign for the counterscarp.—Very right, Trim, quoth my uncle Toby:——And when I had sloped them to your mind, ——an' please your Honour, I would face the glacis, as the finest fortifications are done in Flanders, with sods, ——and as your Honour knows they should be,—and I would make the walls and parapets with sods too.—The best engineers call them gazons, Trim, said my uncle Toby.——Whether they are gazons or sods, is not much matter, replied Trim; your Honour knows they are ten times beyond a facing either of brick or stone.——I know they are, Trim, in some respects,——quoth my uncle Toby, nodding his head;—for a cannon-ball enters into the gazon right onwards, without bringing any rubbish down with it, which might fill the fossé (as was the case at St. Nicolas's gate) and facilitate the passage over it.

Your Honour understands these matters, replied Corporal Trim, better than any officer in his Majesty's service;——but would your Honour please to let the be-speaking of the table alone, and let us but go into the country, I would work under your Honour's directions like a horse, and make fortifications for you something like a tansy, with all their batteries, saps, ditches, and palisadoes, that it should be worth all the world's riding twenty miles to go and see it.

My uncle Toby blushed as red as scarlet as Trim went on;—but it was not a blush of guilt,—of modesty, —or of anger,—it was a blush of joy;—he was fired with Corporal Trim's project and description.——Trim! said my uncle Toby, thou hast said enough.—We might begin the campaign, continued Trim, on the very day that his Majesty and the Allies take the field, and de-molish them town by town as fast as—Trim, quoth my uncle Toby, say no more. Your Honour, continued Trim, might sit in your arm-chair (pointing to it) this fine weather, giving me your orders, and I would——Say no more, Trim, quoth my uncle Toby——Besides, your Honour would get not only pleasure and good pastime, —but good air, and good exercise, and good health,— and your Honour's wound would be well in a month. Thou hast said enough, Trim,—quoth my uncle Toby (putting his hand into his breeches-pocket)——I like thy project mightily.—And if your Honour pleases, I'll this moment go and buy a pioneer's spade to take down with us, and I'll bespeak a shovel and a pick-axe, and a couple of——Say no more, Trim, quoth my uncle Toby, leaping up upon one leg, quite overcome with rapture,— and thrusting a guinea into Trim's hand,—Trim, said

CHAP. V

my uncle Toby, say no more;—but go down, Trim, this moment, my lad, and bring up my supper this instant.

Trim ran down and brought up his master's supper, ——to no purpose:—Trim's plan of operation ran so in my uncle Toby's head, he could not taste it.—Trim, quoth my uncle Toby, get me to bed.—'Twas all one.— Corporal Trim's description had fired his imagination,— my uncle Toby could not shut his eyes.—The more he considered it, the more bewitching the scene appeared to him;—so that, two full hours before daylight, he had come to a final determination, and had concerted the whole plan of his and Corporal Trim's decampment.

My uncle Toby had a little neat country-house of his own, in the village where my father's estate lay at Shandy, which had been left him by an old uncle, with a small estate of about one hundred pounds a-year. Behind this house, and contiguous to it, was a kitchen-garden of about half an acre; and at the bottom of the garden, and cut off from it by a tall yew hedge, was a bowling-green, containing just about as much ground as Corporal Trim wished for;—so that as Trim uttered the words, "A rood and a half of ground to do what they would with,"—this identical bowling-green instantly presented itself, and became curiously painted all at once, upon the retina of my uncle Toby's fancy;—which was the physical cause of making him change colour, or at least of heightening his blush, to that immoderate degree I spoke of.

Never did lover post down to a beloved mistress with more heat and expectation, than my uncle Toby did, to enjoy this self-same thing in private;—I say in private;

—for it was sheltered from the house, as I told you, by a tall yew hedge, and was covered on the other three sides, from mortal sight, by rough holly and thick-set flowering shrubs:—so that the idea of not being seen, did not a little contribute to the idea of pleasure pre-conceived in my uncle Toby's mind.—Vain thought! however thick it was planted about,——or private soever it might seem,—to think, dear uncle Toby, of enjoying a thing which took up a whole rood and a half of ground,—and not have it known!

How my uncle Toby and Corporal Trim managed this matter,—with the history of their campaigns, which were no way barren of events,—may make no uninteresting under-plot in the epitasis and working-up of this drama.—At present the scene must drop,—and change for the parlour fire-side.

Chapter VI

——WHAT can they be doing, brother? said my father. —I think, replied my uncle Toby,—taking, as I told you, his pipe from his mouth, and striking the ashes out of it as he began his sentence;——I think, replied he,—it would not be amiss, brother, if we rung the bell.

Pray, what's all that racket over our heads, Obadiah? ——quoth my father;——my brother and I can scarce hear ourselves speak.

Sir, answered Obadiah, making a bow towards his left shoulder,—my Mistress is taken very badly.—And where's Susannah running down the garden there, as if

CHAP. VI

they were going to ravish her?——Sir, she is running the shortest cut into the town, replied Obadiah, to fetch the old midwife.—Then saddle a horse, quoth my father, and do you go directly for Dr. Slop, the man-midwife, with all our services,—and let him know your mistress is fallen into labour—and that I desire he will return with you with all speed.

It is very strange, says my father, addressing himself to my uncle Toby, as Obadiah shut the door,——as there is so expert an operator as Dr. Slop so near,—that my wife should persist to the very last in this obstinate humour of hers, in trusting the life of my child, who has had one misfortune already, to the ignorance of an old woman;——and not only the life of my child, brother,——but her own life, and with it the lives of all the children I might, peradventure, have begot out of her hereafter.

Mayhap, brother, replied my uncle Toby, my sister does it to save the expense:—A pudding's end,—replied my father,——the Doctor must be paid the same for inaction as action,——if not better,—to keep him in temper.

——Then it can be out of nothing in the whole world, quoth my uncle Toby, in the simplicity of his heart,—but Modesty.—My sister, I dare say, added he, does not care to let a man come so near her ****. I will not say whether my uncle Toby had completed the sentence or not;——'tis for his advantage to suppose he had,——as, I think, he could have added no One Word which would have improved it.

BOOK II

If, on the contrary, my uncle Toby had not fully arrived at the period's end,—then the world stands indebted to the sudden snapping of my father's tobacco-pipe for one of the neatest examples of that ornamental figure in oratory, which Rhetoricians style the Aposiopesis—Just Heaven! how does the *Poco piu* and the *Poco meno* of the Italian artists;—the insensible more or less, determine the precise line of beauty in the sentence, as well as in the statue! How do the slight touches of the chisel, the pencil, the pen, the fiddle-stick, *et caetera*,—give the true swell, which gives the true pleasure!—O my countrymen;—be nice;—be cautious of your language;—and never, O! never let it be forgotten upon what small particles your eloquence and your fame depend.

———"My sister, mayhap," quoth my uncle Toby, "does not choose to let a man come so near her ****." Make this dash,—'tis an Aposiopesis.—Take the dash away, and write Backside,———'tis Bawdy.—Scratch Backside out, and put Covered way in, 'tis a Metaphor; and, I dare say, as fortification ran so much in my uncle Toby's head, that if he had been left to have added one word to the sentence,———that word was it.

But whether that was the case or not the case;—or whether the snapping of my father's tobacco-pipe, so critically, happened through accident or anger, will be seen in due time.

CHAP. VI

CHAPTER VII

Tho' my father was a good natural philosopher,—yet he was something of a moral philosopher too; for which reason, when his tobacco-pipe snapped short in the middle,—he had nothing to do, as such, but to have taken hold of the two pieces, and thrown them gently upon the back of the fire.——He did no such thing;—— he threw them with all the violence in the world;—and, to give the action still more emphasis,—he started upon both his legs to do it.

This looked something like heat;—and the manner of his reply to what my uncle Toby was saying, proved it was so.

—"Not choose," quoth my father, (repeating my uncle Toby's words), "to let a man come so near her!" ——By Heaven, brother Toby! you would try the patience of Job;—and I think I have the plagues of one already without it.——Why?——Where?——Wherein? ——Wherefore?——Upon what account? replied my uncle Toby, in the utmost astonishment.—To think, said my father, of a man living to your age, brother, and knowing so little about women!——I know nothing at all about them,—replied my uncle Toby: And I think, continued he, that the shock I received the year after the demolition of Dunkirk, in my affair with widow Wadman;—which shock you know I should not have received, but from my total ignorance of the sex,—has given me just cause to say, That I neither know nor do pretend to know any thing about 'em or their concerns either.—Methinks, brother, replied my father, you might, at least, know so much as the right end of a woman from the wrong.

It is said in Aristotle's Master Piece, "That when a man doth think of any thing which is past,——he looketh down upon the ground;——but that when he thinketh of something that is to come, he looketh up towards the heavens."

My uncle Toby, I suppose, thought of neither, for he looked horizontally.—Right end! quoth my uncle Toby, muttering the two words low to himself, and fixing his two eyes insensibly as he muttered them, upon a small crevice, formed by a bad joint in the chimney-piece——Right end of a woman!——I declare, quoth my uncle, I know no more which it is than the man in the moon;—— and if I was to think, continued my uncle Toby (keeping his eye still fixed upon the bad joint) this month together, I am sure I should not be able to find it out.

Then, brother Toby, replied my father, I will tell you.

Every thing in this world, continued my father (filling a fresh pipe)—every thing in this world, my dear brother Toby, has two handles.——Not always, quoth my uncle Toby.——At least, replied my father, every one has two hands,—which comes to the same thing. ——Now, if a man was to sit down coolly, and consider within himself the make, the shape, the construction, come-at-ability, and convenience of all the parts which constitute the whole of that animal, called Woman, and compare them analogically —— I never understood

CHAP. VII

rightly the meaning of that word,—quoth my uncle
Toby.—

Analogy, replied my father, is the certain relation
and agreement which different——Here a devil of a rap
at the door snapped my father's definition (like his
tobacco-pipe) in two,—and, at the same time, crushed
the head of as notable and curious a dissertation as ever
was engendered in the womb of speculation;—it was
some months before my father could get an opportunity
to be safely delivered of it:—And, at this hour, it is a
thing full as problematical as the subject of the dissertation itself,—(considering the confusion and distresses of
our domestic misadventures, which are now coming
thick one upon the back of another) whether I shall be
able to find a place for it in the third volume or not.

Chapter VIII

IT is about an hour and a half's tolerable good reading
since my uncle Toby rung the bell, when Obadiah was
ordered to saddle a horse, and go for Dr. Slop, the man-
midwife;—so that no one can say, with reason, that I
have not allowed Obadiah time enough, poetically speaking, and considering the emergency too, both to go and
come;——though, morally and truly speaking, the man
perhaps has scarce had time to get on his boots.

If the hypercritic will go upon this; and is resolved
after all to take a pendulum, and measure the true distance betwixt the ringing of the bell, and the rap at the
door;—and, after finding it to be no more than two

minutes, thirteen seconds, and three fifths,—should take
upon him to insult over me for such a breach in the
unity, or rather probability of time;—I would remind
him, that the idea of duration, and of its simple modes,
is got merely from the train and succession of our ideas,
——and is the true scholastic pendulum,——and by
which, as a scholar, I will be tried in this matter,—ab-
juring and detesting the jurisdiction of all other pendu-
lums whatever.

I would therefore desire him to consider that it is but
poor eight miles from Shandy Hall to Dr. Slop, the man-
midwife's house;—and that whilst Obadiah has been
going those said miles and back, I have brought my
uncle Toby from Namur, quite across all Flanders, into
England:—That I have had him ill upon my hands near
four years;—and have since travelled him and Corporal
Trim in a chariot-and-four, a journey of near two hundred miles down into Yorkshire,——all which put together, must have prepared the reader's imagination for
the entrance of Dr. Slop upon the stage,—as much, at
least (I hope) as a dance, a song, or a concerto between
the acts.

If my hypercritic is intractable, alledging, that two
minutes and thirteen seconds are no more than two minutes and thirteen seconds,—when I have said all I can
about them; and that this plea, though it might save me
dramatically, will damn me biographically, rendering
my book from this very moment, a professed Romance,
which, before, was a book apocryphal:——If I am thus
pressed—I then put an end to the whole objection and

CHAP. VIII

controversy about it all at once,——by acquainting him, that Obadiah had not got above three-score yards from the stable-yard before he met with Dr. Slop;—and indeed he gave a dirty proof that he had met with him, and was within an ace of giving a tragical one too.

Imagine to yourself;—but this had better begin a new chapter.

CHAPTER IX

IMAGINE to yourself a little squat, uncourtly figure of a Doctor Slop, of about four feet and a half perpendicular height, with a breadth of back, and a sesquipedality of belly, which might have done honour to a serjeant in the horse-guards.

Such were the outlines of Dr. Slop's figure, which,—if you have read Hogarth's analysis of beauty, and if you have not, I wish you would;——you must know, may as certainly be caricatured, and conveyed to the mind by three strokes as three hundred.

Imagine such a one,——for such, I say, were the outlines of Dr. Slop's figure, coming slowly along, foot by foot, waddling thro' the dirt upon the vertebræ of a little diminutive pony, of a pretty colour——but of strength,——alack!——scarce able to have made an amble of it, under such a fardel, had the roads been in an ambling condition.——They were not.——Imagine to yourself, Obadiah mounted upon a strong monster of a coach-horse, pricked into a full gallop, and making all practicable speed the adverse way.

BOOK II

Pray, Sir, let me interest you a moment in this description.

Had Dr. Slop beheld Obadiah a mile off, posting in a narrow lane directly towards him, at that monstrous rate,—splashing and plunging like a devil thro' thick and thin, as he approached, would not such a phenomenon, with such a vortex of mud and water moving along with it, round its axis,—have been a subject of juster apprehension to Dr. Slop in his situation, than the worst of Whiston's comets?—To say nothing of the Nucleus; that is, of Obadiah and the coach-horse.—In my idea, the vortex alone of 'em was enough to have involved and carried, if not the doctor, at least the doctor's pony, quite away with it. What then do you think must the terror and hydrophobia of Dr. Slop have been, when you read (which you are just going to do) that he was advancing thus warily along towards Shandy Hall, and had approached to within sixty yards of it, and within five yards of a sudden turn, made by an acute angle of the garden-wall,—and in the dirtiest part of a dirty lane, —when Obadiah and his coach-horse turned the corner, rapid, furious,—pop,—full upon him!—Nothing, I think, in nature, can be supposed more terrible than such a rencounter,—so imprompt! so ill prepared to stand the shock of it as Dr. Slop was.

What could Dr. Slop do?——he crossed himself +
—Pugh!—but the doctor, Sir, was a Papist.—No matter; he had better have kept hold of the pummel.—He had so;—nay, as it happened, he had better have done nothing at all; for in crossing himself he let go his whip,

CHAP. IX

——and in attempting to save his whip betwixt his knee and his saddle's skirt, as it slipped, he lost his stirrup, ——in losing which he lost his seat;——and in the multitude of all these losses (which, by the bye, shews what little advantage there is in crossing) the unfortunate doctor lost his presence of mind. So that without waiting for Obadiah's onset, he left his pony to its destiny, tumbling off it diagonally, something in the style and manner of a pack of wool, and without any other consequence from the fall, save that of being left (as it would

BOOK II

have been) with the broadest part of him sunk about twelve inches deep in the mire.

Obadiah pulled off his cap twice to Dr. Slop;—once as he was falling,—and then again when he saw him seated.——Ill-timed complaisance;—had not the fellow better have stopped his horse, and got off and helped him?—Sir, he did all that his situation would allow; but the Momentum of the coach-horse was so great, that Obadiah could not do it all at once; he rode in a circle three times round Dr. Slop, before he could fully accomplish it any how;—and at the last, when he did stop his beast, 'twas done with such an explosion of mud, that Obadiah had better been a league off. In short, never was a Dr. Slop so beluted, and so transubstantiated, since that affair came into fashion.

CHAPTER X

WHEN Dr. Slop entered the back parlour, where my father and my uncle Toby were discoursing upon the nature of women,——it was hard to determine whether Dr. Slop's figure, or Dr. Slop's presence, occasioned more surprise to them; for as the accident happened so near the house, as not to make it worth while for Obadiah to remount him,——Obadiah had led him in as he was, unwiped, unappointed, unannealed, with all his stains and blotches on him.—He stood like Hamlet's ghost, motionless and speechless, for a full minute and a half at the parlour-door (Obadiah still holding his hand) with all the majesty of mud. His hinder parts, upon which he had received his fall, totally besmeared,——and in every other part of him, blotched over in such a manner with Obadiah's explosion, that you would have sworn (without mental reservation) that every grain of it had taken effect.

Here was a fair opportunity for my uncle Toby to have triumphed over my father in his turn;—for no mortal, who had beheld Dr. Slop in that pickle, could have dissented from so much, at least, of my uncle Toby's opinion, "That mayhap his sister might not care to let such a Dr. Slop come so near her ****." But it was the *Argumentum ad hominem*; and if my uncle Toby was not very expert at it, you may think, he might not care to use it.——No; the reason was,—'twas not his nature to insult.

Dr. Slop's presence at that time, was no less problematical than the mode of it; tho' it is certain, one moment's reflexion in my father might have solved it; for he had apprized Dr. Slop but the week before, that my mother was at her full reckoning; and as the doctor had heard nothing since, 'twas natural and very political too in him, to have taken a ride to Shandy Hall, as he did, merely to see how matters went on.

But my father's mind took unfortunately a wrong turn in the investigation; running, like the hypercritic's, altogether upon the ringing of the bell and the rap upon the door,—measuring their distance, and keeping his mind so intent upon the operation, as to have power to think of nothing else,——commonplace infirmity of the greatest mathematicians! working with might and main at the demonstration, and so wasting all their strength upon it, that they have none left in them to draw the corollary, to do good with.

The ringing of the bell, and the rap upon the door, struck likewise strong upon the sensorium of my uncle Toby,—but it excited a very different train of thoughts; —the two irreconcileable pulsations instantly brought Stevinus, the great engineer, along with them, into my uncle Toby's mind. What business Stevinus had in this affair,—is the greatest problem of all:——It shall be solved,—but not in the next chapter.

Chapter XI

WRITING, when properly managed (as you may be sure I think mine is) is but a different name for conversation. As no one, who knows what he is about in good company, would venture to talk all;——so no author, who understands the just boundaries of decorum and good-breeding, would presume to think all: The truest respect which you can pay to the reader's understanding, is to halve this matter amicably, and leave him something to imagine, in his turn, as well as yourself.

For my own part, I am eternally paying him compliments of this kind, and do all that lies in my power to keep his imagination as busy as my own.

'Tis his turn now;—I have given an ample description of Dr. Slop's sad overthrow, and of his sad appearance in the back parlour;—his imagination must now go on with it for a while.

CHAP. XI

Let the reader imagine then, that Dr. Slop has told his tale—and in what words, and with what aggravations, his fancy chooses;—Let him suppose, that Obadiah has told his tale also, and with such rueful looks of affected concern, as he thinks best will contrast the two figures as they stand by each other.———Let him imagine, that my father has stepped upstairs to see my mother.—And, to conclude this work of imagination,—let him imagine the doctor washed,—rubbed down, and condoled,—felicitated,—got into a pair of Obadiah's pumps, stepping forwards towards the door, upon the very point of entering upon action.

Truce!—truce, good Dr. Slop!—stay thy obstetric hand;—return it safe into thy bosom to keep it warm;—little dost thou know what obstacles,—little dost thou think what hidden causes, retard its operation!—Hast thou, Dr. Slop,—hast thou been intrusted with the secret articles of the solemn treaty, which has brought thee into this place?—Art thou aware that at this instant, a daughter of Lucina is put obstetrically over thy head? Alas!—'tis too true.—Besides, great son of Pilumnus! what canst thou do?—Thou hast come forth unarmed;—thou hast left thy *tire-tête,*—thy new-invented forceps,—thy crotchet,—thy squirt, and all thy instruments of salvation and deliverance, behind thee,—By Heaven! at this moment they are hanging up in a green bays bag, betwixt thy two pistols, at the bed's head!—Ring;—call;—send Obadiah back upon the coach-horse to bring them with all speed.

—Make great haste, Obadiah, quoth my father, and

I'll give thee a crown!—and quoth my uncle Toby, I'll
give him another.

Chapter XII

Your sudden and unexpected arrival, quoth my uncle
Toby, addressing himself to Dr. Slop, (all three of
them sitting down to the fire together, as my uncle Toby
began to speak)—instantly brought the great Stevinus
into my head, who, you must know, is a favourite author
with me.—Then, added my father, making use of the
argument *Ad Crumenam*,—I will lay twenty guineas to a
single crown-piece, (which will serve to give away to
Obadiah when he gets back) that this same Stevinus was
some engineer or other,—or has wrote something or
other, either directly or indirectly, upon the science of
fortification.

He has so,—replied my uncle Toby.—I knew it, said
my father, though, for the soul of me, I cannot see what
kind of connection there can be betwixt Dr. Slop's sudden coming, and a discourse upon fortification;—yet I
feared it.—Talk of what we will, brother,——or let the
occasion be never so foreign or unfit for the subject,—
you are sure to bring it in. I would not, brother Toby,
continued my father,—I declare I would not have my
head so full of curtins and hornworks.—That I dare say
you would not, quoth Dr. Slop, interrupting him, and
laughing most immoderately at his pun.

Dennis the critic could not detest and abhor a pun,
or the insinuation of a pun, more cordially than my

father;—he would grow testy upon it at any time:—but to be broke in upon by one, in a serious discourse, was as bad, he would say, as a fillip upon the nose;——he saw no difference.

Sir, quoth my uncle Toby, addressing himself to Dr. Slop,—the curtins my brother Shandy mentions here, have nothing to do with bedsteads;—tho', I know Du Cange says, "That bed-curtains, in all probability, have taken their name from them";—nor have the horn-works he speaks of, any thing in the world to do with the hornworks of cuckoldom; but the Curtin, Sir, is the word we use in fortification, for that part of the wall or rampart which lies between the two bastions and joins them—Besiegers seldom offer to carry on their attack directly against the curtin, for this reason, because they are so well flanked. ('Tis the case of other curtains, quoth Dr. Slop, laughing.) However, continued my uncle Toby, to make them sure, we generally choose to place ravelins before them, taking care only to extend them beyond the fossé or ditch:——The common men, who know very little of fortification, confound the ravelin and the half-moon together,—tho' they are very differ-ent things; not in their figure or construction, for we make them exactly alike in all points;—for they always consist of two faces, making a salient angle, with the gorges not straight, but in form of a crescent:——Where then lies the difference? (quoth my father, a little testily.) —In their situations, answered my uncle Toby:—For when a ravelin, brother, stands before the curtin, it is a ravelin; and when a ravelin stands before a bastion, then the ravelin is not a ravelin;—it is a half-moon;—a half-moon likewise is a half-moon, and no more, so long as it stands before its bastion;—but was it to change place, and get before the curtin,—'twould be no longer a half-moon; a half-moon, in that case, is not a half-moon;—'tis no more than a ravelin.——I think, quoth my father, that the noble science of defence has its weak sides—— as well as others.

—As for the hornwork (high! ho! sighed my father) which, continued my uncle Toby, my brother was speaking of, they are a very considerable part of an outwork;——they are called by the French engineers, *Ouvrage à corne*, and we generally make them to cover such places as we suspect to be weaker than the rest;—'tis formed by two epaulments or demi-bastions—they are very pretty,—and if you will take a walk, I'll engage to shew you one well worth your trouble.—I own, continued my uncle Toby, when we crown them,—they are much stronger, but then they are very expensive, and take up a great deal of ground, so that, in my opinion, they are most of use to cover or defend the head of a camp; otherwise the double tenaille—By the mother who bore us!— brother Toby, quoth my father, not able to hold out any longer,—you would provoke a saint;—here have you got us, I know not how, not only souse into the middle of the old subject again:—But so full is your head of these confounded works, that though my wife is this moment in the pains of labour, and you hear her cry out, yet nothing will serve you but to carry off the man-midwife.——*Accoucheur*,—if you please, quoth Dr. Slop.

CHAP. XII

——With all my heart, replied my father, I don't care what they call you,—but I wish the whole science of fortification, with all its inventors, at the devil;—it has been the death of thousands,—and it will be mine in the end.—I would not, I would not, brother Toby, have my brains so full of saps, mines, blinds, gabions, pallisadoes, ravelins, half-moons, and such trumpery, to be proprietor of Namur, and of all the towns in Flanders with it.

My uncle Toby was a man patient of injuries;—not from want of courage,—I have told you in a former chapter, "that he was a man of courage":—And will add here, that where just occasions presented, or called it forth,—I know no man under whose arm I would have sooner taken shelter;—nor did this arise from any insensibility or obtuseness of his intellectual parts;—for he felt this insult of my father's as feelingly as a man could do;—but he was of a peaceful, placid nature,—no jarring element in it,—all was mixed up so kindly within him; my uncle Toby had scarce a heart to retaliate upon a fly.

—Go—says he, one day at dinner, to an over-grown one which had buzzed about his nose, and tormented him cruelly all dinner-time,—and which after infinite attempts, he had caught at last, as it flew by him;—I'll not hurt thee, says my uncle Toby, rising from his chair, and going across the room, with the fly in his hand,—— I'll not hurt a hair of thy head:—Go, says he, lifting up the sash, and opening his hand as he spoke, to let it escape;—go, poor devil, get thee gone, why should I hurt thee?—This world surely is wide enough to hold both thee and me.

BOOK II

I was but ten years old when this happened: but
whether it was, that the action itself was more in unison
to my nerves at that age of pity, which instantly set my
whole frame into one vibration of most pleasurable sensation;—or how far the manner and expression of it

CHAP. XII

might go towards it;—or in what degree, or by what secret magic,—a tone of voice and harmony of movement, attuned by mercy, might find a passage to my heart, I know not;—this I know, that the lesson of universal good-will then taught and imprinted by my uncle Toby, has never since been worn out of my mind: And tho' I would not depreciate what the study of the *Literae humaniores*, at the university, have done for me in that respect, or discredit the other helps of an expensive education bestowed upon me, both at home and abroad since;—yet I often think that I owe one half of my philanthropy to that one accidental impression.

☞ This is to serve for parents and governors instead of a whole volume upon the subject.

I could not give the reader this stroke in my uncle Toby's picture, by the instrument with which I drew the other parts of it,—that taking in no more than the mere Hobby-Horsical likeness:—this is a part of his moral character. My father, in this patient endurance of wrongs, which I mention, was very different, as the reader must long ago have noted; he had a much more acute and quick sensibility of nature, attended with a little soreness of temper; tho' this never transported him to any thing which looked like malignancy:—yet in the little rubs and vexations of life, 'twas apt to shew itself in a drollish and witty kind of peevishness:—He was, however, frank and generous in his nature;—at all times open to conviction; and in the little ebullitions of this subacid humour towards others, but particularly towards my uncle Toby, whom he truly loved:—he would feel more pain, ten times told (except in the affair of my aunt Dinah, or where an hypothesis was concerned) than what he ever gave.

The characters of the two brothers, in this view of them, reflected light upon each other, and appeared with great advantage in this affair which arose about Stevinus.

I need not tell the reader, if he keeps a Hobby-Horse, —that a man's Hobby-Horse is as tender a part as he has about him; and that these unprovoked strokes at my uncle Toby's could not be unfelt by him.—No:—as I said above, my uncle Toby did feel them, and very sensibly too.

Pray, Sir, what said he?—How did he behave?—O, Sir!—it was great: For as soon as my father had done insulting his Hobby-Horse,—he turned his head without the least emotion, from Dr. Slop, to whom he was addressing his discourse, and looking up into my father's face, with a countenance spread over with so much good-nature;—so placid;—so fraternal;—so inexpressibly tender towards him:—it penetrated my father to his heart: He rose up hastily from his chair, and seizing hold of both my uncle Toby's hands as he spoke:—Brother Toby, said he—I beg thy pardon;—forgive, I pray thee, this rash humour which my mother gave me.—My dear, dear brother, answered my uncle Toby, rising up by my father's help, say no more about it;—you are heartily welcome, had it been ten times as much, brother. But 'tis ungenerous, replied my father, to hurt any man;—a brother worse;—but to hurt a brother of such gentle

CHAP. XII

manners,—so unprovoking,—and so unresenting;—'tis
base:—By Heaven, 'tis cowardly.—You are heartily
welcome, brother, quoth my uncle Toby,—had it been
fifty times as much.——Besides, what have I to do, my
dear Toby, cried my father, either with your amuse-
ments or your pleasures, unless it was in my power
(which it is not) to increase their measure?

—Brother Shandy, answered my uncle Toby, looking wistfully in his face,—you are much mistaken in this
point:—for you do increase my pleasure very much, in
begetting children for the Shandy family at your time of
life.—But, by that, Sir, quoth Dr. Slop, Mr. Shandy
increases his own.—Not a jot, quoth my father.

BOOK II

Chapter XIII

My brother does it, quoth my uncle Toby, out of principle.—In a family way, I suppose, quoth Dr. Slop.
—Pshaw!—said my father,—'tis not worth talking of.

Chapter XIV

At the end of the last chapter, my father and my uncle
Toby were left both standing, like Brutus and
Cassius, at the close of the scene, making up their ac-
counts.

As my father spoke the three last words,—he sat
down;—my uncle Toby exactly followed his example,
only, that before he took his chair, he rung the bell, to
order Corporal Trim, who was in waiting, to step home
for Stevinus:—my uncle Toby's house being no farther
off than the opposite side of the way.

Some men would have dropped the subject of Stevinus;—but my uncle Toby had no resentment in his
heart, and he went on with the subject, to shew my
father that he had none.

Your sudden appearance, Dr. Slop, quoth my uncle,
resuming his discourse, instantly brought Stevinus into
my head. (My father, you may be sure, did not offer to
lay any more wagers upon Stevinus's head.)—Because,
continued my uncle Toby, the celebrated sailing chariot,
which belonged to Prince Maurice, and was of such
wonderful contrivance and velocity, as to carry half a
dozen people thirty German miles, in I don't know how

few minutes,—was invented by Stevinus, that great mathematician and engineer.

You might have spared your servant the trouble, quoth Dr. Slop (as the fellow is lame), of going for Stevinus's account of it, because in my return from Leyden thro' the Hague, I walked as far as Schevling, which is two long miles, on purpose to take a view of it.

That's nothing, replied my uncle Toby, to what the learned Peireskius did, who walked a matter of five hundred miles, reckoning from Paris to Schevling, and from Schevling to Paris back again, in order to see it,—and nothing else.

Some men cannot bear to be out-gone.

The more fool Peireskius, replied Dr. Slop. But mark, 'twas out of no contempt of Peireskius at all;—but that Peireskius's indefatigable labour in trudging so far on foot, out of love for the sciences, reduced the exploit of Dr. Slop, in that affair, to nothing:—the more fool Peireskius, said he again.—Why so?—replied my father, taking his brother's part, not only to make reparation as fast as he could for the insult he had given him, which sat still upon my father's mind;—but partly, that my father began really to interest himself in the discourse. —Why so?—said he. Why is Peireskius, or any man else, to be abused for an appetite for that, or any other morsel of sound knowledge: For notwithstanding I know nothing of the chariot in question, continued he, the inventor of it must have had a very mechanical head; and tho' I cannot guess upon what principles of philosophy he has achieved it;—yet certainly his machine has been

constructed upon solid ones, be they what they will, or
it could not have answered at the rate my brother mentions.

It answered, replied my uncle Toby, as well, if not
better; for, as Peireskius elegantly expresses it, speaking
of the velocity of its motion, *Tam citus erat, quam erat
ventus;* which, unless I have forgot my Latin, is, that it
was as swift as the wind itself.

But pray, Dr. Slop, quoth my father, interrupting
my uncle (tho' not without begging pardon for it at the
same time) upon what principles was this self-same
chariot set a-going?—Upon very pretty principles to be
sure, replied Dr. Slop:—And I have often wondered,
continued he, evading the question, why none of our
gentry, who live upon large plains like this of ours,—
(especially they whose wives are not past child-bearing)
attempt nothing of this kind; for it would not only be
infinitely expeditious upon sudden calls, to which the
sex is subject,—if the wind only served,—but would be
excellent good husbandry to make use of the winds,
which cost nothing, and which eat nothing, rather than
horses, which (the devil take 'em) both cost and eat a
great deal.

For that very reason, replied my father, "Because
they cost nothing, and because they eat nothing,"—the
scheme is bad;—it is the consumption of our products,
as well as the manufactures of them, which gives bread
to the hungry, circulates trade,—brings in money, and
supports the value of our lands;—and tho', I own, if I
was a Prince, I would generously recompense the scien-

CHAP. XIV

tific head which brought forth such contrivances;—yet I
would as peremptorily suppress the use of them.

My father here had got into his element,—and was
going on as prosperously with his dissertation upon
trade, as my uncle Toby had before, upon his of fortification;—but to the loss of much sound knowledge, the
destinies in the morning had decreed that no dissertation of any kind should be spun by my father that day,
—for as he opened his mouth to begin the next sentence,

Chapter XV

In popped Corporal Trim with Stevinus:—But 'twas
too late,—all the discourse had been exhausted without him, and was running into a new channel.

—You may take the book home again, Trim, said my
uncle Toby, nodding to him.

But prithee, Corporal, quoth my father, drolling,—
look first into it, and see if thou canst spy aught of a
sailing chariot in it.

Corporal Trim, by being in the service, had learned
to obey,—and not to remonstrate;—so taking the book
to a side-table, and running over the leaves; An' please
your Honour, said Trim, I can see no such thing;—however, continued the Corporal, drolling a little in his
turn, I'll make sure work of it, an' please your Honour;
—so taking hold of the two covers of the book, one in
each hand, and letting the leaves fall down, as he bent
the covers back, he gave the book a good sound shake.

There is something falling out, however, said Trim,

an' please your Honour;—but it is not a chariot, or any
thing like one:—Prithee, Corporal, said my father, smiling, what is it then?—I think, answered Trim, stooping
to take it up,—'tis more like a sermon,—for it begins
with a text of scripture, and the chapter and verse;—
and then goes on, not as a chariot, but like a sermon
directly.

The company smiled.

I cannot conceive how it is possible, quoth my uncle
Toby, for such a thing as a sermon to have got into my
Stevinus.

I think 'tis a sermon, replied Trim;—but if it please
your Honours, as it is a fair hand, I will read you a page;
—for Trim, you must know, loved to hear himself read
almost as well as talk.

I have ever a strong propensity, said my father, to
look into things which cross my way, by such strange
fatalities as these;—and as we have nothing better to do,
at least till Obadiah gets back, I shall be obliged to you,
brother, if Dr. Slop has no objection to it, to order the
Corporal to give us a page or two of it,—if he is as able
to do it, as he seems willing. An' please your Honour,
quoth Trim, I officiated two whole campaigns, in
Flanders, as clerk to the chaplain of the regiment.——
He can read it, quoth my uncle Toby, as well as I can.—
Trim, I assure you, was the best scholar in my company,
and should have had the next halberd, but for the poor
fellow's misfortune. Corporal Trim laid his hand upon
his heart, and made an humble bow to his master;—
then laying down his hat upon the floor, and taking up

CHAP. XV

the sermon in his left hand, in order to have his right at
liberty,—he advanced, nothing doubting, into the middle
of the room, where he could best see, and be best seen by
his audience.

Chapter XVI

—If you have any objection,—said my father, addressing himself to Dr. Slop. Not in the least, replied Dr.
Slop;—for it does not appear on which side of the question it is wrote;—it may be a composition of a divine of
our church, as well as yours,—so that we run equal risks.
—'Tis wrote upon neither side, quoth Trim, for 'tis only
upon Conscience, an' please your Honours.

Trim's reason put his audience into good humour,—
all but Dr. Slop, who turning his head about towards
Trim, looked a little angry.

Begin, Trim,—and read distinctly, quoth my father.
—I will, an' please your Honour, replied the Corporal,
making a bow, and bespeaking attention with a slight
movement of his right hand.

Chapter XVII

——But before the Corporal begins, I must first give
you a description of his attitude;—otherwise he
will naturally stand represented, by your imagination,
in an uneasy posture,—stiff,—perpendicular,—dividing
the weight of his body equally upon both legs;—his eye
fixed, as if on duty;—his look determined,—clenching

the sermon in his left hand, like his firelock.—In a word, you would be apt to paint Trim, as if he was standing in his platoon ready for action.—His attitude was as unlike all this as you can conceive.

He stood before them with his body swayed, and bent forwards just so far, as to make an angle of 85 degrees and a half upon the plain of the horizon;—which sound orators, to whom I address this, know very well to be the true persuasive angle of incidence;—in any other angle you may talk and preach;—'tis certain; —and it is done every day;—but with what effect,—I leave the world to judge!

The necessity of this precise angle of 85 degrees and a half to a mathematical exactness,——does it not shew us, by the way, how the arts and sciences mutually befriend each other?

How the deuce Corporal Trim, who knew not so much as an acute angle from an obtuse one, came to hit it so exactly;——or whether it was chance or nature, or good sense or imitation, etc., shall be commented upon in that part of the cyclopædia of arts and sciences, where the instrumental parts of the eloquence of the senate, the pulpit, and the bar, the coffee-house, the bed-chamber, and fire-side, fall under consideration.

He stood,——for I repeat it, to take the picture of him in at one view, with his body swayed, and somewhat bent forwards,—his right leg from under him, sustaining seven-eighths of his whole weight,—the foot of his left leg, the defect of which was no disadvantage to his attitude, advanced a little,—not laterally, nor for-

CHAP. XVII

wards, but in a line betwixt them;—his knee bent, but
that not violently,—but so as to fall within the limits of
the line of beauty;—and I add, of the line of science too;
—for consider, it had one-eighth part of his body to bear
up;—so that in this case the position of the leg is determined,—because the foot could be no further advanced,
or the knee more bent, than what would allow him
mechanically to receive an eighth part of his whole
weight under it, and to carry it too.

    ☞ This I recommend to painters:—need I add,—
to orators!—I think not; for unless they practise it,—
they must fall upon their noses.

    So much for Corporal Trim's body and legs.——He
held the sermon loosely, not carelessly, in his left hand,
raised something above his stomach, and detached a
little from his breast;——his right arm falling negligently by his side, as nature and the laws of gravity
ordered it,——but with the palm of it open and turned
towards his audience, ready to aid the sentiment in case
it stood in need.

    Corporal Trim's eyes and the muscles of his face
were in full harmony with the other parts of him;—he
looked frank,—unconstrained,—something assured,—
but not bordering upon assurance.

    Let not the critic ask how Corporal Trim could come
by all this.——I've told him it should be explained;—
but so he stood before my father, my uncle Toby, and
Dr. Slop,—so swayed his body, so contrasted his limbs,
and with such an oratorical sweep throughout the whole
figure,——a statuary might have modelled from it;——

CHAP. XVII

nay, I doubt whether the oldest Fellow of a College,—or the Hebrew Professor himself, could have much mended it.

Trim made a bow, and read as follows:

The SERMON
Hebrews xiii. 18
——For we trust we have a good Conscience

"Trust!——Trust we have a good conscience!" [Certainly, Trim, quoth my father, interrupting him, you give that sentence a very improper accent; for you curl up your nose, man, and read it with such a sneering tone, as if the Parson was going to abuse the Apostle.

He is, an' please your Honour, replied Trim. Pugh! said my father, smiling.

Sir, quoth Dr. Slop, Trim is certainly in the right; for the writer (who I perceive is a Protestant) by the snappish manner in which he takes up the apostle, is certainly going to abuse him;—if this treatment of him has not done it already. But from whence, replied my father, have you concluded so soon, Dr. Slop, that the writer is of our church?—for aught I can see yet,—he may be of any church.——Because, answered Dr. Slop, if he was of ours,—he durst no more take such a licence, —than a bear by his beard:—If, in our communion, Sir, a man was to insult an apostle,—a saint,—or even the paring of a saint's nail,—he would have his eyes scratched out.—What, by the saint? quoth my uncle Toby. No, replied Dr. Slop, he would have an old house over his head. Pray is the Inquisition an ancient building, answered my uncle Toby, or is it a modern one?—I know nothing of architecture, replied Dr. Slop.—An' please your Honours, quoth Trim, the Inquisition is the vilest ——Prithee spare thy description, Trim, I hate the very name of it, said my father.—No matter for that, answered Dr. Slop,—it has its uses; for tho' I'm no great advocate for it, yet, in such a case as this, he would soon be taught better manners; and I can tell him, if he went on at that rate, would be flung into the Inquisition for his pains. God help him then, quoth my uncle Toby. Amen, added Trim; for Heaven above knows, I have a poor brother who has been fourteen years a captive in it.—I never heard one word of it before, said my uncle Toby, hastily: —How came he there, Trim?——O, Sir! the story will make your heart bleed,—as it has made mine a thousand times;—but it is too long to be told now;—your Honour shall hear it from first to last some day when I am work-ing beside you in our fortifications;—but the short of the story is this;—That my brother Tom went over a servant to Lisbon,—and then married a Jew's widow, who kept a small shop, and sold sausages, which some-how or other, was the cause of his being taken in the middle of the night out of his bed, where he was lying with his wife and two small children, and carried directly to the Inquisition, where, God help him, continued Trim, fetching a sigh from the bottom of his heart,—the poor honest lad lies confined at this hour; he was as honest a soul, added Trim, (pulling out his handker-chief) as ever blood warmed.——

CHAP. XVII

—The tears trickled down Trim's cheeks faster than he could well wipe them away.—A dead silence in the room ensued for some minutes.—Certain proof of pity!

Come, Trim, quoth my father, after he saw the poor fellow's grief had got a little vent,—read on,—and put this melancholy story out of thy head:—I grieve that I interrupted thee; but prithee begin the sermon again;—for if the first sentence in it is matter of abuse, as thou sayest, I have a great desire to know what kind of provocation the apostle has given.

Corporal Trim wiped his face, and returned his handkerchief into his pocket, and, making a bow as he did it, —he began again.]

The SERMON

HEBREWS xiii. 18

——For we trust we have a good Conscience.——

"TRUST! trust we have a good conscience! Surely if there is any thing in this life which a man may depend upon, and to the knowledge of which he is capable of arriving upon the most indisputable evidence, it must be this very thing,—whether he has a good conscience or no."

[I am positive I am right, quoth Dr. Slop.]

"If a man thinks at all, he cannot well be a stranger to the true state of this account;——he must be privy to his own thoughts and desires;—he must remember his past pursuits, and know certainly the true springs and motives, which, in general, have governed the actions of his life."

[I defy him, without an assistant, quoth Dr. Slop.]

"In other matters we may be deceived by false appearances; and, as the wise man complains, 'hardly do we guess aright at the things that are upon the earth, and with labour do we find the things that are before us.' But here the mind has all the evidence and facts within herself;——is conscious of the web she has wove;—— knows its texture and fineness, and the exact share which every passion has had in working upon the several designs which virtue or vice has planned before her."

[The language is good, and I declare Trim reads very well, quoth my father.]

"Now,—as conscience is nothing else but the knowledge which the mind has within herself of this; and the judgment, either of approbation or censure, which it unavoidably makes upon the successive actions of our lives; 'tis plain you will say, from the very terms of the proposition, — whenever this inward testimony goes against a man, and he stands self-accused, that he must necessarily be a guilty man.—And, on the contrary, when the report is favourable on his side, and his heart condemns him not:—that it is not a matter of trust, as the apostle intimates, but a matter of certainty and fact, that the conscience is good, and that the man must be good also."

[Then the apostle is altogether in the wrong, I suppose, quoth Dr. Slop, and the Protestant divine is in the right. Sir, have patience, replied my father, for I think it will presently appear that St. Paul and the Protestant divine are both of an opinion.—As nearly so, quoth Dr.

CHAP. XVII

Slop, as east is to west;—but this, continued he, lifting both hands, comes from the liberty of the press.

It is no more, at the worst, replied my uncle Toby, than the liberty of the pulpit; for it does not appear that the sermon is printed, or ever likely to be.

Go on, Trim, quoth my father.]

"At first sight this may seem to be a true state of the case: and I make no doubt but the knowledge of right and wrong is so truly impressed upon the mind of man, —that did no such thing ever happen, as that the conscience of a man, by long habits of sin, might (as the scripture assures it may) insensibly become hard;—and, like some tender parts of his body, by much stress and continual hard usage, lose by degrees that nice sense and perception with which God and nature endowed it:— Did this never happen; or was it certain that self-love would never hang the least bias upon the judgment;—or that the little interests below could rise up and perplex the faculties of our upper regions, and encompass them about with clouds and thick darkness:—Could no such thing as favour and affection enter this sacred Court:— Did Wit disdain to take a bribe in it;—or was ashamed to shew its face as an advocate for an unwarrantable enjoyment: Or, lastly, were we assured that Interest stood always unconcerned whilst the cause was hearing—and that Passion never got into the judgment-seat, and pronounced sentence in the stead of Reason, which is supposed always to preside and determine upon the case:— Was this truly so, as the objection must suppose;—no doubt then the religious and moral state of a man would be exactly what he himself esteemed it:—and the guilt or innocence of every man's life could be known, in general, by no better measure, than the degrees of his own approbation and censure.

"I own, in one case, whenever a man's conscience does accuse him (as it seldom errs on that side) that he is guilty; and unless in melancholy and hypocondriac cases, we may safely pronounce upon it, that there is always sufficient grounds for the accusation.

"But the converse of the proposition will not hold true;—namely, that whenever there is guilt, the conscience must accuse; and if it does not, that a man is therefore innocent.—This is not fact—So that the common consolation which some good christian or other is hourly administering to himself,—that he thanks God his mind does not misgive him; and that, consequently, he has a good conscience, because he hath a quiet one,— is fallacious;—and as current as the inference is, and as infallible as the rule appears at first sight, yet when you look nearer to it, and try the truth of this rule upon plain facts,—you see it liable to so much error from a false application;—the principle upon which it goes so often perverted;—the whole force of it lost, and sometimes so vilely cast away, that it is painful to produce the common examples from human life, which confirm the account.

"A man shall be vicious and utterly debauched in his principles;—exceptionable in his conduct to the world; shall live shameless, in the open commission of a sin which no reason or pretence can justify,——a sin by

CHAP. XVII

which, contrary to all the workings of humanity, he shall ruin for ever the deluded partner of his guilt;—rob her of her best dowry; and not only cover her own head with dishonour;—but involve a whole virtuous family in shame and sorrow for her sake. Surely, you will think conscience must lead such a man a troublesome life; he can have no rest night or day from its reproaches.

"Alas! Conscience had something else to do all this time, than break in upon him; as Elijah reproached the god Baal,—this domestic god 'was either talking, or pursuing, or was in a journey, or peradventure he slept and could not be awoke.'

"Perhaps He was gone out in company with Honour to fight a duel: to pay off some debt at play;——or dirty annuity, the bargain of his lust; Perhaps Conscience all this time was engaged at home, talking aloud against petty larceny, and executing vengeance upon some such puny crimes as his fortune and rank of life secured him against all temptation of committing; so that he lives as merrily"——[If he was of our church, tho', quoth Dr. Slop, he could not]—"sleeps as soundly in his bed;—and at last meets death as unconcernedly;—perhaps much more so, than a much better man."

[All this is impossible with us, quoth Dr. Slop, turning to my father,—the case could not happen in our church.—It happens in ours, however, replied my father, but too often.——I own, quoth Dr. Slop, (struck a little with my father's frank acknowledgment)—that a man in the Romish church may live as badly;—but then he cannot easily die so.——'Tis little matter, replied my

father, with an air of indifference, —how a rascal dies.—
I mean, answered Dr. Slop, he would be denied the bene-
fits of the last sacraments.—Pray how many have you in
all, said my uncle Toby,—for I always forget?——Seven,
answered Dr. Slop.——Humph!—said my uncle Toby;
tho' not accented as a note of acquiescence,—but as an
interjection of that particular species of surprise, when a
man in looking into a drawer, finds more of a thing than
he expected.—Humph! replied my uncle Toby. Dr. Slop,
who had an ear, understood my uncle Toby as well as if
he had wrote a whole volume against the seven sacraments.——Humph! replied Dr. Slop, (stating my uncle
Toby's argument over again to him)—Why, Sir, are
there not seven cardinal virtues?—Seven mortal sins?—
Seven golden candlesticks?—Seven heavens?—'Tis more
than I know, replied my uncle Toby.——Are there not
seven wonders of the world?—Seven days of the creation?—Seven planets?—Seven plagues?——That there
are, quoth my father with a most affected gravity. But
prithee, continued he, go on with the rest of thy characters, Trim.]

"Another is sordid, unmerciful," (here Trim waved
his right hand) "a strait-hearted, selfish wretch, incapable either of private friendship or public spirit. Take
notice how he passes by the widow and orphan in their
distress, and sees all the miseries incident to human life
without a sigh or a prayer." [An' please your honours,
cried Trim, I think this a viler man than the other.]

"Shall not conscience rise up and sting him on such
occasions?——No; thank God there is no occasion, 'I

CHAP. XVII

pay every man his own;—I have no fornication to
answer to my conscience;—no faithless vows or prom-
ises to make up;—I have debauched no man's wife or
child; thank God, I am not as other men, adulterers, un-
just, or even as this libertine, who stands before me.'

"A third is crafty and designing in his nature. View
his whole life;—'tis nothing but a cunning contexture of
dark arts and unequitable subterfuges, basely to defeat
the true intent of all laws,—plain-dealing and the safe
enjoyment of our several properties.—You will see such
a one working out a frame of little designs upon the ignorance and perplexities of the poor and needy man;—
shall raise a fortune upon the inexperience of a youth, or
the unsuspecting temper of his friend, who would have
trusted him with his life.

"When old age comes on, and repentance calls him
to look back upon his black account, and state it over
again with his conscience—Conscience looks into the
Statutes at Large;—finds no express law broken by what
he has done;—perceives no penalty or forfeiture of goods
and chattels incurred;—sees no scourge waving over his
head, or prison opening his gates upon him:—What is
there to affright his conscience?—Conscience has got
safely entrenched behind the Letter of the Law; sits
there invulnerable, fortified with **Cases** and **Reports** so
strongly on all sides;—that it is not preaching can dis-
possess it of its hold."

[Here Corporal Trim and my uncle Toby exchanged
looks with each other.—Aye, aye, Trim! quoth my uncle
Toby, shaking his head,—these are but sorry fortifica-

tions, Trim.——O! very poor work, answered Trim, to
what your Honour and I make of it.——The character
of this last man, said Dr. Slop, interrupting Trim, is
more detestable than all the rest; and seems to have been
taken from some pettifogging Lawyer amongst you:——
Amongst us, a man's conscience could not possibly continue so long blinded,—three times in a year, at least, he
must go to confession. Will that restore it to sight?
quoth my uncle Toby.——Go on, Trim, quoth my
father, or Obadiah will have got back before thou hast
got to the end of thy sermon.——'Tis a very short one,
replied Trim.——I wish it was longer, quoth my uncle
Toby, for I like it hugely.—Trim went on.]

"A fourth man shall want even this refuge;—shall
break through all their ceremony of slow chicane;—
scorns the doubtful workings of secret plots and cautious
trains to bring about his purpose;——See the barefaced
villain, how he cheats, lies, perjures, robs, murders!—
Horrid!—But indeed much better was not to be expected, in the present case—the poor man was in the
dark!—his priest had got the keeping of his conscience;
—and all he would let him know of it, was, That he must
believe in the Pope;—go to Mass;—cross himself;—tell
his beads;—be a good Catholic, and that this, in all
conscience, was enough to carry him to heaven. What;
—if he perjures!—Why;—he had a mental reservation
in it.—But if he is so wicked and abandoned a wretch as
you represent him;—if he robs,—if he stabs, will not
conscience, on every such act, receive a wound itself?—
Aye,—but the man has carried it to confession;——the

CHAP. XVII

wound digests there, and will do well enough, and in a short time be quite healed up by absolution. O Popery! what hast thou to answer for?——when, not content with the too many natural and fatal ways, thro' which the heart of man is every day thus treacherous to itself above all things;—thou hast wilfully set open the wide gate of deceit before the face of this unwary traveller, too apt, God knows, to go astray of himself; and confidently speak peace to himself, when there is no peace.

"Of this the common instances which I have drawn out of life, are too notorious to require much evidence. If any man doubts the reality of them, or thinks it impossible for a man to be such a bubble to himself,—I must refer him a moment to his own reflections, and will then venture to trust my appeal with his own heart.

"Let him consider in how different a degree of detestation, numbers of wicked actions stand there, tho' equally bad and vicious in their own natures;—he will soon find, that such of them as strong inclination and custom have prompted him to commit, are generally dressed out and painted with all the false beauties which a soft and a flattering hand can give them;—and that the others, to which he feels no propensity, appear, at once, naked and deformed, surrounded with all the true circumstances of folly and dishonour.

"When David surprised Saul sleeping in the cave, and cut off the skirt of his robe—we read his heart smote him for what he had done:—But in the matter of Uriah, where a faithful and gallant servant, whom he ought to have loved and honoured, fell to make way for his lust,

—where conscience had so much greater reason to take the alarm, his heart smote him not. A whole year had almost passed from the first commission of that crime, to the time Nathan was sent to reprove him; and we read not once of the least sorrow or compunction of heart which he testified, during all that time, for what he had done.

"Thus conscience, this once able monitor,——placed on high as a judge within us, and intended by our Maker as a just and equitable one too,—by an unhappy train of causes and impediments, takes often such imperfect cognizance of what passes,——does its office so negligently,——sometimes so corruptly,—that it is not to be trusted alone; and therefore we find there is a necessity, an absolute necessity, of joining another principle with it, to aid, if not govern, its determinations.

"So that if you would form a just judgment of what is of infinite importance to you not to be misled in,—namely, in what degree of real merit you stand either as an honest man, an useful citizen, a faithful subject to your king, or a good servant to your God,——call in religion and morality.—Look, What is written in the law of God?—How readest thou?—Consult calm reason and the unchangeable obligations of justice and truth;——what say they?

"Let Conscience determine the matter upon these reports;——and then if thy heart condemns thee not, which is the case the apostle supposes,—the rule will be infallible";—[Here Dr. Slop fell asleep]—"thou wilt have confidence towards God;——that is, have just grounds

CHAP. XVII

to believe the judgment thou hast passed upon thyself,
is the judgment of God; and nothing else but an antici-
pation of that righteous sentence which will be pronounced upon thee hereafter by that Being, to whom
thou art finally to give an account of thy actions.

" 'Blessed is the man,' indeed, then, as the author of
the book of Ecclesiasticus expresses it, 'who is not
pricked with the multitude of his sins: Blessed is the
man whose heart hath not condemned him; whether he
be rich, or whether he be poor, if he have a good heart'
(a heart thus guided and informed) 'he shall at all times
rejoice in a cheerful countenance; his mind shall tell him
more than seven watch-men that sit above upon a tower
on high.' "—[A tower has no strength, quoth my uncle
Toby, unless 'tis flanked.]—"In the darkest doubts it
shall conduct him safer than a thousand casuists, and
give the state he lives in, a better security for his be-
haviour than all the causes and restrictions put together,
which law-makers are forced to multiply:—'Forced,' I
say, as things stand; human laws not being a matter of
original choice, but of pure necessity, brought in to fence
against the mischievous effects of those consciences
which are no law unto themselves; well intending, by
the many provisions made,—that in all such corrupt and
misguided cases, where principles and the checks of conscience will not make us upright,—to supply their force,
and, by the terrors of gaols and halters, oblige us to it."

[I see plainly, said my father, that this sermon has
been composed to be preached at the Temple,——or at
some Assize.—I like the reasoning,—and am sorry that

Dr. Slop has fallen asleep before the time of his conviction:—for it is now clear, that the Parson, as I thought
at first, never insulted St. Paul in the least;—nor has
there been, brother, the least difference between them.
——A great matter, if they had differed, replied my
uncle Toby,—the best friends in the world may differ
sometimes.——True,—brother Toby, quoth my father,
shaking hands with him—we'll fill our pipes, brother,
and then Trim shall go on.

Well,——what dost thou think of it? said my father,
speaking to Corporal Trim, as he reached his tobaccobox.

I think, answered the Corporal, that the seven watchmen upon the tower, who, I suppose, are all sentinels
there,—are more, an' please your Honour, than were
necessary;—and, to go on at that rate, would harass a
regiment all to pieces, which a commanding officer, who
loves his men, will never do, if he can help it, because
two sentinels, added the Corporal, are as good as twenty.
—I have been a commanding officer myself in the *Corps
de Garde* a hundred times, continued Trim, rising an
inch higher in his figure, as he spoke,—and all the time I
had the honour to serve his Majesty King William, in
relieving the most considerable ports, I never left more
than two in my life.—Very right, Trim, quoth my uncle
Toby,—but you do not consider, Trim, that the towers,
in Solomon's days, were not such things as our bastions,
flanked and defended by other works;—this, Trim, was
an invention since Solomon's death; nor had they hornworks, or ravelins before the curtin, in his time;——or

CHAP. XVII

such a fossé as we make with a curvette in the middle of
it, and with covered ways and counterscarps pallisadoed
along it, to guard against a *Coup de main*:—So that the
seven men upon the tower were a party, I dare say,
from the *Corps de Garde*, set there, not only to look out,
but to defend it.—They could be no more, an' please
your Honour, than a Corporal's Guard.—My father
smiled inwardly, but not outwardly;—the subject being
rather too serious, considering what had happened, to
make a jest of.—So putting his pipe into his mouth,
which he had just lighted,—he contented himself with
ordering Trim to read on. He read on as follows:]

"To have the fear of God before our eyes, and, in our
mutual dealings with each other, to govern our actions
by the eternal measures of right and wrong:——The
first of these will comprehend the duties of religion;—
the second, those of morality, which are so inseparably
connected together, that you cannot divide these two
tables, even in imagination, (tho' the attempt is often
made in practice) without breaking and mutually destroying them both.

"I said the attempt is often made; and so it is;——
there being nothing more common than to see a man
who has no sense at all of religion, and indeed has so
much honesty as to pretend to none, who would take it
as the bitterest affront, should you but hint at a suspicion of his moral character,——or imagine he was not
conscientiously just and scrupulous to the uttermost
mite.

"When there is some appearance that it is so,—tho'

one is unwilling even to suspect the appearance of so
amiable a virtue as moral honesty, yet were we to look
into the grounds of it, in the present case, I am persuaded
we should find little reason to envy such a one the
honour of his motive.

"Let him declaim as pompously as he chooses upon
the subject, it will be found to rest upon no better foundation than either his interest, his pride, his ease, or
some such little and changeable passion as will give us
but small dependence upon his actions in matters of
great distress.

"I will illustrate this by an example.

"I know the banker I deal with, or the physician I
usually call in," [There is no need, cried Dr. Slop, (waking) to call in any physician in this case] "to be neither
of them men of much religion: I hear them make a jest
of it every day, and treat all its sanctions with so much
scorn, as to put the matter past doubt. Well;—notwithstanding this, I put my fortune into the hands of the
one:—and what is dearer still to me, I trust my life to
the honest skill of the other.

"Now let me examine what is my reason for this
great confidence. Why, in the first place, I believe there
is no probability that either of them will employ the
power I put into their hands to my disadvantage;—I
consider that honesty serves the purposes of this life:—
I know their success in the world depends upon the fair-
ness of their characters.—In a word, I'm persuaded that
they cannot hurt me without hurting themselves more.

"But put it otherwise, namely, that interest lay, for

CHAP. XVII

once, on the other side; that a case should happen,
wherein the one, without stain to his reputation, could
secrete my fortune, and leave me naked in the world;—
or that the other could send me out of it, and enjoy an
estate by my death, without dishonour to himself or his
art:—In this case, what hold have I of either of them?—
Religion, the strongest of all motives, is out of the question;—Interest, the next most powerful motive in the
world, is strongly against me:—What have I left to cast
into the opposite scale to balance this temptation?—
Alas! I have nothing,—nothing but what is lighter than
a bubble—I must lie at the mercy of Honour, or some
such capricious principle—Strait security for two of the
most valuable blessings!—my property and myself.

"As, therefore, we can have no dependence upon
morality without religion;—so, on the other hand, there
is nothing better to be expected from religion without
morality; nevertheless, 'tis no prodigy to see a man
whose real moral character stands very low, who yet
entertains the highest notion of himself in the light of a
religious man.

"He shall not only be covetous, revengeful, impla-
cable,—but even wanting in points of common honesty;
yet inasmuch as he talks aloud against the infidelity of
the age,——is zealous for some points of religion,——
goes twice a day to church,—attends the sacraments,—
and amuses himself with a few instrumental parts of religion,—shall cheat his conscience into a judgment, that,
for this, he is a religious man, and has discharged truly
his duty to God: And you will find that such a man,

through force of this delusion, generally looks down with spiritual pride upon every other man who has less affectation of piety,—though, perhaps, ten times more real honesty than himself.

" 'This likewise is a sore evil under the sun'; and I believe, there is no one mistaken principle, which, for its time, has wrought more serious mischiefs.——For a general proof of this,—examine the history of the Romish church";—[Well, what can you make of that? cried Dr. Slop]—"see what scenes of cruelty, murder, rapine, bloodshed,"——[They may thank their own obstinacy, cried Dr. Slop.]——"have all been sanctified by a religion not strictly governed by morality.

"In how many kingdoms of the world"—[Here Trim kept waving his right hand from the sermon to the extent of his arm, returning it backwards and forwards to the conclusion of the paragraph.]

"In how many kingdoms of the world has the crusading sword of this misguided saint-errant, spared neither age nor merit, or sex, or condition?—and, as he fought under the banners of a religion which set him loose from justice and humanity, he shewed none; mercilessly trampled upon both,—heard neither the cries of the unfortunate, nor pitied their distresses."

[I have been in many a battle, an' please your Honour, quoth Trim, sighing, but never in so melancholy a one as this,—I would not have drawn a trigger in it against these poor souls,——to have been made a general officer.——Why? what do you understand of the affair? said Dr. Slop, looking towards Trim, with something

CHAP. XVII

more of contempt than the Corporal's honest heart deserved.—What do you know, friend, about this battle you talk of?—I know, replied Trim, that I never refused quarter in my life to any man who cried out for it;—but to a woman or a child, continued Trim, before I would level my musket at them, I would lose my life a thousand times.——Here's a crown for thee, Trim, to drink with Obadiah to-night, quoth my uncle Toby, and I'll give Obadiah another too.—God bless your Honour, replied Trim,—I had rather these poor women and children had it.——Thou art an honest fellow, quoth my uncle Toby.——My father nodded his head,—as much as to say,—and so he is.——

But prithee, Trim, said my father, make an end,—for I see thou hast but a leaf or two left.

Corporal Trim read on.]

"If the testimony of past centuries in this matter is not sufficient,—consider at this instant, how the votaries of that religion are every day thinking to do service and honour to God, by actions which are a dishonour and scandal to themselves.

"To be convinced of this, go with me for a moment into the prisons of the Inquisition."—[God help my poor brother Tom.]—"Behold Religion, with Mercy and Justice chained down under her feet,——there sitting ghastly upon a black tribunal, propped up with racks and instruments of torment. Hark!—hark! what a piteous groan!"—[Here Trim's face turned as pale as ashes.]——"See the melancholy wretch who uttered it"—[Here the tears began to trickle down.]——"just brought forth to undergo the anguish of a mock trial, and endure the utmost pains that a studied system of cruelty has been able to invent."—[D—n them all, quoth Trim, his colour returning into his face as red as blood.]—"Behold this helpless victim delivered up to his tormentors,—his body so wasted with sorrow and confinement."——[Oh! 'tis my brother, cried poor Trim in a most passionate exclamation, dropping the sermon upon the ground, and clapping his hands together—I fear 'tis poor Tom. My father's and my uncle Toby's heart yearned with sympathy for the poor fellow's distress; even Slop himself acknowledged pity for him.—— Why, Trim, said my father, this is not a history,——'tis a sermon thou art reading; prithee begin the sentence again.]——"Behold this helpless victim delivered up to his tormentors,—his body so wasted with sorrow and confinement, you will see every nerve and muscle as it suffers.

"Observe the last movement of that horrid engine!" —[I would rather face a cannon, quoth Trim, stamping.] —"See what convulsions it has thrown him into!—— Consider the nature of the posture in which he now lies stretched,—what exquisite tortures he endures by it!"— [I hope 'tis not in Portugal.]—"'Tis all nature can bear! Good God! see how it keeps his weary soul hanging upon his trembling lips!" [I would not read another line of it, quoth Trim, for all this world;—I fear, an' please your Honours, all this is in Portugal, where my poor brother Tom is. I tell thee, Trim, again, quoth my father, 'tis not an historical account,—'tis a description.—'Tis only

CHAP. XVII

a description, honest man, quoth Slop, there's not a word of truth in it.——That's another story, replied my father.—However, as Trim reads it with so much concern,—'tis cruelty to force him to go on with it.—Give me hold of the sermon, Trim,—I'll finish it for thee, and thou may'st go. I must stay and hear it too, replied Trim, if your Honour will allow me;—tho' I would not read it myself for a Colonel's pay.——Poor Trim! quoth my uncle Toby. My father went on.]—

"——Consider the nature of the posture in which he now lies stretched,—what exquisite torture he endures by it!—'Tis all nature can bear! Good God! See how it keeps his weary soul hanging upon his trembling lips,—willing to take its leave,——but not suffered to depart! —Behold the unhappy wretch led back to his cell!"— [Then, thank God, however, quoth Trim, they have not killed him.]—"See him dragged out of it again to meet the flames, and the insults in his last agonies, which this principle,—this principle, that there can be religion without mercy, has prepared for him."—[Then, thank God,——he is dead, quoth Trim,—he is out of his pain, —and they have done their worst at him.—O Sirs!— Hold your peace, Trim, said my father, going on with the sermon, lest Trim should incense Dr. Slop,—we shall never have done at this rate.]

"The surest way to try the merit of any disputed notion is, to trace down the consequences such a notion has produced, and compare them with the spirit of Christianity;—'tis the short and decisive rule which our Saviour hath left us, for these and such like cases, and it is worth a thousand arguments—'By their fruits ye shall know them.'

"I will add no further to the length of this sermon, than by two or three short and independent rules deducible from it.

"First, Whenever a man talks loudly against religion, always suspect that it is not his reason, but his passions, which have got the better of his creed. A bad life and a good belief are disagreeable and troublesome neighbours, and where they separate, depend upon it, 'tis for no other cause but quietness' sake.

"Secondly, When a man, thus represented, tells you in any particular instance,——That such a thing goes against his conscience,——always believe he means exactly the same thing, as when he tells you such a thing goes against his stomach;—a present want of appetite being generally the true cause of both.

"In a word,—trust that man in nothing, who has not a Conscience in every thing.

"And, in your own case, remember this plain distinction, a mistake in which has ruined thousands,—that your conscience is not a law:—No, God and reason made the law, and have placed conscience within you to determine;——not, like an Asiatic Cadi, according to the ebbs and flows of his own passions,—but like a British judge in this land of liberty and good sense, who makes no new law, but faithfully declares that law which he knows already written."

F I N I S .

CHAP. XVII

Thou hast read the sermon extremely well, Trim, quoth my father.—If he had spared his comments, replied Dr. Slop,——he would have read it much better. I should have read it ten times better, Sir, answered Trim, but that my heart was so full.—That was the very reason, Trim, replied my father, which has made thee read the sermon as well as thou hast done; and if the clergy of our church, continued my father, addressing himself to Dr. Slop, would take part in what they deliver as deeply as this poor fellow has done,—as their compositions are fine;—[I deny it, quoth Dr. Slop]—I maintain it,—that the eloquence of our pulpits, with such subjects to enflame it, would be a model for the whole world:——But alas! continued my father, and I own it, Sir, with sorrow, that, like French politicians in this respect, what they gain in the cabinet they lose in the field.——'Twere a pity, quoth my uncle, that this should be lost. I like the sermon well, replied my father,——'tis dramatic,—and there is something in that way of writing, when skilfully managed, which catches the attention.——We preach much in that way with us, said Dr. Slop.—I know that very well, said my father,——but in a tone and manner which disgusted Dr. Slop, full as much as his assent, simply, could have pleased him.—— But in this, added Dr. Slop, a little piqued,—our sermons have greatly the advantage, that we never introduce any character into them below a patriarch or a patriarch's wife, or a martyr or a saint.—There are some very bad characters in this, however, said my father, and I do not think the sermon a jot the worse for 'em.

——But pray, quoth my uncle Toby,—who's can this be?—How could it get into my Stevinus? A man must be as great a conjurer as Stevinus, said my father, to resolve the second question:—The first, I think, is not so difficult;—for unless my judgment greatly deceives me,—— I know the author, for 'tis wrote, certainly, by the parson of the parish.

The similitude of the style and manner of it, with those my father constantly had heard preached in his parish-church, was the ground of his conjecture,—proving it as strongly, as an argument *à priori* could prove such a thing to a philosophic mind, That it was Yorick's and no one's else:—It was proved to be so, *à posteriori*, the day after, when Yorick sent a servant to my uncle Toby's house to enquire after it.

It seems that Yorick, who was inquisitive after all kinds of knowledge, had borrowed Stevinus of my uncle Toby, and had carelessly popped his sermon, as soon as he had made it, into the middle of Stevinus; and by an act of forgetfulness, to which he was ever subject, he had sent Stevinus home, and his sermon to keep him company.

Ill-fated sermon! Thou wast lost, after this recovery of thee, a second time, dropped thro' an unsuspected fissure in thy master's pocket, down into a treacherous and a tattered lining,—trod deep into the dirt by the left hind-foot of his Rosinante inhumanly stepping upon thee as thou falledst;—buried ten days in the mire,— raised up out of it by a beggar,—sold for a halfpenny to a parish-clerk,—transferred to his parson,—lost for ever to thy own, the remainder of his days,—nor restored to

CHAP. XVII

his restless Manes till this very moment, that I tell the
world the story.

Can the reader believe, that this sermon of Yorick's
was preached at an assize, in the cathedral of York, before a thousand witnesses, ready to give oath to it, by a
certain prebendary of that church, and actually printed
by him when he had done,——and within so short a
space as two years and three months after Yorick's
death?—Yorick indeed was never better served in his
life;———but it was a little hard to maltreat him after,
and plunder him after he was laid in his grave.

However, as the gentleman who did it was in perfect
charity with Yorick,—and, in conscious justice, printed
but a few copies to give away;—and that I am told he
could moreover have made as good a one himself, had he
thought fit,—I declare I would not have published this
anecdote to the world;—nor do I publish it with an intent to hurt his character and advancement in the
church;—I leave that to others;—but I find myself impelled by two reasons, which I cannot withstand.

The first is, That in doing justice, I may give rest to
Yorick's ghost;—which—as the country-people, and
some others, believe,———still walks.

The second reason is, That, by laying open this story
to the world, I gain an opportunity of informing it,—
That in case the character of parson Yorick, and this
sample of his sermons, is liked,———there are now in the
possession of the Shandy family, as many as will make a
handsome volume, at the world's service,———and much
good may they do it.

BOOK II

CHAPTER XVIII

O BADIAH gained the two crowns without dispute; for he came in jingling, with all the instruments in the green bays bag we spoke of, slung across his body, just as Corporal Trim went out of the room.

It is now proper, I think, quoth Dr. Slop, (clearing up his looks) as we are in a condition to be of some service to Mrs. Shandy, to send up stairs to know how she goes on.

I have ordered, answered my father, the old midwife to come down to us upon the least difficulty;—for you must know, Dr. Slop, continued my father, with a per-plexed kind of a smile upon his countenance, that by express treaty, solemnly ratified between me and my wife, you are no more than an auxiliary in this affair,—and not so much as that,—unless the lean old mother of a midwife above stairs cannot do without you.—Women have their particular fancies, and in points of this nature, continued my father, where they bear the whole burden, and suffer so much acute pain for the advantage of our families, and the good of the species,—they claim a right of deciding, *en Souveraines*, in whose hands, and in what fashion, they choose to undergo it.

They are in the right of it,——quoth my uncle Toby. But, Sir, replied Dr. Slop, not taking notice of my uncle Toby's opinion, but turning to my father,—they had better govern in other points;—and a father of a family, who wishes its perpetuity, in my opinion, had better ex-change this prerogative with them, and give up some other rights in lieu of it.—I know not, quoth my father, answering a little too testily, to be quite dispassionate in what he said,—I know not, quoth he, what we have left to give up, in lieu of who shall bring our children into the world, unless that,—of who shall beget them.——One would almost give up any thing, replied Dr. Slop.—I beg your pardon,—answered my uncle Toby.—Sir, replied Dr. Slop, it would astonish you to know what improvements we have made of late years in all branches of obstetrical knowledge, but particularly in that one single point of the safe and expeditious extraction of the foetus, —which has received such lights, that, for my part (holding up his hands) I declare I wonder how the world has—I wish, quoth my uncle Toby, you had seen what prodigious armies we had in Flanders.

Chapter XIX

I HAVE dropped the curtain over this scene for a minute, —to remind you of one thing,—and to inform you of another.

What I have to inform you, comes, I own, a little out of its due course; for it should have been told a hundred and fifty pages ago, but that I foresaw then 'twould come in pat hereafter, and be of more advantage here than elsewhere.—Writers had need look before them, to keep up the spirit and connection of what they have in hand.

When these two things are done,—the curtain shall

be drawn up again, and my uncle Toby, my father, and Dr. Slop, shall go on with their discourse, without any more interruption.

First, then, the matter which I have to remind you of, is this;—that from the specimens of singularity in my father's notions in the point of Christian-names, and that other previous point thereto,—you was led, I think, into an opinion, (and I am sure I said as much) that my father was a gentleman altogether as odd and whimsical in fifty other opinions. In truth, there was not a stage in the life of man, from the very first act of his begetting,— down to the lean and slippered pantaloon in his second childishness, but he had some favourite notion to himself, springing out of it, as sceptical, and as far out of the high-way of thinking, as these two which have been explained.

—Mr. Shandy, my father, Sir, would see nothing in the light in which others placed it;—he placed things in his own light;—he would weigh nothing in common scales;—no, he was too refined a researcher to lie open to so gross an imposition.—To come at the exact weight of things in the scientific steel-yard, the fulcrum, he would say, should be almost invisible, to avoid all friction from popular tenets;—without this the minutiae of philosophy, which would always turn the balance, will have no weight at all. Knowledge, like matter, he would affirm, was divisible *in infinitum*;—that the grains and scruples were as much a part of it, as the gravitation of the whole world.—In a word, he would say, error was error,—no matter where it fell,—whether in a fraction,—or a pound,

CHAP. XIX

—'twas alike fatal to truth, and she was kept down at the bottom of her well, as inevitably by a mistake in the dust of a butterfly's wing,—as in the disk of the sun, the moon, and all the stars of heaven put together.

He would often lament that it was for want of considering this properly, and of applying it skilfully to civil matters, as well as to speculative truths, that so many things in this world were out of joint;—that the political arch was giving way;—and that the very foundations of our excellent constitution, in church and state, were so sapped as estimators had reported.

You cry out, he would say, we are a ruined, undone people. Why? he would ask, making use of the sorites or syllogism of Zeno and Chrysippus, without knowing it belonged to them.—Why? why are we a ruined people?—Because we are corrupted.—Whence is it, dear Sir, that we are corrupted?—Because we are needy;—our poverty, and not our wills, consent.—And wherefore, he would add, are we needy?—From the neglect, he would answer, of our pence and our halfpence:—Our bank notes, Sir, our guineas,—nay our shillings take care of themselves.

'Tis the same, he would say, throughout the whole circle of the sciences;—the great, the established points of them, are not to be broken in upon.—The laws of nature will defend themselves;—but error—(he would add, looking earnestly at my mother)—error, Sir, creeps in thro' the minute holes and small crevices which human nature leaves unguarded.

This turn of thinking in my father, is what I had to

remind you of:—The point you are to be informed of, and which I have reserved for this place, is as follows.

Amongst the many and excellent reasons, with which my father had urged my mother to accept of Dr. Slop's assistance preferably to that of the old woman,—there was one of a very singular nature; which, when he had done arguing the matter with her as a Christian, and came to argue it over again with her as a philosopher, he had put his whole strength to, depending indeed upon it as his sheet-anchor.——It failed him; tho' from no defect in the argument itself; but that, do what he could, he was not able for his soul to make her comprehend the drift of it.—Cursed luck!—said he to himself, one afternoon, as he walked out of the room, after he had been stating it for an hour and a half to her, to no manner of

CHAP. XIX

purpose;—cursed luck! said he, biting his lip as he shut
the door,——for a man to be master of one of the finest
chains of reasoning in nature,—and have a wife at the
same time with such a head-piece, that he cannot hang
up a single inference within side of it, to save his soul
from destruction.

This argument, though it was entirely lost upon my
mother,—had more weight with him, than all his other
arguments joined together:—I will therefore endeavour
to do it justice,—and set it forth with all the perspicuity
I am master of.

My father set out upon the strength of these two
following axioms:

First, That an ounce of a man's own wit, was worth a
ton of other people's; and,

Secondly, (Which by the bye, was the ground-work
of the first axiom,—tho' it comes last) That every man's
wit must come from every man's own soul,—and no
other body's.

Now, as it was plain to my father that all souls were
by nature equal,—and that the great difference between
the most acute and the most obtuse understanding—
was from no original sharpness or bluntness of one thinking substance above or below another,—but arose merely
from the lucky or unlucky organization of the body, in
that part where the soul principally took up her residence,—he had made it the subject of his enquiry to find
out the identical place.

Now, from the best accounts he had been able to get
of this matter, he was satisfied it could not be where Des

Cartes had fixed it, upon the top of the pineal gland of the brain; which, as he philosophized, formed a cushion for her about the size of a marrow pea; tho', to speak the truth, as so many nerves did terminate all in that one place,—'twas no bad conjecture;—and my father had certainly fallen with that great philosopher plumb into the centre of the mistake, had it not been for my uncle Toby, who rescued him out of it, by a story he told him of a Walloon officer at the battle of Landen, who had one part of his brain shot away by a musket-ball,—and another part of it taken out after by a French surgeon; and after all, recovered, and did his duty very well without it.

If death, said my father, reasoning with himself, is nothing but the separation of the soul from the body; and if it is true that people can walk about and do their business without brains,—then certes the soul does not inhabit there. Q. E. D.

As for that certain, very thin, subtle and very fragrant juice which Coglionissimo Borri, the great Milanese physician affirms, in a letter to Bartholine, to have discovered in the cellulae of the occipital parts of the cerebellum, and which he likewise affirms to be the principal seat of the reasonable soul, (for, you must know, in these latter and more enlightened ages, there are two souls in every man living,—the one, according to the great Metheglingius, being called the *Animus*, the other, the *Anima*;)—as for the opinion, I say, of Borri,—my father could never subscribe to it by any means; the very idea of so noble, so refined, so immaterial, and so ex-

CHAP. XIX

alted a being as the *Anima*, or even the *Animus*, taking
up her residence, and sitting dabbling, like a tadpole all
day long, both summer and winter, in a puddle,—or in a
liquid of any kind, how thick or thin soever, he would
say, shocked his imagination; he would scarce give the
doctrine a hearing.

What, therefore, seemed the least liable to objections
of any, was that the chief sensorium, or headquarters of
the soul, and to which place all intelligences were re-
ferred, and from whence all her mandates were issued,—
was in, or near, the cerebellum,—or rather somewhere
about the medulla oblongata, wherein it was generally
agreed by Dutch anatomists, that all the minute nerves
from all the organs of the seven senses concentered, like
streets and winding alleys, into a square.

So far there was nothing singular in my father's
opinion,—he had the best of philosophers, of all ages and
climates, to go along with him.—But here he took a road
of his own, setting up another Shandean hypothesis
upon these corner-stones they had laid for him;—and
which said hypothesis equally stood its ground; whether
the subtlety and fineness of the soul depended upon the
temperature and clearness of the said liquor, or of the
finer net-work and texture in the cerebellum itself;
which opinion he favoured.

He maintained, that next to the due care to be taken
in the act of propagation of each individual, which required all the thought in the world, as it laid the foundation of this incomprehensible contexture, in which wit,
memory, fancy, eloquence, and what is usually meant

by the name of good natural parts, do consist;—that next to this and his Christian-name, which were the two original and most efficacious causes of all;—that the third cause, or rather what logicians call the *Causa sine quâ non*, and without which all that was done was of no manner of significance,—was the preservation of this delicate and fine-spun web, from the havoc which was generally made in it by the violent compression and crush which the head was made to undergo, by the non-sensical method of bringing us into the world by that foremost.

——This requires explanation.

My father, who dipped into all kinds of books, upon looking into *Lithopaedus Senonesis de Partu difficili*,[1] published by Adrianus Smelvgot, had found out, that the lax and pliable state of a child's head in parturition, the bones of the cranium having no sutures at that time, was such,—that by force of the woman's efforts, which, in strong labour-pains, was equal, upon an average, to the weight of 470 pounds avoirdupois acting perpendicularly upon it;—it so happened, that in 49 instances out of 50, the said head was compressed and moulded into the shape of an oblong conical piece of dough, such as a

---

[1] The author is here twice mistaken;—for Lithopaedus should be wrote thus, *Lithopaedii Senonensis Icon.* The second mistake is, that this Lithopaedus is not an author, but a drawing of a petrified child. The account of this, published by Athosius 1580, may be seen at the end of Cordaeus's works in Spachius. Mr. Tristram Shandy has been led into this error, either from seeing Lithopaedus's name of late in a catalogue of learned writers in Dr. ——, or by mistaking Lithopaedus for Trinecavellius,—from the too great similitude of the names.

CHAP. XIX

pastry-cook generally rolls up in order to make a pie of.
—Good God! cried my father, what havoc and destruction must this make in the infinitely fine and tender texture of the cerebellum!—Or if there is such a juice as
Borri pretends,—is it not enough to make the clearest
liquid in the world both feculent and mothery?

But how great was his apprehension, when he farther
understood, that this force acting upon the very vertex
of the head, not only injured the brain itself, or cerebrum,—but that it necessarily squeezed and propelled
the cerebrum towards the cerebellum, which was the
immediate seat of the understanding!——Angels and
ministers of grace defend us! cried my father,—can any
soul withstand this shock?—No wonder the intellectual
web is so rent and tattered as we see it; and that so many
of our best heads are no better than a puzzled skein of
silk,—all perplexity,—all confusion within-side.

But when my father read on, and was let into the
secret, that when a child was turned topsy-turvy, which
was easy for an operator to do, and was extracted by the
feet;—that instead of the cerebrum being propelled towards the cerebellum, the cerebellum, on the contrary,
was propelled simply towards the cerebrum, where it
could do no manner of hurt:——By heavens! cried he,
the world is in conspiracy to drive out what little wit
God has given us,—and the professors of the obstetric
art are lifted into the same conspiracy.—What is it to me
which end of my son comes foremost into the world,
provided all goes right after, and his cerebellum escapes
uncrushed?

BOOK II

It is the nature of an hypothesis, when once a man has conceived it, that it assimilates every thing to itself, as proper nourishment; and, from the first moment of your begetting it, it generally grows the stronger by every thing you see, hear, read, or understand. This is of great use.

When my father was gone with this about a month, there was scarce a phenomenon of stupidity or of genius, which he could not readily solve by it;—it accounted for the eldest son being the greatest blockhead in the family. —Poor devil, he would say,—he made way for the capacity of his younger brothers.—It unriddled the observations of drivellers and monstrous heads,—shewing *à priori*, it could not be otherwise,—unless **** I don't know what. It wonderfully explained and accounted for the acumen of the Asiatic genius, and that spritelier turn, and a more penetrating intuition of minds, in warmer climates; not from the loose and commonplace solution of a clearer sky, and a more perpetual sunshine, etc.—which for aught we knew, might as well rarefy and dilute the faculties of the soul into nothing, by one extreme,—as they are condensed in colder climates by the other;—but he traced the affair up to its spring-head;— shewed that, in warmer climates, nature had laid a lighter tax upon the fairest parts of the creation;—their pleasures more;—the necessity of their pains less, insomuch that the pressure and resistance upon the vertex was so slight, that the whole organization of the cerebellum was preserved;—nay, he did not believe, in natural births, that so much as a single thread of the net-

CHAP. XIX

work was broke or displaced,—so that the soul might just act as she liked.

When my father had got so far,——what a blaze of light did the accounts of the Caesarean section, and of the towering geniuses who had come safe into the world by it, cast upon this hypothesis? Here you see, he would say, there was no injury done to the sensorium;—no pressure of the head against the pelvis;—no propulsion of the cerebrum towards the cerebellum, either by the *os pubis* on this side, or the *os coxygis* on that;——and pray, what were the happy consequences? Why, Sir, your Julius Caesar, who gave the operation a name;—and your Hermes Trismegistus, who was born so before ever the operation had a name;—your Scipio Africanus; your Manlius Torquatus; our Edward the Sixth,—who, had he lived, would have done the same honour to the hypothesis:—These, and many more who figured high in the annals of fame,—all came side-way, Sir, into the world.

The incision of the abdomen and uterus ran for six weeks together in my father's head;—he had read, and was satisfied, that wounds in the epigastrium, and those in the matrix, were not mortal;—so that the belly of the mother might be opened extremely well to give a passage to the child.—He mentioned the thing one afternoon to my mother,——merely as a matter of fact; but seeing her turn as pale as ashes at the very mention of it, as much as the operation flattered his hopes,—he thought it as well to say no more of it,—contenting himself with admiring,—what he thought was to no purpose to propose.

BOOK II

This was my father Mr. Shandy's hypothesis; concerning which I have only to add, that my brother
Bobby did as great honour to it (whatever he did to the
family) as any one of the great heroes we spoke of: For
happening not only to be christened, as I told you, but
to be born too, when my father was at Epsom,—being
moreover my mother's first child,—coming into the
world with his head foremost,—and turning out afterwards a lad of wonderful slow parts,—my father spelt
all these together into his opinion: and as he had failed
at one end,—he was determined to try the other.

This was not to be expected from one of the sisterhood, who are not easily to be put out of their way,—
and was therefore one of my father's great reasons in
favour of a man of science, whom he could better deal
with.

Of all men in the world, Dr. Slop was the fittest for
my father's purpose;—for though this new invented forceps was the armour he had proved, and what he maintained to be the safest instrument of deliverance, yet, it
seems, he had scattered a word or two in his book, in
favour of the very thing which ran in my father's fancy;
—tho' not with a view to the soul's good in extracting by
the feet, as was my father's system,—but for reasons
merely obstetrical.

This will account for the coalition betwixt my father
and Dr. Slop, in the ensuing discourse, which went a
little hard against my uncle Toby.—In what manner a
plain man, with nothing but common sense, could bear
up against two such allies in science,—is hard to con-

CHAP. XIX

ceive.—You may conjecture upon it, if you please,—and whilst your imagination is in motion, you may encourage it to go on, and discover by what causes and effects in nature it could come to pass, that my uncle Toby got his modesty by the wound he received upon his groin.— You may raise a system to account for the loss of my nose by marriage-articles,—and shew the world how it could happen, that I should have the misfortune to be called Tristram, in opposition to my father's hypothesis, and the wish of the whole family, Godfathers and Godmothers not excepted.—These, with fifty other points left yet unravelled, you may endeavour to solve if you have time;—but I tell you beforehand it will be in vain, for not the sage Alquife, the magician in *Don Belianis of Greece*, nor the no less famous Urganda, the sorceress, his wife, (were they alive) could pretend to come within a league of the truth.

The reader will be content to wait for a full explanation of these matters till the next year,—when a series of things will be laid open which he little expects.

BOOK II

BOOK III

Multitudinis imperitae non formido judicia; meis tamen, rogo,
parcant opusculis——in quibus fuit propositi semper, a jocis
ad seria, a seriis vicissim ad jocos transire.
      —Joan. Saresberiensis,
       Episcopus Lugdun.

CHAPTER I

——"I wish, Dr. Slop," quoth my uncle Toby, (repeating his wish for Dr. Slop a second time, and with a degree of more zeal and earnestness in his manner of wishing, than he had wished at first)——"I wish, Dr. Slop," quoth my uncle Toby, "you had seen what prodigious armies we had in Flanders."

My uncle Toby's wish did Dr. Slop a disservice which his heart never intended any man,—Sir, it confounded him—and thereby putting his ideas first into confusion, and then to flight, he could not rally them again for the soul of him.

In all disputes,—male or female,—whether for honour, for profit, or for love,—it makes no difference in the case;—nothing is more dangerous, Madam, than a wish coming sideways in this unexpected manner upon a man: the safest way in general to take off the force of the wish, is for the party wished at, instantly to get upon his legs —and wish the wisher something in return, of pretty near the same value,—so balancing the account upon the spot, you stand as you were—nay sometimes gain the advantage of the attack by it.

This will be fully illustrated to the world in my chapter of wishes.—

Dr. Slop did not understand the nature of this defence;—he was puzzled with it, and it put an entire stop to the dispute for four minutes and a half;—five had been fatal to it:—my father saw the danger—the dispute was one of the most interesting disputes in the world, "Whether the child of his prayers and endeavours should be born without a head or with one":—he waited to the last moment, to allow Dr. Slop, in whose behalf the wish was made, his right of returning it; but perceiving, I say, that he was confounded, and continued looking with that perplexed vacuity of eye which puzzled souls generally stare with—first in my uncle Toby's face—then in his—then up—then down—then east—east and by east, and so on,—coasting it along by the plinth of the wainscot till he had got to the opposite point of the compass, —and that he had actually begun to count the brass nails upon the arm of his chair,—my father thought there was no time to be lost with my uncle Toby, so took up the discourse as follows.

Chapter II

"—WHAT prodigious armies you had in Flanders!"— Brother Toby, replied my father, taking his wig from off his head with his right hand, and with his left pulling out a striped India handkerchief from his right coat pocket, in order to rub his head, as he argued the point with my uncle Toby.—

—Now, in this I think my father was much to blame; and I will give you my reasons for it.

Matters of no more seeming consequence in themselves than, "Whether my father should have taken off his wig with his right hand or with his left,"—have

CHAP. II

divided the greatest kingdoms, and made the crowns of
the monarchs who governed them, to totter upon their
heads.—But need I tell you, Sir, that the circumstances
with which every thing in this world is begirt, give every
thing in this world its size and shape!—and by tighten-
ing it, or relaxing it, this way or that, make the thing to
be, what it is—great—little—good—bad—indifferent or
not indifferent, just as the case happens?

As my father's India handkerchief was in his right
coat pocket, he should by no means have suffered his
right hand to have got engaged: on the contrary, instead
of taking off his wig with it, as he did, he ought to have
committed that entirely to the left; and then, when the
natural exigency my father was under of rubbing his
head, called out for his handkerchief, he would have had
nothing in the world to have done, but to have put his
right hand into his right coat pocket and taken it out;—
which he might have done without any violence, or the
least ungraceful twist in any one tendon or muscle of his
whole body.

In this case, (unless, indeed, my father had been resolved to make a fool of himself by holding the wig stiff
in his left hand—or by making some nonsensical angle or
other at his elbow-joint, or arm-pit)—his whole attitude
had been easy—natural—unforced: Reynolds himself,
as great and gracefully as he paints, might have painted
him as he sat.

Now as my father managed this matter,—consider
what a devil of a figure my father made of himself.

In the latter end of Queen Anne's reign, and in the

BOOK III

beginning of the reign of King George the First—"Coat pockets were cut very low down in the skirt."—I need say no more—the father of mischief, had he been hammering at it a month, could not have contrived a worse fashion for one in my father's situation.

CHAPTER III

IT was not an easy matter in any king's reign (unless you were as lean a subject as myself) to have forced your hand diagonally, quite across your whole body, so as to gain the bottom of your opposite coat pocket.—In the year one thousand seven hundred and eighteen, when this happened, it was extremely difficult; so that when my uncle Toby discovered the transverse zig-zaggery of my father's approaches towards it, it instantly brought into his mind those he had done duty in, before the gate of St. Nicolas;—the idea of which drew off his attention so entirely from the subject in debate, that he had got his right hand to the bell to ring up Trim to go and fetch his map of Namur, and his compasses and sector along with it, to measure the returning angles of the traverses of that attack,—but particularly of that one, where he received his wound upon his groin.

My father knit his brows, and as he knit them, all the blood in his body seemed to rush up into his face— my uncle Toby dismounted immediately.

——I did not apprehend your uncle Toby was o' horseback.——

Chapter IV

A MAN's body and his mind, with the utmost reverence to both I speak it, are exactly like a jerkin, and a jerkin's lining;—rumple the one,—you rumple the other. There is one certain exception however in this case, and that is, when you are so fortunate a fellow, as to have had your jerkin made of gum-taffeta, and the body-lining to it of a sarcenet, or thin persian.

Zeno, Cleanthes, Diogenes Babylonius, Dionysius Heracleotes, Antipater, Panaetius, and Posidonius amongst the Greeks;—Cato and Varro and Seneca amongst the Romans;—Pantaenus and Clemens Alexandrinus and Montaigne amongst the Christians; and a score and a half of good, honest, unthinking Shandean people as ever lived, whose names I can't recollect,—all pretended that their jerkins were made after this fashion,—you might have rumpled and crumpled, and doubled and creased, and fretted and fridged the outside of them all to pieces;—in short, you might have played the very devil with them, and at the same time, not one of the insides of them would have been one button the worse, for all you had done to them.

I believe in my conscience that mine is made up somewhat after this sort:—for never poor jerkin has been tickled off at such a rate as it has been these last nine months together,—and yet I declare, the lining to it,——as far as I am a judge of the matter, it is not a three-penny piece the worse;—pell-mell, helter-skelter, ding-dong, cut and thrust, back stroke and fore stroke,

side way and long way, have they been trimming it for
me:—had there been the least gumminess in my lining,
—by heaven! it had all of it long ago been frayed and
fretted to a thread.

——You Messrs. the Monthly reviewers!—how could
you cut and slash my jerkin as you did?—how did you
know but you would cut my lining too?

Heartily and from my soul, to the protection of that
Being who will injure none of us, do I recommend you
and your affairs,—so God bless you;—only next month,
if any one of you should gnash his teeth, and storm and
rage at me, as some of you did last May (in which I remember the weather was very hot)—don't be exasper-
ated, if I pass it by again with good temper,—being
determined as long as I live or write (which in my case
means the same thing) never to give the honest gentleman a worse word or a worse wish than my uncle Toby
gave the fly which buzzed about his nose all dinner-time,
——"Go,—go, poor devil," quoth he,—"get thee gone,
—why should I hurt thee? This world is surely wide
enough to hold both thee and me."

CHAPTER V

ANY man, Madam, reasoning upwards, and observing
the prodigious suffusion of blood in my father's
countenance,—by means of which (as all the blood in his
body seemed to rush into his face, as I told you) he must
have reddened, pictorially and scientifically speaking,
six whole tints and a half, if not a full octave above his

CHAP. V

natural colour:—any man, Madam, but my uncle Toby, who had observed this, together with the violent knitting of my father's brows, and the extravagant contortion of his body during the whole affair,—would have concluded my father in a rage; and taking that for granted,—had he been a lover of such kind of concord as arises from two such instruments being put in exact tune,—he would instantly have screwed up his, to the same pitch;—and then the devil and all had broke loose—the whole piece, Madam, must have been played off like the sixth of Avison Scarlatti—*con furia*,—like mad.—Grant me patience!——What has *con furia*,—*con strepito*,—or any other hurly burly whatever to do with harmony?

Any man, I say, Madam, but my uncle Toby, the benignity of whose heart interpreted every motion of the body in the kindest sense the motion would admit of, would have concluded my father angry, and blamed him too. My uncle Toby blamed nothing but the tailor who cut the pocket hole;—so sitting still till my father had got his handkerchief out of it, and looking all the time up in his face with inexpressible good-will—my father, at length, went on as follows.

CHAPTER VI

"WHAT prodigious armies you had in Flanders!"—— Brother Toby, quoth my father, I do believe thee to be as honest a man, and with as good and as upright a heart as ever God created;—nor is it thy fault, if all the children which have been, may, can, shall, will, or ought to be begotten, come with their heads foremost into the world:—but believe me, dear Toby, the accidents which unavoidably way-lay them, not only in the article of our begetting 'em—though these, in my opinion, are well worth considering,—but the dangers and difficulties our children are beset with, after they are got forth into the world, are enow—little need is there to expose them to unnecessary ones in their passage to it.——Are these dangers, quoth my uncle Toby, laying his hand upon my father's knee, and looking up seriously in his face for an answer,—are these dangers greater now o' days, brother, than in times past? Brother Toby, answered my father, if a child was but fairly begot, and born alive, and healthy, and the mother did well after it,—our fore-fathers never looked farther.——My uncle Toby in-stantly withdrew his hand from off my father's knee, re-clined his body gently back in his chair, raised his head till he could just see the cornice of the room, and then directing the buccinatory muscles along his cheeks, and the orbicular muscles around his lips to do their duty—he whistled *Lillabullero*.

CHAPTER VII

WHILST my uncle Toby was whistling *Lillabullero* to my father,—Dr. Slop was stamping, and cursing and damning at Obadiah at a most dreadful rate,——it would have done your heart good, and cured you, Sir, for ever of the vile sin of swearing, to have heard him; I am determined therefore to relate the whole affair to you.

CHAP. VII

When Dr. Slop's maid delivered the green baize bag
with her master's instruments in it, to Obadiah, she very
sensibly exhorted him to put his head and one arm
through the strings, and ride with it slung across his
body: so undoing the bow-knot, to lengthen the strings
for him, without any more ado, she helped him on with
it. However, as this, in some measure, unguarded the
mouth of the bag, lest any thing should bolt out in
galloping back, at the speed Obadiah threatened, they
consulted to take it off again; and in the great care and
caution of their hearts, they had taken the two strings
and tied them close (pursing up the mouth of the bag
first) with half a dozen hard knots, each of which
Obadiah, to make all safe, had twitched and drawn together with all the strength of his body.

This answered all that Obadiah and the maid intended; but was no remedy against some evils which
neither he nor she foresaw. The instruments, it seems, as
tight as the bag was tied above, had so much room to
play in it, towards the bottom (the shape of the bag
being conical) that Obadiah could not make a trot of it,
but with such a terrible jingle, what with the *tire-tête*,
forceps, and squirt, as would have been enough, had
Hymen been taking a jaunt that way, to have frightened
him out of the country; but when Obadiah accelerated
his motion, and from a plain trot assayed to prick his
coach-horse into a full gallop—by Heaven! Sir, the jingle
was incredible.

As Obadiah had a wife and three children—the tur-
pitude of fornication, and the many other political ill

consequences of this jingling, never once entered his
brain,—he had however his objection, which came home
to himself, and weighed with him, as it has oft-times
done with the greatest patriots.——"The poor fellow,
Sir, was not able to hear himself whistle."

Chapter VIII

As Obadiah loved wind-music preferably to all the instrumental music he carried with him,—he very
considerately set his imagination to work, to contrive
and to invent by what means he should put himself in a
condition of enjoying it.

In all distresses (except musical) where small cords
are wanted, nothing is so apt to enter a man's head as
his hat-band:——the philosophy of this is so near the
surface—I scorn to enter into it.

As Obadiah's was a mixed case—mark, Sirs,—I say,
a mixed case; for it was obstetrical,—scriptical, squirtical,
papistical—and as far as the coach-horse was concerned
in it,—caball-istical—and only partly musical;—Obadiah made no scruple of availing himself of the first expedient which offered;—so taking hold of the bag and
instruments, and griping them hard together with one
hand, and with the finger and thumb of the other putting the end of the hat-band betwixt his teeth, and then
slipping his hand down to the middle of it,—he tied and
cross-tied them all fast together from one end to the
other (as you would cord a trunk) with such a multi-
plicity of roundabouts and intricate cross turns, with a

hard knot at every intersection or point where the strings met,—that Dr. Slop must have had three fifths of Job's patience at least to have unloosed them.—I think in my conscience, that had Nature been in one of her nimble moods, and in humour for such a contest—and she and Dr. Slop both fairly started together—there is no man living who had seen the bag with all that Obadiah had done to it,—and known likewise the great speed the Goddess can make when she thinks proper, who would have had the least doubt remaining in his mind—which of the two would have carried off the prize. My mother, Madam, had been delivered sooner than the green bag

BOOK III

infallibly——at least by twenty *knots*.——Sport of small accidents, Tristram Shandy! that thou art, and ever will be! had that trial been for thee, and it was fifty to one but it had,—thy affairs had not been so depressed— (at least by the depression of thy nose) as they have been; nor had the fortunes of thy house and the occasions of making them, which have so often presented themselves in the course of thy life, to thee, been so often, so vexatiously, so tamely, so irrecoverably abandoned—as thou hast been forced to leave them;——but 'tis over,——all but the account of 'em, which cannot be given to the curious till I am got out into the world.

CHAPTER IX

GREAT wits jump: for the moment Dr. Slop cast his eyes upon his bag (which he had not done till the dispute with my uncle Toby about midwifery put him in mind of it)—the very same thought occurred.—'Tis God's mercy, quoth he (to himself) that Mrs. Shandy has had so bad a time of it,——else she might have been brought to bed seven times told, before one half of these knots could have got untied.——But here you must distinguish —the thought floated only in Dr. Slop's mind, without sail or ballast to it, as a simple proposition; millions of which, as your worship knows, are every day swimming quietly in the middle of the thin juice of a man's understanding, without being carried backwards or forwards, till some little gusts of passion or interest drive them to one side.

CHAP. IX

A sudden trampling in the room above, near my
mother's bed, did the proposition the very service I am
speaking of. By all that's unfortunate, quoth Dr. Slop,
unless I make haste, the thing will actually befall me as
it is.

CHAPTER X

IN the case of knots,—by which, in the first place, I
would not be understood to mean slip-knots—because
in the course of my life and opinions—my opinions concerning them will come in more properly when I mention
the catastrophe of my great uncle Mr. Hammond
Shandy,—a little man,—but of high fancy:—he rushed
into the duke of Monmouth's affair:—nor, secondly, in
this place, do I mean that particular species of knots
called bow-knots;—there is so little address, or skill, or
patience required in the unloosing them, that they are
below my giving any opinion at all about them.—But by
the knots I am speaking of, may it please your reverences to believe, that I mean good, honest, devilish
tight, hard knots, made *bona fide*, as Obadiah made his;
—in which there is no quibbling provision made by the
duplication and return of the two ends of the strings
thro' the annulus or noose made by the second implica-
tion of them—to get them slipped and undone by.——I
hope you apprehend me.

In the case of these knots then, and of the several ob-
structions, which, may it please your reverences, such
knots cast in our way in getting through life—every
hasty man can whip out his penknife and cut through

them.——'Tis wrong. Believe me, Sirs, the most virtuous way, and which both reason and conscience dictate
—is to take our teeth or our fingers to them.—Dr. Slop
had lost his teeth—his favourite instrument, by extracting in a wrong direction, or by some misapplication of it,
unfortunately slipping, he had formerly, in a hard labour,
knocked out three of the best of them with the handle of
it:——he tried his fingers—alas; the nails of his fingers
and thumbs were cut close.——The deuce take it! I can
make nothing of it either way, cried Dr. Slop.——The
trampling over head near my mother's bed-side increased.—Pox take the fellow! I shall never get the knots
untied as long as I live.——My mother gave a groan.
——Lend me your penknife——I must e'en cut the
knots at last—pugh!—psha!—Lord! I have cut my
thumb quite across to the very bone——curse the fellow
—if there was not another man-midwife within fifty
miles——I am undone for this bout—I wish the scoundrel hanged—I wish he was shot—I wish all the devils in
hell had him for a blockhead!——

My father had a great respect for Obadiah, and could
not bear to hear him disposed of in such a manner—he
had moreover some little respect for himself—and could
as ill bear with the indignity offered to himself in it.

Had Dr. Slop cut any part about him, but his thumb
——my father had passed it by—his prudence had triumphed: as it was, he was determined to have his revenge.

Small curses, Dr. Slop, upon great occasions, quoth
my father (condoling with him first upon the accident)

CHAP. X

are but so much waste of our strength and soul's health
to no manner of purpose.—I own it, replied Dr. Slop.—
They are like sparrow-shot, quoth my uncle Toby (suspending his whistling) fired against a bastion.——They
serve, continued my father, to stir the humours——but
carry off none of their acrimony:—for my own part, I
seldom swear or curse at all—I hold it bad——but if I
fall into it by surprise, I generally retain so much presence of mind (right, quoth my uncle Toby) as to make it
answer my purpose——that is, I swear on till I find myself easy. A wise and a just man however would always
endeavour to proportion the vent given to these humours,
not only to the degree of them stirring within himself—
but to the size and ill intent of the offence upon which
they are to fall.—"Injuries come only from the heart,"
—quoth my uncle Toby. For this reason, continued my
father, with the most Cervantic gravity, I have the
greatest veneration in the world for that gentleman,
who, in distrust of his own discretion in this point, sat
down and composed (that is at his leisure) fit forms of
swearing suitable to all cases, from the lowest to the
highest provocation which could possibly happen to him
—which forms being well considered by him, and such
moreover as he could stand to, he kept them ever by him
on the chimney-piece, within his reach, ready for use.—I
never apprehended, replied Dr. Slop, that such a thing
was ever thought of—much less executed. I beg your
pardon, answered my father; I was reading, though not
using, one of them to my brother Toby this morning,
whilst he poured out the tea—'tis here upon the shelf

over my head;—but if I remember right, 'tis too violent
for a cut of the thumb.—Not at all, quoth Dr. Slop—the
devil take the fellow.——Then, answered my father,
'Tis much at your service, Dr. Slop—on condition you
will read it aloud;——so rising up and reaching down a
form of excommunication of the church of Rome, a copy

CHAP. X

Textus de Ecclesiâ Roffensi, per Ernulfum Episcopum.

CAP. XI

EXCOMMUNICATIO

Ex auctoritate Dei omnipotentis, Patris, et Filij, et Spiritus Sancti, et sanctorum canonum, sanctaeque et intemeratae Virginis Dei genetricis Mariae,—

As the genuineness of the consultation of the Sorbonne upon the question of baptism, was doubted by some, and denied by others——'twas thought proper to print the original of this excommunication; for the copy of which Mr. Shandy returns thanks to the chapter clerk of the dean and chapter of Rochester.

BOOK III

of which, my father (who was curious in his collections) had procured out of the leger-book of the church of Rochester, writ by Ernulphus the bishop—with a most affected seriousness of look and voice, which might have cajoled Ernulphus himself—he put it into Dr. Slop's hands.—Dr. Slop wrapt his thumb up in the corner of his handkerchief, and with a wry face, though without any suspicion, read aloud, as follows——my uncle Toby whistling *Lillabullero* as loud as he could all the time.

CHAPTER XI

"BY the authority of God Almighty, the Father, Son, and Holy Ghost, and of the holy canons, and of the undefiled Virgin Mary, mother and patroness of our Saviour." I think there is no necessity, quoth Dr. Slop, dropping the paper down to his knee, and addressing himself to my father—as you have read it over, Sir, so lately, to read it aloud—and as Captain Shandy seems to have no great inclination to hear it——I may as well read it to myself. That's contrary to treaty, replied my father:—besides, there is something so whimsical, especially in the latter part of it, I should grieve to lose the pleasure of a second reading. Dr. Slop did not altogether like it,——but my uncle Toby offering at that instant to give over whistling, and read it himself to them;——Dr. Slop thought he might as well read it under the cover of my uncle Toby's whistling——as suffer my uncle Toby to read it alone;——so raising up the paper to his face, and holding it quite parallel to it, in order to hide his

———Atque omnium coelestium virtutum, angelorum, archangelorum, thronorum, dominationum, potestatum, cherubin ac seraphin, & sanctorum patriarcharum, prophetarum, & omnium apostolorum & evangelistarum, & sanctorum innocentum, qui in conspectu Agni soli digni inventi sunt canticum cantare novum, et sanctorum martyrum et sanctorum confessorum, et sanctarum virginum, atque omnium simul sanctorum et electorum

Dei,———Excommunicamus, et anathematizamus hunc *vel* os

furem, vel hunc malefactorem, N. N. et a liminibus sanctae Dei ecclesiae sequestramus, et aeternis suppliciis

excruciandus, mancipetur, cum Dathan et Abiram, et cum his qui dixerunt Domino Deo, Recede à nobis, scientiam viarum tuarum nolumus: et sicut aquâ ignis

extinguitur, sic extinguatur lucerna ejus in secula seculorum nisi resipuerit, et ad satisfactionem venerit. Amen.

Maledicat illum Deus Pater qui hominem creavit.

Maledicat illum Dei Filius qui pro homine passus est.

Maledicat illum Spiritus Sanctus qui in baptismo effusus est. Maledicat illum sancta crux, quam Christus pro nostrâ salute hostem triumphans ascendit.

chagrin——he read it aloud as follows——my uncle Toby
whistling *Lillabullero*, though not quite so loud as before.

"By the authority of God Almighty, the Father, Son,
and Holy Ghost, and of the undefiled Virgin Mary,
mother and patroness of our Saviour, and of all the
celestial virtues, angels, archangels, thrones, dominions,
powers, cherubins and seraphins, and of all the holy
patriarchs, prophets, and of all the apostles and evangelists, and of the holy innocents, who in the sight of the
Holy Lamb, are found worthy to sing the new song of
the holy martyrs and holy confessors, and of the holy
virgins, and of all the saints, together with the holy and
elect of God,——May he" (Obadiah) "be damned" (for
tying these knots)——"We excommunicate, and anathe-
matize him, and from the thresholds of the holy church
of God Almighty we sequester him, that he may be tormented, disposed, and delivered over with Dathan and
Abiram, and with those who say unto the Lord God,
Depart from us, we desire none of thy ways. And as fire
is quenched with water, so let the light of him be put out
for evermore, unless it shall repent him" (Obadiah, of
the knots which he has tied) "and make satisfaction"
(for them) "Amen."

"May the Father who created man, curse him.——
May the Son who suffered for us, curse him.——May
the Holy Ghost, who was given to us in baptism, curse
him (Obadiah)——May the holy cross which Christ, for
our salvation triumphing over his enemies, ascended,
curse him.

CHAP. XI

Maledicat illum sancta Dei genetrix et perpetua Virgo

Maria. Maledicat illum sanctus Michael, animarum sus-

ceptor sacrarum. Maledicant illum omnes angeli et
archangeli, principatus et potestates, omnisque militia
coelestis.

Maledicat illum patriarcharum et prophetarum lau-

dabilis numerus. Maledicat illum sanctus Johannes Praecursor et Baptista Christi, et sanctus Petrus, et sanctus
Paulus, atque sanctus Andreas, omnesque Christi apos-
toli, simul et caeteri discipuli, quatuor quoque evange-
listae, qui sua praedicatione mundum universum con-

verterunt. Maledicat illum cuneus martyrum et confessorum mirificus, qui Deo bonis operibus placitus in-
ventus est.

Maledicant illum sacrarum virginum chori, quae
mundi vana causa honoris Christi respuenda contempse-

runt. Maledicant illum omnes sancti qui ab initio mundi
usque in finem seculi Deo dilecti inveniuntur.

Maledicant illum coeli et terra, et omnia sancta in eis
manentia.

BOOK III

"May the holy and eternal Virgin Mary, mother of God, curse him.——May St. Michael, the advocate of holy souls, curse him.——May all the angels and archangels, principalities and powers, and all the heavenly armies, curse him." [Our armies swore terribly in Flanders, cried my uncle Toby,—but nothing to this.—For my own part I could not have a heart to curse my dog so.]

"May St. John, the Praecursor, and St. John the Baptist, and St. Peter and St. Paul, and St. Andrew, and all other Christ's apostles, together curse him. And may the rest of his disciples and four evangelists, who by their preaching converted the universal world, and may the holy and wonderful company of martyrs and confessors who by their holy works are found pleasing to God Almighty, curse him" (Obadiah).

"May the holy choir of the holy virgins, who for the honour of Christ have despised the things of the world, damn him——May all the saints, who from the beginning of the world to everlasting ages are found to be beloved of God, damn him——

"May the heavens and earth, and all the holy things remaining therein, damn him," (Obadiah) "or her," (or who ever else had a hand in tying these knots).

CHAP. XI

Maledictus sit ubicunque fuerit, sive in domo, sive in agro, sive in viâ, sive in semitâ, sive in silvâ, sive in aquâ, sive in ecclesiâ.

Maledictus sit vivendo, moriendo,———————
——————— ——————— ——— ——————— ——————— ——— ———
——————— ——————— —— ——————— ——————— ——————— ——
——— ——————— ——————— ——————— ——————— ——— ———

manducando, bibendo, esuriendo, sitiendo, jejunando, dormitando, dormiendo, vigilando, ambulando, stando, sedendo, jacendo, operando, quiescendo, mingendo, cacando, flebotomando.

Maledictus sit in totis viribus corporis,

Maledictus sit intus et exterius.

Maledictus sit in capillis; maledictus sit in cerebro.

Maledictus sit in vertice, in temporibus, in fronte, in auriculis, in superciliis, in oculis, in genis, in maxillis, in naribus, in dentibus, mordacibus, sive molaribus, in labiis, in guttere, in humeris, in harnis, in brachiis, in manubus, in digitis, in pectore, in corde, et in omnibus interioribus stomacho tenus, in renibus, in inguinibus, in femore, in genitalibus, in coxis, in genubus, in cruribus, in pedibus, et in inguibus.

"May he (Obadiah) be damned wherever he be——whether in the house or the stables, the garden or the field, or the highway, or in the path, or in the wood, or in the water, or in the church.——May he be cursed in living, in dying." [Here my uncle Toby, taking the advantage of a minim in the second bar of his tune, kept whistling one continued note to the end of the sentence. ——Dr. Slop, with his division of curses moving under him, like a running bass all the way.] "May he be cursed in eating and drinking, in being hungry, in being thirsty, in fasting, in sleeping, in slumbering, in walking, in standing, in sitting, in lying, in working, in resting, in pissing, in shitting, and in blood-letting!"

"May he" (Obadiah) "be cursed in all the faculties of his body!

"May he be cursed inwardly and outwardly!——May he be cursed in the hair of his head!——May he be cursed in his brains, and in his vertex," (that is a sad curse, quoth my father) "in his temples, in his forehead, in his ears, in his eye-brows, in his cheeks, in his jaw-bones, in his nostrils, in his fore-teeth and grinders, in his lips, in his throat, in his shoulders, in his wrists, in his arms, in his hands, in his fingers!

"May he be damned in his mouth, in his breast, in his heart and purtenance, down to the very stomach!

"May he be cursed in his reins, and in his groin," (God in heaven forbid! quoth my uncle Toby) "in his thighs, in his genitals," (my father shook his head) "and in his hips, and in his knees, his legs, and feet, and toe-nails!

CHAP. XI

Maledictus sit in totis compagibus membrorum, a vertice capitis, usque ad plantam pedis—non sit in eo sanitas.

Maledicat illum Christus Filius Dei vivi toto suae majestatis imperio.——

——et insurgat adversus illum coelum cum omnibus virtutibus quae in eo moventur ad *damnandum* eum, nisi penituerit et ad satisfactionem venerit. Amen. Fiat, fiat. Amen.

BOOK III

"May he be cursed in all the joints and articulations of his members, from the top of his head to the sole of his foot! May there be no soundness in him!

"May the Son of the living God, with all the glory of his Majesty"——[Here my uncle Toby, throwing back his head, gave a monstrous, long, loud Whew—w—w ——something betwixt the interjectional whistle of Hey-day! and the word itself.——

——By the golden beard of Jupiter—and of Juno (if her majesty wore one) and by the beards of the rest of your heathen worships, which by the bye was no small number, since what with the beards of your celestial gods, and gods aerial and aquatic—to say nothing of the beards of town-gods and country-gods, or of the celestial goddesses your wives, or of the infernal goddesses your whores and concubines (that is in case they wore 'em) ——all which beards, as Varro tells me, upon his word and honour, when mustered up together, made no less than thirty thousand effective beards upon the pagan establishment;——every beard of which claimed the rights and privileges of being stroken and sworn by—by all these beards together then——I vow and protest, that of the two bad cassocks I am worth in the world, I would have given the better of them, as freely as ever Cid Hamet offered his——to have stood by, and heard my uncle Toby's accompaniment.]

—"Curse him!" continued Dr. Slop,—"and may heaven, with all the powers which move therein, rise up against him, curse and damn him" (Obadiah) "unless he repent and make satisfaction! Amen. So be it,—so be it. Amen."

CHAP. XI

I declare, quoth my uncle Toby, my heart would not let me curse the devil himself with so much bitterness.— He is the father of curses, replied Dr. Slop.—So am not I, replied my uncle.—But he is cursed and damned already, to all eternity, replied Dr. Slop.

I am sorry for it, quoth my uncle Toby.

Dr. Slop drew up his mouth, and was just beginning to return my uncle Toby the compliment of his Whu—u—u—or interjectional whistle—when the door hastily opening in the next chapter but one—put an end to the affair.

Chapter XII

Now don't let us give ourselves a parcel of airs, and pretend that the oaths we make free with in this land of liberty of ours are our own; and because we have the spirit to swear them,—imagine that we have had the wit to invent them too.

I'll undertake this moment to prove it to any man in the world, except to a connoisseur:—though I declare I object only to a connoisseur in swearing,—as I would do to a connoisseur in painting, etc., etc., the whole set of 'em are so hung round and befetished with the bobs and trinkets of criticism,—or to drop my metaphor, which by the bye is a pity,—for I have fetched it as far as from the coast of Guiney;—their heads, Sir, are stuck so full of rules and compasses, and have that eternal propensity to apply them upon all occasions, that a work of genius had better go to the devil at once, than stand to be pricked and tortured to death by 'em.

—And how did Garrick speak the soliloquy last
night?—Oh, against all rule, my Lord,—most ungram-
matically! betwixt the substantive and the adjective,
which should agree together in number, case, and gender, he made a breach thus,—stopping, as if the point
wanted settling;—and betwixt the nominative case,
which your lordship knows should govern the verb, he
suspended his voice in the epilogue a dozen times three
seconds and three fifths by a stop-watch, my Lord, each
time.—Admirable grammarian!—But in suspending his
voice—was the sense suspended likewise? Did no expression of attitude or countenance fill up the chasm?—
Was the eye silent? Did you narrowly look?—I looked
only at the stop-watch, my Lord.—Excellent observer!

And what of this new book the whole world makes
such a rout about?—Oh! 'tis out of all plumb, my Lord,
——quite an irregular thing!—not one of the angles at
the four corners was a right angle.—I had my rule and
compasses, etc., my Lord, in my pocket.—Excellent
critic!

—And for the epic poem your lordship bid me look
at—upon taking the length, breadth, height, and depth
of it, and trying them at home upon an exact scale of
Bossu's—'tis out, my Lord, in every one of its dimen-
sions.—Admirable connoisseur!

—And did you step in, to take a look at the grand
picture in your way back?—'Tis a melancholy daub! my
Lord; not one principle of the pyramid in any one group!
—and what a price!—for there is nothing of the colouring of Titian—the expression of Rubens—the grace of

CHAP. XII

Raphael—the purity of Dominichino—the corregiescity of Corregio—the learning of Poussin—the airs of Guido —the taste of the Carrachis—or the grand contour of Angelo.—Grant me patience, just Heaven!—Of all the cants which are canted in this canting world—though the cant of hypocrites may be the worst—the cant of criticism is the most tormenting!

I would go fifty miles on foot, for I have not a horse worth riding on, to kiss the hand of that man whose generous heart will give up the reins of his imagination into his author's hands—be pleased he knows not why, and cares not wherefore.

Great Apollo! if thou art in a giving humour—give me—I ask no more, but one stroke of native humour, with a single spark of thy own fire along with it—and send Mercury, with the rules and compasses, if he can be spared, with my compliments to—no matter.

Now to any one else I will undertake to prove, that all the oaths and imprecations which we have been puffing off upon the world for these two hundred and fifty years last past as originals—except St. Paul's thumb— God's flesh and God's fish, which were oaths monarchical, and, considering who made them, not much amiss; and as kings' oaths, 'tis not much matter whether they were fish or flesh;—else I say, there is not an oath, or at least a curse amongst them, which has not been copied over and over again out of Ernulphus a thousand times; but, like all other copies, how infinitely short of the force and spirit of the original!—It is thought to be no bad oath—and by itself passes very well—"G—d damn you."

BOOK III

—Set it beside Ernulphus's—"God Almighty the Father
damn you—God the Son damn you—God the Holy
Ghost damn you"—you see 'tis nothing.—There is an
orientality in his, we cannot rise up to: besides, he is
more copious in his invention—possessed more of the
excellencies of a swearer—had such a thorough knowledge of the human frame, its membranes, nerves, ligaments, knittings of the joints, and articulations,—that
when Ernulphus cursed—no part escaped him.—'Tis
true there is something of a hardness in his manner—
and, as in Michael Angelo, a want of grace—but then
there is such a greatness of gusto!

My father, who generally looked upon every thing in
a light very different from all mankind, would, after all,
never allow this to be an original.—He considered rather
Ernulphus's anathema as an institute of swearing, in
which, as he suspected, upon the decline of swearing in
some milder pontificate, Ernulphus, by order of the
succeeding pope, had with great learning and diligence
collected together all the laws of it;—for the same reason
that Justinian, in the decline of the empire, had ordered
his chancellor Tribonian to collect the Roman or civil
laws all together into one code or digest—lest, through
the rust of time—and the fatality of all things committed
to oral tradition—they should be lost to the world for
ever.

For this reason my father would oft-times affirm,
there was not an oath, from the great and tremendous
oath of William the Conqueror (By the splendour of
God) down to the lowest oath of a scavenger (Damn

your eyes) which was not to be found in Ernulphus.—In short, he would add—I defy a man to swear *out* of it.

The hypothesis is, like most of my father's, singular and ingenious too;—nor have I any objection to it, but that it overturns my own.

CHAPTER XIII

—**B**LESS my soul!—my poor mistress is ready to faint —and her pains are gone—and the drops are done —and the bottle of julap is broke—and the nurse has cut her arm—(and I, my thumb, cried Dr. Slop,) and the child is where it was, continued Susannah,—and the midwife has fallen backwards upon the edge of the fender, and bruised her hip as black as your hat.—I'll look at it, quoth Dr. Slop.—There is no need of that, replied Susannah,—you had better look at my mistress—but the midwife would gladly first give you an account how things are, so desires you would go up stairs and speak to her this moment.

Human nature is the same in all professions.

The midwife had just before been put over Dr. Slop's head—He had not digested it.—No, replied Dr. Slop, 'twould be full as proper, if the midwife came down to me.—I like subordination, quoth my uncle Toby,—and but for it, after the reduction of Lisle, I know not what might have become of the garrison of Ghent, in the mutiny for bread, in the year Ten.—Nor, replied Dr. Slop, (parodying my uncle Toby's hobby-horsical reflection; though full as hobby-horsical himself)——do I know, Captain Shandy, what might have become of the garrison above stairs, in the mutiny and confusion I find all things are in at present, but for the subordination of fingers and thumbs to ******——the application of which, Sir, under this accident of mine, comes in so *à propos*, that without it, the cut upon my thumb might have been felt by the Shandy family, as long as the Shandy family had a name.

Chapter XIV

LET us go back to the ******——in the last chapter. It is a singular stroke of eloquence (at least it was so, when eloquence flourished at Athens and Rome, and would be so now, did orators wear mantles) not to mention the name of a thing, when you had the thing about you *in petto*, ready to produce, pop, in the place you want

it. A scar, an axe, a sword, a pinked doublet, a rusty hel-
met, a pound and a half of pot-ashes in an urn, or a three-
halfpenny pickle pot—but above all, a tender infant
royally accoutred.—Tho' if it was too young, and the
oration as long as Tully's second Philippic—it must certainly have beshit the orator's mantle.—And then again,
if too old,—it must have been unwieldy and incommo-
dious to his action—so as to make him lose by his child
almost as much as he could gain by it.—Otherwise,
when a state orator has hit the precise age to a minute—
hid his BAMBINO in his mantle so cunningly that no
mortal could smell it—and produced so critically, that
no soul could say, it came in by head and shoulders—
Oh Sirs! it has done wonders—It has opened the sluices,
and turned the brains, and shook the principles, and un-
hinged the politics of half a nation.

These feats however are not to be done, except in
those states and times, I say, where orators wore mantles
—and pretty large ones too, my brethren, with some
twenty or five-and-twenty yards of good purple, superfine, marketable cloth in them—with large flowing folds
and doubles, and in a great style of design.—All which
plainly shews, may it please your worships, that the
decay of eloquence, and the little good service it does at
present, both within and without doors, is owing to
nothing else in the world, but short coats, and the disuse
of trunk-hose.—We can conceal nothing under ours,
Madam, worth shewing.

Chapter XV

D r. Slop was within an ace of being an exception to
all this argumentation: for happening to have his
green baize bag upon his knees, when he began to parody
my uncle Toby—'twas as good as the best mantle in the
world to him: for which purpose, when he foresaw the
sentence would end in his new-invented forceps, he
thrust his hand into the bag in order to have them ready
to clap in, where your reverences took so much notice of
the ***, which had he managed—my uncle Toby had
certainly been overthrown: the sentence and the argument in that case jumping closely in one point, so like
the two lines which form the salient angle of a ravelin,—
Dr. Slop would never have given them up;—and my
uncle Toby would as soon have thought of flying, as
taking them by force: but Dr. Slop fumbled so vilely in
pulling them out, it took off the whole effect, and what
was a ten times worse evil (for they seldom come alone
in this life) in pulling out his forceps, his forceps unfortunately drew out the squirt along with it.

When a proposition can be taken in two senses—'tis
a law in disputation, That the respondent may reply to
which of the two he pleases, or finds most convenient for
him.—This threw the advantage of the argument quite
on my uncle Toby's side.—"Good God!" cried my uncle
Toby, "are children brought into the world with a
squirt?"

CHAP. XV

Chapter XVI

—Upon my honour, Sir, you have tore every bit of
skin quite off the back of both my hands with your
forceps, cried my uncle Toby—and you have crushed all
my knuckles into the bargain with them to a jelly. 'Tis
your own fault, said Dr. Slop—you should have clinched
your two fists together into the form of a child's head as
I told you, and sat firm.—I did so, answered my uncle
Toby.—Then the points of my forceps have not been
sufficiently armed, or the rivet wants closing—or else
the cut on my thumb has made me a little awkward—or
possibly—'Tis well, quoth my father, interrupting the
detail of possibilities—that the experiment was not first
made upon my child's head-piece.——It would not have
been a cherry-stone the worse, answered Dr. Slop.—I
maintain it, said my uncle Toby, it would have broke
the cerebellum (unless indeed the skull had been as hard
as a granado) and turned it all into a perfect posset.——
Pshaw! replied Dr. Slop, a child's head is naturally as
soft as the pap of an apple;—the sutures give way—and
besides, I could have extracted by the feet after.—Not
you, said she.—I rather wish you would begin that way,
quoth my father.

Pray do, added my uncle Toby.

Chapter XVII

—And pray, good woman, after all, will you take upon you to say, it may not be the child's hip, as well as the child's head?——'Tis most certainly the head, replied the midwife. Because, continued Dr. Slop (turning to my father) as positive as these old ladies generally are —'tis a point very difficult to know—and yet of the greatest consequence to be known;—because, Sir, if the hip is mistaken for the head—there is a possibility (if it is a boy) that the forceps * * * * * * * * * * * * * *

—What the possibility was, Dr. Slop whispered very low to my father, and then to my uncle Toby.—There is no such danger, continued he, with the head.—No, in truth, quoth my father—but when your possibility has taken place at the hip—you may as well take off the head too.

—It is morally impossible the reader should understand this—'tis enough Dr. Slop understood it:—so taking the green baize bag in his hand, with the help of Obadiah's pumps, he tripped pretty nimbly, for a man of his size, across the room to the door—and from the door was shewn the way, by the good old midwife, to my mother's apartment.

Chapter XVIII

It is two hours, and ten minutes—and no more—cried my father, looking at his watch, since Dr. Slop and Obadiah arrived—and I know not how it happens, brother Toby—but to my imagination it seems almost an age.

—Here—pray, Sir, take hold of my cap—nay, take the bell along with it, and my pantoufles too.

Now, Sir, they are all at your service; and I freely make you a present of 'em, on condition you give me all your attention to this chapter.

Though my father said, "he knew not how it happened,"—yet he knew very well how it happened;—and at the instant he spoke it, was pre-determined in his mind to give my uncle Toby a clear account of the matter by a metaphysical dissertation upon the subject of duration and its simple modes, in order to show my uncle Toby by what mechanism and mensurations in the brain it came to pass, that the rapid succession of their ideas, and the eternal scampering of the discourse from one thing to another, since Dr. Slop had come into the room, had lengthened out so short a period to so inconceivable an extent.—"I know not how it happens—cried my father,—but it seems an age."

—'Tis owing entirely, quoth my uncle Toby, to the succession of our ideas.

My father, who had an itch, in common with all philosophers, of reasoning upon every thing which happened, and accounting for it too—proposed infinite pleasure to himself in this, of the succession of ideas, and had not the least apprehension of having it snatched out of his hands by my uncle Toby, who (honest man!) generally took every thing as it happened;—and who, of all things in the world, troubled his brain the least with abstruse thinking;—the ideas of time and space—or how we came by those ideas—or of what stuff they were made—or whether they were born with us—or we picked them up afterwards as we went along—or whether we did it in frocks—or not till we had got into breeches—with a thousand other inquiries and disputes about Infinity, Prescience, Liberty, Necessity, and so forth, upon whose desperate and unconquerable theories so many fine heads have been turned and cracked—never did my uncle Toby's the least injury at all; my father knew it—and was no less surprised than he was disappointed, with my uncle's fortuitous solution.

Do you understand the theory of that affair? replied my father.

Not I, quoth my uncle.

—But you have some ideas, said my father, of what you talk about?—

No more than my horse, replied my uncle Toby.

Gracious heaven! cried my father, looking upwards, and clasping his two hands together—there is a worth in thy honest ignorance, brother Toby—'twere almost a pity to exchange it for a knowledge.—But I'll tell thee.—

To understand what time is aright, without which we never can comprehend infinity, insomuch as one is a portion of the other—we ought seriously to sit down and consider what idea it is we have of duration, so as to give a satisfactory account how we came by it.—What is that to any body? quoth my uncle Toby. [1]For if you will turn your eyes inwards upon your mind, continued my father,

[1] *Vide* Locke.

CHAP. XVIII

and observe attentively, you will perceive, brother, that whilst you and I are talking together, and thinking, and smoking our pipes, or whilst we receive successively ideas in our minds, we know that we do exist, and so we estimate the existence, or the continuation of the existence of ourselves, or any thing else, commensurate to the succession of any ideas in our minds, the duration of ourselves, or any such other thing co-existing with our thinking—and so according to that preconceived——— You puzzle me to death, cried my uncle Toby.

———'Tis owing to this, replied my father, that in our computations of time, we are so used to minutes, hours, weeks, and months—and of clocks (I wish there was not a clock in the kingdom) to measure out their several portions to us, and to those who belong to us—that 'twill be well, if in time to come, the succession of our ideas be of any use or service to us at all.

Now, whether we observe it or no, continued my father, in every sound man's head, there is a regular succession of ideas of one sort or other, which follow each other in train just like———A train of artillery? said my uncle Toby—A train of a fiddle-stick!—quoth my father—which follow and succeed one another in our minds at certain distances, just like the images in the inside of a lanthorn turned round by the heat of a candle. —I declare, quoth my uncle Toby, mine are more like a smoke-jack.—Then, brother Toby, I have nothing more to say to you upon the subject, said my father.

Chapter XIX

—WHAT a conjuncture was here lost!—My father in one of his best explanatory moods—in eager pursuit of a metaphysical point into the very regions, where clouds and thick darkness would soon have encompassed it about;—my uncle Toby in one of the finest dispositions for it in the world; his head like a smoke-jack; —the funnel unswept, and the ideas whirling round and round about in it, all obfuscated and darkened over with fuliginous matter!—By the tombstone of Lucian—if it is in being—if not, why then by his ashes! by the ashes of my dear Rabelais, and dearer Cervantes!——my father and my uncle Toby's discourse upon Time and Eternity —was a discourse devoutly to be wished for! and the petulancy of my father's humour, in putting a stop to it as he did, was a robbery of the Ontologic Treasury of such a jewel, as no coalition of great occasions and great men are ever likely to restore to it again.

Chapter XX

THO' my father persisted in not going on with the discourse—yet he could not get my uncle Toby's smoke-jack out of his head—piqued as he was at first with it;— there was something in the comparison at the bottom, which hit his fancy; for which purpose, resting his elbow upon the table, and reclining the right side of his head upon the palm of his hand—but looking first stedfastly in the fire—he began to commune with himself, and

CHAP. XX

philosophize about it: but his spirits being wore out with the fatigues of investigating new tracts, and the constant exertion of his faculties upon that variety of subjects which had taken their turn in the discourse—— the idea of the smoke-jack soon turned all his ideas upside down—so that he fell asleep almost before he knew what he was about.

As for my uncle Toby, his smoke-jack had not made a dozen revolutions, before he fell asleep also.—Peace be with them both!—Dr. Slop is engaged with the midwife and my mother above stairs.—Trim is busy in turning an old pair of jack-boots into a couple of mortars, to be employed in the siege of Messina next summer—and is this instant boring the touch-holes with the point of a hot poker.—All my heroes are off my hands;—'tis the first time I have had a moment to spare—and I'll make use of it, and write my preface.

THE AUTHOR'S PREFACE

No, I'll not say a word about it——here it is;—in publishing it—I have appealed to the world—and to the world I leave it;—it must speak for itself.

All I know of the matter is—when I sat down, my intent was to write a good book; and so far as the tenuity of my understanding would hold out—a wise, aye, and a discreet—taking care only, as I went along, to put into it all the wit and the judgment, (be it more or less) which the great Author and Bestower of them had thought fit originally to give me——so that, as your worships see— 'tis just as God pleases.

BOOK III

Now, Agelastes (speaking dispraisingly) sayeth, That
there may be some wit in it, for aught he knows—but no
judgment at all. And Triptolemus and Phutatorius agree-
ing thereto, ask, How is it possible there should? for that
wit and judgment in this world never go together; inasmuch as they are two operations differing from each
other as wide as east from west——So, says Locke—so
are farting and hiccuping, say I. But in answer to this,
Didius the great church lawyer, in his code *de fartendi et
illustrandi fallaciis*, doth maintain and make fully appear, That an illustration is no argument—nor do I
maintain the wiping of a looking-glass clean to be a
syllogism;—but you all, may it please your worships,
see the better for it——so that the main good these
things do is only to clarify the understanding, previous
to the application of the argument itself, in order to free
it from any little motes, or specks of opacular matter,
which, if left swimming therein, might hinder a conception and spoil all.

Now, my dear Anti-Shandeans, and thrice able
critics, and fellow-labourers (for to you I write this
Preface)——and to you, most subtle statesmen and discreet doctors (do—pull off your beards) renowned for
gravity and wisdom;—Monopolus, my politician—
Didius, my counsel; Kysarcius, my friend;—Phutatorius, my guide;—Gastripheres, the preserver of my
life; Somnolentius, the balm and repose of it—not for-
getting all others, as well sleeping as waking, ecclesiastical as civil, whom for brevity, but out of no resentment
to you, I lump all together.—Believe me, right worthy.

CHAP. XX

My most zealous wish and fervent prayer in your behalf, and in my own too, in case the thing is not done already for us—is, that the great gifts and endowments both of wit and judgment, with every thing which usually goes along with them——such as memory, fancy, genius, eloquence, quick parts, and what not, may this precious moment, without stint or measure, let or hindrance, be poured down warm as each of us could bear it—scum and sediment and all (for I would not have a drop lost) into the several receptacles, cells, cellules, domiciles, dormitories, refectories, and spare places of our brains ——in such sort, that they might continue to be injected and tunned into, according to the true intent and meaning of my wish, until every vessel of them both great and small, be so replenished, saturated, and filled up therewith, that no more, would it save a man's life, could possibly be got either in or out.

Bless us!—what noble work we should make!—how should I tickle it off!—and what spirits should I find myself in, to be writing away for such readers!—and you— just heaven!—with what raptures would you sit and read—but oh!—'tis too much—I am sick—I faint away deliciously at the thoughts of it—'tis more than nature can bear!—lay hold of me—I am giddy—I am stone blind—I'm dying—I am gone.—Help! Help! Help!— But hold—I grow something better again, for I am beginning to foresee, when this is over, that as we shall all of us continue to be great wits—we should never agree amongst ourselves, one day to an end:—there would be so much satire and sarcasm—scoffing and

[229]

flouting, with rallying and reparteeing of it—thrusting
and parrying in one corner or another—there would be
nothing but mischief among us—Chaste stars! what
biting and scratching, and what a racket and a clatter
we should make, what with breaking of heads, rapping
of knuckles, and hitting of sore places—there would be
no such thing as living for us.

But then again, as we should all of us be men of
great judgment, we should make up matters as fast as
ever they went wrong; and though we should abominate
each other ten times worse than so many devils or devil-
esses, we should nevertheless, my dear creatures, be all
courtesy and kindness, milk and honey—'twould be a
second land of promise—a paradise upon earth, if there
was such a thing to be had—so that upon the whole we
should have done well enough.

All I fret and fume at, and what most distresses my
invention at present, is how to bring the point itself to
bear; for as your worships well know, that of these heavenly emanations of wit and judgment, which I have so
bountifully wished both for your worships and myself—
there is but a certain *quantum* stored up for us all for the
use and behoof of the whole race of mankind; and such
small modicums of 'em are only sent forth into this wide
world, circulating here and there in one bye corner or
another—and in such narrow streams, and at such prodigious intervals from each other, that one would wonder
how it holds out, or could be sufficient for the wants and
emergencies of so many great estates, and populous
empires.

CHAP. XX

Indeed there is one thing to be considered, that in Nova Zembla, North Lapland, and in all those cold and dreary tracts of the globe, which lie more directly under the arctic and antarctic circles, where the whole province of man's concernments lies for near nine months together within the narrow compass of his cave—where the spirits are compressed almost to nothing—and where the passions of a man, with every thing which belongs to them, are as frigid as the zone itself—there the least quantity of judgment imaginable does the business—and of wit—there is a total and an absolute saving—for as not one spark is wanted—so not one spark is given. Angels and ministers of grace defend us! what a dismal thing would it have been to have governed a kingdom, to have fought a battle, or made a treaty, or run a match, or wrote a book, or got a child, or held a provincial chapter there, with so plentiful a lack of wit and judgment about us! For mercy's sake, let us think no more about it, but travel on as fast as we can southwards into Norway—crossing over Swedeland, if you please, through the small triangular province of Angermania to the lake of Bothnia; coasting along it through east and west Bothnia, down to Carelia, and so on, through all those states and provinces which border upon the far side of the Gulf of Finland, and the north-east of the Baltic, up to Petersbourg, and just stepping into Ingria;—then stretching over directly from thence through the north parts of the Russian empire—leaving Siberia a little upon the left hand, till we got into the very heart of Russian and Asiatic Tartary.

Now throughout this long tour which I have led you,
you observe the good people are better off by far, than
in the polar countries which we have just left:—for if
you hold your hand over your eyes, and look very attentively, you may perceive some small glimmerings (as it
were) of wit, with a comfortable provision of good plain
household judgment, which, taking the quality and
quantity of it together, they make a very good shift
with——and had they more of either the one or the
other, it would destroy the proper balance betwixt them,
and I am satisfied moreover they would want occasions
to put them to use.

Now, Sir, if I conduct you home again into this
warmer and more luxuriant island, where you perceive
the springtide of our blood and humours runs high—
where we have more ambition, and pride, and envy, and
lechery, and other whoreson passions upon our hands to
govern and subject to reason—the height of our wit, and
the depth of our judgment, you see, are exactly proportioned to the length and breadth of our necessities—and
accordingly we have them sent down amongst us in such
a flowing kind of descent and creditable plenty, that no
one thinks he has any cause to complain.

It must however be confessed on this head, that, as
our air blows hot and cold—wet and dry, ten times in a
day, we have them in no regular and settled way;—so
that sometimes for near half a century together, there
shall be very little wit or judgment either to be seen or
heard of amongst us:—the small channels of them shall
seem quite dried up—then all of a sudden the sluices

CHAP. XX

shall break out, and take a fit of running again like fury
—you would think they would never stop:—and then it
is, that in writing, and fighting, and twenty other gallant
things, we drive all the world before us.

It is by these observations, and a wary reasoning by
analogy in that kind of argumentative process, which
Suidas calls dialectic induction——that I draw and set
up this position as most true and veritable;

That of these two luminaries so much of their irradi-
ations are suffered from time to time to shine down upon
us, as he, whose infinite wisdom which dispenses every
thing in exact weight and measure, knows will just serve
to light us on our way in this night of our obscurity; so
that your reverences and worships now find out, nor is it
a moment longer in my power to conceal it from you,
That the fervent wish in your behalf with which I set
out, was no more than the first insinuating How d'ye of
a caressing prefacer, stifling his reader, as a lover sometimes does a coy mistress, into silence. For alas! could
this effusion of light have been as easily procured, as the
exordium wished it—I tremble to think how many thousands for it, of benighted travellers (in the learned
sciences at least) must have groped and blundered on in
the dark, all the nights of their lives—running their
heads against posts, and knocking out their brains without ever getting to their journies' end;—some falling
with their noses perpendicularly into sinks—others horizontally with their tails into kennels. Here one half of a
learned profession tilting full butt against the other half
of it, and then tumbling and rolling one over the other

in the dirt like hogs.—Here the brethren of another profession, who should have run in opposition to each other,
flying on contrary like a flock of wild geese, all in a row
the same way.—What confusion!—what mistakes!—
fiddlers and painters judging by their eyes and ears—
admirable!—trusting to the passions excited—in an air
sung, or a story painted to the heart—instead of measuring them by a quadrant.

In the fore-ground of this picture, a statesman turning the political wheel, like a brute, the wrong way
round—against the stream of corruption—by Heaven!
—instead of with it.

In this corner, a son of the divine Esculapius, writing
a book against predestination; perhaps worse—feeling
his patient's pulse, instead of his apothecary's—a brother
of the faculty in the back-ground upon his knees in tears
—drawing the curtains of a mangled victim to beg his
forgiveness;—offering a fee—instead of taking one.

In that spacious Hall, a coalition of the gown, from
all the bars of it, driving a damned, dirty, vexatious
cause before them, with all their might and main, the
wrong way!—kicking it *out* of the great doors, instead of,
in—and with such fury in their looks, and such a degree
of inveteracy in their manner of kicking it, as if the laws
had been originally made for the peace and preservation
of mankind;——perhaps a more enormous mistake committed by them still—a litigated point fairly hung up;
——for instance, Whether John o'Nokes his nose could
stand in Tom o'Stiles his face, without a trespass, or not
—rashly determined by them in five-and-twenty min-

CHAP. XX

utes, which, with the cautious pros and cons required in so intricate a proceeding, might have taken up as many months—and if carried on upon a military plan, as your honours know an Action should be, with all the stratagems practicable therein,——such as feints,—forced marches,—surprises—ambuscades—mask-batteries, and a thousand other strokes of generalship, which consist in catching at all advantages on both sides——might reasonably have lasted them as many years, finding food and raiment all that term for a centumvirate of the profession.

As for the clergy—No—if I say a word against them, I'll be shot.—I have no desire;—and besides, if I had—I durst not for my soul touch upon the subject—with such weak nerves and spirits, and in the condition I am in at present, 'twould be as much as my life was worth, to deject and contrist myself with so bad and melancholy an account—and therefore 'tis safer to draw a curtain across, and hasten from it, as fast as I can, to the main and principal point I have undertaken to clear up—and that is, How it comes to pass, that your men of least wit are reported to be men of most judgment.—But mark— I say, reported to be—for it is no more, my dear sirs, than a report, and which, like twenty others taken up every day upon trust, I maintain to be a vile and a malicious report into the bargain.

This by the help of the observation already premised, and I hope already weighed and perpended by your reverences and worships, I shall forthwith make appear.

I hate set dissertations—and above all things in the

world, 'tis one of the silliest things in one of them, to
darken your hypothesis by placing a number of tall,
opaque words, one before another, in a right line, betwixt your own and your reader's conception—when in
all likelihood, if you had looked about, you might have
seen something standing, or hanging up, which would
have cleared the point at once—"for what hindrance,
hurt, or harm doth the laudable desire of knowledge
bring to any man, if even from a sot, a pot, a fool, a
stool, a winter-mitten, a truckle for a pully, the lid of a
goldsmith's crucible, an oil bottle, an old slipper, or a
cane chair?"—I am this moment sitting upon one. Will
you give me leave to illustrate this affair of wit and
judgment, by the two knobs on the top of the back of it?
—they are fastened on, you see, with two pegs stuck
slightly into two gimlet-holes, and will place what I have
to say in so clear a light, as to let you see through the
drift and meaning of my whole preface, as plainly as if
every point and particle of it was made up of sun-beams.

I now enter directly upon the point.

—Here stands Wit—and there stands Judgment,
close beside it, just like the two knobs I'm speaking of,
upon the back of this self-same chair on which I am
sitting.

—You see they are the highest and most ornamental
parts of its frame—as wit and judgment are of ours—
and like them too, indubitably both made and fitted to
go together, in order, as we say in all such cases of
duplicated embellishments——to answer one another.

Now for the sake of an experiment, and for the

CHAP. XX

clearer illustrating this matter—let us for a moment take off one of these two curious ornaments (I care not which) from the point or pinnacle of the chair it now stands on—nay, don't laugh at it,—but did you ever see, in the whole course of your lives, such a ridiculous business as this has made of it?—Why, 'tis as miserable a sight as a sow with one ear; and there is just as much sense and symmetry in the one as in the other:—do pray, get off your seats only to take a view of it.—Now would any man who valued his character a straw, have turned a piece of work out of his hand in such a condition?—nay, lay your hands upon your hearts, and answer this plain question, Whether this one single knob, which now stands here like a blockhead by itself, can serve any purpose upon earth, but to put one in mind of the want of the other?—and let me further ask, in case the chair was your own, if you would not in your conscience think, rather than be as it is, that it would be ten times better without any knob at all.

Now these two knobs—or top ornaments of the mind of man, which crown the whole entablature—being, as I said, wit and judgment, which of all others, as I have proved it, are the most needful—the most prized—the most calamitous to be without, and consequently the hardest to come at—for all these reasons put together, there is not a mortal among us, so destitute of a love of good fame or feeding—or so ignorant of what will do him good therein—who does not wish and stedfastly resolve in his own mind, to be, or to be thought at least, master of the one or the other, and indeed of both of

them, if the thing seems anyway feasible, or likely to be
brought to pass.

Now your graver gentry having little or no kind of
chance in aiming at the one—unless they laid hold of the
other,—pray what do you think would become of them?
—Why, Sirs, in spite of all their gravities, they must e'en
have been contented to have gone with their insides
naked—this was not to be borne, but by an effort of
philosophy not to be supposed in the case we are upon—
so that no one could well have been angry with them,
had they been satisfied with what little they could have
snatched up and secreted under their cloaks and great
perriwigs, had they not raised a hue and cry at the same
time against the lawful owners.

I need not tell your worships, that this was done with
so much cunning and artifice—that the great Locke,
who was seldom outwitted by false sounds—was nevertheless bubbled here. The cry, it seems, was so deep and
solemn a one, and what with the help of great wigs,
grave faces, and other implements of deceit, was rendered so general a one against the poor wits in this matter,
that the philosopher himself was deceived by it—it was
his glory to free the world from the lumber of a thousand
vulgar errors;—but this was not of the number; so that
instead of sitting down coolly, as such a philosopher
should have done, to have examined the matter of fact
before he philosophized upon it—on the contrary he
took the fact for granted, and so joined in with the cry,
and hallooed it as boisterously as the rest.

This has been made the *Magna Charta* of stupidity

CHAP. XX

ever since—but your reverences plainly see, it has been obtained in such a manner, that the title to it is not worth a groat:—which by the bye is one of the many and vile impositions which gravity and grave folks have to answer for hereafter.

As for great wigs, upon which I may be thought to have spoken my mind too freely—I beg leave to qualify whatever has been unguardedly said to their dispraise or prejudice, by one general declaration—That I have no abhorrence whatever, nor do I detest and abjure either great wigs or long beards, any farther than when I see they are bespoke and let grow on purpose to carry on this self-same imposture—for any purpose—peace be with them!— mark only—I write not for them.

Chapter XXI

EVERY day for at least ten years together did my father resolve to have it mended—'tis not mended yet;—no family but ours would have borne with it an hour—and what is most astonishing, there was not a subject in the world upon which my father was so eloquent, as upon that of door-hinges.—And yet at the same time, he was certainly one of the greatest bubbles to them, I think, that history can produce: his rhetoric and conduct were at perpetual handy-cuffs.—Never did the parlour-door open—but his philosophy or his principles fell a victim to it;—three drops of oil with a feather, and a smart stroke of a hammer, had saved his honour for ever.

—Inconsistent soul that man is!—languishing under

wounds, which he has the power to heal!—his whole life
a contradiction to his knowledge!—his reason, that precious gift of God to him—(instead of pouring in oil)
serving but to sharpen his sensibilities—to multiply his
pains, and render him more melancholy and uneasy
under them!—Poor unhappy creature, that he should do
so!—Are not the necessary causes of misery in this life
enow, but he must add voluntary ones to his stock of
sorrow;—struggle against evils which cannot be avoided,
and submit to others, which a tenth part of the trouble
they create him would remove from his heart for ever?

By all that is good and virtuous, if there are three
drops of oil to be got, and a hammer to be found within
ten miles of Shandy Hall—the parlour door hinge shall
be mended this reign.

CHAPTER XXII

WHEN Corporal Trim had brought his two mortars
to bear, he was delighted with his handy-work beyond measure; and knowing what a pleasure it would be
to his master to see them, he was not able to resist the
desire he had of carrying them directly into his parlour.

Now next to the moral lesson I had in view in men-
tioning the affair of hinges, I had a speculative consideration arising out of it, and it is this.

Had the parlour door opened and turned upon its
hinges, as a door should do—

Or for example, as cleverly as our government has
been turning upon its hinges—(that is, in case things

CHAP. XXII

have all along gone well with your worship,—otherwise
I give up my simile)—in this case, I say, there had been
no danger either to master or man, in Corporal Trim's
peeping in: the moment he had beheld my father and
my uncle Toby fast asleep—the respectfulness of his
carriage was such, he would have retired as silent as
death, and left them both in their arm-chairs, dreaming
as happy as he had found them: but the thing was,
morally speaking, so very impracticable, that for the
many years in which this hinge was suffered to be out of
order, and amongst the hourly grievances my father
submitted to upon its account—this was one; that he
never folded his arms to take his nap after dinner, but
the thoughts of being unavoidably awakened by the first
person who should open the door, was always upper-
most in his imagination, and so incessantly stepped in
betwixt him and the first balmy presage of his repose, as
to rob him, as he often declared, of the whole sweets of it.

"When things move upon bad hinges, an' please
your lordships, how can it be otherwise?"

Pray what's the matter? Who is there? cried my
father, waking, the moment the door began to creak.—I
wish the smith would give a peep at that confounded
hinge.—'Tis nothing, an' please your honour, said Trim,
but two mortars I am bringing in.—They shan't make a
clatter with them here, cried my father hastily.—If Dr.
Slop has any drugs to pound, let him do it in the kitchen.
—May it please your honour, cried Trim, they are two
mortar-pieces for a siege next summer, which I have
been making out of a pair of jack-boots, which Obadiah

told me your honour had left off wearing.—By Heaven!
cried my father, springing out of his chair, as he swore—
I have not one appointment belonging to me, which I
set so much store by as I do by these jack-boots—they
were our great grandfather's, brother Toby—they were
hereditary. Then I fear, quoth my uncle Toby, Trim has

CHAP. XXII

cut off the entail.—I have only cut off the tops, an'
please your honour, cried Trim—I hate perpetuities as
much as any man alive, cried my father—but these jack-
boots, continued he (smiling, though very angry at the
same time) have been in the family, brother, ever since
the civil wars;—Sir Roger Shandy wore them at the
battle of Marston-Moor.—I declare I would not have
taken ten pounds for them.—I'll pay you the money,
brother Shandy, quoth my uncle Toby, looking at the
two mortars with infinite pleasure, and putting his hand
into his breeches pocket as he viewed them—I'll pay
you the ten pounds this moment with all my heart and
soul.—

Brother Toby, replied my father, altering his tone,
you care not what money you dissipate and throw away,
provided, continued he, 'tis but upon a siege.—Have I
not one hundred and twenty pounds a year, besides my
half pay? cried my uncle Toby.—What is that—replied
my father hastily—to ten pounds for a pair of jack-
boots?—twelve guineas for your pontoons?—half as
much for your Dutch draw-bridge?—to say nothing of
the train of little brass artillery you bespoke last week,
with twenty other preparations for the siege of Messina:
believe me, dear brother Toby, continued my father,
taking him kindly by the hand—these military operations of yours are above your strength;—you mean well,
brother—but they carry you into greater expenses than
you were first aware of;—and take my word, dear Toby,
they will in the end quite ruin your fortune, and make a
beggar of you.—What signifies it if they do, brother,

replied my uncle Toby, so long as we know 'tis for the good of the nation?—

My father could not help smiling for his soul—his anger at the worst was never more than a spark;—and the zeal and simplicity of Trim—and the generous (though hobby-horsical) gallantry of my uncle Toby, brought him into perfect good-humour with them in an instant.

Generous souls!—God prosper you both, and your mortar-pieces too! quoth my father to himself.

CHAPTER XXIII

ALL is quiet and hush, cried my father, at least above stairs—I hear not one foot stirring.—Prithee, Trim, who's in the kitchen? There is no one soul in the kitchen, answered Trim, making a low bow as he spoke, except Dr. Slop.—Confusion! cried my father (getting up upon his legs a second time)—not one single thing has gone right this day! had I faith in astrology, brother, (which, by the bye, my father had) I would have sworn some retrograde planet was hanging over this unfortunate house of mine,—and turning every individual thing in it out of its place.—Why, I thought Dr. Slop had been above stairs with my wife, and so said you.—What can the fellow be puzzling about in the kitchen?—He is busy, an' please your honour, replied Trim, in making a bridge.—'Tis very obliging in him, quoth my uncle Toby:——pray, give my humble service to Dr. Slop, Trim, and tell him I thank him heartily.

You must know, my uncle Toby mistook the bridge
—as widely as my father mistook the mortars;—but to
understand how my uncle Toby could mistake the
bridge—I fear I must give you an exact account of the
road which led to it;—or to drop my metaphor (for there
is nothing more dishonest in an historian than the use of
one)—in order to conceive the probability of this error
in my uncle Toby aright, I must give you some account
of an adventure of Trim's, though much against my
will, I say much against my will, only because the story,
in one sense, is certainly out of its place here; for by
right it should come in, either amongst the anecdotes of
my uncle Toby's amours with widow Wadman, in which
Corporal Trim was no mean actor—or else in the middle
of his and my uncle Toby's campaigns on the bowling-
green—for it will do very well in either place;—but then
if I reserve it for either of those parts of my story—I
ruin the story I'm upon;—and if I tell it here—I antici-
pate matters, and ruin it there.

—What would your worships have me do in this
case?

—Tell it, Mr. Shandy, by all means.—You are a
fool, Tristram, if you do.

O ye Powers! (for powers ye are, and great ones too)
—which enable mortal man to tell a story worth the
hearing——that kindly shew him, where he is to begin
it—and where he is to end it—what he is to put into it
—and what he is to leave out—how much of it he is to
cast into a shade—and whereabouts he is to throw his
light!—Ye, who preside over this vast empire of bio-

graphical freebooters, and see how many scrapes and plunges your subjects hourly fall into;—will you do one thing?

I beg and beseech you (in case you will do nothing better for us) that wherever in any part of your dominions it so falls out, that three several roads meet in one point, as they have done just here—that at least you set up a guide-post in the centre of them, in mere charity, to direct an uncertain devil which of the three he is to take.

Chapter XXIV

Tho' the shock my uncle Toby received the year after the demolition of Dunkirk, in his affair with widow Wadman, had fixed him in a resolution never more to think of the sex—or of aught which belonged to it;—yet Corporal Trim had made no such bargain with himself. Indeed in my uncle Toby's case there was a strange and unaccountable concurrence of circumstances, which insensibly drew him in, to lay siege to that fair and strong citadel.—In Trim's case there was a concurrence of nothing in the world, but of him and Bridget in the kitchen;—though in truth, the love and veneration he bore his master was such, and so fond was he of imitating him in all he did, that had my uncle Toby employed his time and genius in tagging of points—I am persuaded the honest corporal would have laid down his arms, and followed his example with pleasure. When therefore my uncle Toby sat down before the mistress—Corporal Trim incontinently took ground before the maid.

Now, my dear friend Garrick, whom I have so much cause to esteem and honour—(why, or wherefore, 'tis no matter)—can it escape your penetration—I defy it—that so many play-wrights, and opificers of chit-chat have ever since been working upon Trim's and my uncle Toby's pattern.—I care not what Aristotle, or Pacuvius, or Bossu, or Ricaboni say—(though I never read one of them)—there is not a greater difference between a single-horse chair and madam Pompadour's *vis-à-vis*; than betwixt a single amour, and an amour thus nobly doubled, and going upon all four, prancing throughout a grand drama—Sir, a simple, single, silly affair of that kind—is quite lost in five acts;—but that is neither here nor there.

After a series of attacks and repulses in a course of nine months on my uncle Toby's quarter, a most minute account of every particular of which shall be given in its proper place, my uncle Toby, honest man! found it necessary to draw off his forces and raise the siege somewhat indignantly.

Corporal Trim, as I said, had made no such bargain either with himself—or with any one else—the fidelity however of his heart not suffering him to go into a house which his master had forsaken with disgust—he contented himself with turning his part of the siege into a blockade;—that is, he kept others off;—for though he never after went to the house, yet he never met Bridget in the village, but he would either nod or wink, or smile, or look kindly at her—or (as circumstances directed) he would shake her by the hand—or ask her lovingly how she did—or would give her a ribbon—and now-and-then, though never but when it could be done with decorum, would give Bridget a—

Precisely in this situation, did these things stand for five years; that is, from the demolition of Dunkirk in the year 13, to the latter end of my uncle Toby's campaign in the year 18, which was about six or seven weeks before the time I'm speaking of.—When Trim, as his custom was, after he had put my uncle Toby to bed, going down one moonshiny night to see that every thing was right at his fortifications—in the lane separated from the bowling-green with flowering shrubs and holly—he espied his Bridget.

As the Corporal thought there was nothing in the world so well worth shewing as the glorious works which he and my uncle Toby had made, Trim courteously and gallantly took her by the hand, and led her in: this was not done so privately, but that the foul-mouthed trumpet of Fame carried it from ear to ear, till at length it reached my father's, with this untoward circumstance along with it, that my uncle Toby's curious drawbridge, constructed and painted after the Dutch fashion, and which went quite across the ditch—was broke down, and somehow or other crushed all to pieces that very night.

My father, as you have observed, had no great esteem for my uncle Toby's hobby-horse, he thought it the most ridiculous horse that ever gentleman mounted; and indeed unless my uncle Toby vexed him about it, could never think of it once, without smiling at it—so

CHAP. XXIV

that it could never get lame or happen any mischance,
but it tickled my father's imagination beyond measure;
for this being an accident much more to his humour than
any one which had yet befallen it, it proved an inexhaustible fund of entertainment to him.—Well—but, dear
Toby! my father would say, do tell me seriously how
this affair of the bridge happened.—How can you tease
me so much about it? my uncle Toby would reply—I
have told it you twenty times, word for word as Trim
told it me.—Prithee, how was it then, Corporal? my
father would cry, turning to Trim.—It was a mere misfortune, an' please your honour;—I was shewing Mrs.
Bridget our fortifications, and in going too near the edge
of the fossé, I unfortunately slipped in—Very well,
Trim! my father would cry—(smiling mysteriously, and
giving a nod—but without interrupting him)—and being
linked fast, an' please your honour, arm in arm with
Mrs. Bridget, I dragged her after me, by means of which
she fell backwards soss against the bridge—and Trim's
foot (my uncle Toby would cry, taking the story out of
his mouth) getting into the curvette, he tumbled full
against the bridge too.—It was a thousand to one, my
uncle Toby would add, that the poor fellow did not
break his leg.——Ay truly, my father would say—a
limb is soon broke, brother Toby, in such encounters.—
And so, an' please your honour, the bridge, which your
honour knows was a very slight one, was broke down
betwixt us, and splintered all to pieces.

At other times, but especially when my uncle Toby
was so unfortunate as to say a syllable about cannons,

bombs, or petards—my father would exhaust all the
stores of his eloquence (which indeed were very great) in
a panegyric upon the battering-rams of the ancients—
the vinea which Alexander made use of at the siege of
Troy.—He would tell my uncle Toby of the catapultae
of the Syrians, which threw such monstrous stones so
many hundred feet, and shook the strongest bulwarks
from their very foundation:—he would go on and describe the wonderful mechanism of the ballista which
Marcellinus makes so much rout about!—the terrible
effects of the pyroboli, which cast fire;—the danger of
the terebra and scorpio, which cast javelins.——But
what are these, would he say, to the destructive machinery of Corporal Trim?—Believe me, brother Toby, no
bridge, or bastion, or sally-port, that ever was con-

CHAP. XXIV

structed in this world, can hold out against such artillery.

My uncle Toby would never attempt any defence against the force of this ridicule, but that of redoubling the vehemence of smoking his pipe; in doing which, he raised so dense a vapour one night after supper, that it set my father, who was a little phthisical, into a suffocating fit of violent coughing: my uncle Toby leaped up without feeling the pain upon his groin—and, with infinite pity, stood beside his brother's chair, tapping his back with one hand, and holding his head with the other, and from time to time wiping his eyes with a clean cambric handkerchief, which he pulled out of his pocket. —The affectionate and endearing manner in which my uncle Toby did these little offices cut my father thro' his reins, for the pain he had just been giving him.— May my brains be knocked out with a battering-ram or a catapulta, I care not which, quoth my father to himself—if ever I insult this worthy soul more!

Chapter XXV

THE draw-bridge being held irreparable, Trim was ordered directly to set about another——but not upon the same model: for cardinal Alberoni's intrigues at that time being discovered, and my uncle Toby rightly foreseeing that a flame would inevitably break out betwixt Spain and the Empire, and that the operations of the ensuing campaign must in all likelihood be either in Naples or Sicily—he determined upon an Italian bridge —(my uncle Toby, by the bye, was not far out of his

conjectures)—but my father, who was infinitely the
better politician, and took the lead as far of my uncle
Toby in the cabinet, as my uncle Toby took it of him in
the field——convinced him, that if the king of Spain and
the Emperor went together by the ears, England and
France and Holland must, by force of their pre-engage-
ments, all enter the lists too;—and if so, he would say,
the combatants, brother Toby, as sure as we are alive,
will fall to it again, pell-mell, upon the old prize-fighting
stage of Flanders;—then what will you do with your
Italian bridge?

—We will go on with it then upon the old model,
cried my uncle Toby.

When Corporal Trim had about half finished it in
that style—my uncle Toby found out a capital defect in
it, which he had never thoroughly considered before. It
turned, it seems, upon hinges at both ends of it, opening
in the middle, one half of which turning to one side of
the fossé, and the other to the other; the advantage of
which was this, that by dividing the weight of the bridge
into two equal portions, it empowered my uncle Toby to
raise it up or let it down with the end of his crutch, and
with one hand, which, as his garrison was weak, was as
much as he could well spare—but the disadvantages of
such a construction were insurmountable;—for by this
means, he would say, I leave one half of my bridge in my
enemy's possession—and pray of what use is the other?

The natural remedy for this was, no doubt, to have
his bridge fast only at one end with hinges, so that the
whole might be lifted up together, and stand bolt up-

CHAP. XXV

right——but that was rejected for the reason given above.

For a whole week after he was determined in his mind to have one of that particular construction which is made to draw back horizontally, to hinder a passage; and to thrust forwards again to gain a passage—of which sorts your worship might have seen three famous ones at Spires before its destruction—and one now at Brisac, if I mistake not;—but my father advising my uncle Toby, with great earnestness, to have nothing more to do with thrusting bridges—and my uncle foreseeing moreover that it would but perpetuate the memory of the Corporal's misfortune—he changed his mind for that of the marquis d'Hôpital's invention, which the younger Bernouilli has so well and learnedly described, as your worships may see——*Act. Erud. Lips.* an. 1695—to these a lead weight is an eternal balance, and keeps watch as well as a couple of sentinels, inasmuch as the construction of them was a curve line approximating to a cycloid ——if not a cycloid itself.

My uncle Toby understood the nature of a parabola as well as any man in England—but was not quite such a master of the cycloid;—he talked however about it every day—the bridge went not forwards.—We'll ask somebody about it, cried my uncle Toby to Trim.

Chapter XXVI

WHEN Trim came in and told my father, that Dr. Slop was in the kitchen, and busy in making a bridge— my uncle Toby—the affair of the jack-boots having just then raised a train of military ideas in his brain—took it instantly for granted that Dr. Slop was making a model of the marquis d'Hôpital's bridge.—'Tis very obliging in him, quoth my uncle Toby;—pray give my humble service to Dr. Slop, Trim, and tell him I thank him heartily.

Had my uncle Toby's head been a Savoyard's box, and my father peeping in all the time at one end of it— it could not have given him a more distinct conception of the operations of my uncle Toby's imagination, than what he had; so, notwithstanding the catapulta and battering-ram, and his bitter imprecation about them, he was just beginning to triumph—

When Trim's answer, in an instant, tore the laurel from his brows, and twisted it to pieces.

Chapter XXVII

—THIS unfortunate draw-bridge of yours, quoth my father—God bless your honour, cried Trim, 'tis a bridge for master's nose.—In bringing him into the world with his vile instruments, he has crushed his nose, Susannah says, as flat as a pancake to his face, and he is making a false bridge with a piece of cotton and a thin piece of whalebone out of Susannah's stays, to raise it up.

—Lead me, brother Toby, cried my father, to my room this instant.

CHAP. XXVII

Chapter XXVIII

FROM the first moment I sat down to write my life for the amusement of the world, and my opinions for its instruction, has a cloud insensibly been gathering over my father.—A tide of little evils and distresses has been setting in against him.—Not one thing, as he observed himself, has gone right: and now is the storm thickened and going to break, and pour down full upon his head.

I enter upon this part of my story in the most pensive and melancholy frame of mind that ever sympathetic breast was touched with.—My nerves relax as I tell it.—Every line I write, I feel an abatement of the quickness of my pulse, and of that careless alacrity with it, which every day of my life prompts me to say and write a thousand things I should not—And this moment that I last dipped my pen into my ink, I could not help taking notice what a cautious air of sad composure and solemnity there appeared in my manner of doing it.—Lord! how different from the rash jerks and hair-brained squirts thou art wont, Tristram, to transact it with in other humours—dropping thy pen—spurting thy ink about thy table and thy books—as if thy pen and thy ink, thy books and furniture cost thee nothing.

Chapter XXIX

I WON'T go about to argue the point with you—'tis so— and I am persuaded of it, madam, as much as can be, "That both man and woman bear pain or sorrow (and,

for aught I know, pleasure too) best in a horizontal
position."

The moment my father got up into his chamber, he
threw himself prostrate across his bed in the wildest disorder imaginable, but at the same time in the most
lamentable attitude of a man borne down with sorrows,
that ever the eye of pity dropped a tear for.—The palm
of his right hand, as he fell upon the bed, receiving his
forehead, and covering the greatest part of both his eyes,

CHAP. XXIX

gently sunk down with his head (his elbow giving way backwards) till his nose touched the quilt;—his left arm hung insensible over the side of the bed, his knuckles reclining upon the handle of the chamber-pot, which peeped out beyond the valance—his right leg (his left being drawn up towards his body) hung half over the side of the bed, the edge of it pressing upon his shinbone—He felt it not. A fixed, inflexible sorrow took possession of every line of his face.—He sighed once—heaved his breast often—but uttered not a word.

An old set-stitched chair, valanced and fringed around with party-coloured worsted bobs, stood at the bed's head, opposite to the side where my father's head reclined.—My uncle Toby sat him down in it.

Before an affliction is digested—consolation ever comes too soon;—and after it is digested—it comes too late: so that you see, madam, there is but a mark between these two, as fine almost as a hair, for a comforter to take aim at: my uncle Toby was always either on this side, or on that of it, and would often say, he believed in his heart he could as soon hit the longitude; for this reason, when he sat down in the chair, he drew the curtain a little forwards, and having a tear at every one's service—he pulled out a cambric handkerchief—gave a low sigh—but held his peace.

Chapter XXX

—"ALL is not gain that is got into the purse."—So that notwithstanding my father had the happiness of reading the oldest books in the universe, and had moreover, in himself, the oddest way of thinking that ever man in it was blessed with, yet it had this drawback upon him after all——that it laid him open to some of the oddest and most whimsical distresses; of which this particular one, which he sunk under at present, is as strong an example as can be given.

No doubt, the breaking down of the bridge of a child's nose, by the edge of a pair of forceps—however scientifically applied—would vex any man in the world, who was at so much pains in begetting a child, as my father was—yet it will not account for the extravagance of his affliction, nor will it justify the unchristian manner he abandoned and surrendered himself up to.

To explain this, I must leave him upon the bed for half an hour—and my uncle Toby in his old fringed chair sitting beside him.

Chapter XXXI

—I THINK it a very unreasonable demand—cried my great-grandfather, twisting up the paper, and throwing it upon the table.—By this account, madam, you have but two thousand pounds fortune, and not a shilling more—and you insist upon having three hundred pounds a year jointure for it.——

CHAP. XXXI

—"Because," replied my great-grandmother, "you have little or no nose, Sir."—

Now before I venture to make use of the word Nose a second time—to avoid all confusion in what will be said upon it, in this interesting part of my story, it may not be amiss to explain my own meaning, and define, with all possible exactness and precision, what I would willingly be understood to mean by the term: being of opinion, that 'tis owing to the negligence and perverseness of writers in despising this precaution, and to nothing else—that all the polemical writings in divinity are not as clear and demonstrative as those upon a Will o' the Wisp, or any other sound part of philosophy, and natural pursuit; in order to which, what have you to do, before you set out, unless you intend to go puzzling on to the day of judgment—but to give the world a good definition, and stand to it, of the main word you have most occasion for—changing it, Sir, as you would a guinea, into small coin?—which done—let the father of confusion puzzle you, if he can; or put a different idea either into your head, or your reader's head, if he knows how.

In books of strict morality and close reasoning, such as this I am engaged in—the neglect is inexcusable; and Heaven is witness, how the world has revenged itself upon me for leaving so many openings to equivocal strictures—and for depending so much as I have done, all along, upon the cleanliness of my readers' imaginations.

—Here are two senses, cried Eugenius, as we walked along, pointing with the fore finger of his right hand to

the word Crevice, in the one hundred and seventy-eighth
page of the first volume of this book of books;——here
are two senses—quoth he—And here are two roads, replied I, turning short upon him—a dirty and a clean one
—which shall we take?—The clean, by all means, replied Eugenius. Eugenius, said I, stepping before him,
and laying my hand upon his breast—to define—is to
distrust.—Thus I triumphed over Eugenius; but I triumphed over him as I always do, like a fool.—'Tis my
comfort, however, I am not an obstinate one: therefore

I define a nose as follows—intreating only before-
hand, and beseeching my readers, both male and female,
of what age, complexion, and condition soever, for the
love of God and their own souls, to guard against the
temptations and suggestions of the devil, and suffer him
by no art or wile to put any other ideas into their minds,
than what I put into my definition—For by the word
Nose, throughout all this long chapter of noses, and in
every other part of my work, where the word Nose
occurs—I declare, by that word I mean a nose, and
nothing more, or less.

Chapter XXXII

—"Because," quoth my great-grandmother, repeating the words again—"you have little or no
nose, Sir."——

'Sdeath! cried my great-grandfather, clapping his
hand upon his nose,—'tis not so small as that comes to;
—'tis a full inch longer than my father's.—Now, my

great-grandfather's nose was for all the world like unto the noses of all the men, women, and children, whom Pantagruel found dwelling upon the island of Ennasin.
——By the way, if you would know the strange way of getting a-kin amongst so flat-nosed a people—you must read the book;—find it out yourself, you never can.—
—'Twas shaped, Sir, like an ace of clubs.
—'Tis a full inch, continued my grandfather, pressing up the ridge of his nose with his finger and thumb; and repeating his assertion—'tis a full inch longer, madam, than my father's—You must mean your uncle's, replied my great-grandmother.
——My great-grandfather was convinced.—He untwisted the paper, and signed the article.

Chapter XXXIII

—WHAT an unconscionable jointure, my dear, do we pay out of this small estate of ours, quoth my grandmother to my grandfather.

My father, replied my grandfather, had no more nose, my dear, saving the mark, than there is upon the back of my hand.

—Now, you must know, that my great-grandmother outlived my grandfather twelve years; so that my father had the jointure to pay, a hundred and fifty pounds half-yearly—(on Michaelmas and Lady-day,)—during all that time.

No man discharged pecuniary obligations with a better grace than my father.——And as far as a hundred pounds went, he would fling it upon the table, guinea by guinea, with that spirited jerk of an honest welcome, which generous souls, and generous souls only, are able to fling down money: but as soon as ever he entered upon the odd fifty—he generally gave a loud Hem! rubbed the side of his nose leisurely with the flat part of his fore finger—inserted his hand cautiously betwixt his head and the caul of his wig—looked at both sides of every guinea as he parted with it—and seldom could get to the end of the fifty pounds, without pulling out his handkerchief, and wiping his temples.

Defend me, gracious Heaven! from those persecuting spirits who make no allowances for these workings within us.—Never—O never may I lay down in their tents, who cannot relax the engine, and feel pity for the force of education, and the prevalence of opinions long derived from ancestors!

For three generations at least this tenet in favour of long noses had gradually been taking root in our family. ——Tradition was all along on its side, and Interest was every half-year stepping in to strengthen it; so that the whimsicality of my father's brain was far from having the whole honour of this, as it had of almost all his other strange notions.—For in a great measure he might be said to have sucked this in with his mother's milk. He did his part however.—If education planted the mistake (in case it was one) my father watered it, and ripened it to perfection.

He would often declare, in speaking his thoughts upon the subject, that he did not conceive how the

CHAP. XXXIII

greatest family in England could stand it out against an uninterrupted succession of six or seven short noses.——And for the contrary reason, he would generally add, That it must be one of the greatest problems in civil life, where the same number of long and jolly noses, following one another in a direct line, did not raise and hoist it up into the best vacancies in the kingdom.——He would often boast that the Shandy family ranked very high in King Harry the VIIIth's time, but owed its rise to no state engine—he would say—but to that only;—but that, like other families, he would add—it had felt the turn of the wheel, and had never recovered the blow of my great-grandfather's nose.——It was an ace of clubs indeed, he would cry, shaking his head—and as vile a one for an unfortunate family as ever turned up trumps.

——Fair and softly, gentle reader!——where is thy fancy carrying thee?—If there is truth in man, by my great-grandfather's nose, I mean the external organ of smelling, or that part of man which stands prominent in his face—and which painters say, in good jolly noses and well-proportioned faces, should comprehend a full third —that is, measured downwards from the setting on of the hair.——

—What a life of it has an author, at this pass!

Chapter XXXIV

IT is a singular blessing, that nature has formed the mind of man with the same happy backwardness and renitency against conviction, which is observed in old dogs—"of not learning new tricks."

What a shuttlecock of a fellow would the greatest philosopher that ever existed be whisked into at once, did he read such books, and observe such facts, and think such thoughts, as would eternally be making him change sides!

Now, my father, as I told you last year, detested all this—He picked up an opinion, Sir, as a man in a state of nature picks up an apple.—It becomes his own—and if he is a man of spirit, he would lose his life rather than give it up.

I am aware that Didius, the great civilian, will contest this point; and cry out against me, Whence comes this man's right to this apple? *ex confesso*, he will say— things were in a state of nature—The apple, as much Frank's apple as John's. Pray, Mr. Shandy, what patent has he to shew for it? and how did it begin to be his? was it, when he set his heart upon it? or when he gathered it? or when he chewed it? or when he roasted it? or when he peeled, or when he brought it home? or when he digested?—or when he—?—for 'tis plain, Sir, if the first picking up of the apple, made it not his—that no subsequent act could.

Brother Didius, Tribonius will answer—(now Tribonius the civilian and church lawyer's beard being three inches and a half and three eighths longer than Didius his beard—I'm glad he takes up the cudgels for me, so I give myself no farther trouble about the answer).— Brother Didius, Tribonius will say, it is a decreed case, as you may find it in the fragments of Gregorius and Hermogenes's codes, and in all the codes from Justinian's down to the codes of Louis and Des Eaux—That the sweat of a man's brows, and the exsudations of a man's brains, are as much a man's own property as the breeches upon his backside;—which said exsudations, etc., being dropped upon the said apple by the labour of finding it, and picking it up; and being moreover indissolubly wasted, and as indissolubly annexed, by the picker up, to the thing picked up, carried home, roasted, peeled, eaten, digested, and so on;—'tis evident that the gatherer of the apple, in so doing, has mixed up something which was his own, with the apple which was not his own, by which means he has acquired a property;—or, in other words, the apple is John's apple.

By the same learned chain of reasoning my father stood up for all his opinions; he had spared no pains in picking them up, and the more they lay out of the common way, the better still was his title.—No mortal claimed them; they had cost him moreover as much labour in cooking and digesting as in the case above, so that they might well and truly be said to be of his own goods and chattels.—Accordingly he held fast by 'em, both by teeth and claws—would fly to whatever he could lay his hands on—and, in a word, would intrench and fortify them round with as many circumvallations and breast-works, as my uncle Toby would a citadel.

There was one plaguy rub in the way of this—the scarcity of materials to make any thing of a defence with, in case of a smart attack; inasmuch as few men of great genius had exercised their parts in writing books upon the subject of great noses: by the trotting of my lean horse, the thing is incredible! and I am quite lost in my understanding, when I am considering what a treasure of precious time and talents together has been wasted upon worse subjects—and how many millions of books in all languages, and in all possible types and bindings, have been fabricated upon points not half so much tending to the unity and peace-making of the world. What was to be had, however, he set the greater store by; and though my father would oft-times sport with my uncle Toby's library—which, by the bye, was ridiculous enough—yet at the very same time he did it, he collected every book and treatise which had been systematically wrote upon noses, with as much care as my honest uncle Toby had done those upon military architecture.—'Tis true, a much less table would have held them—but that was not thy transgression, my dear uncle.—

Here—but why here—rather than in any other part of my story—I am not able to tell:——but here it is—— my heart stops me to pay to thee, my dear uncle Toby, once for all, the tribute I owe thy goodness.—Here let me thrust my chair aside, and kneel down upon the ground, whilst I am pouring forth the warmest sentiment of love for thee, and veneration for the excellency

CHAP. XXXIV

of thy character, that ever virtue and nature kindled in a nephew's bosom.—Peace and comfort rest for evermore upon thy head!—Thou enviedst no man's comforts—insultedst no man's opinions—Thou blackenedst no man's character—devouredst no man's bread: gently, with faithful Trim behind thee, didst thou amble round the little circle of thy pleasures, jostling no creature in thy way:—for each one's sorrows, thou hadst a tear,—for each man's need, thou hadst a shilling.

Whilst I am worth one, to pay a weeder—thy path from thy door to thy bowling-green shall never be grown up.—Whilst there is a rood and a half of land in the Shandy family, thy fortifications, my dear uncle Toby, shall never be demolished.

Chapter XXXV

My father's collection was not great, but to make amends, it was curious; and consequently he was some time in making it; he had the great good fortune however, to set off well, in getting Bruscambille's prologue upon long noses, almost for nothing—for he gave no more for Bruscambille than three half-crowns; owing indeed to the strong fancy which the stall-man saw my father had for the book the moment he laid his hands upon it.—There are not three Bruscambilles in Christendom—said the stall-man, except what are chained up in the libraries of the curious. My father flung down the money as quick as lightning—took Bruscambille into his bosom—hied home from Piccadilly to Coleman Street with it, as he would have hied home with a treasure, without taking his hand once off from Bruscambille all the way.

To those who do not yet know of which gender Bruscambille is——inasmuch as a prologue upon long noses might easily be done by either——'twill be no objection against the simile—to say, That when my father got home, he solaced himself with Bruscambille after the manner in which, 'tis ten to one, your worship solaced yourself with your first mistress——that is, from morning even unto night: which, by the bye, how delightful soever it may prove to the inamorato—is of little or no entertainment at all to by-standers.—Take notice, I go no farther with the simile—my father's eye was greater than his appetite—his zeal greater than his knowledge—he cooled—his affections became divided—he got hold of Prignitz—purchased Scroderus, Andrea Paraeus, Bouchet's Evening Conferences, and above all, the great

CHAP. XXXV

and learned Hafen Slawkenbergius; of which, as I shall
have much to say by and bye—I will say nothing now.

Chapter XXXVI

Of all the tracts my father was at the pains to procure
and study in support of his hypothesis, there was
not any one wherein he felt a more cruel disappointment at
first, than in the celebrated dialogue between Pamphagus
and Cocles, written by the chaste pen of the great and
venerable Erasmus, upon the various uses and seasonable applications of long noses.——Now don't let Satan,
my dear girl, in this chapter, take advantage of any one
spot of rising ground to get astride of your imagination,
if you can any ways help it; or if he is so nimble as to
slip on—let me beg of you, like an unbacked filly, to
frisk it, to squirt it, to jump it, to rear it, to bound it—and
to kick it, with long kicks and short kicks, till, like Tickletoby's mare, you break a strap or a crupper, and throw
his worship into the dirt.—You need not kill him.—

—And pray who was Tickletoby's mare?—'tis just
as discreditable and unscholarlike a question, Sir, as to
have asked what year (*ab urb. con.*) the second Punic
war broke out.—Who was Tickletoby's mare?—Read,
read, read, read, my unlearned reader! read—or by the
knowledge of the great saint Paraleipomenon—I tell you
before-hand, you had better throw down the book at
once; for without much reading, by which your reverence knows I mean much knowledge, you will no more
be able to penetrate the moral of the next marbled page

CHAP. XXXVI

(motley emblem of my work!) than the world with all its sagacity has been able to unravel the many opinions, transactions, and truths which still lie mystically hid under the dark veil of the black one.

Chapter XXXVII

"*Nihil me paenitet hujus nasi,*" quoth Pamphagus;—that is—"My nose has been the making of me."—"*Nec est cur paeniteat,*" replies Cocles; that is, "How the deuce should such a nose fail?"

The doctrine, you see, was laid down by Erasmus, as my father wished it, with the utmost plainness; but my father's disappointment was, in finding nothing more from so able a pen, but the bare fact itself; without any of that speculative subtlety or ambidexterity of argumentation upon it, which Heaven had bestowed upon man on purpose to investigate truth, and fight for her on all sides.—My father pished and pughed at first most terribly——'tis worth something to have a good name. As the dialogue was of Erasmus, my father soon came to himself, and read it over and over again with great application, studying every word and every syllable of it thro' and thro' in its most strict and literal interpretation—he could still make nothing of it, that way. Mayhap there is more meant, than is said in it, quoth my father.—Learned men, brother Toby, don't write dialogues upon long noses for nothing.——I'll study the mystic and the allegoric sense—here is some room to turn a man's self in, brother.

My father read on.——

Now I find it needful to inform your reverences and worships, that besides the many nautical uses of long noses enumerated by Erasmus, the dialogist affirmeth that a long nose is not without its domestic conveniences also; for that in a case of distress—and for want of a pair of bellows, it will do excellently well, *ad excitandum focum* (to stir up the fire).

Nature had been prodigal in her gifts to my father beyond measure, and had sown the seeds of verbal criticism as deep within him as she had done the seeds of all other knowledge——so that he got out his pen-knife, and was trying experiments upon the sentence, to see if he could not scratch some better sense into it.—I've got within a single letter, brother Toby, cried my father, of Erasmus his mystic meaning.—You are near enough, brother, replied my uncle, in all conscience.——Pshaw! cried my father, scratching on—I might as well be seven miles off.—I've done it—said my father, snapping his fingers—See, my dear brother Toby, how I have mended the sense.—But you have marred a word, replied my uncle Toby.—My father put on his spectacles—bit his lip—and tore out the leaf in a passion.

CHAPTER XXXVIII

O SLAWKENBERGIUS! thou faithful analyzer of my Disgrazias—thou sad foreteller of so many of the whips and short turns which in one stage or other of my life have come slap upon me from the shortness of my nose, and no other cause that I am conscious of.—Tell me, Slawkenbergius! what secret impulse was it? what intonation of voice? whence came it? how did it sound in thy ears?—art thou sure thou heard'st it?—which first cried out to thee——go——go, Slawkenbergius! dedicate the labours of thy life—neglect thy pastimes—— call forth all the powers and faculties of thy nature— macerate thyself in the service of mankind, and write a grand Folio for them, upon the subject of their noses.

How the communication was conveyed into Slawkenbergius's sensorium—so that Slawkenbergius should know whose finger touched the key—and whose hand it was that blew the bellows—as Hafen Slawkenbergius has been dead and laid in his grave above fourscore and ten years——we can only raise conjectures.

Slawkenbergius was played upon, for aught I know, like one of Whitefield's disciples—that is, with such a distinct intelligence, Sir, of which of the two masters it was that had been practising upon his instrument——as to make all reasoning upon it needless.

——For in the account which Hafen Slawkenbergius gives the world of his motives and occasions for writing, and spending so many years of his life upon this one work—towards the end of his prolegomena, which by the bye should have come first—but the bookbinder has most injudiciously placed it betwixt the analytical contents of the book, and the book itself—he informs his reader, that ever since he had arrived at the age of discernment, and was able to sit down coolly, and consider within himself the true state and condition of man, and

distinguish the main end and design of his being;—or—
to shorten my translation, for Slawkenbergius's book is
in Latin, and not a little prolix in this passage—ever
since I understood, quoth Slawkenbergius, any thing—
or rather what was what—and could perceive that the
point of long noses had been too loosely handled by all
who had gone before;—have I, Slawkenbergius, felt a
strong impulse, with a mighty and unresistible call within me, to gird up myself to this undertaking.

And to do justice to Slawkenbergius, he has entered
the list with a stronger lance, and taken a much larger
career in it than any one man who had ever entered it
before him—and indeed, in many respects, deserves to
be en-niched as a prototype for all writers, of voluminous
works at least, to model their books by—for he has taken
in, Sir, the whole subject—examined every part of it
dialectically——then brought it into full day; dilucidat-
ing it with all the light which either the collision of his
own natural parts could strike—or the profoundest
knowledge of the sciences had impowered him to cast
upon it—collating, collecting, and compiling——begging, borrowing, and stealing, as he went along, all that
had been wrote or wrangled thereupon in the schools and
porticos of the learned: so that Slawkenbergius his book
may properly be considered, not only as a model—but
as a thorough-stitched digest and regular institute of
noses, comprehending in it all that is or can be needful to
be known about them.

For this cause it is that I forbear to speak of so many
(otherwise) valuable books and treatises of my father's

CHAP. XXXVIII

collecting, wrote either, plump upon noses—or collaterally touching them;——such for instance as Prignitz, now lying upon the table before me, who with infinite learning, and from the most candid and scholar-like examination of above four thousand different skulls, in upwards of twenty charnel-houses in Silesia, which he had rummaged——has informed us, that the mensuration and configuration of the osseous or bony parts of human noses, in any given tract of country, except Crim Tartary, where they are all crushed down by the thumb, so that no judgment can be formed upon them—are much nearer alike, than the world imagines;—the difference amongst them being, he says, a mere trifle, not worth taking notice of;—but that the size and jollity of every individual nose, and by which one nose ranks above another, and bears a higher price, is owing to the cartilaginous and muscular parts of it, into whose ducts and sinuses the blood and animal spirits being impelled and driven by the warmth and force of the imagination, which is but a step from it (bating the case of idiots whom Prignitz, who had lived many years in Turky, supposes under the more immediate tutelage of Heaven) —it so happens, and ever must, says Prignitz, that the excellency of the nose is in a direct arithmetical proportion to the excellency of the wearer's fancy.

It is for the same reason, that is, because 'tis all comprehended in Slawkenbergius, that I say nothing likewise of Scroderus (Andrea) who, all the world knows, set himself to oppugn Prignitz with great violence—proving it in his own way, first logically, and then by a series of

stubborn facts, "That so far was Prignitz from the truth,
in affirming that the fancy begat the nose, that on the
contrary—the nose begat the fancy."

—The learned suspected Scroderus of an indecent
sophism in this—and Prignitz cried out aloud in the dispute, that Scroderus had shifted the idea upon him—
but Scroderus went on, maintaining his thesis.

My father was just balancing within himself, which
of the two sides he should take in this affair; when Ambrose Paraeus decided it in a moment, and by overthrow-
ing the systems, both of Prignitz and Scroderus, drove
my father out of both sides of the controversy at once.

Be witness——

I don't acquaint the learned reader—in saying it, I
mention it only to shew the learned, I know the fact
myself——

That this Ambrose Paraeus was chief surgeon and
nose-mender to Francis the Ninth of France, and in high
credit with him and the two preceding, or succeeding
kings (I know not which)—and that, except in the slip
he made in his story of Taliacotius's noses, and his
manner of setting them on—he was esteemed by the
whole college of physicians at that time, as more knowing in matters of noses, than any one who had ever taken
them in hand.

Now Ambrose Paraeus convinced my father, that
the true and efficient cause of what had engaged so much
the attention of the world, and upon which Prignitz and
Scroderus had wasted so much learning and fine parts—
was neither this nor that—but that the length and good-

CHAP. XXXVIII

ness of the nose was owing simply to the softness and flaccidity in the nurse's breast——as the flatness and shortness of puisne noses was to the firmness and elastic repulsion of the same organ of nutrition in the hale and lively—which, tho' happy for the woman, was the undoing of the child, inasmuch as his nose was so snubbed, so rebuffed, so rebated, and so refrigerated thereby, as never to arrive *ad mensuram suam legitimam;*—but that in case of the flaccidity and softness of the nurse or mother's breast—by sinking into it, quoth Paraeus, as into so much butter, the nose was comforted, nourished, plumped up, refreshed, refocillated, and set a-growing for ever.

I have but two things to observe of Paraeus; first, That he proves and explains all this with the utmost chastity and decorum of expression:—for which may his soul for ever rest in peace!

And, secondly, that besides the systems of Prignitz and Scroderus, which Ambrose Paraeus his hypothesis effectually overthrew—it overthrew at the same time the system of peace and harmony of our family; and for three days together, not only embroiled matters between my father and my mother, but turned likewise the whole house and every thing in it, except my uncle Toby, quite upside down.

Such a ridiculous tale of a dispute between a man and his wife, never surely in any age or country got vent through the key-hole of a street-door.

My mother, you must know——but I have fifty things more necessary to let you know first—I have a

hundred difficulties which I have promised to clear up,
and a thousand distresses and domestic misadventures
crowding in upon me thick and threefold, one upon the
neck of another. A cow broke in (to-morrow morning) to
my uncle Toby's fortifications, and eat up two rations
and a half of dried grass, tearing up the sods with it,
which faced his horn-work and covered-way.—Trim in-
sists upon being tried by a court-martial—the cow to be
shot—Slop to be crucifixed—myself to be tristramed
and at my very baptism made a martyr of;—poor unhappy devils that we all are!—I want swaddling——but
there is no time to be lost in exclamations——I have
left my father lying across his bed, and my uncle Toby
in his old fringed chair, sitting beside him, and promised
I would go back to them in half an hour; and five-and-
thirty minutes are lapsed already.——Of all the perplexities a mortal author was ever seen in—this certainly
is the greatest, for I have Hafen Slawkenbergius's folio,
Sir, to finish—a dialogue between my father and my
uncle Toby, upon the solution of Prignitz, Scroderus,
Ambrose Paraeus, Ponocrates, and Grangousier to relate—a tale out of Slawkenbergius to translate, and all
this in five minutes less than no time at all;——such a
head!—would to Heaven my enemies only saw the inside
of it!

Chapter XXXIX

THERE was not any one scene more entertaining in our
family—and to do it justice in this point;——and I
here put off my cap and lay it upon the table close beside

my ink-horn, on purpose to make my declaration to the world concerning this one article the more solemn—that I believe in my soul (unless my love and partiality to my understanding blinds me) the hand of the supreme Maker and first Designer of all things never made or put a family together (in that period at least of it which I have sat down to write the story of)—where the characters of it were cast or contrasted with so dramatic a felicity as ours was, for this end; or in which the capacities of affording such exquisite scenes, and the powers of shifting them perpetually from morning to night, were lodged and intrusted with so unlimited a confidence, as in the Shandy Family.

Not any one of these was more diverting, I say, in this whimsical theatre of ours—than what frequently arose out of this self-same chapter of long noses—— especially when my father's imagination was heated with the enquiry, and nothing would serve him but to heat my uncle Toby's too.

My uncle Toby would give my father all possible fair play in this attempt; and with infinite patience would sit smoking his pipe for whole hours together, whilst my father was practising upon his head, and trying every accessible avenue to drive Prignitz and Scroderus's solutions into it.

Whether they were above my uncle Toby's reason— or contrary to it—or that his brain was like damp timber, and no spark could possibly take hold—or that it was so full of saps, mines, blinds, curtins, and such military disqualifications to his seeing clearly into Prignitz and

Scroderus's doctrines—I say not—let schoolmen—scullions, anatomists, and engineers, fight for it among themselves—

'Twas some misfortune, I make no doubt, in this affair, that my father had every word of it to translate for the benefit of my uncle Toby, and render out of Slawkenbergius's Latin, of which, as he was no great master, his translation was not always of the purest—and generally least so where 'twas most wanted.—This naturally opened a door to a second misfortune;—that in the warmer paroxysms of his zeal to open my uncle Toby's eyes—my father's ideas ran on as much faster than the translation, as the translation outmoved my uncle Toby's——neither the one nor the other added much to the perspicuity of my father's lecture.

Chapter XL

THE gift of ratiocination and making syllogisms—I mean in man—for in superior classes of beings, such as angels and spirits—'tis all done, may it please your worships, as they tell me, by Intuition;—and beings inferior, as your worships all know—syllogize by their noses: though there is an island swimming in the sea (though not altogether at its ease) whose inhabitants, if my intelligence deceives me not, are so wonderfully gifted, as to syllogize after the same fashion, and ofttimes to make very well out too:——but that's neither here nor there——

The gift of doing it as it should be, amongst us, or—

CHAP. XL

the great and principal act of ratiocination in man, as
logicians tell us, is the finding out the agreement or dis-
agreement of two ideas one with another, by the inter-
vention of a third (called the *medius terminus*); just as a
man, as Locke well observes, by a yard, finds two men's
ninepin-alleys to be of the same length, which could not
be brought together, to measure their equality, by juxta-
position.

Had the same great reasoner looked on, as my father
illustrated his systems of noses, and observed my uncle
Toby's deportment—what great attention he gave to
every word—and as oft as he took his pipe from his
mouth, with what wonderful seriousness he contem-
plated the length of it—surveying it transversely as he
held it betwixt his finger and his thumb——then fore-
right——then this way, and then that, in all its possible
directions and foreshortenings——he would have concluded my uncle Toby had got hold of the *medius
terminus*, and was syllogizing and measuring with it the
truth of each hypothesis of long noses, in order, as my
father laid them before him. This, by the bye, was more
than my father wanted—his aim in all the pains he was
at in these philosophic lectures—was to enable my uncle
Toby not to discuss—but comprehend—to hold the
grains and scruples of learning—not to weigh them.—
My uncle Toby, as you will read in the next chapter, did
neither the one nor the other.

Chapter XLI

'TIS a pity, cried my father one winter's night, after a three hours' painful translation of Slawkenbergius—'tis a pity, cried my father, putting my mother's thread-paper into the book for a mark, as he spoke—that truth, brother Toby, should shut herself up in such impregnable fastnesses, and be so obstinate as not to surrender herself sometimes upon the closest siege.——

Now it happened then, as indeed it had often done before, that my uncle Toby's fancy, during the time of my father's explanation of Prignitz to him——having nothing to stay it there, had taken a short flight to the bowling-green;——his body might as well have taken a turn there too—so that with all the semblance of a deep school-man intent upon the *medius terminus*——my uncle Toby was in fact as ignorant of the whole lecture, and all its pros and cons, as if my father had been translating Hafen Slawkenbergius from the Latin tongue into the Cherokee. But the word "siege," like a talismanic power, in my father's metaphor, wafting back my uncle Toby's fancy, quick as a note could follow the touch—he opened his ears—and my father observing that he took his pipe out of his mouth, and shuffled his chair nearer the table, as with a desire to profit—my father with great pleasure began his sentence again—changing only the plan, and dropping the metaphor of the siege of it, to keep clear of some dangers my father apprehended from it.

'Tis a pity, said my father, that truth can only be on

one side, brother Toby——considering what ingenuity these learned men have all shewn in their solutions of noses.—Can noses be dissolved? replied my uncle Toby.

——My father thrust back his chair——rose up—put on his hat——took four long strides to the door——jerked it open—thrust his head half way out—shut the door again—took no notice of the bad hinge—returned to the table—plucked my mother's thread-paper out of Slawkenbergius's book——went hastily to his bureau—walked slowly back—twisted my mother's thread-paper about his thumb—unbuttoned his waistcoat—threw my mother's thread-paper into the fire—bit her satin pincushion in two, filled his mouth with bran—confounded it;—but mark!—the oath of confusion was levelled at my uncle Toby's brain—which was e'en confused enough already—the curse came charged only with the bran—the bran, may it please your honours, was no more than powder to the ball.

'Twas well my father's passions lasted not long; for so long as they did last, they led him a busy life on't; and it is one of the most unaccountable problems that ever I met with in my observations of human nature, that nothing should prove my father's mettle so much, or make his passions go off so like gunpowder, as the un-expected strokes his science met with from the quaint simplicity of my uncle Toby's questions.—Had ten dozen of hornets stung him behind in so many different places all at one time—he could not have exerted more mechan-ical functions in fewer seconds——or started half so much, as with one single *quaere* of three words unseasonably popping in full upon him in his hobby-horsical career.

'Twas all one to my uncle Toby——he smoked his pipe on with unvaried composure—his heart never intended offence to his brother—and as his head could seldom find out where the sting of it lay—he always gave my father the credit of cooling by himself.—He was five minutes and thirty-five seconds about it in the present case.

By all that's good! said my father, swearing, as he came to himself, and taking the oath out of Ernulphus's digest of curses—(though to do my father justice it was a fault (as he told Dr. Slop in the affair of Ernulphus) which he as seldom committed as any man upon earth) ——By all that's good and great! brother Toby, said my father, if it was not for the aids of philosophy, which befriend one so much as they do—you would put a man beside all temper.—Why, by the solutions of noses, of which I was telling you, I meant, as you might have known, had you favoured me with one grain of attention, the various accounts which learned men of different kinds of knowledge have given the world of the causes of the short and long noses.—There is no cause but one, replied my uncle Toby—why one man's nose is longer than another's, but because that God pleases to have it so.—That is Grangousier's solution, said my father.— 'Tis he, continued my uncle Toby, looking up, and not regarding my father's interruption, who makes us all, and frames and puts us together in such forms and proportions, and for such ends, as is agreeable to his infinite

CHAP. XLI

wisdom.—'Tis a pious account, cried my father, but not philosophical—there is more religion in it than sound science. 'Twas no inconsistent part of my uncle Toby's character—that he feared God, and reverenced religion. —So the moment my father finished his remark—my uncle Toby fell a-whistling *Lillabullero* with more zeal (though more out of tune) than usual.—

What is become of my wife's thread-paper?

CHAPTER XLII

No matter—as an appendage to seamstressy, the thread-paper might be of some consequence to my mother—of none to my father, as a mark in Slawkenbergius. Slawkenbergius in every page of him was a rich treasure of inexhaustible knowledge to my father—he could not open him amiss; and he would often say in closing the book, that if all the arts and sciences in the world, with the books which treated of them, were lost —should the wisdom and policies of governments, he would say, through disuse, ever happen to be forgot, and all that statesmen had wrote or caused to be written, upon the strong or the weak sides of courts and kingdoms, should they be forgot also—and Slawkenbergius only left—there would be enough in him in all conscience, he would say, to set the world a-going again. A treasure therefore was he indeed! an institute of all that was necessary to be known of noses, and every thing else—at matin, noon, and vespers was Hafen Slawkenbergius his recreation and delight: 'twas for ever in his hands—you would have sworn, Sir, it had been a canon's prayer-book—so worn, so glazed, so contrited and attrited was it with fingers and with thumbs in all its parts, from one end even unto the other.

I am not such a bigot to Slawkenbergius as my father; —there is a fund in him, no doubt: but in my opinion, the best, I don't say the most profitable, but the most amusing part of Hafen Slawkenbergius, is his tales—— and, considering he was a German, many of them told not without fancy:——these take up his second book, containing nearly one half of his folio, and are compre-hended in ten decads, each decad containing ten tales ——Philosophy is not built upon tales; and therefore 'twas certainly wrong in Slawkenbergius to send them into the world by that name!—there are a few of them in his eighth, ninth, and tenth decads, which I own seem rather playful and sportive, than speculative—but in general they are to be looked upon by the learned as a detail of so many independent facts, all of them turning round somehow or other upon the main hinges of his subject, and collected by him with great fidelity, and added to his work as so many illustrations upon the doctrines of noses.

As we have leisure enough upon our hands—if you give me leave, madam, I'll tell you the ninth tale of his tenth decad.

CHAP. XLII

BOOK IV

SLAWKENBERGII
FABELLA [1]

*V*ESPERA *quâdam frigidulâ, posteriori in parte mensis Augusti, peregrinus, mulo fusco colore insidens, manticâ a tergo, paucis indusiis, binis calceis, braccisque sericis coccineis repleta,* Argentoratum *ingressus est.*

Militi eum percontanti, quum portas intraret, dixit, se apud Nasorum promontorium fuisse, Francofurtum *proficisci, et* Argentoratum, *transitu ad fines Sarmatiae mensis intervallo, reversurum.*

Miles peregrini in faciem suspexit—Dî boni, nova forma nasi!

At multum mihi profuit, inquit peregrinus, carpum amento extrahens, e quo pependit acinaces: Loculo manum inseruit, et magnâ cum urbanitate, pilei parte anteriore tactâ manu sinistrâ, ut extendit dextram, militi florinum dedit et processit.

Dolet mihi, ait miles, tympanistam nanum et vulgam alloquens, virum adeo urbanum vaginam perdidisse: iti-

---

[1] As Hafen Slawkenbergius *de Nasis* is extremely scarce, it may not be unacceptable to the learned reader to see the specimen of a few pages of his original; I will make no reflection upon it, but that his story-telling Latin is much more concise than his philosophic—and, I think, has more of Latinity in it.

BOOK IV

SLAWKENBERGIUS's
TALE

IT was one cool refreshing evening, at the close of a
very sultry day, in the latter end of the month of
August, when a stranger, mounted upon a dark mule,
with a small cloak-bag behind him, containing a few
shirts, a pair of shoes, and a crimson-satin pair of
breeches, entered the town of Strasburg.

He told the sentinel, who questioned him as he entered
the gates, that he had been at the Promontory of Noses
—was going on to Frankfort—and should be back again
at Strasburg that day month, in his way to the borders
of Grim Tartary.

The sentinel looked up into the stranger's face—he
never saw such a Nose in his life!

—I have made a very good venture of it, quoth the
stranger—so slipping his wrist out of the loop of a black
ribbon, to which a short scimetar was hung, he put his
hand into his pocket, and with great courtesy touching
the fore part of his cap with his left hand, as he extended
his right—he put a florin into the sentinel's hand, and
passed on.

It grieves me, said the sentinel, speaking to a little
dwarfish bandy-legged drummer, that so courteous a
soul should have lost his scabbard——he cannot travel
without one to his scimetar, and will not be able to get a

nerari haud poterit nudâ acinaci; neque vaginam toto Argentorato *habilem inveniet.*———*Nullam unquam habui, respondit peregrinus respiciens*———*seque comiter inclinans —hoc more gesto, nudam acinacem elevans, mulo lentò progrediente, ut nasum tueri possim.*

Non immerito, benigne peregrine, respondit miles.

Nihili aestimo, ait ille tympanista, e pergamenâ factitius est.

Prout christianus sum, inquit miles, nasus ille, ni sexties major sit, meo esset conformis.

Crepitare audivi ait tympanista.

Mehercule! sanguinem emisit, respondit miles.

Miseret me, inquit tympanista, qui non ambo tetigimus!

Eodem temporis puncto, quo haec res argumentata fuit inter militem et tympanistam, disceptabatur ibidem tubicine et uxore suâ qui tunc accesserunt, et peregrino praetereunte, restiterunt.

Quantus nasus! aeque longus est, ait tubicina, ac tuba.

Et ex eodem metallo, ait tubicen, velut sternutamento audias.

Tantum abest, respondit illa, quod fistulam dulcedine vincit.

Aeneus est, ait tubicen.

Nequaquam, respondit uxor.

Rursum affirmo, ait tubicen, quod aeneus est.

Rem penitus explorabo; prius enim digito tangam, ait uxor, quam dormivero.

BOOK IV

scabbard to fit it in all Strasburg.—I never had one, replied the stranger, looking back to the sentinel, and
putting his hand up to his cap as he spoke—I carry it,
continued he, thus—holding up his naked scimetar, his
mule moving on slowly all the time—on purpose to
defend my nose.

It is well worth it, gentle stranger, replied the sentinel.

—'Tis not worth a single stiver, said the bandy-
legged drummer—'tis a nose of parchment.

As I am a true catholic—except that it is six times as
big—'tis a nose, said the sentinel, like my own.

—I heard it crackle, said the drummer.

By dunder, said the sentinel, I saw it bleed.

What a pity, cried the bandy-legged drummer, we
did not both touch it!

At the very time that this dispute was maintaining
by the sentinel and the drummer—was the same point
debating betwixt a trumpeter and a trumpeter's wife,
who were just then coming up, and had stopped to see
the stranger pass by.

Benedicity!——What a nose! 'tis as long, said the
trumpeter's wife, as a trumpet.

And of the same metal, said the trumpeter, as you
hear by its sneezing.

'Tis as soft as a flute, said she.

—'Tis brass, said the trumpeter.

—'Tis a pudding's end, said his wife.

I tell thee again, said the trumpeter, 'tis a brazen nose.

I'll know the bottom of it, said the trumpeter's wife,
for I will touch it with my finger before I sleep.

Mulus peregrini gradu lento progressus est, ut unumquodque verbum controversiae, non tantum inter militem et tympanistam, verum etiam inter tubicinem et uxorem ejus, audiret.

Nequaquam, ait ille, in muli collum fraena demittens, et manibus ambabus in pectus positis, (mulo lentè progrediente) nequaquam, ait ille respiciens, non necesse est ut res isthaec dilucidata foret. Minime gentium! meus nasus nunquam tangetur, dum spiritus hos reget artus—Ad quid agendum? ait uxor burgomagistri.

Peregrinus illi non respondit. Votum faciebat tunc temporis sancto Nicolao; quo facto, in sinum dextrum inserens, e quâ negligenter pependit acinaces, lento gradu processit per plateam Argentorati latam quae ad diversorium templo ex adversum ducit.

Peregrinus mulo descendens stabulo includi, et manticam inferri jussit: quâ apertâ et coccineis sericis femoralibus extractis cum argenteo laciniato Περιζώμαντὲ, his sese induit, statimque, acinaci in manu, ad forum deambulavit.

The stranger's mule moved on at so slow a rate, that he heard every word of the dispute, not only betwixt the sentinel and the drummer, but betwixt the trumpeter and trumpeter's wife.

No! said he, dropping his reins upon his mule's neck, and laying both his hands upon his breast, the one over the other, in a saint-like position (his mule going on easily all the time)—No! said he, looking up—I am not such a debtor to the world—slandered and disappointed as I have been—as to give it that conviction—no! said he, my nose shall never be touched whilst Heaven gives me strength—To do what? said a burgomaster's wife.

The stranger took no notice of the burgomaster's wife——he was making a vow to Saint Nicolas; which done, having uncrossed his arms with the same solemnity with which he crossed them, he took up the reins of his bridle with his left hand, and putting his right hand into his bosom, with his scimetar hanging loosely to the wrist of it, he rode on, as slowly as one foot of the mule could follow another, through the principal streets of Strasburg, till chance brought him to the great inn in the market-place over-against the church.

The moment the stranger alighted, he ordered his mule to be led into the stable, and his cloak-bag to be brought in; then opening, and taking out of it his crimson-satin breeches, with a silver-fringed—(appendage to them, which I dare not translate)—he put his breeches, with his fringed codpiece on, and forthwith, with his short scimetar in his hand, walked out to the grand parade.

*Quod ubi peregrinus esset ingressus, uxorem tubicinis
obviam euntem aspicit; illico cursum flectit, metuens ne
nasus suus exploraretur, atque ad diversorium regressus
est—exuit se vestibus; braccas coccineas sericas manticae
imposuit mulumque educi jussit.*

*Francofurtum proficiscor, ait ille, et Argentoratum
quatuor abhinc hebdomadis revertar.*
*Bene curasti hoc jumentum? (ait) muli faciem manu
demulcens—me, manticamque meam, plus sexcentis mille
passibus portavit.*

*Longa via est! respondet hospes, nisi plurimum esset
negoti.—Enimvero, ait peregrinus, a Nasorum promontorio redii, et nasum speciosissimum, egregiosissimumque
quem unquam quisquam sortitus est, acquisivi.*

*Dum peregrinus hanc miram rationem de seipso reddit,
hospes et uxor ejus, oculis intentis, peregrini nasum con-
templantur—Per sanctos sanctasque omnes, ait hospitis
uxor, nasis duodecim maximis in toto Argentorato major
est!—estne, ait illa mariti in aurem insusurrans, nonne
est nasus praegrandis?*

Dolus inest, anime mî, ait hospes—nasus est falsus.

Verus est, respondit uxor—
Ex abiete factus est, ait ille, terebinthinum olet——

BOOK IV

The stranger had just taken three turns upon the parade, when he perceived the trumpeter's wife at the opposite side of it—so turning short, in pain lest his nose should be attempted, he instantly went back to his inn—undressed himself, packed up his crimson-satin breeches, etc., in his cloak-bag, and called for his mule.

I am going forwards, said the stranger, for Frankfort —and shall be back at Strasburg this day month.

I hope, continued the stranger, stroking down the face of his mule with his left hand as he was going to mount it, that you have been kind to this faithful slave of mine—it has carried me and my cloak-bag, continued he, tapping the mule's back, above six hundred leagues.

—'Tis a long journey, Sir, replied the master of the inn—unless a man has great business.—Tut! tut! said the stranger, I have been at the Promontory of Noses; and have got me one of the goodliest, thank Heaven, that ever fell to a single man's lot.

Whilst the stranger was giving this odd account of himself, the master of the inn and his wife kept both their eyes fixed full upon the stranger's nose—By Saint Radagunda, said the inn-keeper's wife to herself, there is more of it than in any dozen of the largest noses put together in all Strasburg! is it not, said she, whispering her husband in his ear, is it not a noble nose?

'Tis an imposture, my dear, said the master of the inn—'tis a false nose.

'Tis a true nose, said his wife.

'Tis made of fir-tree, said he, I smell the turpentine.——

Carbunculus inest, ait uxor.
Mortuus est nasus, respondit hospes.
Vivus est, ait illa,—et si ipsa vivam tangam.

Votum feci sancto Nicolao, ait peregrinus, nasum meum intactum fore usque ad—Quodnam tempus? illico respondit illa.

Minimo tangetur, inquit ille (manibus in pectus compositis) usque ad illam horam——Quam horam? ait illa ——Nullam, respondit peregrinus, donec pervenio ad— Quem locum,—obsecro? ait illa——Peregrinus nil respondens mulo conscenso discessit.

BOOK IV

There's a pimple on it, said she.

'Tis a dead nose, replied the inn-keeper.

'Tis a live nose, and if I am alive myself, said the inn-keeper's wife, I will touch it.

I have made a vow to Saint Nicolas this day, said the stranger, that my nose shall not be touched till— Here the stranger, suspending his voice, looked up.—— Till when? said she hastily.

It never shall be touched, said he, clasping his hands and bringing them close to his breast, till that hour— What hour? cried the inn-keeper's wife.—Never!— never! said the stranger, never till I am got—For Heaven's sake, into what place? said she——The stranger rode away without saying a word.

The stranger had not got half a league on his way towards Frankfort before all the city of Strasburg was in an uproar about his nose. The Compline bells were just ringing to call the Strasburgers to their devotions, and shut up the duties of the day in prayer:—no soul in all Strasburg heard 'em—the city was like a swarm of bees ——men, women, and children (the Compline bells tinkling all the time) flying here and there—in at one door, out at another—this way and that way—long ways and cross ways—up one street, down another street —in at this alley, out of that——did you see it? did you see it? did you see it? O! did you see it?——who saw it? who did see it? for mercy's sake, who saw it?

Alack o' day! I was at vespers!—I was washing, I was starching, I was scouring, I was quilting——God help me! I never saw it——I never touched it!——would

I had been a sentinel, a bandy-legged drummer, a trumpeter, a trumpeter's wife, was the general cry and lamentation in every street and corner of Strasburg.

Whilst all this confusion and disorder triumphed throughout the great city of Strasburg, was the courteous stranger going on as gently upon his mule in his way to Frankfort, as if he had no concern at all in the affair——talking all the way he rode in broken sentences sometimes to his mule—sometimes to himself—sometimes to his Julia.

O Julia, my lovely Julia!—nay I cannot stop to let thee bite that thistle—that ever the suspected tongue of a rival should have robbed me of enjoyment when I was upon the point of tasting it.—

—Pugh!—'tis nothing but a thistle—never mind it —thou shalt have a better supper at night.

—Banished from my country—my friends—from thee.—

Poor devil, thou'rt sadly tired with thy journey!— come—get on a little faster—there's nothing in my cloak-bag but two shirts—a crimson-satin pair of breeches, and a fringed——Dear Julia!

—But why to Frankfort?—is it that there is a hand unfelt, which secretly is conducting me through these meanders and unsuspected tracts?

—Stumbling! by Saint Nicolas! every step—why, at this rate we shall be all night in getting in——

—To happiness—or am I to be the sport of fortune and slander—destined to be driven forth unconvicted— unheard—untouched—if so, why did I not stay at Stras-

burg, where justice—but I had sworn! Come, thou shalt drink—to Saint Nicolas—O Julia!——What dost thou prick up thy ears at?—'tis nothing but a man, etc.

The stranger rode on communing in this manner with his mule and Julia—till he arrived at his inn, where, as soon as he arrived, he alighted——saw his mule, as he had promised it, taken good care of—took off his cloak-bag, with his crimson-satin breeches, etc., in it—called for an omelet to his supper, went to his bed about twelve o'clock and in five minutes fell fast asleep.

It was about the same hour when the tumult in Strasburg being abated for that night,—the Strasburgers had all got quietly into their beds—but not like the stranger, for the rest either of their minds or bodies; Queen Mab, like an elf as she was, had taken the stranger's nose, and without reduction of its bulk, had that night been at the pains of slitting and dividing it into as many noses of different cuts and fashions, as there were heads in Strasburg to hold them. The abbess of Quedlinburg, who with the four great dignitaries of her chapter, the prioress, the deaness, the sub-chantress, and senior canoness, had that week come to Strasburg to consult the university upon a case of conscience relating to their placket-holes——was ill all the night.

The courteous stranger's nose had got perched upon the top of the pineal gland of her brain, and made such rousing work in the fancies of the four great dignitaries of her chapter, they could not get a wink of sleep the whole night thro' for it—there was no keeping a limb still amongst them—in short, they got up like so many ghosts.

The penitentiaries of the third order of Saint Francis
—the nuns of mount Calvary—the Praemonstratenses
—the Clunienses[1]—the Carthusians, and all the severer
orders of nuns who lay that night in blankets or hair-
cloth, were still in a worse condition than the abbess of
Quedlinburg—by tumbling and tossing, and tossing and
tumbling from one side of their beds to the other the
whole night long—the several sisterhoods had scratched
and mauled themselves all to death—they got out of
their beds almost flayed alive—every body thought
Saint Antony had visited them for probation with his
fire—they had never once, in short, shut their eyes the
whole night long from vespers to matins.

The nuns of Saint Ursula acted the wisest—they
never attempted to go to bed at all.

The dean of Strasburg, the prebendaries, the capitu-
lars and domiciliars (capitularly assembled in the morning to consider the case of buttered buns) all wished they
had followed the nuns of Saint Ursula's example.——

In the hurry and confusion every thing had been in
the night before, the bakers had all forgot to lay their
leaven—there were no buttered buns to be had for break-
fast in all Strasburg—the whole close of the cathedral
was in one eternal commotion—such a cause of restlessness and disquietude, and such a zealous inquiry into
the cause of that restlessness, had never happened in
Strasburg, since Martin Luther, with his doctrines, had
turned the city upside down.

[1] Hafen Slawkenbergius means the Benedictine nuns of Cluny, founded in
the year 940, by Odo, abbé de Cluny.

If the stranger's nose took this liberty of thrusting himself thus into the dishes[1] of religious orders, etc., what a carnival did his nose make of it, in those of the laity!— 'tis more than my pen, worn to the stump as it is, has power to describe; tho' I acknowledge, (cries Slawkenbergius, with more gaiety of thought than I could have expected from him) that there is many a good simile now subsisting in the world which might give my countrymen some idea of it; but at the close of such a folio as this, wrote for their sakes, and in which I have spent the greatest part of my life—tho' I own to them the simile is in being, yet would it not be unreasonable in them to expect I should have either time or inclination to search for it? Let it suffice to say, that the riot and disorder it occasioned in the Strasburgers' fantasies was so general —such an overpowering mastership had it got of all the faculties of the Strasburgers' minds—so many strange things, with equal confidence on all sides, and with equal eloquence in all places, were spoken and sworn to concerning it, that turned the whole stream of all discourse and wonder towards it—every soul, good and bad —rich and poor—learned and unlearned—doctor and student—mistress and maid—gentle and simple—nun's flesh and woman's flesh, in Strasburg spent their time in hearing tidings about it—every eye in Strasburg languished to see it—every finger—every thumb in Strasburg burned to touch it.

[1] Mr. Shandy's compliments to orators—is very sensible that Slawkenbergius has here changed his metaphor——which he is very guilty of:—that as a translator, Mr. Shandy has all along done what he could to make him stick to it—but that here 'twas impossible.

Now what might add, if any thing may be thought
necessary to add, to so vehement a desire—was this,
that the sentinel, the bandy-legged drummer, the trumpeter, the trumpeter's wife, the burgomaster's widow,
the master of the inn, and the master of the inn's wife,
how widely soever they all differed every one from
another in their testimonies and description of the
stranger's nose—they all agreed together in two points
—namely, that he was gone to Frankfort, and would not
return to Strasburg till that day month; and secondly,
whether his nose was true or false, that the stranger himself was one of the most perfect paragons of beauty—
the finest-made man—the most genteel!—the most generous of his purse—the most courteous in his carriage,
that had ever entered the gates of Strasburg—that as he
rode, with scimetar slung loosely to his wrist, thro' the
streets—and walked with his crimson-satin breeches
across the parade—'twas with so sweet an air of careless
modesty, and so manly withal—as would have put the
heart in jeopardy (had his nose not stood in his way) of
every virgin who had cast her eyes upon him.

I call not upon that heart which is a stranger to the
throbs and yearnings of curiosity, so excited, to justify
the abbess of Quedlinburg, the prioress, the deaness,
and sub-chantress, for sending at noon-day for the
trumpeter's wife: she went through the streets of Strasburg with her husband's trumpet in her hand,—the best
apparatus the straitness of the time would allow her, for
the illustration of her theory—she staid no longer than
three days.

BOOK IV

The sentinel and bandy-legged drummer!—nothing
on this side of old Athens could equal them! they read
their lectures under the city-gates to comers and goers,
with all the pomp of a Chrysippus and a Crantor in their
porticos.

The master of the inn, with his ostler on his left-
hand, read his also in the same style—under the portico
or gateway of his stable-yard—his wife, hers more privately in a back room: all flocked to their lectures; not
promiscuously—but to this or that, as is ever the way,
as faith and credulity marshalled them—in a word, each
Strasburger came crowding for intelligence—and every
Strasburger had the intelligence he wanted.

'Tis worth remarking, for the benefit of all demonstrators in natural philosophy, etc., that as soon as the
trumpeter's wife had finished the abbess of Quedlinburg's private lecture, and had begun to read in public,
which she did upon a stool in the middle of the great
parade,—she incommoded the other demonstrators
mainly, by gaining incontinently the most fashionable
part of the city of Strasburg for her auditory—But when
a demonstrator in philosophy (cries Slawkenbergius) has
a trumpet for an apparatus, pray what rival in science
can pretend to be heard besides him?

Whilst the unlearned, thro' these conduits of intelligence, were all busied in getting down to the bottom of
the well, where Truth keeps her little court——were the
learned in their way as busy in pumping her up thro' the
conduits of dialect induction—they concerned themselves not with facts——they reasoned——

Not one profession had thrown more light upon this subject than the Faculty—had not all their disputes about it run into the affair of Wens and oedematous swellings, they could not keep clear of them for their bloods and souls——the stranger's nose had nothing to do either with wens or oedematous swellings.

It was demonstrated however very satisfactorily, that such a ponderous mass of heterogeneous matter could not be congested and conglomerated to the nose, whilst the infant was *in Utero*, without destroying the statical balance of the foetus, and throwing it plump upon its head nine months before the time.——

—The opponents granted the theory—they denied the consequences.

And if a suitable provision of veins, arteries, etc., said they, was not laid in, for the due nourishment of such a nose, in the very first stamina and rudiments of its formation, before it came into the world (bating the case of Wens) it could not regularly grow and be sustained afterwards.

This was all answered by a dissertation upon nutriment, and the effect which nutriment had in extending the vessels, and in the increase and prolongation of the muscular parts to the greatest growth and expansion imaginable—In the triumph of which theory, they went so far as to affirm, that there was no cause in nature, why a nose might not grow to the size of the man himself.

The respondents satisfied the world this event could never happen to them so long as a man had but one

stomach and one pair of lungs—For the stomach, said
they, being the only organ destined for the reception of
food, and turning it into chyle—and the lungs the only
engine of sanguification—it could possibly work off no
more, than what the appetite brought it: or admitting
the possibility of a man's overloading his stomach,
nature had set bounds however to his lungs—the engine
was of a determined size and strength, and could elab-
orate but a certain quantity in a given time——that is,
it could produce just as much blood as was sufficient for
one single man, and no more; so that, if there was as
much nose as man—they proved a mortification must
necessarily ensue; and forasmuch as there could not be a
support for both, that the nose must either fall off from
the man, or the man inevitably fall off from his nose.

Nature accommodates herself to these emergencies,
cried the opponents—else what do you say to the case of
a whole stomach—a whole pair of lungs, and but half a
man, when both his legs have been unfortunately shot
off.

He dies of a plethora, said they—or must spit blood,
and in a fortnight or three weeks go off in a consumption.——

—It happens otherwise—replied the opponents.—

It ought not, said they.

The more curious and intimate inquirers after Nature
and her doings, though they went hand in hand a good
way together, yet they all divided about the nose at last,
almost as much as the Faculty itself.

They amicably laid it down, that there was a just

and geometrical arrangement and proportion of the several parts of the human frame to its several destinations, offices, and functions, which could not be transgressed but within certain limits—that nature, though she sported—she sported within a certain circle;—and they could not agree about the diameter of it.

The logicians stuck much closer to the point before them than any of the classes of the literati;——they began and ended with the word Nose; and had it not been for a *petitio principii*, which one of the ablest of them ran his head against in the beginning of the combat, the whole controversy had been settled at once.

A nose, argued the logician, cannot bleed without blood—and not only blood—but blood circulating in it to supply the phenomenon with a succession of drops—(a stream being but a quicker succession of drops, that is included, said he).—Now death, continued the logician, being nothing but the stagnation of the blood—

I deny the definition—Death is the separation of the soul from the body, said his antagonist—Then we don't agree about our weapons, said the logician—Then there is an end of the dispute, replied the antagonist.

The civilians were still more concise: what they offered being more in the nature of a decree—than a dispute.

Such a monstrous nose, said they, had it been a true nose, could not possibly have been suffered in civil society—and if false—to impose upon society with such false signs and tokens, was a still greater violation of its rights, and must have had still less mercy shown it.

BOOK IV

The only objection to this was, that if it proved any thing, it proved the stranger's nose was neither true nor false.

This left room for the controversy to go on. It was maintained by the advocates of the ecclesiastic court, that there was nothing to inhibit a decree, since the stranger *ex mero motu* had confessed he had been at the Promontory of Noses, and had got one of the goodliest, etc. etc.——To this it was answered, it was impossible there should be such a place as the Promontory of Noses, and the learned be ignorant where it lay. The commissary of the bishop of Strasburg undertook the advocates, explained this matter in a treatise upon proverbial phrases, showing them, that the Promontory of Noses was a mere allegoric expression, importing no more than that nature had given him a long nose: in proof of which, with great learning, he cited the underwritten authorities,[1] which had decided the point incontestably, had it not appeared that a dispute about some franchises of dean and chapter-lands had been determined by it nineteen years before.

[1] Nonnulli ex nostratibus eadem loquendi formulâ utun. Quinimo & Logistae & Canonistae—Vid. Parce Barne Jas in d. L. Provincial. Constitut. de conjec. vid. Vol. Lib. 4. Titul. 1. n. 7. quâ etiam in re conspir. Om de Promontorio Nas. Tichmak. ff. d. tit. 3. fol. 189. passim. Vid. Glos. de contrahend. empt. &c. necnon J. Scrudr. in cap. § refut. per totum. Cum his cons. Rever. J. Tubal, Sentent. & Prov. cap. 9. ff. 11, 12. obiter. V. & Librum, cui Tit. de Terris & Phras. Belg. ad finem, cum comment. N. Bardy Belg. Vid. Scrip. Argentotarens. de Antiq. Ecc. in Episc. Archiv. fid. coll. per Von Jacobum Koinshoven Folio Argent. 1583. praecip. ad finem. Quibus add. Rebuff in L. obvenire de Signif. Nom. ff. fol. & de jure Gent. & Civil. de protib. aliena feud. per federa, test. Joha. Luxius in prolegom. quem velim videas, de Analy. Cap. 1, 2, 3. Vid. Idea.

It happened—I must not say unluckily for Truth, because they were giving her a lift another way in so doing; that the two universities of Strasburg—the Lutheran, founded in the year 1538 by Jacobus Surmis, counsellor of the senate,—and the Popish, founded by Leopold, archduke of Austria, were, during all this time, employing the whole depth of their knowledge (except just what the affair of the abbess of Quedlinburg's placket-holes required)—in determining the point of Martin Luther's damnation.

The Popish doctors had undertaken to demonstrate *à priori*, that from the necessary influence of the planets on the twenty-second day of October 1483——when the moon was in the twelfth house, Jupiter, Mars, and Venus in the third, the Sun, Saturn, and Mercury, all got together in the fourth—that he must in course, and unavoidably, be a damned man—and that his doctrines, by a direct corollary, must be damned doctrines too.

By inspection into his horoscope, where five planets were in coition all at once with Scorpio[1] (in reading this my father would always shake his head) in the ninth house, which the Arabians allotted to religion—it appeared that Martin Luther did not care one stiver about the matter——and that from the horoscope directed to

---

[1] Haec mira, satisque horrenda Planetarum coitio sub Scorpio Asterismo in nona coeli statione, quam Arabes religioni deputabant, efficit Martinum Lutherum sacrilegum hereticum, Christianae religionis hostem acerrimum atque prophanum, ex horoscopi directione ad Martis coitum, religiosissimus obiit, ejus Anima scelestissima ad infernos navigavit—ab Alecto, Tisiphone & Megara flagellis igneis cruciata perenniter.

—Lucas Gauricus in Tractatu astrologico de praeteritis multorum hominum accidentibus per genituras examinatis.

the conjunction of Mars—they made it plain likewise he must die cursing and blaspheming—with the blast of which his soul (being steeped in guilt) sailed before the wind, in the lake of hell-fire.

The little objection of the Lutheran doctors to this, was, that it must certainly be the soul of another man, born Oct. 22, 83, which was forced to sail down before the wind in that manner—inasmuch as it appeared from the register of Eisleben in the county of Mansfelt, that Luther was not born in the year 1483, but in 84; and not on the 22nd day of October, but on the 10th of November, the eve of Martinmas day, from whence he had the name of Martin.

[—I must break off my translation for a moment; for if I did not, I know I should no more be able to shut my eyes in bed, than the abbess of Quedlinburg—It is to tell the reader, that my father never read this passage of Slawkenbergius to my uncle Toby, but with triumph ——not over my uncle Toby, for he never opposed him in it—but over the whole world.

—Now you see, brother Toby, he would say, looking up, "that christian names are not such indifferent things";——had Luther here been called by any other name but Martin, he would have been damned to all eternity——Not that I look upon Martin, he would add, as a good name—far from it—'tis something better than a neutral, and but a little—yet little as it is, you see it was of some service to him.

My father knew the weakness of this prop to his hypothesis, as well as the best logician could shew him—

yet so strange is the weakness of man at the same time,
as it fell in his way, he could not for his life but make use
of it; and it was certainly for this reason, that though
there are many stories in Hafen Slawkenbergius's
Decads full as entertaining as this I am translating, yet
there is not one amongst them which my father read
over with half the delight——it flattered two of his
strangest hypotheses together—his Names and his
Noses.—I will be bold to say, he might have read all the
books in the Alexandrian Library, had not fate taken
other care of them, and not have met with a book or
passage in one, which hit two such nails as these upon
the head at one stroke.]

The two universities of Strasburg were hard tugging
at this affair of Luther's navigation. The Protestant
doctors had demonstrated, that he had not sailed right
before the wind, as the Popish doctors had pretended;
and as every one knew there was no sailing full in the
teeth of it—they were going to settle, in case he had
sailed, how many points he was off; whether Martin had
doubled the cape, or had fallen upon a lee-shore; and no
doubt, as it was an enquiry of much edification, at least
to those who understood this sort of Navigation, they
had gone on with it in spite of the size of the stranger's
nose, had not the size of the stranger's nose drawn off
the attention of the world from what they were about—
it was their business to follow.

The abbess of Quedlinburg and her four dignitaries
was no stop; for the enormity of the stranger's nose
running full as much in their fancies as their case of

conscience—the affair of their placket-holes kept cold—
in a word, the printers were ordered to distribute their
types—all controversies dropped.

'Twas a square cap with a silver tassel upon the
crown of it—to a nut-shell—to have guessed on which
side of the nose the two universities would split.

'Tis above reason, cried the doctors on one side.

'Tis below reason, cried the others.

'Tis faith, one cried.

'Tis a fiddle-stick, said the other.

'Tis possible, cried the one.

'Tis impossible, said the other.

God's power is infinite, cried the Nosarians, he can
do any thing.

He can do nothing, replied the Antinosarians, which
implies contradictions.

He can make matter think, said the Nosarians.

As certainly as you can make a velvet cap out of a
sow's ear, replied the Antinosarians.

He cannot make two and two five, replied the Popish
doctors.—'Tis false, said their other opponents.—

Infinite power is infinite power, said the doctors who
maintained the reality of the nose.—It extends only to
all possible things, replied the Lutherans.

By God in heaven, cried the Popish doctors, he can
make a nose, if he thinks fit, as big as the steeple of
Strasburg.

Now the steeple of Strasburg being the biggest and
the tallest church-steeple to be seen in the whole world,
the Antinosarians denied that a nose of 575 geometrical

feet in length could be worn, at least by a middle-sized man—The Popish doctors swore it could—The Lutheran doctors said No;—it could not.

This at once started a new dispute, which they pursued a great way, upon the extent and limitation of the moral and natural attributes of God—That controversy led them naturally into Thomas Aquinas, and Thomas Aquinas to the devil.

The stranger's nose was no more heard of in the dispute—it just served as a frigate to launch them into the gulf of school-divinity—and then they all sailed before the wind.

Heat is in proportion to the want of true knowledge.

The controversy about the attributes, etc., instead of cooling, on the contrary had inflamed the Strasburgers' imaginations to a most inordinate degree—The less they understood of the matter, the greater was their wonder about it—they were left in all the distresses of desire unsatisfied—saw their doctors, the Parchmentarians, the Brassarians, the Turpentarians, on one side—the Popish doctors on the other, like Pantagruel and his companions in quest of the oracle of the bottle, all embarked out of sight.

—The poor Strasburgers left upon the beach!

—What was to be done?—No delay—the uproar increased—every one in disorder—the city gates set open.—

Unfortunate Strasburgers! was there in the storehouse of nature——was there in the lumber-rooms of learning——was there in the great arsenal of chance, one single engine left undrawn forth to torture your curiosities, and stretch your desires, which was not pointed by the hand of Fate to play upon your hearts!— I dip not my pen into my ink to excuse the surrender of yourselves—'tis to write your panegyric. Shew me a city so macerated with expectation—who neither eat, or drank, or slept, or prayed, or hearkened to the calls either of religion or nature for seven-and-twenty days together, who could have held out one day longer.

On the twenty-eighth the courteous stranger had promised to return to Strasburg.

Seven thousand coaches (Slawkenbergius must certainly have made some mistake in his numeral characters); 7,000 coaches—15,000 single-horse chairs—20,000 waggons, crowded as full as they could all hold with senators, counsellors, syndics—beguines, widows, wives, virgins, canons, concubines, all in their coaches—The abbess of Quedlinburg, with the prioress, the deaness and sub-chantress, leading the procession in one coach, and the dean of Strasburg, with the four great dignitaries of his chapter, on her left-hand—the rest following higglety-pigglety as they could; some on horseback —some on foot—some led—some driven—some down the Rhine—some this way—some that—all set out at sun-rise to meet the courteous stranger on the road.

Haste we now towards the catastrophe of my tale ——I say Catastrophe (cries Slawkenbergius) inasmuch as a tale, with parts rightly disposed, not only rejoiceth (*gaudet*) in the Catastrophe and Peripetia of a Drama, but rejoiceth moreover in all the essential and integrant parts of it—it has its Protasis, Epitasis, Catastasis, its Catastrophe or Peripetia growing one out of the other in it, in the order Aristotle first planted them—without which a tale had better never been told at all, says Slawkenbergius, but be kept to a man's self.

In all my ten tales, in all my ten decads, have I Slawkenbergius tied down every tale of them as tightly to this rule, as I have done this of the stranger and his nose.

—From his first parley with the sentinel, to his leaving the city of Strasburg, after pulling off his crimson-satin pair of breeches, is the Protasis or first entrance—where the characters of the *Personae Dramatis* are just touched in, and the subject slightly begun.

The Epitasis, wherein the action is more fully entered upon and heightened, till it arrives at its state or height called the Catastasis, and which usually takes up the 2nd and 3rd act, is included within that busy period of my tale, betwixt the first night's uproar about the nose, to the conclusion of the trumpeter's wife's lectures upon it in the middle of the grand parade: and from the first embarking of the learned in the dispute—to the doctors finally sailing away, and leaving the Strasburgers upon the beach in distress, is the Catastasis or the ripening of the incidents and passions for their bursting forth in the fifth act.

This commences with the setting out of the Strasburgers in the Frankfort road, and terminates in unwinding the labyrinth and bringing the hero out of a state of agitation (as Aristotle calls it) to a state of rest and quietness.

BOOK IV

This, says Hafen Slawkenbergius, constitutes the Catastrophe or Peripetia of my tale—and that is the part of it I am going to relate.

We left the stranger behind the curtain asleep—he enters now upon the stage.

—What dost thou prick up thy ears at?—'tis nothing but a man upon a horse—was the last word the stranger uttered to his mule. It was not proper then to tell the reader, that the mule took his master's word for it; and without any more *ifs* or *ands*, let the traveller and his horse pass by.

The traveller was hastening with all diligence to get to Strasburg that night. What a fool am I, said the traveller to himself, when he had rode about a league farther, to think of getting into Strasburg this night.—Strasburg!—the great Strasburg!—Strasburg, the capital of all Alsatia! Strasburg, an imperial city! Strasburg, a sovereign state! Strasburg, garrisoned with five thousand of the best troops in all the world!—Alas! if I was at the gates of Strasburg this moment, I could not gain admittance into it for a ducat—nay a ducat and half—'tis too much—better go back to the last inn I have passed—than lie I know not where—or give I know not what. The traveller, as he made these reflections in his mind, turned his horse's head about, and three minutes after the stranger had been conducted into his chamber, he arrived at the same inn.

——We have bacon in the house, said the host, and bread——and till eleven o'clock this night had three eggs in it—but a stranger, who arrived an hour ago, has had them dressed into an omelet, and we have nothing.——

Alas! said the traveller, harassed as I am, I want nothing but a bed.——I have one as soft as is in Alsatia, said the host.

—The stranger, continued he, should have slept in it, for 'tis my best bed, but upon the score of his nose.—— He has got a defluxion, said the traveller.—Not that I know, cried the host.—But 'tis a camp-bed, and Jacinta, said he, looking towards the maid, imagined there was not room in it to turn his nose in.——Why so? cried the traveller, starting back.—It is so long a nose, replied the host.—The traveller fixed his eyes upon Jacinta, then upon the ground—kneeled upon his right knee—had just got his hand laid upon his breast——Trifle not with my anxiety, said he, rising up again.—'Tis no trifle, said Jacinta, 'tis the most glorious nose!—The traveller fell upon his knee again—laid his hand upon his breast— then, said he, looking up to heaven, thou hast conducted me to the end of my pilgrimage—'Tis Diego.

The traveller was the brother of the Julia, so often invoked that night by the stranger as he rode from Strasburg upon his mule; and was come, on her part, in quest of him. He had accompanied his sister from Valladolid across the Pyrenean mountains through France, and had many an entangled skein to wind off in pursuit of him through the many meanders and abrupt turnings of a lover's thorny tracks.

—Julia had sunk under it——and had not been able to go a step farther than to Lyons, where, with the many disquietudes of a tender heart, which all talk of—but

few feel—she sickened, but had just strength to write a
letter to Diego; and having conjured her brother never
to see her face till he had found him out, and put the
letter into his hands, Julia took to her bed.

Fernandez (for that was her brother's name)—tho'
the camp-bed was as soft as any one in Alsace, yet he
could not shut his eyes in it.—As soon as it was day he
rose, and hearing Diego was risen too, he entered his
chamber, and discharged his sister's commission.

The letter was as follows:

"Seig. DIEGO,

"Whether my suspicions of your nose were justly
excited or not——'tis not now to inquire—it is enough I
have not had firmness to put them to farther trial.

"How could I know so little of myself, when I sent
my Duenna to forbid your coming more under my
lattice? or how could I know so little of you, Diego, as to
imagine you would not have stayed one day in Valladolid to have given ease to my doubts?—Was I to be
abandoned, Diego, because I was deceived? or was it
kind to take me at my word, whether my suspicions
were just or no, and leave me, as you did, a prey to much
uncertainty and sorrow?

"In what manner Julia has resented this—my brother, when he puts this letter into your hands, will tell you;
He will tell you in how few moments she repented of the
rash message she had sent you—in what frantic haste
she flew to her lattice, and how many days and nights
together she leaned immoveably upon her elbow, look-

ing through it towards the way which Diego was wont to come.

"He will tell you, when she heard of your departure —how her spirits deserted her—how her heart sickened —how piteously she mourned—how low she hung her head. O Diego! how many weary steps has my brother's pity led me by the hand languishing to trace out yours; how far has desire carried me beyond strength—and how oft have I fainted by the way, and sunk into his arms, with only power to cry out—O my Diego!

"If the gentleness of your carriage has not belied your heart, you will fly to me, almost as fast as you fled from me—haste as you will—you will arrive but to see me expire.——'Tis a bitter draught, Diego, but oh! 'tis embittered still more by dying un——"

She could proceed no farther.

Slawkenbergius supposes the word intended was "unconvinced," but her strength would not enable her to finish her letter. The heart of the courteous Diego overflowed as he read the letter——he ordered his mule forthwith and Fernandez's horse to be saddled; and as no vent in prose is equal to that of poetry in such conflicts—chance, which as often directs us to remedies as to diseases, having thrown a piece of charcoal into the window—Diego availed himself of it, and whilst the hostler was getting ready his mule, he eased his mind against the wall as follows.

ODE

Harsh and untuneful are the notes of love,
Unless my Julia strikes the key,
Her hand alone can touch the part,
Whose dulcet move-
ment charms the heart,
And governs all the man with sympathetic sway.

2nd.

O Julia!

The lines were very natural—for they were nothing
at all to the purpose, says Slawkenbergius, and 'tis a
pity there were no more of them; but whether it was
that Seig. Diego was slow in composing verses—or the
hostler quick in saddling mules—is not averred; certain
it was, that Diego's mule and Fernandez's horse were
ready at the door of the inn, before Diego was ready for
his second stanza; so without staying to finish his ode,
they both mounted, sallied forth, passed the Rhine,
traversed Alsace, shaped their course towards Lyons,
and before the Strasburgers and the abbess of Quedlinburg had set out on their cavalcade, had Fernandez,
Diego, and his Julia crossed the Pyrenean mountains,
and got safe to Valladolid.

'Tis needless to inform the geographical reader, that
when Diego was in Spain, it was not possible to meet the
courteous stranger in the Frankfort road; it is enough to
say, that of all restless desires, curiosity being the strongest—the Strasburgers felt the full force of it; and that

for three days and nights they were tossed to and fro in the Frankfort road, with the tempestuous fury of this passion, before they could submit to return home.—When alas! an event was prepared for them, of all other, the most grievous that could befall a free people.

As this revolution of the Strasburgers' affairs is often spoken of, and little understood, I will, in ten words, says Slawkenbergius, give the world an explanation of it, and with it put an end to my tale.

Every body knows of the grand system of Universal Monarchy, wrote by order of Mons. Colbert, and put in manuscript into the hands of Lewis the fourteenth, in the year 1664.

'Tis as well known, that one branch out of many of that system, was the getting possession of Strasburg, to favour an entrance at all times into Suabia, in order to disturb the quiet of Germany—and that in consequence of this plan, Strasburg unhappily fell at length into their hands.

It is the lot of a few to trace out the true springs of this and such like revolutions—The vulgar look too high for them—Statesmen look too low—Truth (for once) lies in the middle.

What a fatal thing is the popular pride of a free city! cries one historian—The Strasburgers deemed it a diminution of their freedom to receive an imperial garrison—so fell a prey to a French one.

The fate, says another, of the Strasburgers, may be a warning to all free people to save their money.——They anticipated their revenues—brought themselves under taxes, exhausted their strength, and in the end became so weak a people, they had not strength to keep their gates shut, and so the French pushed them open.

Alas! alas! cries Slawkenbergius, 'twas not the French,—'twas curiosity pushed them open——The French indeed, who are ever upon the catch, when they saw the Strasburgers, men, women, and children, all marched out to follow the stranger's nose—each man followed his own, and marched in.

Trade and manufactures have decayed and gradually grown down ever since—but not from any cause which commercial heads have assigned; for it is owing to this only, that noses have ever so run in their heads, that the Strasburgers could not follow their business.

Alas! alas! cries Slawkenbergius, making an exclamation—it is not the first—and I fear will not be the last fortress that has been either won—or lost by noses.

The *END* of *Slawkenbergius's* TALE.

CHAPTER I

WITH all this learning upon noses running perpetually in my father's fancy—with so many family prejudices—and ten decads of such tales running on for ever along with them—how was it possible with such exquisite —was it a true nose?—That a man with such exquisite feelings as my father had, could bear the shock at all below stairs—or indeed above stairs, in any other posture, but the very posture I have described?

—Throw yourself down upon the bed, a dozen times

—taking care only to place a looking-glass first in a chair on one side of it, before you do it—But was the stranger's nose a true nose, or was it a false one?

To tell that before-hand, madam, would be to do injury to one of the best tales in the Christian-world; and that is the tenth of the tenth decad, which immediately follows this.

This tale, cried Slawkenbergius, somewhat exultingly, has been reserved by me for the concluding tale of my whole work; knowing right well, that when I shall have told it, and my reader shall have read it thro'— 'twould be even high time for both of us to shut up the book; inasmuch, continues Slawkenbergius, as I know of no tale which could possibly ever go down after it.

—'Tis a tale indeed!

This sets out with the first interview in the inn at Lyons, when Fernandez left the courteous stranger and his sister Julia alone in her chamber, and is over-written

The INTRICACIES OF *Diego* and *Julia.*

Heavens! thou art a strange creature, Slawkenbergius! what a whimsical view of the involutions of the heart of woman hast thou opened! how this can ever be translated, and yet if this specimen of Slawkenbergius's tales, and the exquisitiveness of his moral, should please the world—translated shall a couple of volumes be.—— Else, how this can ever be translated into good English, I have no sort of conception—There seems in some passages to want a sixth sense to do it rightly.—What can he mean by the lambent pupilability of slow, low, dry chat, five notes below the natural tone—which you know, madam, is little more than a whisper? The moment I pronounced the words, I could perceive an attempt towards a vibration in the strings, about the region of the heart.——The brain made no acknowledgment.—There's often no good understanding betwixt 'em—I felt as if I understood it.—I had no ideas.—The movement could not be without cause.—I'm lost. I can make nothing of it—unless, may it please your worships, the voice, in that case being little more than a whisper, unavoidably forces the eyes to approach not only within six inches of each other—but to look into the pupils—is not that dangerous?—But it can't be avoided—for to look up to the ceiling, in that case the two chins unavoidably meet—and to look down into each other's lap, the foreheads come to immediate contact, which at once puts an end to the conference—I mean to the sentimental part of it.—What is left, madam, is not worth stooping for.

Chapter II

My father lay stretched across the bed as still as if the hand of death had pushed him down, for a full hour and a half before he began to play upon the floor with the toe of that foot which hung over the bed-side; my uncle Toby's heart was a pound lighter for it.——In a few moments, his left-hand, the knuckles of which had all the time reclined upon the handle of the chamber-pot, came to its feeling—he thrust it a little more within the valance—drew up his hand, when he had done, into his bosom—gave a hem! My good uncle Toby, with infinite pleasure, answered it; and full gladly would have ingrafted a sentence of consolation upon the opening it afforded: but having no talents, as I said, that way, and fearing moreover that he might set out with something which might make a bad matter worse, he contented himself with resting his chin placidly upon the cross of his crutch.

Now whether the compression shortened my uncle Toby's face into a more pleasurable oval—or that the philanthropy of his heart, in seeing his brother beginning to emerge out of the sea of his afflictions, had braced up his muscles—so that the compression upon his chin only doubled the benignity which was there before, is not hard to decide.—My father, in turning his eyes, was struck with such a gleam of sunshine in his face, as melted down the sullenness of his grief in a moment.

He broke silence as follows.

Chapter III

Did ever man, brother Toby, cried my father, raising himself upon his elbow, and turning himself round to the opposite side of the bed, where my uncle Toby was sitting in his old fringed chair, with his chin resting upon his crutch—did ever a poor unfortunate man, brother Toby, cried my father, receive so many lashes?—The most I ever saw given, quoth my uncle Toby (ringing the bell at the bed's head for Trim) was to a grenadier, I think in Mackay's regiment.

——Had my uncle Toby shot a bullet through my father's heart, he could not have fallen down with his nose upon the quilt more suddenly.

Bless me! said my uncle Toby.

CHAPTER IV

W AS it Mackay's regiment, quoth my uncle Toby, where the poor grenadier was so unmercifully whipped at Bruges about the ducats?—O Christ! he was innocent! cried Trim, with a deep sigh.—And he was whipped, may it please your honour, almost to death's door.—They had better have shot him outright, as he begged, and he had gone directly to heaven, for he was as innocent as your honour.——I thank thee, Trim, quoth my uncle Toby.—I never think of his, continued Trim, and my poor brother Tom's misfortunes, for we were all three school-fellows, but I cry like a coward.—Tears are no proof of cowardice, Trim.—I drop them oft-times myself, cried my uncle Toby.—I know your honour does, replied Trim, and so am not ashamed of it myself.—But to think, may it please your honour, continued Trim, a tear stealing into the corner of his eye as he spoke—to think of two virtuous lads with hearts as warm in their bodies, and as honest as God could make them—the children of honest people, going forth with gallant spirits to seek their fortunes in the world—and fall into such evils!—poor Tom! to be tortured upon a rack for nothing —but marrying a Jew's widow who sold sausages— honest Dick Johnson's soul to be scourged out of his

body, for the ducats another man put into his knapsack!
—O!—these are misfortunes, cried Trim,—pulling out
his handkerchief—these are misfortunes, may it please
your honour, worth lying down and crying over.

—My father could not help blushing.

'Twould be a pity, Trim, quoth my uncle Toby, thou
shouldst ever feel sorrow of thy own—thou feelest it so
tenderly for others.—Alack-o-day, replied the Corporal,
brightening up his face——your honour knows I have
neither wife or child—I can have no sorrows in this
world.—My father could not help smiling.—As few as
any man, Trim, replied my uncle Toby; nor can I see
how a fellow of thy light heart can suffer, but from the
distress of poverty in thy old age—when thou art passed
all services, Trim—and hast outlived thy friends.—An'
please your honour, never fear, replied Trim, cheerily.—
But I would have thee never fear, Trim, replied my
uncle Toby, and therefore, continued my uncle Toby,
throwing down his crutch, and getting up upon his legs
as he uttered the word "therefore"—in recompense,
Trim, of thy long fidelity to me, and that goodness of
thy heart I have had such proofs of—whilst thy master
is worth a shilling—thou shalt never ask elsewhere,
Trim, for a penny. Trim attempted to thank my uncle
Toby—but had not power—tears trickled down his
cheeks faster than he could wipe them off—He laid his
hands upon his breast—made a bow to the ground, and
shut the door.

—I have left Trim my bowling-green, cried my uncle
Toby.—My father smiled.——I have left him moreover

a pension, continued my uncle Toby.—My father looked grave.

CHAPTER V

I s this a fit time, said my father to himself, to talk of Pensions and Grenadiers?

CHAPTER VI

W HEN my uncle Toby first mentioned the grenadier, my father, I said, fell down with his nose flat to the quilt, and as suddenly as if my uncle Toby had shot him; but it was not added that every other limb and member of my father instantly relapsed with his nose into the same precise attitude in which he lay first described; so that when Corporal Trim left the room, and my father found himself disposed to rise off the bed—he had all the little preparatory movements to run over again, before he could do it. Attitudes are nothing, madam —'tis the transition from one attitude to another—like the preparation and resolution of the discord into harmony, which is all in all.

For which reason my father played the same jig over again with his toe upon the floor—pushed the chamber-pot still a little further within the valance—gave a hem —raised himself up upon his elbow—and was just beginning to address himself to my uncle Toby—when recollecting the unsuccessfulness of his first effort in that attitude—he got upon his legs, and in making the third turn across the room, he stopped short before my uncle

Toby; and laying the three first fingers of his right-hand in the palm of his left, and stooping a little, he addressed himself to my uncle Toby as follows:

CHAPTER VII

WHEN I reflect, brother Toby, upon Man; and take a view of that dark side of him which represents his life as open to so many causes of trouble—when I consider, brother Toby, how oft we eat the bread of affliction, and that we are born to it, as to the portion of our inheritance——I was born to nothing, quoth my uncle Toby, interrupting my father—but my commission. Zooks! said my father, did not my uncle leave you a hundred and twenty pounds a year?——What could I have done without it? replied my uncle Toby——That's another concern, said my father testily—But I say, Toby, when one runs over the catalogue of all the cross-reckonings and sorrowful Items with which the heart of man is overcharged, 'tis wonderful by what hidden resources the mind is enabled to stand out, and bear itself up, as it does, against the impositions laid upon our nature.—— 'Tis by the assistance of Almighty God, cried my uncle Toby, looking up, and pressing the palms of his hands close together—'tis not from our own strength, brother Shandy—a sentinel in a wooden sentry-box might as well pretend to stand it out against a detachment of fifty men.—We are upheld by the grace and the assistance of the best of Beings.

—That is cutting the knot, said my father, instead of

BOOK IV

untying it.—But give me leave to lead you, brother Toby, a little deeper into the mystery.

With all my heart, replied my uncle Toby.

My father instantly exchanged the attitude he was in, for that in which Socrates is so finely painted by Raffael in his school of Athens; which your connoisseurship knows is so exquisitely imagined, that even the particular manner of the reasoning of Socrates is expressed by it—for he holds the fore-finger of his left-hand between the fore-finger and the thumb of his right, and seems as if he was saying to the libertine he is reclaiming——"You grant me this—and this: and this, and this, I don't ask of you—they follow of themselves in course."

So stood my father, holding fast his fore-finger betwixt his finger and his thumb, and reasoning with my uncle Toby as he sat in his old fringed chair, valanced around with party-coloured worsted bobs—O Garrick! —what a rich scene of this would thy exquisite powers make! and how gladly would I write such another to avail myself of thy immortality, and secure my own behind it.

CHAPTER VIII

THOUGH man is of all others the most curious vehicle, said my father, yet at the same time 'tis of so slight a frame, and so totteringly put together, that the sudden jerks and hard jostlings it unavoidably meets with in this rugged journey, would overset and tear it to pieces a dozen times a day—was it not, brother Toby, that there is a secret spring within us.—Which spring, said my uncle Toby, I take to be Religion.—Will that set my child's nose on? cried my father, letting go his finger, and striking one hand against the other.—It makes every thing straight for us, answered my uncle Toby.— Figuratively speaking, dear Toby, it may, for aught I know, said my father; but the spring I am speaking of, is that great and elastic power within us of counterbalancing evil, which, like a secret spring in a well-ordered machine, though it can't prevent the shock—at least it imposes upon our sense of it.

Now, my dear brother, said my father, replacing his fore-finger, as he was coming closer to the point—had my child arrived safe into the world, unmartyred in that precious part of him—fanciful and extravagant as I may appear to the world in my opinion of christian names, and of that magic bias which good or bad names irresistibly impress upon our characters and conducts—Heaven is witness! that in the warmest transports of my wishes for the prosperity of my child, I never once wished to crown his head with more glory and honour than what George or Edward would have spread around it.

But alas! continued my father, as the greatest evil has befallen him—I must counteract and undo it with the greatest good.

He shall be christened Trismegistus, brother.

I wish it may answer—replied my uncle Toby, rising up.

CHAPTER IX

WHAT a chapter of chances, said my father, turning himself about upon the first landing, as he and my uncle Toby were going downstairs—what a long chapter of chances do the events of this world lay open to us! Take pen and ink in hand, brother Toby, and calculate it fairly—I know no more of calculation than this balluster,

CHAP. IX

said my uncle Toby (striking short of it with his crutch, and hitting my father a desperate blow souse upon his shin-bone)—'Twas a hundred to one—cried my uncle Toby—I thought, quoth my father, (rubbing his shin) you had known nothing of calculations, brother Toby. 'Tis a mere chance, said my uncle Toby.——Then it adds one to the chapter—replied my father.

The double success of my father's repartees tickled off the pain of his shin at once—it was well it so fell out —(chance! again)—or the world to this day had never known the subject of my father's calculation—to guess it—there was no chance—What a lucky chapter of chances has this turned out! for it has saved me the trouble of writing one express, and in truth I have enough already upon my hands without it.—Have not I promised the world a chapter of knots? two chapters upon the right and the wrong end of a woman? a chapter upon whiskers? a chapter upon wishes?—a chapter of noses?—No, I have done that—a chapter upon my uncle Toby's modesty? to say nothing of a chapter upon chapters, which I will finish before I sleep—by my great-grandfather's whiskers, I shall never get half of 'em through this year.

Take pen and ink in hand, and calculate it fairly, brother Toby, said my father, and it will turn out a million to one, that of all the parts of the body, the edge of the forceps should have the ill luck just to fall upon and break down that one part, which should break down the fortunes of our house with it.

It might have been worse, replied my uncle Toby.—

BOOK IV

I don't comprehend, said my father.——Suppose the hip had presented, replied my uncle Toby, as Dr. Slop foreboded.

My father reflected half a minute—looked down— touched the middle of his forehead slightly with his finger——

—True, said he.

CHAPTER X

Is it not a shame to make two chapters of what passed in going down one pair of stairs? for we are got no farther yet than to the first landing, and there are fifteen more steps down to the bottom; and for aught I know, as my father and my uncle Toby are in a talking humour, there may be as many chapters as steps:—let that be as it will, Sir, I can no more help it than my destiny:—A sudden impulse comes across me—drop the curtain, Shandy—I drop it—Strike a line here across the paper, Tristram—I strike it—and hey for a new chapter.

The deuce of any other rule have I to govern myself by in this affair—and if I had one—as I do all things out of all rule—I would twist it and tear it to pieces, and throw it into the fire when I had done—Am I warm? I am, and the cause demands it—a pretty story! is a man to follow rules——or rules to follow him?

Now this, you must know, being my chapter upon chapters, which I promised to write before I went to sleep, I thought it meet to ease my conscience entirely before I laid down, by telling the world all I knew about

the matter at once: Is not this ten times better than to
set out dogmatically with a sententious parade of wisdom, and telling the world a story of a roasted horse—
that chapters relieve the mind—that they assist—or impose upon the imagination—and that in a work of this
dramatic cast they are as necessary as the shifting of
scenes—with fifty other cold conceits, enough to ex-
tinguish the fire which roasted him?—O! but to understand this, which is a puff at the fire of Diana's temple—
you must read Longinus—read away—if you are not a
jot the wiser by reading him the first time over—never
fear—read him again—Avicenna and Licetus read Aristotle's metaphysics forty times through a-piece, and
never understood a single word.—But mark the consequence—Avicenna turned out a desperate writer at all
kinds of writing—for he wrote books *de omni scribili*;
and for Licetus (Fortunio) though all the world knows
he was born a foetus,[1] of no more than five and a half
inches in length, yet he grew to that astonishing height in

---

[1] Ce Foetus n'étoit pas plus grand que la paume de la main; mais son père
l'ayant examiné en qualité de Médecin, & ayant trouvé que c'étoit quelque
chose de plus qu'un Embryon, le fit transporter tout vivant à Raqallo, où il
le fit voir à Jérôme Bardi & à d'autres Médecins du lieu. On trouva qu'il ne
lui manquoit rien d'essentiel à la vie; & son père pour faire voir un essai de
son expérience, entreprit d'achever l'ouvrage de la Nature, & de travailler à
la formation de l'Enfant avec le même artifice que celui dont on se sert pour
faire éclore les Poulets en Egypte. Il instruisit une Nourrice de tout ce
qu'elle avoit à faire, & ayant fait mettre son fils dans un four proprement
accommodé, il réussit à l'élever & à lui faire prendre ses accroissemens
nécessaires, par l'uniformité d'une chaleur étrangère mesurée exactement sur
les dégrés d'un Thermomètre, ou d'un autre instrument équivalent. (Vide

literature, as to write a book with a title as long as himself——the learned know I mean his Gonopsychanthropologia, upon the origin of the human soul.

So much for my chapter upon chapters, which I hold
to be the best chapter in my whole work; and take my
word, whoever reads it, is full as well employed, as in
picking straws.

CHAPTER XI

W E shall bring all things to rights, said my father,
setting his foot upon the first step from the landing.—This Trismegistus, continued my father, drawing
his leg back and turning to my uncle Toby—was the
greatest (Toby) of all earthly beings—he was the greatest
king—the greatest law-giver—the greatest philosopher
—and the greatest priest—and engineer—said my uncle
Toby.

——In course, said my father.

Mich. Giustinian negli Scritt. Liguri à Cart. 223. 488.)
On auroit toujours été très satisfait de l'industrie d'un père si expéri-
menté dans l'Art de la Génération, quand il n'auroit pu prolonger la vie à
sons fils que pour quelques mois, ou pour peu d'années.
Mais quand on se représente que l'Enfant a vecu près de quatre-vingts
ans, & qu'il a composé quatre-vingts Ouvrages différents tous fruits d'une
longue lecture—il faut convenir que tout ce qui est incroyable n'est pas
toujours faux, & que la Vraisemblance n'est pas toujours du côté de la Vérité.
Il n'avoit que dix neuf ans lorsqu'il composa Gonopsychanthropologia
de Origine Animae humanae.
(Les Enfans célèbres, revu & corrigé par M. de la Monnoye de l'Aca-
démie Françoise.)

Chapter XII

—And how does your mistress? cried my father, taking the same step over again from the landing, and calling to Susannah, whom he saw passing by the foot of the stairs with a huge pincushion in her hand—how does your mistress? As well, said Susannah, tripping by, but without looking up, as can be expected.—What a fool am I! said my father, drawing his leg back again—let things be as they will, brother Toby, 'tis ever the precise answer—And how is the child, pray?—No answer. And where is Dr. Slop? added my father, raising his voice aloud, and looking over the ballusters—Susannah was out of hearing.

Of all the riddles of a married life, said my father, crossing the landing in order to set his back against the wall, whilst he propounded it to my uncle Toby—of all the puzzling riddles, said he, in a marriage state,—of which you may trust me, brother Toby, there are more asses' loads than all Job's stock of asses could have carried—there is not one that has more intricacies in it than this—that from the very moment the mistress of the house is brought to bed, every female in it, from my lady's gentlewoman down to the cinder-wench, becomes an inch taller for it; and give themselves more airs upon that single inch, than all the other inches put together.

I think rather, replied my uncle Toby, that 'tis we who sink an inch lower.—If I meet but a woman with child—I do it.—'Tis a heavy tax upon that half of our fellow-creatures, brother Shandy, said my uncle Toby—

'Tis a piteous burden upon 'em, continued he, shaking his head—Yes, yes, 'tis a painful thing—said my father, shaking his head too—but certainly since shaking of heads came into fashion, never did two heads shake together, in concert, from two such different springs.

God bless ⎰'em all——said my uncle Toby and my
Deuce take ⎱father, each to himself.

Chapter XIII

HOLLA!—you, chairman!—here's sixpence—do step into that bookseller's shop, and call me a day-tall critic. I am very willing to give any one of 'em a crown to help me with his tackling, to get my father and my uncle Toby off the stairs, and to put them to bed.

—'Tis even high time; for except a short nap, which they both got whilst Trim was boring the jack-boots—and which, by the bye, did my father no sort of good, upon the score of the bad hinge—they have not else shut their eyes, since nine hours before the time that Dr. Slop was led into the back parlour in that dirty pickle by Obadiah.

Was every day of my life to be as busy a day as this—and to take up—Truce.

I will not finish that sentence till I have made an observation upon the strange state of affairs between the reader and myself, just as things stand at present—an observation never applicable before to any one biographical writer since the creation of the world, but to myself—and I believe, will never hold good to any other, until its final destruction—and therefore, for the very novelty of it alone, it must be worth your worships attending to.

I am this month one whole year older than I was this time twelve-month; and having got, as you perceive, almost into the middle of my fourth volume[1]—and no farther than to my first day's life—'tis demonstrative that I have three hundred and sixty-four days more life to write just now, than when I first set out; so that instead of advancing, as a common writer, in my work with what I have been doing at it—on the contrary, I am just thrown so many volumes back—was every day of my life to be as busy a day as this—And why not?— and the transactions and opinions of it to take up as much description—And for what reason should they be cut short? as at this rate I should just live 364 times faster than I should write—It must follow, an' please your worships, that the more I write, the more I shall have to write—and consequently, the more your worships will have to read.

Will this be good for your worships' eyes?

It will do well for mine; and, was it not that my Opinions will be the death of me, I perceive I shall lead a fine life of it out of this self-same life of mine; or, in other words, shall lead a couple of fine lives together.

As for the proposal of twelve volumes a year, or a volume a month, it no way alters my prospect—write as I will, and rush as I may into the middle of things, as Horace advises—I shall never overtake myself whipped

[1 *i.e.* According to the original editions.]

and driven to the last pinch; at the worst I shall have one day the start of my pen—and one day is enough for two volumes—and two volumes will be enough for one year.—

Heaven prosper the manufacturers of paper under this propitious reign, which is now opened to us—as I trust its providence will prosper every thing else in it that is taken in hand.—

As for the propagation of Geese—I give myself no concern—Nature is all bountiful—I shall never want tools to work with.

—So then, friend! you have got my father and my uncle Toby off the stairs, and seen them to bed?—— And how did you manage it?—You dropped a curtain at the stair-foot—I thought you had no other way for it ——Here's a crown for your trouble.

Chapter XIV

—THEN reach me my breeches off the chair, said my father to Susannah.—There is not a moment's time to dress you, Sir, cried Susannah—the child is as black in the face as my—As your what? said my father, for like all orators, he was a dear searcher into comparisons. —Bless me, Sir, said Susannah, the child's in a fit.—And where's Mr. Yorick?—Never where he should be, said Susannah, but his curate's in the dressing-room, with the child upon his arm, waiting for the name—and my mistress bid me run as fast as I could to know, as captain

Shandy is the godfather, whether it should not be called after him.

Were one sure, said my father to himself, scratching his eye-brow, that the child was expiring, one might as well compliment my brother Toby as not—and it would be a pity, in such a case, to throw away so great a name as Trismegistus upon him—but he may recover.

No, no,—said my father to Susannah, I'll get up—— There is no time, cried Susannah, the child's as black as my shoe. Trismegistus, said my father——But stay—thou art a leaky vessel, Susannah, added my father; canst thou carry Trismegistus in thy head, the length of the gallery without scattering?——Can I? cried Susannah, shutting the door in a huff.—If she can, I'll be shot, said my father, bouncing out of bed in the dark, and groping for his breeches.

BOOK IV

Susannah ran with all speed along the gallery.

My father made all possible speed to find his breeches.

Susannah got the start, and kept it.—'Tis Tris—something, cried Susannah—There is no christian-name in the world, said the curate, beginning with Tris—but Tristram. Then 'tis Tristram-gistus, quoth Susannah.

—There is no gistus to it, noddle!—'tis my own name, replied the curate, dipping his hand, as he spoke, into the bason—Tristram! said he, etc. etc. etc. etc., so Tristram was I called, and Tristram shall I be to the day of my death.

My father followed Susannah, with his night-gown across his arm, with nothing more than his breeches on, fastened through haste with but a single button, and that button through haste thrust only half into the button-hole.

CHAP. XIV

—She has not forgot the name? cried my father, half opening the door.—No, no, said the curate, with a tone of intelligence.—And the child is better, cried Susannah. —And how does your mistress? As well, said Susannah, as can be expected.—Pish! said my father, the button of his breeches slipping out of the button-hole—So that whether the interjection was levelled at Susannah, or the button-hole—whether Pish was an interjection of contempt or an interjection of modesty, is a doubt, and must be a doubt till I shall have time to write the three following favourite chapters, that is, my chapter of chamber-maids, my chapter of pishes, and my chapter of button-holes.

All the light I am able to give the reader at present is this, that the moment my father cried Pish! he whisked himself about—and with his breeches held up by one hand, and his night-gown thrown across the arm of the other, he turned along the gallery to bed, something slower than he came.

Chapter XV

I wish I could write a chapter upon sleep.

A fitter occasion could never have presented itself, than what this moment offers, when all the curtains of the family are drawn—the candles put out—and no creature's eyes are open but a single one, for the other has been shut these twenty years, of my mother's nurse.

It is a fine subject!

And yet, as fine as it is, I would undertake to write a

BOOK IV

CHAP. XV

dozen chapters upon button-holes, both quicker and with more fame, than a single chapter upon this.

Button-holes! there is something lively in the very idea of 'em—and trust me, when I get amongst 'em—You gentry with great beards—look as grave as you will——I'll make merry work with my button-holes—I shall have 'em all to myself—'tis a maiden subject—I shall run foul of no man's wisdom or fine sayings in it.

But for sleep—I know I shall make nothing of it before I begin—I am no dab at your fine sayings in the first place—and in the next, I cannot for my soul set a grave face upon a bad matter, and tell the world—'tis the refuge of the unfortunate—the enfranchisement of the prisoner—the downy lap of the hopeless, the weary, and the broken-hearted; nor could I set out with a lie in my mouth, by affirming, that of all the soft and delicious functions of our nature, by which the great Author of it, in his bounty, has been pleased to recompense the sufferings wherewith his justice and his good pleasure has wearied us—that this is the chiefest (I know pleasures worth ten of it); or what a happiness it is to man, when the anxieties and passions of the day are over, and he lies down upon his back, that his soul shall be so seated within him, that whichever way she turns her eyes, the heavens shall look calm and sweet above her—no desire —or fear—or doubt that troubles the air, nor any difficulty past, present, or to come, that the imagination may not pass over without offence, in that sweet secession.

"God's blessing," said Sancho Pança, "be upon the man who first invented this self-same thing called sleep

—it covers a man all over like a cloak." Now there is more to me in this, and it speaks warmer to my heart and affections, than all the dissertations squeezed out of the heads of the learned together upon the subject.

—Not that I altogether disapprove of what Montaigne advances upon it—'tis admirable in its way—(I quote by memory).

The world enjoys other pleasures, says he, as they do that of sleep, without tasting or feeling it as it slips and passes by.—We should study and ruminate upon it, in order to render proper thanks to him who grants it to us. —For this end I cause myself to be disturbed in my sleep, that I may the better and more sensibly relish it. —And yet I see few, says he again, who live with less sleep, when need requires; my body is capable of a firm, but not of a violent and sudden agitation—I evade of late all violent exercises—I am never weary with walking—but from my youth I never liked to ride upon pavements. I love to lie hard and alone, and even without my wife—This last word may stagger the faith of the world—but remember, "La Vraisemblance (as Bayle says in the affair of Liceti) n'est pas toujours du Côté de la Verité." And so much for sleep.

Chapter XVI

If my wife will but venture him—brother Toby, Trismegistus shall be dressed and brought down to us, whilst you and I are getting our breakfasts together.

—Go, tell Susannah, Obadiah, to step here.

CHAP. XVI

She is run up stairs, answered Obadiah, this very instant, sobbing and crying, and wringing her hands as if her heart would break.

We shall have a rare month of it, said my father, turning his head from Obadiah, and looking wistfully in my uncle Toby's face for some time—we shall have a devilish month of it, brother Toby, said my father, setting his arms a-kimbo, and shaking his head; fire, water, women, wind—brother Toby!—'Tis some misfortune, quoth my uncle Toby.—That it is, cried my father—to have so many jarring elements breaking loose, and riding triumph in every corner of a gentleman's house—Little boots it to the peace of a family, brother Toby, that you and I possess ourselves, and sit here silent and unmoved—whilst such a storm is whistling over our heads.——

And what's the matter, Susannah? They have called the child Tristram—and my mistress is just got out of an hysteric fit about it—No!—'tis not my fault, said Susannah—I told him it was Tristram-gistus.

—Make tea for yourself, brother Toby, said my father, taking down his hat—but how different from the sallies and agitations of voice and members which a common reader would imagine!

—For he spake in the sweetest modulation—and took down his hat with the genteelest movement of limbs, that ever affliction harmonized and attuned together.

—Go to the bowling-green for Corporal Trim, said my uncle Toby, speaking to Obadiah, as soon as my father left the room.

Chapter XVII

WHEN the misfortune of my nose fell so heavily upon my father's head;—the reader remembers that he walked instantly up stairs, and cast himself down upon his bed; and from hence, unless he has a great insight into human nature, he will be apt to expect a rotation of the same ascending and descending movements from him, upon this misfortune of my name;—no.

The different weight, dear Sir—nay even the different package of two vexations of the same weight—makes a very wide difference in our manner of bearing and getting through with them.—It is not half an hour ago, when (in the great hurry and precipitation of a poor devil's writing for daily bread) I threw a fair sheet, which I had just finished, and carefully wrote out, slap into the fire, instead of the foul one.

Instantly I snatched off my wig, and threw it perpendicularly, with all imaginable violence, up to the top of the room—indeed I caught it as it fell—but there was an end of the matter; nor do I think any thing else in Nature would have given such immediate ease: She, dear Goddess, by an instantaneous impulse, in all provoking cases, determines us to a sally of this or that member—or else she thrusts us into this or that place, or posture of body, we know not why—But mark, madam, we live amongst riddles and mysteries—the most obvious things, which come in our way, have dark sides, which the quickest sight cannot penetrate into; and even the clearest and most exalted understandings amongst

CHAP. XVII

us find ourselves puzzled and at a loss in almost every cranny of nature's works: so that this, like a thousand other things, falls out for us in a way, which tho' we cannot reason upon it—yet we find the good of it, may it please your reverences and your worships—and that's enough for us.

Now, my father could not lie down with this affliction for his life—nor could he carry it up stairs like the other—he walked composedly out with it to the fishpond.

Had my father leaned his head upon his hand, and reasoned an hour which way to have gone——reason, with all her force, could not have directed him to any thing like it: there is something, Sir, in fish-ponds—but what it is, I leave to system-builders and fish-pond-diggers betwixt 'em to find out—but there is something,

BOOK IV

under the first disorderly transport of the humours, so
unaccountably becalming in an orderly and a sober walk
towards one of them, that I have often wondered that
neither Pythagoras, nor Plato, nor Solon, nor Lycurgus,
nor Mahomet, nor any one of your noted lawgivers, ever
gave order about them.

Chapter XVIII

Your honour, said Trim, shutting the parlour-door before he began to speak, has heard, I imagine, of this
unlucky accident——O yes, Trim, said my uncle Toby,
and it gives me great concern.—I am heartily concerned
too, but I hope your honour, replied Trim, will do me
the justice to believe, that it was not in the least owing
to me.—To thee—Trim?—cried my uncle Toby, looking
kindly in his face——'twas Susannah's and the curate's
folly betwixt them.——What business could they have
together, an' please your honour, in the garden?—In the
gallery thou meanest, replied my uncle Toby.

Trim found he was upon a wrong scent, and stopped
short with a low bow—Two misfortunes, quoth the corporal to himself, are twice as many at least as are needful to be talked over at one time;—the mischief the cow
has done in breaking into the fortifications, may be told
his honour hereafter.—Trim's casuistry and address,
under the cover of his low bow, prevented all suspicion
in my uncle Toby, so he went on with what he had to
say to Trim as follows:

——For my own part, Trim, though I can see little

or no difference betwixt my nephew's being called Tristram or Trismegistus—yet as the thing sits so near my
brother's heart, Trim——I would freely have given a
hundred pounds rather than it should have happened.—
A hundred pounds, an' please your honour! replied Trim,
—I would not give a cherry-stone to boot.—Nor would
I, Trim, upon my own account, quoth my uncle Toby
——but my brother, whom there is no arguing with in
this case—maintains that a great deal more depends,
Trim, upon christian-names, than what ignorant people
imagine—for he says there never was a great or heroic
action performed since the world began by one called
Tristram—nay, he will have it, Trim, that a man can
neither be learned, or wise, or brave.—'Tis all fancy, an'
please your honour—I fought just as well, replied the
corporal, when the regiment called me Trim, as when
they called me James Butler.—And for my own part,
said my uncle Toby, though I should blush to boast of
myself, Trim—yet had my name been Alexander, I
could have done no more at Namur than my duty.—
Bless your honour! cried Trim, advancing three steps as
he spoke, does a man think of his christian-name when
he goes upon the attack?——Or when he stands in the
trench, Trim? cried my uncle Toby, looking firm.—Or
when he enters a breach? said Trim, pushing in between
two chairs.—Or forces the lines? cried my uncle, rising
up, and pushing his crutch like a pike.—Or facing a
platoon? cried Trim, presenting his stick like a firelock.—
Or when he marches up the glacis? cried my uncle Toby,
looking warm and setting his foot upon his stool.——

BOOK IV

Chapter XIX

M Y father was returned from his walk to the fish-pond
—and opened the parlour-door in the very height
of the attack, just as my uncle Toby was marching up the
glacis—Trim recovered his arms—never was my uncle
Toby caught in riding at such a desperate rate in his life!
Alas! my uncle Toby! had not a weightier matter called
forth all the ready eloquence of my father—how hadst
thou then and thy poor Hobby-Horse too been insulted!
My father hung up his hat with the same air he took

CHAP. XIX

it down; and after giving a slight look at the disorder of the room, he took hold of one of the chairs which had formed the corporal's breach, and placing it over-against my uncle Toby, he sat down in it, and as soon as the tea-things were taken away, and the door shut, he broke out in a lamentation as follows.

MY FATHER'S LAMENTATION

It is vain longer, said my father, addressing himself as much to Ernulphus's curse, which was laid upon the corner of the chimney-piece—as to my uncle Toby, who sat under it—it is in vain longer, said my father, in the most querulous monotony imaginable, to struggle as I have done against this most uncomfortable of human persuasions—I see it plainly, that either for my own sins, brother Toby, or the sins and follies of the Shandy family, Heaven has thought fit to draw forth the heaviest of its artillery against me; and that the prosperity of my child is the point upon which the whole force of it is directed to play.——Such a thing would batter the whole universe about our ears, brother Shandy, said my uncle Toby—if it was so—Unhappy Tristram! child of wrath! child of decrepitude! interruption! mistake! and discontent! What one misfortune or disaster in the book of embryotic evils, that could unmechanize thy frame, or entangle thy filaments! which has not fallen upon thy head, or ever thou camest into the world—what evils in thy passage into it!——what evils since!—produced into being, in the decline of thy father's days—when the powers of his imagination and of his body were waxing

feeble—when radical heat and radical moisture, the elements which should have tempered thine, were drying
up; and nothing left to found thy stamina in, but nega-
tions—'tis pitiful——brother Toby, at the best, and
called out for all the little helps that care and attention
on both sides could give it. But how were we defeated!
You know the event, brother Toby—'tis too melancholy
a one to be repeated now—when the few animal spirits
I was worth in the world, and with which memory, fancy,
and quick parts should have been conveyed——were all
dispersed, confused, confounded, scattered, and sent to
the devil.——

Here then was the time to have put a stop to this
persecution against him;——and tried an experiment at
least——whether calmness and serenity of mind in your
sister, with a due attention, brother Toby, to her evacuations and repletions——and the rest of her non-
naturals, might not, in a course of nine months' gesta-
tion, have set all things to rights.——My child was
bereft of these!——What a teazing life did she lead herself, and consequently her foetus too, with that non-
sensical anxiety of hers about lying-in in town! I thought
my sister submitted with the greatest patience, replied
my uncle Toby——I never heard her utter one fretful
word about it.——She fumed inwardly, cried my father;
and that, let me tell you, brother, was ten times worse
for the child—and then! what battles did she fight with
me, and what perpetual storms about the midwife.——
There she gave vent, said my uncle Toby.——Vent!
cried my father, looking up.

CHAP. XIX

But what was all this, my dear Toby, to the injuries done us by my child's coming head foremost into the world, when all I wished, in this general wreck of his frame, was to have saved this little casket unbroke, un-rifled.——

With all my precautions, how was my system turned topside-turvy in the womb with my child! his head exposed to the hand of violence, and a pressure of 470 pounds avoirdupois weight acting so perpendicularly upon its apex—that at this hour 'tis ninety per cent. insurance, that the fine net-work of the intellectual web be not rent and torn to a thousand tatters.

—Still we could have done.—Fool, coxcomb, puppy —give him but a Nose—Cripple, Dwarf, Driveller, Goosecap——(shape him as you will) the door of fortune stands open—O Licetus! Licetus! had I been blest with a foetus five inches long and a half, like thee—Fate might have done her worst.

Still, brother Toby, there was one cast of the die left for our child after all—O Tristram! Tristram! Tristram!

We will send for Mr. Yorick, said my uncle Toby.

—You may send for whom you will, replied my father.

CHAPTER XX

WHAT a rate have I gone on at, curveting and frisking it away, two up and two down for four volumes[1] together, without looking once behind, or even on one side of me, to see whom I trod upon!—I'll tread upon

[1 *i.e.* According to the original editions.]

no one—quoth I to myself when I mounted——I'll take
a good rattling gallop; but I'll not hurt the poorest jack-
ass upon the road.—So off I set—up one lane——down
another, through this turnpike—over that, as if the
arch-jockey of jockeys had got behind me.

Now ride at this rate with what good intention and
resolution you may—'tis a million to one you'll do some
one a mischief, if not yourself——He's flung—he's off—
he's lost his hat—he's down——he'll break his neck—
see!—if he has not galloped full among the scaffolding of
the undertaking critics!—he'll knock his brains out
against some of their posts—he's bounced out!—look—
he's now riding like a mad-cap full tilt through a whole
crowd of painters, fiddlers, poets, biographers, physicians, lawyers, logicians, players, schoolmen, church-
men, statesmen, soldiers, casuists, connoisseurs, prelates,
popes, and engineers—Don't fear, said I—I'll not hurt
the poorest jack-ass upon the king's highway.—But
your horse throws dirt; see you've splashed a bishop—I
hope in God, 'twas only Ernulphus, said I.——But you
have squirted full in the faces of Mess. Le Moyne, De
Romigny, and De Marcilly, doctors of the Sorbonne.
——That was last year, replied I.—But you have trod
this moment upon a king.—Kings have bad times on't,
said I, to be trod upon by such people as me.

You have done it, replied my accuser.

I deny it, quoth I, and so have got off, and here am I
standing with my bridle in one hand, and with my cap in
the other, to tell my story.——And what is it? You shall
hear in the next chapter.

CHAP. XX

Chapter XXI

As Francis the First of France was one winterly night warming himself over the embers of a wood fire, and talking with his first minister of sundry things for the good of the state[1]—It would not be amiss, said the king, stirring up the embers with his cane, if this good understanding betwixt ourselves and Switzerland was a little strengthened.—There is no end, Sire, replied the minister, in giving money to these people—they would swallow up the treasury of France.—Poo! poo! answered the king—there are more ways, Mons. le Premier, of bribing states, besides that of giving money—I'll pay Switzerland the honour of standing godfather for my next child.—Your majesty, said the minister, in so doing, would have all the grammarians in Europe upon your back;—Switzerland, as a republic, being a female, can in no construction be godfather.—She may be godmother, replied Francis hastily—so announce my intentions by a courier to-morrow morning.

I am astonished, said Francis the First, (that day fortnight) speaking to his minister as he entered the closet, that we have had no answer from Switzerland.—Sire, I wait upon you this moment, said Mons. le Premier, to lay before you my dispatches upon that business.—They take it kindly, said the king.—They do, Sire, replied the minister, and have the highest sense of the honour your majesty has done them—but the republic, as godmother, claims her right, in this case, of naming the child.

[1] *Vide* Menagiana, vol. i.

In all reason, quoth the king—she will christen him
Francis, or Henry, or Lewis, or some name that she
knows will be agreeable to us. Your majesty is deceived,
replied the minister—I have this hour received a dispatch from our resident, with the determination of the
republic on that point also.—And what name has the
republic fixed upon for the Dauphin?—Shadrach, Me-
shech, Abed-nego, replied the minister.—By Saint
Peter's girdle, I will have nothing to do with the Swiss,
cried Francis the First, pulling up his breeches and walking hastily across the floor.

Your majesty, replied the minister calmly, cannot
bring yourself off.

We'll pay them in money——said the king.

Sire, there are not sixty thousand crowns in the
treasury, answered the minister.—I'll pawn the best
jewel in my crown, quoth Francis the First.

Your honour stands pawned already in this matter,
answered Monsieur le Premier.

Then, Mons. le Premier, said the king, by——we'll
go to war with 'em.

CHAPTER XXII

ALBEIT, gentle reader, I have lusted earnestly, and en-
deavoured carefully (according to the measure of
such a slender skill as God has vouchsafed me, and as convenient leisure from other occasions of needful profit and
healthful pastime have permitted) that these little books
which I here put into thy hands, might stand instead of

many bigger books—yet have I carried myself towards
thee in such fanciful guise of careless disport, that right
sore am I ashamed now to intreat thy lenity seriously
——in beseeching thee to believe it of me, that in the
story of my father and his christian-names—I have no
thoughts of treading upon Francis the First—nor in the
affair of the nose—upon Francis the Ninth—nor in the
character of my uncle Toby—of characterizing the mili-
tiating spirits of my country—the wound upon his groin,
is a wound to every comparison of that kind—nor by
Trim—that I meant the Duke of Ormond—or that my
book is wrote against predestination, or free-will, or
taxes—If 'tis wrote against any thing,—'tis wrote, an'
please your worships, against the spleen! in order, by a
more frequent and a more convulsive elevation and depression of the diaphragm, and the succussations of the
intercostal and abdominal muscles in laughter, to drive
the gall and other bitter juices from the gall-bladder,
liver, and sweet-bread of his majesty's subjects, with all
the inimicitious passions which belong to them, down
into their duodenums.

Chapter XXIII

—But can the thing be undone, Yorick? said my father
—for in my opinion, continued he, it cannot. I am
a vile canonist, replied Yorick—but of all evils, holding
suspense to be the most tormenting, we shall at least know
the worst of this matter. I hate these great dinners—
said my father—The size of the dinner is not the point,

answered Yorick—we want, Mr. Shandy, to dive into the bottom of this doubt, whether the name can be changed or not—and as the beards of so many commissaries, officials, advocates, proctors, registers, and of the most eminent of our school-divines, and others, are all to meet in the middle of one table, and Didius has so pressingly invited you—who in your distress would miss such an occasion? All that is requisite, continued Yorick, is to apprise Didius, and let him manage a conversation after dinner so as to introduce the subject.—Then my brother Toby, cried my father, clapping his two hands together, shall go with us.

—Let my old tie-wig, quoth my uncle Toby, and my laced regimentals, be hung to the fire all night, Trim.

CHAP. XXIII

Chapter XXV

—No doubt, Sir,—there is a whole chapter wanting here—and a chasm of ten pages made in the book by it—but the book-binder is neither a fool, or a knave, or a puppy—nor is the book a jot more imperfect (at least upon that score)—but, on the contrary, the book is more perfect and complete by wanting the chapter, than having it, as I shall demonstrate to your reverences in this manner.—I question first, by the bye, whether the same experiment might not be made as successfully upon sundry other chapters——but there is no end, an' please your reverences, in trying experiments upon chapters——we have had enough of it—So there's an end of that matter.

But before I begin my demonstration, let me only tell you, that the chapter which I have torn out, and which otherwise you would all have been reading just now, instead of this—was the description of my father's, my uncle Toby's, Trim's, and Obadiah's setting out and journeying to the visitation at ****.

We'll go in the coach, said my father—Prithee, have the arms been altered, Obadiah?—It would have made my story much better to have begun with telling you, that at the time my mother's arms were added to the Shandys', when the coach was re-painted upon my father's marriage, it had so fallen out, that the coach-painter, whether by performing all his works with the left-hand, like Turpilius the Roman, or Hans Holbein of

Basil—or whether 'twas more from the blunder of his head than hand—or whether, lastly, it was from the sinister turn which every thing relating to our family was apt to take—it so fell out, however, to our reproach, that instead of the bend-dexter, which since Harry the Eighth's reign was honestly our due——a bend-sinister, by some of these fatalities, had been drawn quite across the field of the Shandy arms. 'Tis scarce credible that the mind of so wise a man as my father was, could be so much incommoded with so small a matter. The word coach—let it be whose it would—or coach-man, or coach-horse, or coach-hire, could never be named in the family, but he constantly complained of carrying this vile mark of illegitimacy upon the door of his own; he never once was able to step into the coach, or out of it, without turning round to take a view of the arms, and making a vow at the same time, that it was the last time he would ever set his foot in it again, till the bend-sinister was taken out—but like the affair of the hinge, it was one of the many things which the Destinies had set down in their books ever to be grumbled at (and in wiser families than ours)—but never to be mended.

—Has the bend-sinister been brushed out, I say? said my father.—There has been nothing brushed out, Sir, answered Obadiah, but the lining. We'll go o' horseback, said my father, turning to Yorick.—Of all things in the world, except politics, the clergy know the least of heraldry, said Yorick.—No matter for that, cried my father—I should be sorry to appear with a blot in my escutcheon before them.—Never mind the bend-sinister,

CHAP. XXV

said my uncle Toby, putting on his tie-wig.—No, indeed, said my father—you may go with my aunt Dinah to a visitation with a bend-sinister, if you think fit—My poor uncle Toby blushed. My father was vexed at himself.——No—my dear brother Toby, said my father, changing his tone—but the damp of the coach-lining about my loins, may give me the sciatica again, as it did December, January, and February last winter—so if you please you shall ride my wife's pad—and as you are to preach, Yorick, you had better make the best of your way before—and leave me to take care of my brother Toby, and to follow at our own rates.

Now the chapter I was obliged to tear out, was the description of this cavalcade, in which Corporal Trim and Obadiah, upon two coach-horses a-breast, led the way as slow as a patrole—whilst my uncle Toby, in his laced regimentals and tie-wig, kept his rank with my father, in deep roads and dissertations alternately upon the advantage of learning and arms, as each could get the start.

—But the painting of this journey, upon reviewing it, appears to be so much above the style and manner of any thing else I have been able to paint in this book, that it could not have remained in it, without depreciating every other scene; and destroying at the same time that necessary equipoise and balance, (whether of good or bad) betwixt chapter and chapter, from whence the just proportions and harmony of the whole work results. For my own part, I am but just set up in the business, so know little about it—but, in my opinion, to write a book is for all the world like humming a song—be but in tune with yourself, madam, 'tis no matter how high or how low you take it.

—This is the reason, may it please your reverences, that some of the lowest and flattest compositions pass off very well—(as Yorick told my uncle Toby one night)— by siege.—My uncle Toby looked brisk at the sound of the word siege, but could make neither head or tail of it.

I'm to preach at court next Sunday, said Homenas— run over my notes—so I hummed over doctor Homenas's notes—the modulation's very well—'twill do, Homenas, if it holds on at this rate—so on I hummed—and a tolerable tune I thought it was; and to this hour, may it please your reverences, had never found out how low, how flat, how spiritless and jejune it was, but that all of a sudden, up started an air in the middle of it, so fine, so rich, so heavenly,—it carried my soul up with it into the other world; now had I (as Montaigne complained in a parallel accident)—had I found the declivity easy, or the ascent accessible——certes I had been outwitted.

——Your notes, Homenas, I should have said, are good notes;—but it was so perpendicular a precipice—so wholly cut off from the rest of the work, that by the first note I hummed I found myself flying into the other world, and from thence discovered the vale from whence I came, so deep, so low, and dismal, that I shall never have the heart to descend into it again.

☞ A dwarf who brings a standard along with him to measure his own size—take my word, is a dwarf in

CHAP. XXV

more articles than one.—And so much for tearing out of chapters.

CHAPTER XXVI

—SEE if he is not cutting it into slips, and giving them about him to light their pipes!—'Tis abominable, answered Didius; it should not go unnoticed, said doctor Kysarcius——☞ he was of the Kysarcii of the Low Countries.

Methinks, said Didius, half rising from his chair, in order to remove a bottle and a tall decanter, which stood in a direct line betwixt him and Yorick—you might have spared this sarcastic stroke, and have hit upon a more proper place, Mr. Yorick—or at least upon a more proper occasion to have shewn your contempt of what we have been about: If the sermon is of no better worth than to light pipes with—'twas certainly, Sir, not good enough to be preached before so learned a body; and if 'twas good enough to be preached before so learned a body—'twas certainly, Sir, too good to light their pipes with afterwards.

—I have got him fast hung up, quoth Didius to himself, upon one of the two horns of my dilemma—let him get off as he can.

I have undergone such unspeakable torments, in bringing forth this sermon, quoth Yorick, upon this occasion——that I declare, Didius, I would suffer martyrdom—and if it was possible my horse with me, a thousand times over, before I would sit down and make such

another: I was delivered of it at the wrong end of me—
it came from my head instead of my heart——and it is
for the pain it gave me, both in the writing and the
preaching of it, that I revenge myself of it, in this
manner—To preach, to shew the extent of our reading,
or the subtleties of our wit—to parade in the eyes of the
vulgar with the beggarly accounts of a little learning,
tinselled over with a few words which glitter, but convey
little light and less warmth—is a dishonest use of the
poor single half hour in a week which is put into our
hands—'Tis not preaching the gospel—but ourselves—
For my own part, continued Yorick, I had rather direct
five words point-blank to the heart.—

As Yorick pronounced the word point-blank, my
uncle Toby rose up to say something upon projectiles—
when a single word and no more uttered from the opposite side of the table drew every one's ears towards it—a
word of all others in the dictionary the last in that place
to be expected—a word I am ashamed to write—yet
must be written—must be read—illegal—uncanonical—
guess ten thousand guesses, multiplied into themselves
—rack—torture your invention for ever, you're where
you was——In short, I'll tell it in the next chapter.

CHAP. XXVI

Chapter XXVII

Z OUNDS! ——————————————————

————Z——ds! cried Phutatorius, partly to himself
—and yet high enough to be heard—and what seemed
odd, 'twas uttered in a construction of look, and in a
tone of voice, somewhat between that of a man in
amazement and one in bodily pain.

One or two who had very nice ears, and could distinguish the expression and mixture of the two tones as
plainly as a third or a fifth, or any other chord in music
—were the most puzzled and perplexed with it—the
concord was good in itself—but then 'twas quite out of
the key, and no way applicable to the subject started;—
so that with all their knowledge, they could not tell what
in the world to make of it.

Others who knew nothing of musical expression, and
merely lent their ears to the plain import of the word,
imagined that Phutatorius, who was somewhat of a
choleric spirit, was just going to snatch the cudgels out
of Didius's hands, in order to bemaul Yorick to some
purpose—and that the desperate monosyllable Z——ds
was the exordium to an oration, which, as they judged
from the sample, presaged but a rough kind of handling
of him; so that my uncle Toby's good-nature felt a pang
for what Yorick was about to undergo. But seeing
Phutatorius stop short, without any attempt or desire to
go on—a third party began to suppose, that it was no
more than an involuntary respiration, casually forming

CHAP. XXVII

itself into the shape of a twelve-penny oath—without the sin or substance of one.

Others, and especially one or two who sat next him, looked upon it on the contrary as a real and substantial oath, propensely formed against Yorick, to whom he was known to bear no good liking—which said oath, as my father philosophized upon it, actually lay fretting and fuming at that very time in the upper regions of Phutatorius's purtenance; and so was naturally, and according to the due course of things, first squeezed out by the sudden influx of blood which was driven into the right ventricle of Phutatorius's heart, by the stroke of surprise which so strange a theory of preaching had excited.

How finely we argue upon mistaken facts!

There was not a soul busied in all these various reasonings upon the monosyllable which Phutatorius uttered—who did not take this for granted, proceeding upon it as from an axiom, namely, that Phutatorius's mind was intent upon the subject of debate which was arising between Didius and Yorick; and indeed as he looked first towards the one and then towards the other, with the air of a man listening to what was going forwards—who would not have thought the same? But the truth was, that Phutatorius knew not one word or one syllable of what was passing—but his whole thoughts and attention were taken up with a transaction which was going forwards at that very instant within the precincts of his own Galligaskins, and in a part of them, where of all others he stood most interested to watch accidents: So that notwithstanding he looked with all the attention in the world, and had gradually screwed up every nerve and muscle in his face, to the utmost pitch the instrument would bear, in order, as it was thought, to give a sharp reply to Yorick, who sat over-against him—yet, I say, was Yorick never once in any one domicile of Phutatorius's brain—but the true cause of his exclamation lay at least a yard below.

This I will endeavour to explain to you with all imaginable decency.

You must be informed then, that Gastripheres, who had taken a turn into the kitchen a little before dinner, to see how things went on—observing a wicker-basket of fine chestnuts standing upon the dresser, had ordered that a hundred or two of them might be roasted and sent in, as soon as dinner was over—Gastripheres inforcing his orders about them, that Didius, but Phutatorius especially, were particularly fond of 'em.

About two minutes before the time that my uncle Toby interrupted Yorick's harangue—Gastripheres's chestnuts were brought in—and as Phutatorius's fondness for 'em was uppermost in the waiter's head, he laid them directly before Phutatorius, wrapt up hot in a clean damask napkin.

Now whether it was physically impossible, with half a dozen hands all thrust into the napkin at a time—but that some one chestnut, of more life and rotundity than the rest, must be put in motion—it so fell out, however, that one was actually sent rolling off the table; and as Phutatorius sat straddling under—it fell perpendicularly into that particular aperture of Phutatorius's breeches,

CHAP. XXVII

for which, to the shame and indelicacy of our language be it spoke, there is no chaste word throughout all Johnson's dictionary—let it suffice to say—it was that particular aperture which, in all good societies, the laws of decorum do strictly require, like the temple of Janus (in peace at least) to be universally shut up.

The neglect of this punctilio in Phutatorius (which by the bye should be a warning to all mankind) had opened a door to this accident.—

Accident I call it, in compliance to a received mode of speaking——but in no opposition to the opinion either of Acrites or Mythogeras in this matter; I know they were both prepossessed and fully persuaded of it—and are so to this hour, That there was nothing of accident in the whole event—but that the chestnut's taking that particular course, and in a manner of its own accord—and then falling with all its heat directly into that one particular place, and no other—was a real judgment upon Phutatorius, for that filthy and obscene treatise *de Concubinis retinendis*, which Phutatorius had published about twenty years ago—and was that identical week going to give the world a second edition of.

It is not my business to dip my pen in this contro-versy—much undoubtedly may be wrote on both sides of the question—all that concerns me as a historian, is to represent the matter of fact, and render it credible to the reader, that the hiatus in Phutatorius's breeches was sufficiently wide to receive the chestnut;—and that the chestnut, somehow or other, did fall perpendicularly and piping hot into it, without Phutatorius's perceiving it, or any one else at that time.   BOOK IV

The genial warmth which the chestnut imparted, was not undelectable for the first twenty or five-and-twenty seconds—and did no more than gently solicit Phutatorius's attention towards the part:——But the heat gradually increasing, and in a few seconds more getting beyond the point of all sober pleasure, and then advancing with all speed into the regions of pain, the soul of Phutatorius, together with all his ideas, his thoughts, his attention, his imagination, judgment, resolution, deliberation, ratiocination, memory, fancy, with ten battalions of animal spirits, all tumultuously crowded down, through different defiles and circuits, to the place of danger, leaving all his upper regions, as you may imagine, as empty as my purse.

With the best intelligence which all these messengers could bring him back, Phutatorius was not able to dive into the secret of what was going forwards below, nor could he make any kind of conjecture, what the devil was the matter with it: However, as he knew not what the true cause might turn out, he deemed it most prudent, in the situation he was in at present, to bear it, if possible, like a Stoic; which, with the help of some wry faces and compursions of the mouth, he had certainly accomplished, had his imagination continued neuter;— but the sallies of the imagination are ungovernable in things of this kind—a thought instantly darted into his mind, that tho' the anguish had the sensation of glowing heat—it might, notwithstanding that, be a bite as well as a burn; and if so, that possibly a newt or an asker, or some such detested reptile, had crept up, and was fasten-

CHAP. XXVII

ing his teeth—the horrid idea of which, with a fresh glow of pain arising that instant from the chestnut, seized Phutatorius with a sudden panic, and in the first terrifying disorder of the passion, it threw him, as it has done the best generals upon earth, quite off his guard:—the effect of which was this, that he leapt incontinently up, uttering as he rose that interjection of surprise so much descanted upon, with the aposiopestic break after it, marked thus, Z——ds—which, though not strictly canonical, was still as little as any man could have said upon the occasion;——and which, by the bye, whether canonical or not, Phutatorius could no more help than he could the cause of it.

Though this has taken up some time in the narrative, it took up little more time in the transaction, than just to allow time for Phutatorius to draw forth the chestnut, and throw it down with violence upon the floor—and for Yorick to rise from his chair, and pick the chestnut up.

It is curious to observe the triumph of slight incidents over the mind:—What incredible weight they have in forming and governing our opinions, both of men and things—that trifles, light as air, shall waft a belief into the soul, and plant it so immoveably within it—that Euclid's demonstrations, could they be brought to batter it in breach, should not all have power to overthrow it.

Yorick, I said, picked up the chestnut which Phutatorius's wrath had flung down—the action was trifling—I am ashamed to account for it—he did it, for no reason, but that he thought the chestnut not a jot worse for the adventure—and that he held a good chestnut worth

BOOK IV

stooping for.——But this incident, trifling as it was, wrought differently in Phutatorius's head: He considered this act of Yorick's in getting off his chair and picking up the chestnut, as a plain acknowledgment in him, that the chestnut was originally his—and in course, that it must have been the owner of the chestnut, and no one else, who could have played him such a prank with it: What greatly confirmed him in this opinion, was this, that the table being parallelogramical and very narrow, it afforded a fair opportunity for Yorick, who sat directly over against Phutatorius, of slipping the chestnut in— and consequently that he did it. The look of something more than suspicion, which Phutatorius cast full upon Yorick as these thoughts arose, too evidently spoke his opinion—and as Phutatorius was naturally supposed to know more of the matter than any person besides, his opinion at once became the general one;—and for a reason very different from any which have been yet given—in a little time it was put out of all manner of dispute.

When great or unexpected events fall out upon the stage of this sublunary world—the mind of man, which is an inquisitive kind of a substance, naturally takes a flight behind the scenes to see what is the cause and first spring of them.—The search was not long in this instance.

It was well known that Yorick had never a good opinion of the treatise which Phutatorius had wrote *de Concubinis retinendis*, as a thing which he feared had done hurt in the world—and 'twas easily found out, that

CHAP. XXVII

there was a mystical meaning in Yorick's prank—and
that his chucking the chestnut hot into Phutatorius's
—**, was a sarcastical fling at his book—the doctrines of which, they said, had enflamed many an honest
man in the same place.

This conceit awakened Somnolentus—made Agelastes
smile—and if you can recollect the precise look and air
of a man's face intent in finding out a riddle——it threw
Gastripheres's into that form—and in short was thought
by many to be a master-stroke of arch-wit.

This, as the reader has seen from one end to the
other, was as groundless as the dreams of philosophy:
Yorick, no doubt, as Shakespeare said of his ancestor
——"was a man of jest," but it was tempered with something which withheld him from that, and many other
ungracious pranks, of which he as undeservedly bore the
blame;—but it was his misfortune all his life long to bear
the imputation of saying and doing a thousand things,
of which (unless my esteem blinds me) his nature was
incapable. All I blame him for—or rather, all I blame
and alternately like him for, was that singularity of his
temper, which would never suffer him to take pains to
set a story right with the world, however in his power.
In every ill usage of that sort, he acted precisely as in
the affair of his lean horse——he could have explained it
to his honour, but his spirit was above it; and besides, he
ever looked upon the inventor, the propagator and be-
liever of an illiberal report alike so injurious to him—he
could not stoop to tell his story to them—and so trusted
to time and truth to do it for him.

BOOK IV

This heroic cast produced him inconveniences in many respects—in the present it was followed by the fixed resentment of Phutatorius, who, as Yorick had just made an end of his chestnut, rose up from his chair a second time, to let him know it—which indeed he did with a smile; saying only—that he would endeavour not to forget the obligation.

But you must mark and carefully separate and distinguish these two things in your mind.

—The smile was for the company.

—The threat was for Yorick.

Chapter XXVIII

—CAN you tell me, quoth Phutatorius, speaking to Gastripheres who sat next to him—for one would not apply to a surgeon in so foolish an affair—can you tell me, Gastripheres, what is best to take out the fire?— Ask Eugenius, said Gastripheres.—That greatly depends, said Eugenius, pretending ignorance of the adventure, upon the nature of the part—If it is a tender part, and a part which can conveniently be wrapt up ——It is both the one and the other, replied Phutatorius, laying his hand as he spoke, with an emphatical nod of his head, upon the part in question, and lifting up his right leg at the same time to ease and ventilate it. ——If that is the case, said Eugenius, I would advise you, Phutatorius, not to tamper with it by any means; but if you will send to the next printer, and trust your cure to such a simple thing as a soft sheet of paper just come off the press—you need do nothing more than twist it round.—The damp paper, quoth Yorick (who sat next to his friend Eugenius) though I know it has a refreshing coolness in it—yet I presume is no more than the vehicle—and that the oil and lamp-black with which the paper is so strongly impregnated, does the business. —Right, said Eugenius, and is, of any outward application I would venture to recommend, the most anodyne and safe.

Was it my case, said Gastripheres, as the main thing is the oil and lamp-black, I should spread them thick upon a rag, and clap it on directly.——That would make a very devil of it, replied Yorick.—And besides, added Eugenius, it would not answer the intention, which is the extreme neatness and elegance of the prescription, which the Faculty hold to be half in half;—for consider, if the type is a very small one (which it should be) the sanative particles, which come into contact in this form, have the advantage of being spread so infinitely thin, and with such a mathematical equality (fresh paragraphs and large capitals excepted) as no art or management of the spatula can come up to.——It falls out very luckily, replied Phutatorius, that the second edition of my treatise *de Concubinis retinendis* is at this instant in the press.——You may take any leaf of it, said Eugenius——no matter which.—Provided, quoth Yorick, there is no bawdry in it.——

They are just now, replied Phutatorius, printing off the ninth chapter—which is the last chapter but one in the book.—Pray what is the title of that chapter? said

Yorick; making a respectful bow to Phutatorius as he spoke.——I think, answered Phutatorius, 'tis that *de re concubinariâ*.

For Heaven's sake keep out of that chapter, quoth Yorick.

—By all means—added Eugenius.

CHAPTER XXIX

—Now, quoth Didius, rising up, and laying his right hand with his fingers spread upon his breast—had such a blunder about a christian-name happened before the Reformation——[It happened the day before yesterday, quoth my uncle Toby to himself] and when baptism was administered in Latin—['Twas all in English, said my uncle]——many things might have coincided with it, and upon the authority of sundry decreed cases, to have pronounced the baptism null, with a power of giving the child a new name—Had a priest, for instance, which was no uncommon thing, through ignorance of the Latin tongue, baptized a child of Tom o' Stiles, *in nomine patriae & filia & spiritum sanctos*—the baptism was held null.—I beg your pardon, replied Kysarcius—in that case, as the mistake was only the terminations, the baptism was valid—and to have rendered it null, the blunder of the priest should have fallen upon the first syllable of each noun——and not, as in your case, upon the last.

My father delighted in subtleties of this kind, and listened with infinite attention.

Gastripheres, for example, continued Kysarcius, baptizes a child of John Stradling's in *Gomine* gatris, etc. etc., instead of *in Nomine* patris, etc.—is this a baptism? No—say the ablest canonists; inasmuch as the radix of each word is hereby torn up, and the sense and meaning of them removed and changed quite to another object; for *Gomine* does not signify a name, nor *gatris* a father. —What do they signify? said my uncle Toby.—Nothing at all——quoth Yorick.—Ergo, such a baptism is null, said Kysarcius.—

In course, answered Yorick, in a tone two parts jest and one part earnest.—

But in the case cited, continued Kysarcius, where *patriae* is put for *patris*, *filia* for *filii*, and so on—as it is a fault only in the declension, and the roots of the words continue untouched, the inflections of their branches either this way or that, does not in any sort hinder the baptism, inasmuch as the same sense continues in the words as before.—But then, said Didius, the intention of the priest's pronouncing them grammatically must have been proved to have gone along with it.——Right, answered Kysarcius; and of this, brother Didius, we have an instance in a decree of the decretals of Pope Leo the IIId.—But my brother's child, cried my uncle Toby, has nothing to do with the Pope——'tis the plain child of a Protestant gentleman, christened Tristram against the wills and wishes both of his father and mother, and all who are a-kin to it.—

If the wills and wishes, said Kysarcius, interrupting my uncle Toby, of those only who stand related to Mr. Shandy's child, were to have weight in this matter, Mrs.

Shandy, of all people, has the least to do in it.—My uncle Toby laid down his pipe, and my father drew his chair still closer to the table, to hear the conclusion of so strange an introduction.

—It has not only been a question, Captain Shandy, amongst the[1] best lawyers and civilians in this land, continued Kysarcius, "Whether the mother be of kin to her child,"—but, after much dispassionate enquiry and jactitation of the arguments on all sides—it has been adjudged for the negative—namely, "That the mother is not of kin to her child."[2] My father instantly clapped his hand upon my uncle Toby's mouth, under colour of whispering in his ear;—the truth was, he was alarmed for *Lillabullero*—and having a great desire to hear more of so curious an argument—he begged my uncle Toby, for Heaven's sake, not to disappoint him in it.—My uncle Toby gave a nod—resumed his pipe, and contenting himself with whistling *Lillabullero* inwardly—Kysarcius, Didius, and Triptolemus went on with the discourse as follows.

This determination, continued Kysarcius, how contrary soever it may seem to run to the stream of vulgar ideas, yet had reason strongly on its side; and has been put out of all manner of dispute from the famous case, known commonly by the name of the Duke of Suffolk's case.——It is cited in Brook, said Triptolemus——And taken notice of by Lord Coke, added Didius.—And you may find it in Swinburn on Testaments, said Kysarcius.

[1] *Vide* Swinburn on Testaments, Part 7, § 8.
[2] *Vide* Brook, Abridg. Tit. Administr. N. 47.

CHAP. XXIX

The case, Mr. Shandy, was this.

In the reign of Edward the Sixth, Charles duke of Suffolk having issue a son by one venter, and a daughter by another venter, made his last will, wherein he devised goods to his son, and died; after whose death the son died also—but without will, without wife, and without child—his mother and his sister by the father's side (for she was born of the former venter) then living. The mother took the administration of her son's goods, according to the statute of the 21st of Harry the Eighth, whereby it is enacted, That in case any person die intestate, the administration of his goods shall be committed to the next of kin.

The administration being thus (surreptitiously) granted to the mother, the sister by the father's side commenced a suit before the Ecclesiastical Judge, alleging, 1st, That she herself was next of kin; and 2ndly, That the mother was not of kin at all to the party deceased; and therefore prayed the court, that the administration granted to the mother might be revoked, and be committed unto her, as next of kin to the deceased, by force of the said statute.

Hereupon, as it was a great cause, and much depending upon its issue—and many causes of great property likely to be decided in times to come, by the precedent to be then made—the most learned, as well in the laws of this realm, as in the civil law, were consulted together, whether the mother was of kin to her son, or no.—Whereunto not only the temporal lawyers—but the church lawyers—the juris-consulti—the juris-prudents

—the civilians—the advocates—the commissaries—the judges of the consistory and prerogative courts of Canterbury and York, with the master of the faculties, were all unanimously of opinion, That the mother was not of[1] kin to her child.—

And what said the duchess of Suffolk to it? said my uncle Toby.

The unexpectedness of my uncle Toby's question, confounded Kysarcius more than the ablest advocate— He stopped a full minute, looking in my uncle Toby's face without replying—and in that single minute Triptolemus put by him, and took the lead as follows.

'Tis a ground and principle in the law, said Triptolemus, that things do not ascend, but descend in it; and I make no doubt 'tis for this cause, that however true it is, that the child may be of the blood and seed of its parents—that the parents, nevertheless, are not of the blood and seed of it; inasmuch as the parents are not begot by the child, but the child by the parents—For so they write, *Liberi sunt de sanguine patris & matris, sed pater & mater non sunt de sanguine liberorum.*

—But this, Triptolemus, cried Didius, proves too much—for from this authority cited it would follow, not only what indeed is granted on all sides, that the mother is not of kin to her child—but the father likewise.—It is held, said Triptolemus, the better opinion; because the father, the mother, and the child, though they be three persons, yet are they but (*una caro*[2]) one flesh; and con-

---

[1] Mater non numeratur inter consanguineos, Bald. in ult. C. de Verb. signific.

[2] *Vide* Brook, Abridg. Tit. Administr. N. 47.

CHAP. XXIX

sequently no degree of kindred—or any method of ac-
quiring one in nature.—There you push the argument
again too far, cried Didius—for there is no prohibition
in nature, though there is in the Levitical law—but that
a man may beget a child upon his grandmother—in
which case, supposing the issue a daughter, she would
stand in relation both of—But who ever thought, cried
Kysarcius, of lying with his grandmother?——The
young gentleman, replied Yorick, whom Selden speaks
of—who not only thought of it, but justified his intention to his father by the argument drawn from the law
of retaliation.—"You lay, Sir, with my mother," said
the lad—"why may not I lie with yours?"—'Tis the
Argumentum commune, added Yorick.—'Tis as good,
replied Eugenius, taking down his hat, as they deserve.

The company broke up.

Chapter XXX

—And pray, said my uncle Toby, leaning upon Yorick,
as he and my father were helping him leisurely
down the stairs—don't be terrified, madam, this stair-
case conversation is not so long as the last—And pray,
Yorick, said my uncle Toby, which way is this said affair
of Tristram at length settled by these learned men? Very
satisfactorily, replied Yorick; no mortal, Sir, has any concern with it—for Mrs. Shandy the mother is nothing at
all a-kin to him—and as the mother's is the surest side—
Mr. Shandy, in course, is still less than nothing——In
short, he is not as much a-kin to him, Sir, as I am.—

————That may well be, said my father, shaking his head.

————Let the learned say what they will, there must certainly, quoth my uncle Toby, have been some sort of consanguinity betwixt the duchess of Suffolk and her son.

The vulgar are of the same opinion, quoth Yorick, to this hour.

Chapter XXXI

Though my father was hugely tickled with the subtleties of these learned discourses——'twas still but like the anointing of a broken bone——The moment he got home, the weight of his afflictions returned upon him but so much the heavier, as is ever the case when the staff we lean on slips from under us.—He became pensive —walked frequently forth to the fish-pond—let down one loop of his hat—sighed often—forbore to snap—and, as the hasty sparks of temper, which occasion snapping, so much assist perspiration and digestion, as Hippocrates tells us—he had certainly fallen ill with the extinction of them, had not his thoughts been critically drawn off, and his health rescued by a fresh train of disquietudes left him, with a legacy of a thousand pounds, by my aunt Dinah.

My father had scarce read the letter, when taking the thing by the right end, he instantly began to plague and puzzle his head how to lay it out mostly to the honour of his family.—A hundred-and-fifty odd projects took possession of his brains by turns—he would do this, and that, and t'other—He would go to Rome—he would go to law—he would buy stock—he would buy John Hobson's farm—he would new forefront his house, and add a new wing to make it even—There was a fine water-mill on this side, and he would build a wind-mill on the other side of the river in full view to answer it— But above all things in the world, he would enclose the great Ox-moor, and send out my brother Bobby immediately upon his travels.

But as the sum was finite, and consequently could not do every thing—and in truth very few of these to any purpose—of all the projects which offered themselves upon this occasion, the two last seemed to make the deepest impression; and he would infallibly have determined upon both at once, but for the small inconvenience hinted at above, which absolutely put him under a necessity of deciding in favour either of the one or the other.

This was not altogether so easy to be done; for though 'tis certain my father had long before set his heart upon this necessary part of my brother's education, and like a prudent man had actually determined to carry it into execution, with the first money that returned from the second creation of actions in the Mississippi-scheme, in which he was an adventurer—yet the Ox-moor, which was a fine, large, whinny, undrained, unimproved common, belonging to the Shandy-estate, had almost as old a claim upon him: he had long and affectionately set his heart upon turning it likewise to some account.

But having never hitherto been pressed with such a conjuncture of things, as made it necessary to settle either the priority or justice of their claims—like a wise man he had refrained entering into any nice or critical examination about them: so that upon the dismission of every other project at this crisis——the two old projects, the Ox-moor and my Brother, divided him again; and so equal a match were they for each other, as to become the occasion of no small contest in the old gentleman's mind—which of the two should be set o'going first.

—People may laugh as they will—but the case was this.

It had ever been the custom of the family, and by length of time was almost become a matter of common right, that the eldest son of it should have free ingress, egress, and regress into foreign parts before marriage—not only for the sake of bettering his own private parts, by the benefit of exercise and change of so much air—but simply for the mere delectation of his fancy, by the feather put into his cap, of having been abroad—*tantum valet*, my father would say, *quantum sonat*.

Now as this was a reasonable, and in course a most christian indulgence—to deprive him of it, without why or wherefore—and thereby make an example of him, as the first Shandy unwhirled about Europe in a post-chaise, and only because he was a heavy lad—would be using him ten times worse than a Turk.

On the other hand, the case of the Ox-moor was full as hard.

Exclusive of the original purchase-money, which was eight hundred pounds—it had cost the family eight hun-

CHAP. XXXI

dred pounds more in a law-suit about fifteen years before —besides the Lord knows what trouble and vexation.

It had been moreover in possession of the Shandy-family ever since the middle of the last century; and though it lay full in view before the house, bounded on one extremity by the water-mill, and on the other by the projected wind-mill spoken of above—and for all these reasons seemed to have the fairest title of any part of the estate to the care and protection of the family—yet by an unaccountable fatality, common to men, as well as the ground they tread on—it had all along most shamefully been overlooked; and to speak the truth of it, had suffered so much by it, that it would have made any man's heart have bled (Obadiah said) who understood the value of the land, to have rode over it, and only seen the condition it was in.

However, as neither the purchasing this tract of ground—nor indeed the placing of it where it lay, were either of them, properly speaking, of my father's doing —he had never thought himself any way concerned in the affair——till the fifteen years before, when the breaking out of that cursed law-suit mentioned above (and which had arose about its boundaries)——which being altogether my father's own act and deed, it naturally awakened every other argument in its favour, and upon summing them all up together, he saw, not merely in interest, but in honour, he was bound to do something for it—and that now or never was the time.

I think there must certainly have been a mixture of ill-luck in it, that the reasons on both sides should happen to be so equally balanced by each other; for though my father weighed them in all humours and conditions——spent many an anxious hour in the most profound and abstracted meditation upon what was best to be done—reading books of farming one day——books of travels another—laying aside all passion whatever—viewing the arguments on both sides in all their lights and circumstances—communing every day with my uncle Toby—arguing with Yorick, and talking over the whole affair of the Ox-moor with Obadiah——yet nothing in all that time appeared so strongly in behalf of the one, which was not either strictly applicable to the other, or at least so far counterbalanced by some consideration of equal weight, as to keep the scales even.

For to be sure, with proper helps, and in the hands of some people, tho' the Ox-moor would undoubtedly have made a different appearance in the world from what it did, or ever could do in the condition it lay—yet every tittle of this was true, with regard to my brother Bobby —let Obadiah say what he would.——

In point of interest—the contest, I own, at first sight, did not appear so undecisive betwixt them; for whenever my father took pen and ink in hand, and set about calculating the simple expense of paring and burning, and fencing in the Ox-moor, etc. etc.—with the certain profit it would bring him in return—the latter turned out so prodigiously in his way of working the account, that you would have sworn the Ox-moor would have carried all before it. For it was plain he should reap a hundred lasts of rape, at twenty pounds a last, the very

CHAP. XXXI

first year—besides an excellent crop of wheat the year following—and the year after that, to speak within bounds, a hundred—but in all likelihood, a hundred and fifty——if not two hundred quarters of pease and beans —besides potatoes without end.—But then, to think he was all this while breeding up my brother, like a hog to eat them—knocked all on the head again, and generally left the old gentleman in such a state of suspense—that, as he often declared to my uncle Toby—he knew no more than his heels what to do.

No body, but he who has felt it, can conceive what a plaguing thing it is to have a man's mind torn asunder by two projects of equal strength, both obstinately pulling in a contrary direction at the same time: for to say nothing of the havoc, which by a certain consequence is unavoidably made by it all over the finer system of the nerves, which you know convey the animal spirits and more subtle juices from the heart to the head, and so on —it is not to be told in what a degree such a wayward kind of friction works upon the more gross and solid parts, wasting the fat and impairing the strength of a man every time as it goes backwards and forwards.

My father had certainly sunk under this evil, as certainly as he had done under that of my Christian name —had he not been rescued out of it, as he was out of that, by a fresh evil——the misfortune of my brother Bobby's death.

What is the life of man! Is it not to shift from side to side?——from sorrow to sorrow?——to button up one cause of vexation——and unbutton another?

BOOK IV

Chapter XXXII

From this moment I am to be considered as heir-apparent to the Shandy family—and it is from this point properly, that the story of my Life and my Opinions sets out. With all my hurry and precipitation, I have but been clearing the ground to raise the building—and such a building do I foresee it will turn out, as never was planned, and as never was executed since Adam. In less than five minutes I shall have thrown my pen into the fire, and the little drop of thick ink which is left remaining at the bottom of my ink-horn, after it—I have but half a score things to do in the time—I have a thing to name—a thing to lament—a thing to hope—a thing to promise, and a thing to threaten—I have a thing to suppose—a thing to declare—a thing to conceal—a thing to choose, and a thing to pray for——This chapter, therefore, I name the chapter of Things——and my next chapter to it, that is, the first chapter of my next volume, if I live, shall be my chapter upon Whiskers, in order to keep up some sort of connection in my works.

The thing I lament is, that things have crowded in so thick upon me, that I have not been able to get into that part of my work, towards which I have all the way looked forwards, with so much earnest desire; and that is the Campaigns, but especially the amours of my uncle Toby, the events of which are of so singular a nature, and so Cervantic a cast, that if I can so manage it, as to convey but the same impressions to every other brain, which the occurrences themselves excite in my own—I will answer for it the book shall make its way in the world, much better than its master has done before it.—Oh Tristram! Tristram! can this but be once brought about—the credit, which will attend thee as an author, shall counterbalance the many evils which have befallen thee as a man——thou wilt feast upon the one—when thou hast lost all sense and remembrance of the other!—

No wonder I itch so much as I do, to get at these amours—They are the choicest morsel of my whole story! and when I do get at 'em—assure yourselves, good folks—(nor do I value whose squeamish stomach takes offence at it) I shall not be at all nice in the choice of my words!—and that's the thing I have to declare.——I shall never get all through in five minutes, that I fear—and the thing I hope is, that your worships and reverences are not offended—if you are, depend upon't I'll give you something, my good gentry, next year to be offended at—that's my dear Jenny's way—but who my Jenny is—and which is the right and which the wrong end of a woman, is the thing to be concealed—it shall be told you in the next chapter but one to my chapter of Button-holes—and not one chapter before.

And now that you have just got to the end of these four volumes[1]—the thing I have to ask is, how you feel your heads? my own aches dismally!——as for your healths, I know, they are much better.—True Shandeism, think what you will against it, opens the heart and lungs, and like all those affections which partake of

[1 According to the original editions.]

its nature, it forces the blood and other vital fluids of the body to run freely through its channels, makes the wheel of life run long and cheerfully round.

Was I left, like Sancho Pança, to choose my kingdom, it should not be maritime—or a kingdom of blacks to make a penny of;—no, it should be a kingdom of hearty laughing subjects: And as the bilious and more saturnine passions, by creating disorders in the blood and humours, have as bad an influence, I see, upon the body politic as body natural—and as nothing but a habit of virtue can fully govern those passions, and subject them to reason——I should add to my prayer—that God would give my subjects grace to be as wise as they are merry; and then should I be the happiest monarch, and they the happiest people under heaven.

And so, with this moral for the present, may it please your worships and your reverences, I take my leave of you till this time twelve-month, when, (unless this vile cough kills me in the mean time) I'll have another pluck at your beards, and lay open a story to the world you little dream of.

END of the FIRST VOLUME

CHAP. XXXII